QUANTUM ARROW

G. B. HOLLEY

Also by G. B. Holley

ARKLIGHT Ancient Alien Adventure Novels

ARKLIGHT Revelations
ARKLIGHT Recondite
ARKLIGHT Regulus

QUANTUM ARROW

G. B. HOLLEY

Spirit Owl Books, LLC
P.O. Box 3547
Seminole, Fl 33775

First Edition: December 2020

Library of Congress Control Number: 2020916107

Holley, G. B.

Quantum Arrow
ISBN: 978-1-7320128-9-9 (hardback)
ISBN: 978-1-7356513-0-9 (e-book)
ISBN: 978-1-7356513-1-6 (paperback)

Printed in the United States of America

Book cover, interior design, and formatting by: Jera Publishing, Roswell, GA

For my Mom, Jacquelyn Lee
and
for my Dad, William A.

PROLOGUE

Largo, Florida — November 11, 1969 — 0300 hours

Alone sniper maintained his watch over the only access road, which wound its way from the main road to the back of the two-story manufacturing plant. From his rooftop sniper's hide, he had a clear view of an unmarked tractor-trailer as it rolled slowly toward a loading dock at the rear of the facility. Two black SUV's followed the semi. He knew all three vehicles belonged to a nuclear material transport team and that nuclear weapons technicians were waiting for the truck at the loading bay.

The semi backed up to the loading dock. Several men quickly attached steel barricades to the rear of the trailer to prevent anyone from seeing what would be unloaded. Armed security personnel positioned themselves behind the escort SUVs, which had parked on each side of the semi.

"All clear," the sniper radioed.

The grating sound of the semi's armored rear doors opening carried across the field in the crisp night air. Security was much tighter than it appeared. It had to be. The work being done at the plant was one of America's most closely guarded secrets. The men and women who worked there were responsible for manufacturing neutron generators used to trigger nuclear weapons. The sniper knew that the delivery this morning was a mix of radioactive materials, and that fully operational neutron generators would be loaded on the semi for transport to Texas.

The sniper had worked at the facility for years. The Pinellas Plant wasn't like any other in Florida. Although a GE symbol was affixed over the main entrance to the one hundred and sixty thousand square-foot concrete building, it was actually operated by the Atomic Energy Commission. Built on one hundred acres of pastureland in the 1950s, it was surrounded by dense woods and was accessible only from a two-lane road on the south side of the building. A tall chain-link fence surrounded the entire property, and two reinforced concrete moats bracketed the entrance to the building and a security checkpoint, limiting access to the restricted property.

Attached to the back of the building was a new addition, accessable only through a single corridor inside the plant. Built like a bunker, it was designated off limits to all but a few. Anyone attempting to gain unauthorized entry to the new building would be stopped by armed security personnel. Their standing orders allowed them to make only a single challenge before using lethal force.

Tonight was supposed to be a routine operation. The sniper watched the armed security guards patrolling the grounds and the fenceline that surrounded the facility. In the darkness, they were nearly invisible in their camouflage fatigues. He scanned and listened for any sign of a threat.

Joe Peterson was hidden among thick, strategically planted shrubs. The foliage surrounded a concrete slab, where he sat with his rifle across his lap. From this position Peterson could watch the north and west fencelines. His post was considered a secondary line of defense. There was an identical post three hundred yards to the east of him. If anyone managed to get past the perimeter sentries during a nuclear offload, he and his counterpart would do whatever was required to stop the threat. If they failed, the sniper on the roof was the last resort.

The cooler temperature was a welcome change. He was used to sitting at his post in the sweltering heat and listening to mosquitos buzzing around his face. But tonight, not a single one of them had dined on him. Occasionally, he'd quietly dispatch a rattlesnake that slithered into the bushes near him. He'd preferred shooting them, but his position couldn't be compromised. Peterson raised his M16A1 automatic rifle, looked through the Starlight scope, and scanned the area. A raccoon ambled out of the woods and then scurried back into the brush as if frightened.

As a Vietnam War veteran and Silver Star recipient, sitting in the bush was nothing new to him. His muscular physique and close-cropped hair, along with the scar that ran across his cheek, gave him a hardened warrior's appearance. He'd seen plenty of combat in Nam. Too much. After his discharge from the Marines, the Pinellas Plant security job had provided him a way to readjust to civilian life. Most of the security personnel were former military, and he knew how lucky he was to have secured the position.

Peterson put the rifle in his lap and leaned back to stretch. Just then, a blinding white light blasted out of the night sky, illuminating the building and the field. Peterson squinted as he tried to locate the source. Suddenly, his security radio crackled to life with static. Because of his proximity to the plant, he could hear people shouting.

Peterson lifted his weapon when two figures floated down from what had to be the biggest aircraft he'd ever seen. A second later, a narrow beam of blue light encircled him and he couldn't move. He couldn't talk. He couldn't even pull the trigger on the rifle he had pointed at one of the beings. A moment later, a humanoid and a small brown creature stood in front of him. His rifle and radio dropped to the ground as he was lifted skyward. Then his world went black.

Three nights later

Joe Peterson awoke to find himself standing in an open field behind the GE plant in the darkness. When he looked up, a huge craft rocketed away and blended into the star field. A moment later, he heard the sound of people running toward him.

"Joe, is that really you?" Barry Guall asked as he came to a stop in front of him.

Peterson tried to swallow, but his throat felt as if he'd been in the desert for days.

"Joe, are you alright?" Guall asked.

Peterson cleared his throat, and with a strained voice said, "Yeah. What happened? What was that light?" Then the memories flooded over him, and he knew what the light was and where he'd been.

"F-4 Phantoms buzzed the field," Guall said. "Their landing lights lit up the whole area as they flew over. After they left, we couldn't find you. All we found was your rifle and radio. What happened to you?"

Peterson looked at Guall, then at the man next to him, Reggie James. "Jets and landing lights? What the hell are you talking about?" He looked toward the loading dock. "Where are the transport vehicles?"

Reggie replied, "They left. Joe, you've been MIA for three days."

"That's not possible."

"I'm telling you the truth," Reggie said. "You disappeared three days ago. The boss thought you'd been scared off by the jets."

"What about the alien ship? Did the jets catch up to it?"

"Don't go talking crazy," Guall warned.

"Didn't you see the ship and the two beings that took me away? A human-looking thing and a small brown creature. Someone had to have seen me. What about the sniper?"

"No one reported seeing anything," Guall replied. "It was just low-flying jets headed for MacDill. Let's get you inside. You seem confused."

"I'm not confused. I know what happened to me. No one saw the alien ship bring me back? How did you know I was out here?"

Reggie replied, "There wasn't any ship. One of the thermal sensors spotted you a minute ago. We were dispatched to see who was out here."

"I need to speak to the boss," Peterson said. "It's important. I have a message that needs to be delivered to the president."

"The president?" Reggie said. "You mean the President of the United States?"

"That's exactly who I mean. The aliens gave me a message to give to President Nixon."

"He's lost it," Reggie said.

Guall moved closer to Peterson, put his hand on his shoulder, and said, "You need to stow that talk about spacemen and alien spaceships. You aren't going to tell Nixon anything. If you tell the boss that story, your security clearance will be revoked, and you'll be looking for a new job. Understand?"

"But I have to deliver a warning that comes from the alien beings. I need to see Chairman Seaborg. He can get me in to see the president."

Guall looked at Reggie and said, "We need to get him to the infirmary. Now!"

"I'm fine," Peterson said. "I don't need the infirmary. I need our boss to put me in touch with Atomic Energy Commission Chairman Seaborg."

"You aren't fine," Guall said. "You need to tell the boss that you went on a three-day bender after seeing the jets. You had a flashback to Nam, and thought you were being targeted. You ran for cover and couldn't bring yourself to tell anyone what happened to you, so you went off and got drunk."

The radio crackled, "Guall, report!" Supervisor Jackson ordered.

"Joe, don't say anything about aliens," Guall implored. "They won't fire you if you tell them you thought you were back in Nam. You'll get a reprimand or a short suspension for abandoning your post, but you'll keep your job."

Peterson couldn't believe what he was hearing. He had to tell them that the world was going to end, about the message he'd been given. It was his duty to report what had happened.

"We found Peterson," Guall reported. "He's a little rattled. It looks like postwar trauma. You were right, the jets brought back bad memories, and he sought cover."

"Get him back in here," Jackson commanded.

"Yes, sir," Guall replied. "Joe, you're my best friend, so please, no talking about aliens. Melanie is flying in from New York next week, and you said that you wanted to convince her to move to Florida. Do you remember telling me that you want to marry her?"

"Yeah," Peterson said. "But this has nothing to do with Melanie."

"You start talking about aliens and she may not move down. You said she was a religious woman."

"She is," Peterson replied in understanding.

"Aliens aren't compatible with scripture." Guall leaned in closer and added, "Joe, I believe you think you had an encounter, but you can't tell anyone what happened to you, even if it's true. They'll cart you off and put you in a padded cell. You won't be able to get another federal job, and Melanie won't marry you."

Peterson nodded with reluctant acceptance.

"Reggie, Joe didn't say anything about aliens. Got it?"

"I won't say anything."

Peterson walked with the others across the field in silence. The aliens had given him a warning to relay, but the end of the world wouldn't come for decades. He knew his friend was right. No one would believe his story, and they'd think he was crazy. He stopped and looked up at the stars.

"Joe, what are doing?" Guall asked.

"Just wondering if the aliens will return someday. Maybe tell someone else, and they can sound the alarm."

"There are no aliens," Guall said. "I don't want to hear another word about them."

Peterson sighed, then said, "They exist, but you're probably right. No one will believe me. Hell, you don't even believe me. I won't say another word about them."

PART ONE

> "If the future and the past do exist, I want to know where they are. I may not yet be capable of such knowledge, but at least I know that, wherever they are, they are not there as future or past, but as present."
>
> W. H. AUDEN

ONE

The sky was clear, and a blue canvas stretched to the horizon. Trent McDougal was enjoying the view from his Cessna 172 as he piloted the last leg of his flight. He'd taken off from the Ocala International Airport two hours earlier. A tailwind had cut some time off of his trip to Key West. The Cessna was equipped with the latest upgrades in glass panel cockpits. He was on an instrument flight plan, and he knew that Miami Center would momentarily begin directing his descent for a landing at Key West International. He could just make out the shadowy outline of Key West on the horizon. He entered the IFR landing procedure into the primary flight display, then entered the approach to land on runway nine. With the winds out of the northeast at a brisk eighteen knots, he planned to crab a little on the approach, then cross-control the aircraft to straighten it out just before landing.

Trent loved to fly. He had earned his private pilot certificate ten years ago. He'd waited until he was thirty-three to take up flying, taking lessons at a flight school at the Albert Whitted Airport in St. Petersburg, Florida. He'd wanted to become a pilot since he was a child, but life always seemed to get in the way. After his mother died, he decided life was too short not to pursue his dreams.

Trent went on to get an instrument rating, and now he traveled extensively across the southeast. He'd bought his Cessna 172 Skyhawk to save time and money. At least that's how he had rationalized the purchase. His management consulting business was thriving. Almost weekly he was in another city providing leadership training seminars. He also provided consulting services and assisted companies with finding ways to improve efficiency and cost savings. Trent really needed a faster aircraft, but he was notoriously frugal, and the Cessna served the purpose, plus it was fun to fly. The little reliable plane got him anywhere he needed to go, and it was a tax write-off.

He'd finished teaching his portion of a week-long leadership seminar for a small group of resort executives in Ocala, Florida, earlier in the morning. Trent used his executive privilege and turned the seminar over to one of his senior associates for the afternoon session. Leaving early allowed him the opportunity to start his trip to Key West while the weather was good. A woman waited for him there, and he couldn't wait to see her. Trent knew she was probably at the beach snorkeling.

He'd planned this romantic rendezvous for a special occasion. He was going to ask the woman to marry him. A one-point-five carat diamond engagement ring was snuggly secured in its little blue box in his coat pocket.

Alexa was three years his junior, and she was anxious to start a family. Trent was pretty sure she knew he was going to propose this weekend. This would be the first marriage for both of them. They were career-oriented people, but their biological clocks were ticking. Trent found it hard to believe that he would be almost eligible for Social Security just after his children graduated from college.

Trent had been with Alexa Padget for over two years, and they shared a home in Kissimmee, Florida. Both had an office in Orlando. Alexa was the CEO of a twenty-employee security and consulting firm that specialized in providing executive protection to dignitaries and VIPs while they visited the Sunshine State. She had started the company three years ago after leaving the United States Secret Service. She'd served twelve years as a special agent before deciding to open her own company. Born in Tampa and raised in Lakeland, Florida, Alexa had earned a BA degree in criminal justice at the University of South Florida before joining the Secret Service.

Trent had fallen in love with her on their first date, and fortunately, Alexa had felt the same way about him. They were living together a few months later. They shared common interests in water sports and enjoyed sailing and scuba diving—when time permitted.

He'd completed his business degree at the University of Florida and joined Disney right out of college, taking advantage of the company's strong leadership development program. He eventually found himself teaching the course. Then he figured out that he could make a living doing the same thing on his own. Trent left Disney when he was twenty-seven and founded the McDougal Leadership and Consulting Group. He quickly discovered teaching leadership for an established company was far easier than finding clients and marketing a business. It took a decade of very lean times before his company began seeing substantial profits.

"Six Tango Golf descend to five thousand," the Miami Center controller advised.

"Down to five thousand for Six Tango Golf," Trent acknowledged. He dialed in the altitude on the autopilot, throttled back, and began the descent.

A few minutes later, Trent leveled off at the assigned altitude. An intense white light reflected off the passenger window. When he turned he could see that the light was getting brighter as it approached the right side of his aircraft. It had appeared out of nowhere. *What the hell is that?* A second later, the passenger window was obscured by the blazing light.

"Miami Center, this is Six Tango Golf. There's a strange light off the right side of my aircraft." Trent was trying to keep his voice calm. Giving way to panic was the worst thing he could do now. "Is the Naval Air Station at Key West testing anything in my area?"

The controller said, "Negative, Six Tango Golf. The nearest traffic I have in your vicinity is a Piper Arrow fifteen miles to the north of you at nine thousand."

"Miami, this isn't an aircraft." Trent's voice cracked. "It appears to be a ball of light, and it's traveling alongside the right side of my aircraft. It's matching my speed and altitude."

"Six Tango Golf, I have you at five thousand, twenty miles north of Key West. I have no other aircraft in your area."

As the light grew more intense, Trent began to feel lightheaded. The instrument readings on the PFD and the multifunction display panel were still operational, but the magnetic compass was spinning like a top. Trent pushed the autopilot release button on the yoke and went into a hard sixty-degree-banking turn away from the light.

"Miami, I'm turning to 090 to get away from this thing," Trent yelled.

"Copy Six Tango Golf," the controller replied. "I still have negative radar contact with any other traffic in your area."

"The damn thing's slightly below me now, and it's on my new heading. It's as bright as the sun. My compass is spinning and I'm feeling lightheaded."

"Six Tango Golf, maneuver at your discretion."

The computerized instrument panel on Trent's plane went dark, and the engine suddenly died. The only sound Trent heard came from the air passing over the aircraft as he glided toward the sea. The brilliant white light enveloped his plane. Only his training kept him from becoming totally disoriented. His only sense of his surroundings came from watching his backup instruments. The plane's magnetic compass was still spinning and his sense of direction was lost. He was losing altitude, but his wings were level, and the aircraft was trimmed to glide speed. The radio wasn't functional with all electronics gone. He reached for a portable radio in his flight bag to transmit the call no pilot wants to make.

"Mayday, Mayday, Mayday! Six Tango Golf—engine out—all electrical gone. The cockpit is illuminated with a bright white light. I've lost visual reference. I'm going down. Mayday, do you copy?"

No one heard Trent's radio call. The little Cessna disappeared from radar.

"Six Tango Golf has disappeared," Brent Stone announced. He signaled for his supervisor, David Webster, to join him. Stone had been a controller for twenty years and always dreaded hearing a distress call. This time the call wasn't like anything he'd heard before.

"Any emergency locator transmission?" Webster asked as he approached Stone's console.

"Nothing. Tango Golf was at three thousand MSL when he just vanished from the scope. Navy says they have nothing in the area."

"See if anyone else saw anything," Webster said.

Stone contacted all of the aircraft within thirty miles of the airplane's last reported location. Their answers were all negative.

"I'll issue the alert," Webster said.

Over the next several weeks, search teams scoured the area for Trent's aircraft without success. The NTSB investigators reviewed the radar and radio recordings. There were no indications from the radar recordings that there was any other aircraft in the area. Brett Stone was interviewed by the NTSB, and later by someone claiming to be from Homeland Security, although Stone suspected the man was CIA. This man told Stone not to talk to anyone about what he'd heard or seen, including family and friends, and especially not any of the media, under severe penalty of the law. Stone had known what the not-so-veiled threat meant. He was cleared of any mishandling of the event and restored to full status. He was certain that Webster had received similar instructions.

Neither of them discussed what had happened again.

Key West — January 25th

Alexa Padget was frustrated by the lack of progress in finding any sign of Trent or his plane. After the Coast Guard suspended the search ten days earlier, she'd organized a civilian flotilla in Key West to continue searching for some piece of wreckage. She was determined not to leave Key West until she had an answer as to what had happened to him.

She'd learned that the searchers and the NTSB were also puzzled by the complete absence of any debris, especially because they knew the exact location where Trent's plane had disappeared. She'd been told by the NTSB that Trent's Cessna had vanished in midair, but there was no indication of an explosion. She'd also been assured that something would be found, because the area around the islands was too well traveled. Alexa had asked to speak to the controller and to listen to Trent's final transmissions, but she'd been denied access to both. In her opinion, she was being stonewalled for some reason, which only added to her frustration.

Her anger had boiled over after an NTSB investigator insinuated that Trent had committed suicide or that he had faked his death so they could split his life insurance. Harsh words had been exchanged, and the interview degenerated into a shouting match. That had been the last official meeting with anyone involved in the investigation, and she hadn't heard anything officially in over a week. She was beginning to wonder if the investigator had provoked her so that she would stop calling them.

Twenty Miles North of Key West – February 02 – 1340 hours

Trent McDougal regained control of the aircraft when the light disappeared. The plane's engine and electronics were operating normally again. Even the magnetic compass wasn't spinning anymore. He looked around and didn't see any sign of the light, but he knew something was wrong. The sky was different. It was hazier and it looked as if a frontal boundary now extended south of the Lower Keys.

"Miami Center, Six Tango Golf, how do you copy?"

"What the hell?" The hair on the back of Miami air traffic controller Stone's neck stood on end, and gooseflesh rose on his arms. "Boss, you need to hear this."

David Webster hurried to his side.

"Miami Center, this is Six Tango Golf, at three thousand, twenty miles north of Key West. Do you read me?"

"Six Tango Golf, I copy you," Stone responded. "Please ident."

"That *can't* be the same plane that disappeared," Webster said.

"It's the same radio call sign and he just sent the same transponder code," Stone replied, looking up from the radar screen. "I recognize his voice. I'll never forget it. He's right where he was when he disappeared."

Webster said, "Let's be sure before I make the calls."

"Radar contact twenty miles north of Key West, heading 090, at three thousand," Stone said.

"Miami Center, I'm clear of the light. My electrical system and engine are operating normally. I'm not sure what happened. I would like direct vectors to Key West. I want to land as soon as possible, Six Tango Golf."

"Six Tango Golf, turn to heading 210 until reestablished on the Victor 539 airway."

Trent repeated the instructions.

"That's definitely him," Stone said. "He even mentioned the light."

"You're not going to ask him, are you?" Webster asked.

"I know better."

"I'll make the call to the NTSB and Homeland. You know this isn't going to end well. You ever been through one of these?"

"Nope. Heard rumors about them."

"They can get interesting." Webster walked away.

A few minutes later, Webster returned. "Instruct him to land his plane at the NAS Key West and give him the vectors. Tell him not to deviate. He is not to land at Key West International."

"I understand," Stone said. "Six Tango Golf, turn to heading 165, descend to two thousand. I will give you vectors to the Naval Air Station."

Trent turned to the new heading and descended. "Why NAS? I'm not a military aircraft. I'm filed for KEYW."

"Six Tango Golf, you are directed to land at NAS, Key West. Do not deviate from your vectors. The Boca Chica Field tower frequency is 118.575. I'll hand you off. Your new Squawk Code is 7200." Stone's voice sounded hard, almost cold.

Trent repeated the instructions. The only explanation for him being directed to the Naval Air Station was that he'd seen something he shouldn't have. Maybe he'd stumbled across a super-secret military weapon. Landing on the military base gave the government more control. He was certain the military wanted to debrief him or, more probably, scare the crap out of him to make sure he didn't talk about what he'd witnessed.

"Six Tango Golf, frequency change approved," Stone said. "And good luck."

Trent entered the new frequency and contacted the NAS tower. After landing, he was instructed to follow the escort vehicle waiting for him at the end of the runway. Trent taxied behind the patrol car to an open hangar, where it pulled inside, and Trent was directed to follow it. Once Trent's plane was inside the hangar, he was directed to shut the engine down and ordered to remain in the aircraft.

"This can't be good," he said aloud.

Once the propeller stopped, the escort vehicle parked directly in front of his plane. A Navy law enforcement officer immediately exited his vehicle and stood by the driver's door, his hand on his weapon. Three more patrol vehicles arrived and surrounded him. He wasn't going anywhere, even if he wanted to leave.

As the knot in his stomach grew, Trent opened a side window and asked, "Hey, what's going on?"

"Close your window and stay in your aircraft," a Master-at-Arms standing in front of his plane barked. A Master-at-Arms, or MA, is responsible for law enforcement and force protection in the Navy. Ten more MAs appeared, some carrying automatic weapons. They took up positions behind the patrol vehicles.

"Will do." Trent replied, and closed the window. He removed the computer tablet that had been attached to his leg and stowed it in his flight bag. Next he took off his headset, gathered the charts, and secured them in the bag. When he looked up he saw two more military vehicles driving toward him. "They better not try to seize my plane," he muttered.

T W O

Alexa was sitting with friends at a waterfront bar grabbing a bite to eat before they resumed their search. She really wasn't hungry, but she knew she had to eat. Her long, curly brown hair was pulled over her sunburned shoulder. The dark patches under her blue eyes reflected the exhaustion she felt. Her face showed no sign of emotion as she stared at the boats in the marina. She'd lost ten pounds over the last three weeks, weight she couldn't afford to lose. Alexa had a runner's physique, but she was starting to look anorexic.

Alexa and her friends had been searching for any sign of wreckage around the islands from sunrise to sunset, returning to the marina only for fuel and food. It was the same routine, over and over again, every day. Even though the Coast Guard had officially stopped searching, she'd persuaded the Coast Guard station commander to allow one of their small boats to *unofficially* continue searching the area for training purposes. The Coast Guard had been responsive to her daily requests on sea current updates, which had narrowed their search grids. But still they had found nothing.

Alexa took a long swig of her white wine, then put the empty glass down on her cocktail napkin. She played with the edges of the small napkin for a moment. *Schooners Reef Bar* was printed on it. She looked around at the people in the bar. Some were laughing, some she could tell were tourists enjoying the island ambiance, and they all had one thing in common—they were living their lives. Trent was gone, and she knew she needed to come to grips with that fact. They could search for months and still not find anything.

Alexa looked at Sue Calder, her best friend since high school. Sue wasn't a fashion model—far from it—but she had a cute freckled face. All the time they'd spent on the water searching had given Sue a glowing tan, and her mouse-brown, shoulder-length hair was showing signs of sun-bleaching. Sue had flown down on a private plane from Tampa as soon as Alexa had called and told her Trent's plane had gone down. She hadn't left Alexa's side since arriving. They'd seen each other through bad times before, but this was the most difficult, and prolonged, and Alexa was glad that Sue was with her.

Alexa stifled her need to cry.

Marvin Thanos sat next to Sue. He was not only a great friend, but he had worked for Alexa since his discharge from the Marine Corps. He was six feet tall and two hundred and fifty pounds of solid muscle. His dark skin came from a Greek father and an African-American mother. Alexa thought back to the day she'd met Marvin on the sponge docks in Tarpon Springs, Florida. He was helping his father unload their catch from his boat. Marvin's skin had a sheen to it, and she thought that he looked like an ancient Greek warrior. They'd struck up a conversation on the dock and later met for drinks. They'd talked for hours, but in the end they had both decided that they would be better friends than a couple. Marvin had told her that his family name meant "immortal" in Greek, and she believed that he could be. After learning Marvin was ex-military, she decided he'd make a great addition to her fledgling security and consulting business and offered him a job.

She knew her friends would stay with her and continue the search for as long as she needed in order to find closure, but she also understood it was time to face reality.

Alexa cleared her throat and said, "It's time to call it quits." Her voice cracked as tears filled her eyes. "Thank you both for everything. But you have your own lives to get back to, and Trent is gone." She couldn't bring herself to say he was dead.

Sue shook her head. "Alexa, I can stay as long as you need me."

"It's time to end this. You both have been so great. Your support has meant more than you can imagine." Alexa heard her phone chirp with a text message. She pulled the phone from her purse. She couldn't believe what she saw. She looked at Sue. "It's a text message . . . from Trent."

"This had better not be someone's sick idea of a joke." Marvin said, sounding truly incensed. His clenched jaw reflected his anger.

"Alexa, before you open it, when was it sent?" Sue asked. "It could have been sent weeks ago and somehow got caught in a buffer." She leaned her rotund five-foot frame toward Alexa, trying to read the date of the text. Alexa held it up for her to see the date and time stamp.

"It was sent one minute ago," Alexa answered. She opened the text and read it aloud.

"It says, '*I'm at the Key West Naval Air Station. Meet you at the hotel as soon as I can. Sorry – Trent.*'"

"How the hell could he be at the Naval Air Station?" Marvin asked. "And why didn't he just call you. This has to be a joke."

Alexa didn't wait. She dialed Trent's cell phone.

The phone rang once and Trent answered. "Hey there. Let me call you back in a bit. I have company that won't take kindly to me having a conversation right now."

"Trent, is that you?" Alexa blubbered.

"Yes. It's me. You called me, remember. What's wrong? You sound funny."

"Is it him?" Sue asked.

Alexa nodded. Sue grabbed her arm and Marvin leaned back in his chair in disbelief.

"Are you alright?" Alexa asked.

"Yes. I'll explain everything when I see you. I can't talk right now. I'm surrounded by a bunch of Navy law enforcement officers dressed in blue fatigues with *big* guns. I was instructed to land here, and they haven't let me out of the plane yet. I saw something on my way to Key West that I'm guessing was classified."

"Where have you been?" Alexa asked, sounding confused.

"What do you mean? I've been in the air since I left Ocala. What's wrong with you?"

"I don't think he knows," Alexa said, looking over at Marvin and Sue.

"I don't know what?" Trent said.

"Trent, we're on our way," Marvin bellowed.

"Marvin? What's he doing down here? Uh-oh, I'll call you right back. The Navy guys don't look happy. Later."

"No, wait," Alexa cried. "He hung up. Let's head for the base."

Trent stashed the phone in his flight bag. One of the officers yanked open the door of the Cessna.

"Get out." The sailor ordered.

"Hey, I was told to stay in the plane. No one said I couldn't answer my phone."

The officer pulled Trent out of the plane, then reached inside and picked up Trent's flight bag. He checked around the inside of the plane, then said, "Hand over the phone."

"It's in the flight bag. I'll need both of those back."

A tall, thin man with graying hair, wearing a dark suit, got out of one of the cars that had just pulled up to the hangar. He walked over to Trent. "Mr. McDougal, my name is NCIS Special Agent Anthony Dobson. I need you to come with me." Agent Dobson motioned toward his car.

Trent didn't move. "If you don't want one of your play toys to be seen, you shouldn't use it in public view."

The Master-at-Arms seized Trent by the arm and forcibly walked him to the car. Trent was sure his opening statement wasn't the smartest way to start a dialog, especially under the circumstances. Trent got into the backseat and was forced to slide over as Agent Dobson sat down next to him.

"It would be best for everyone if you didn't say anything," Dobson said.

Trent glared at him. "Is this the NCIS version of the Miranda Warning?"

Dobson smirked. "I wish—but no. I'd appreciate you keeping your mouth shut until asked to open it. I've been instructed to keep you on the base. I imagine you will be taken to a regional office in due time."

"Where's the regional office?"

"Mayport."

"Mayport—as in Jacksonville? I have no intention of going to Jacksonville. My girlfriend is here, and I'm planning to propose to her tonight. She knows I'm on the base, and so do her friends. I haven't done anything wrong. I demand that you release me."

Dobson said to the driver, "Let's go." He looked at Trent and said, "Your friends knowing that you're here is most unfortunate for everyone, Mr. McDougal."

As the car left the hangar, Trent looked back to see the Navy personnel closing the hangar door. "I'm going to want my plane back."

Boca Chica NAS, Key West — 1435 hours

Standing next to their rented white Mercedes SUV at the entrance gate to Boca Chica, NAS, Marvin was trying to look intimidating while Alexa yelled at the Navy security officer.

Sue touched Alexa's arm.

"I already explained this to you," Master-at-Arms Peter Wilson said. "Let me try again. The base is on lockdown. No one gets in, and no one gets out. Now turn your car around and leave the area."

"What are you going to do if I don't? Are you going to arrest me and lock me up on the base? Then do it. My boyfriend is in there. His name is Trent McDougal. He's been missing for three weeks, and I want to see him. Call the base commander."

Additional Navy MAs arrived at the gate and took up positions behind the security building near the entrance.

"Last chance," Wilson said, pointing behind her. "I will have you arrested if you don't leave immediately."

Alexa turned and saw a Monroe County Sheriff's cruiser pull up behind their SUV.

"This isn't looking good," Marvin muttered.

"Alexa, let's wait for Trent to call us back," Sue said. "We know he's here, we know he's alive, and the last thing he would want is for you to get arrested. We can wait down the road for his call and be back here in just a minute."

Alexa sighed heavily. She turned to Sue, then saw a deputy sheriff walking toward them. "I guess you're right." She faced the deputy. "I apologize. I'm just very tired. I spoke to my boyfriend, Trent McDougal, a few minutes ago. He told me he'd just landed at the base. I don't understand what's happening."

She sat down on the curb.

Sue knelt next to her, gave her a hug, then said, "Everything will be okay. I'm sure Trent will call again soon."

Marvin leaned down, put his hands under her arms, and pulled Alexa up. She gave him a conspiratorial wink. He nodded his understanding. She was only stalling.

The deputy said with a calm, soothing southern accent, "Folks, you can't go on the base. You all need to leave—now."

"We're going," Marvin said as he led Alexa away.

Another MA approached the gate and said, "Wilson, there was a small aircraft that landed here a half-hour ago. I was on the security detail. The pilot's in custody."

Alexa turned and hurried back to the gate. "That has to be him, Trent McDougal. He's a white male, forty-three, six feet tall, about one hundred and ninety pounds, brown hair, brown eyes."

"Check on it," Wilson ordered. The MA walked into the security building.

"Thank you so much," Alexa said, her hope restored that she might see Trent.

A few minutes later the MA returned. "I have been instructed to tell you that the aircraft that landed wasn't being flown by Trent McDougal."

"What?" Alexa cried. "Where is he?"

"Ma'am, I checked." The MA said in a softer tone. "The aircraft had to make an emergency landing, but the pilot is not Mr. McDougal. I have been ordered to see that you leave the area. Deputy, please escort her away."

Alexa balled her fists as if ready to throw a punch, when Marvin grabbed her from behind and lifted her off the ground in a bear hug.

"We're leaving," Marvin said, carrying Alexa toward the SUV.

Alexa squirmed in his grip, but Marvin had her arms pinned. Sue held the back door open, and Marvin shoved her inside.

"Stay put," Marvin said. He turned to the deputy. "Please don't arrest her. She's been through so much the last few weeks. She's exhausted and really frustrated. She'll calm down in a minute."

The deputy nodded and said, "I'm Deputy Todd Griffin. I need to get some information from you all. I know you're trying to help your friend here, but somehow I don't think I've seen the last of her."

Marvin smiled at Griffin. "I sincerely hope you have. I'm Marvin Thanos."

Alexa yelled a string of profanities.

"Can we follow you somewhere, away from the base?" Marvin asked. "I want to give Alexa time to calm down. I'll explain everything then. I hope you can help us."

"Sure." Griffin said. He waved at the MAs still at the checkpoint. "They're leaving." Griffin turned back to Marvin. "Follow me back to the office. It's not far from here. It's just across the bridge."

"Will do, thanks," Marvin said. He waved at the base security team.

When Marvin got behind the wheel, Alexa said, "That was his plane. They're hiding something."

"I know," Marvin replied. "But we can't storm the base. Let's see if the deputy will make some inquiries for us. So play nice."

Marvin started the car and followed the deputy on US 1 toward Key West.

Naval Air Station – NCIS Office – 1535 hours

Trent sat across the table from Agent Dobson in the secure interview room. He was handcuffed to the table, still not understanding what he had done wrong. He hadn't broken any laws, and no one had told him why he was under arrest. "I'm not a terrorist," Trent said, for the fifth time.

Dobson looked at him. "Since you obviously aren't going to sit quietly, why don't you tell me what happened."

Trent smiled. "I thought you'd never ask. I was flying to Key West to spend a romantic weekend with my girlfriend. Her name is Alexa Padget. I'm going to propose to her tonight. The ring is in my flight bag."

"I don't care about your love life. Tell me what happened to you."

Trent described everything he had experienced in detail.

When he was finished, Dobson said, "That's quite a story. You said you felt lightheaded? Were you smoking dope, doing drugs, or just drunk?"

"None of the above. Look, I don't know what I saw. If it was one of your new toys, I'm impressed. If it wasn't one of ours, then I don't know what to say."

"When you talked to your girlfriend, Alexa, what did you tell her?"

"I told her where I was, that I was sorry that I would be late, and I would talk to her later. Look, I really want to save what's left of the weekend. Do you want me to sign something saying I didn't see anything?" Trent shifted in the uncomfortably hard chair, his handcuffs clinking against the metal table.

"Alexa was at the front gate earlier wanting to see you."

"Good. Can I see her?"

"No." Dobson picked up a pen and tapped it on the table. "I can't help but wonder if she isn't in on this charade."

"What charade?"

"The fact that you disappeared three weeks ago and then suddenly reappeared today."

Trent felt stunned. "What do you mean I disappeared three weeks ago? I left Ocala just a few hours ago. What kind of game are you playing?"

Dobson's cold, grey eyes narrowed. "You left Ocala a few hours ago?"

"Yes. I filed a flight plan. You can check."

"I don't need to. I think you and your friends have concocted some elaborate scheme so you can make some money off this adventure. You guys planning to sell your story and get your fifteen minutes of fame?"

"What the hell are you talking about?" Trent shouted. He knew he needed to calm down.

"Did you think this stunt would drum up business? I can see the headline now. 'Leadership Guru abducted by aliens.' Your future wife can add a new specialty to her security business as a novelty. How am I doing?" Dobson twirled his pen in his fingers.

"I think you're the one who's been smoking something. I have no idea what you are talking about. There is no conspiracy or scheme. If I told anyone about a close encounter, I would *lose* credibility, and so would Alexa. It's not the kind of publicity we would want to generate."

Trent took a deep breath. "Have I really been gone for three weeks?"

"Yes."

"So you're telling me that the big ball of light was not a military weapon?"

Dobson stared at Trent for a moment, then said, "Let me ask you this. What do you think you saw?"

Trent decided to roll the dice, which for him was never a good idea. "I believe what I saw was a distorted image, maybe a light reflection cast by an airliner above me. I became confused and hyperventilated, which is what caused the lightheadedness."

"You didn't see a spaceship?"

"Nope."

"Are you absolutely sure?"

"Yes. I did *not* see an alien spaceship. Can I go now?"

"How do you explain the missing three weeks? Not to mention the large amount of money the government spent trying to find you."

Trent shook his head and said, "I can't. What's the date?"

"Today is February 2, Groundhog Day."

"I really don't understand. Look at the date on my watch." If it were true that he'd been gone for three weeks, that would explain Alexa's confusion. But where had he been?

Dobson looked at the date on Trent's watch face and confirmed it read the 10th. He sat back in his chair.

"Look, I'm really confused right now," Trent said. "I can't explain where I've been. If you want me to say this was a hoax, I will, if it'll get me out of here. It won't be true, but I promise not to say anything to anyone about what I've seen." Trent was growing more frustrated by the minute. *Where the hell have I been?*

Dobson stopped twirling the pen and leaned toward him. "As I see it, I have a couple of options. I can hold you in Mayport until we discover where you really were for the last three weeks and how you managed to disappear from the FAA radar. I could also have you sent to Gitmo under the Patriot Act and have you held there until we discover the stealth technology you used to cloak your radar signature and where you acquired it. Or you can answer my questions truthfully, and I will see what can be done to expedite your processing."

Trent shook his head. "I'm not a terrorist. My Cessna doesn't have any stealth capability. Check it out. I probably should be medically screened and you may not want to be sitting so close to me if I was abducted by aliens."

Dobson leaned back. "That is a very good idea. A blood draw and screening for drugs or alcohol may help explain some things while I wait to hear from my superiors."

"I have no problem with that. I don't do drugs and I don't drink when I'm flying."

Dobson's eyes narrowed. "You aren't lying, are you?"

"No, Agent Dobson, I'm not. I thought the light was a new weapon the military was testing. If I've been gone for three weeks, then you must be playing with a time machine or there's an alien component to all of this. I'm guessing the latter since you seem as perplexed as I am."

"Let's get the medical screening started," Dobson said. "You'll get a full medical workup when you get to Mayport. But we will take some blood here and a give you a physical before you leave. I wouldn't want a little alien creature coming out of your chest on the way there."

"Can I at least call Alexa so she knows where I'm going?"

"No." There was a knock on the door. "Yes?" Dobson said, sounding annoyed.

The door opened. "Sir, there's a call for you. I was instructed to interrupt you."

Dobson glared at Trent. "We're not done yet." Dobson stood.

"Can I at least use the bathroom, or the head as you Navy guys call it?"

"No." Dobson left, closing the door behind him.

Trent sat quietly in thought, trying to piece it all together.

Monroe County Sheriff's Office — Key West — 1600 hours

Deputy Todd Griffin sat behind an old wooden desk. Marvin, Sue, and Alexa sat on the other side. He believed that they'd received a call from Trent McDougal. Alexa's credentials had checked out. There'd be no reason for her to make up a story about the call. Plus, he'd overheard the MA telling her that a plane had landed there.

Having followed the disappearance and the search effort, he was curious about what was going on. The Sheriff's office had used their helicopter to search the shorelines around the islands for wreckage. What he couldn't reconcile was how Trent could reappear after three weeks and supposedly end up being held at the Naval Air Station. Someone could be playing a trick on them, but the evidence said otherwise. Alexa had showed him the text message from Trent. It was dated today, and it was from his cell phone. She'd also shown him the time stamp of her call to Trent's phone. If McDougal was on the base and had just landed today, what was the Navy hiding?

Marvin had already led him down the conspiracy highway. He couldn't dispute what they'd told him. The evidence corroborated their story. Still, the Navy denied that Trent was on the base. Nothing added up.

Griffin said, "As I see it, there are two possibilities. One, the Navy is holding Trent for some unknown reason. Two, someone created an elaborate hoax or a sick joke. Maybe someone found Trent's phone washed up on a beach."

"No, I recognized Trent's voice," Alexa replied. "He's on that base."

"Okay. I think you spoke to Trent. I also think that he's on the base." Griffin opened his desk drawer, and found the paper he was looking for. "Let me see if I can clear this up."

Marvin squeezed Alexa's hand.

Griffin dialed the NTSB Field Office in Miami. A moment later, someone answered.

"NTSB, Miami. How may I direct your call?"

Griffin noticed the woman's sexy voice. "Hi, I'm Deputy Todd Griffin. I'm with the Monroe County Sheriff's Office in Key West. I need to speak to the person in charge of the Trent McDougal disappearance."

"One moment, please," she replied. He was put on hold.

"Investigator John Garland."

Griffin identified himself. "Investigator Garland, is it possible to get an update on the investigation into the disappearance of Trent McDougal?"

"There's no new information to report. He's still listed as missing. Did you find some debris?"

"No. Actually the reason I'm calling is . . ." Griffin wasn't sure how to phrase what he needed to say. "It's possible Mr. McDougal landed at the Naval Air Station Key West today."

Garland chuckled. "Are you saying that he's no longer missing?"

"I can't actually answer that question." Griffin told him what he knew and what had happened at the base. When he was finished, there was a long period of silence on the line.

"That's quite a story, Deputy Griffin. What's a good number where I can call you back?"

Griffin gave Garland his office and cell phone numbers, then hung up.

"That was Investigator John Garland," Griffin said. "He's going to check into this and call us back."

"Alexa, they'll get to the bottom of this," Marvin told her reassuringly.

"I hope so," Alexa said. "But none of this sits well with me. Trent's in trouble. More than he probably even realizes." She looked at Sue. "What do you think?"

"Trent's on the base, and for some reason somebody doesn't want us to know it. The Navy cop confirmed an aircraft had landed there."

"I agree." Alexa looked at Deputy Griffin. "Will you call the Key West airport tower and ask them if they can confirm that a Cessna 172 landed at the Naval Air Station? If so, get the tail number?"

Griffin nodded. "I can do that, but don't you want to wait to hear from the NTSB? They may answer the question for us."

"No. From my years of working in the Secret Service, I know if the government wants to cover something up, they can. The longer we wait, the easier it will be for them to destroy evidence and get to those who know what happened and silence them. If the Navy, or whoever, wants to cover this up, time isn't on our side."

"You think the government wants to keep Trent sequestered?" Griffin asked. "Why would they do that?"

"I wish I knew. I know how easy it is to hide things from the public." Alexa sat back in her chair. "Maybe he stumbled onto a secret government program that the military doesn't want disclosed."

Deputy Griffin wasn't sure what to say. He wanted to laugh, but he could tell Alexa was serious. "Let me call a buddy of mine in our Aviation Unit. The guys working in the tower may feel more at ease talking to him. I think we should wait, but I can see you all are anxious to get this resolved."

"Thank you," Alexa said.

Deputy Griffin called one of his pilot friends in the aviation unit, explained what was happening, and his friend said that he would make the call immediately. Griffin hung up and said, "Now we wait."

THREE

NCIS Agent Dobson sat at a desk in the office adjacent to where Trent McDougal was being held. Dobson was shaking his head after talking to his boss, Special Agent in Charge, Gordon Sullivan, at Mayport. SAIC Sullivan wasn't happy to hear that he had questioned Trent, especially considering his story. Dobson explained that no one told him not to talk to Trent, and since he was familiar with the plane's disappearance, he figured that was what he was supposed to do. Sullivan explained loudly, and in painful detail, what detaining someone meant, and that it didn't involve asking questions. The FBI and Homeland Security wanted Trent held until someone in Washington made a decision as to which agency was to take the lead in the investigation. The SAIC made it very clear that he wasn't to ask Trent any more questions. His job was to watch him. He was not to allow Trent to have contact with anyone else, and he was ordered to secure Trent's clothing and all personal items, especially his watch. Of course, Sullivan wouldn't have thought to tell him to keep that unless he'd mentioned it to him. He was also instructed not to let anyone get near Trent's airplane.

Dobson didn't like stepping into someone else's mess, especially when he wasn't sure who's mess it was. He knew McDougal's disappearance had nothing to do with any domestic terrorist threat. He was starting to believe that Trent didn't know he'd been missing for three weeks, and his story of a mysterious light was starting to take root as an alien encounter. He needed to keep that opinion to himself. There was more to Trent's disappearance than what he needed to know, and now he was neck deep in the muck. He was only four years away from retiring and he knew how it felt when an assignment was going sideways. He had that feeling now.

Monroe County Sheriff's Office –1635 hours

The phone rang, and Deputy Griffin answered. Alexa knew it was bad news by the expression on Griffin's face. He obviously wasn't very good at hiding his emotions.

Griffin hung up the phone and said, "My friend in the aviation unit said that a small plane did land at the Naval Air Station. When the controller tried to get the N-number of the plane, he was blocked from someone higher up in the FAA food chain. The conversation was terminated for national security reasons. The controller had been ordered not to provide any information about the aircraft to anyone, including law enforcement."

Alexa bit her lower lip. Her face flushed. "I knew it. They're trying to bury this already."

"Let's wait for NTSB Investigator Garland to call us back before jumping to any conclusions," Griffin said. "He may still be able to shed some light on what's happened. You know how government agencies don't talk to each other. There's still hope."

"You want me to wait!" Alexa exclaimed. "That's exactly what the people covering this up want us to do. I'm willing to wager Investigator Garland will either not call us back or, if he does, he won't give you any information." Alexa was furious.

Marvin leaned toward Griffin and said, "Is there really nothing you can do?"

"I wish there was something, but no. If Mr. McDougal is on the base, I can't do anything to get him released. It's a federal matter. You know what happens when they play the national security card."

"Yes, I do," Alexa said.

"Your boyfriend is on the base and safe," Griffin said. "The fact the base is locked down after a small plane landed there, coupled with this now being a national security issue, is enough evidence to confirm it."

Alexa said, "With Trent already being presumed dead, making him disappear will be easier for them."

"I see your point," Griffin replied. "Your boyfriend may very well be at the epicenter of some highly classified operation. Which means he may be held for a while, but I think eventually he'll be released. None of us may ever learn what has really happened, but I'm sure you'll see him again."

Alexa stood and walked to the door, then turned and said, "Deputy Griffin, if the government knows we all know that Trent is alive, what do you think will happen to us?"

"I hadn't thought about that."

"Well, you better start thinking about it."

The phone on the desk rang again, and Griffin answered. He put it on speaker.

"Deputy Griffin, this is John Garland, at NTSB."

"Thanks for calling back. What were you able to find out?"

"Actually, not very much through normal channels. The Navy is denying they have Mr. McDougal or his airplane at the base. After a little digging, I learned from a friend of mine at Miami Center that an aircraft with McDougal's registration number was picked up on radar about twenty miles north of Key West earlier today. It was in the same airspace as it was when it vanished. The aircraft was directed to land at the Naval Air Station. That's all my friend could tell me."

"That's good news," Griffin said, giving a thumbs-up gesture.

Alexa walked back to her chair and sat down.

"Well, that's only part of the news," Garland said. "When I called my boss in Washington to let him know what had happened and that I was going to the base to conduct a follow-up investigation, he told me the NTSB was no longer responsible for the investigation. He said I should forward all related files to Washington. Then he ordered me not to go anywhere near Boca Chica and that the investigation was closed."

"Isn't that a bit unusual?" Griffin asked.

"Very unusual. I've been investigating aircraft accidents for twenty-five years, and I've never been ordered to close an investigation just when the aircraft has been confirmed as found. I'm sorry, but I no longer have any official involvement in the investigation. I can't be of any further assistance."

Griffin nodded. "I bet being removed from an investigation doesn't sit well with you. I know how I feel when my cases are reassigned. Do you have any idea which agency is taking over the investigation?"

"Not a clue. I've never heard of anything like this happening. I probably shouldn't have told you what I have, but I wasn't instructed not to cooperate with local law enforcement."

"And you're pissed off," Griffin added.

"You got that right. So, now you know what I know. I have a feeling Mr. McDougal is alive and well, but I can't say that officially. I hope you have better luck than I did cracking this nut."

"Thanks very much for your help. Could you let me know if anything changes?"

"I will, unless instructed otherwise. Good luck."

After Griffin disconnected, he said, "You heard him. We have positive confirmation."

"I knew they'd start circling the wagons," Alexa said. "Damn it!"

"Alexa, you need to calm down," Marvin said. "This emotional rollercoaster ride is going to land you in the hospital."

Griffin said, "I think it's obvious there's more going on here than a missing plane. Someone wants it kept quiet. It sure looks like someone high up in the government is calling the shots. They don't want your boyfriend going public with whatever has happened to him. But that doesn't mean they'll make him disappear."

"Maybe we should contact the media and tell them that Trent is being held by the Navy," Sue said. "We could make up some signs and get our friends to stand outside the main gate and create a media event."

Alexa shook her head. "That won't work. They'll simply bury him deeper. They can fly him out at any time. He may already be off the base." Alexa stood and extended her hand. "Deputy Griffin, you have been a big help. I wish you the best."

"I wish I could do more," Griffin said. He stood and shook her hand.

She could tell he meant it. "I know and I appreciate it. But you've taken this as far as you can. I think things are going to get interesting, and you don't need to be involved any more than you already are."

"You're not going to do anything crazy, like storm the gates, are you?"

Alexa smiled at him for the first time. "Deputy Griffin, I won't be that overt. I still have resources working in very secret places that most people don't even know exist. If whoever is behind this cover-up wants to play games, then I'll take them on."

"For what it's worth, I'm here if you need me. I'd like to see you and your boyfriend reunited. It isn't right what's happening." Griffin took out a business card and wrote his personal cell phone number on it. "Anytime you need something, just give me a call."

"I appreciate it."

Alexa, Marvin, and Sue left the office.

Once they were in the parking lot, Marvin asked, "What now?"

"Now we take on the government," Alexa replied. "Marvin, are you up for a little adventure?"

"Always," Marvin replied with a smile.

"I need you to drop Sue and me at the hotel. Then I'd like you to drive back to the base and find a place where you can covertly monitor the front gate."

"You think they're going to drive him out of the front gate?" Sue asked.

"No, I don't. But I'm willing to bet there'll be an increase of vehicle traffic at the gate and an increase of air traffic, too. Marvin, I need you to monitor the aircraft landing and taking off. Even if that means losing sight of the front gate. I want you to record all aircraft registration numbers. You know the drill."

"So we're going to just sit and watch?" Sue asked.

"There's really nothing else we can do. I'm betting they'll airlift him and his plane out of here as soon as they can."

"What are you going to do?" Marvin asked.

"I'm going to take a shower, change into some clean clothes, and make some calls to friends in Washington, Maryland, and Utah. If the response to my calls goes as planned, you and I will be flying out first thing in the morning."

"What am I going to do?" Sue asked.

"Sue, my dear friend, you are going home. You've done enough, and its time you get back to living your life. I don't want you any more involved than you already are."

"I'm not going home until this is over," Sue said. "You're going to need my help."

"Listen to me. You're going home."

"No, I'm not," Sue said firmly. "You've been my best friend for over twenty years. Where you go, I go. End of discussion."

Alexa nodded, then smiled at Sue. "I can see that your mind's made up. Okay, but promise me that if things get intense that you'll find safe haven."

"I promise. This sounds exciting."

"You may not think so tomorrow," Alexa replied. "Marvin, take us back to the hotel."

NAS Key West – NCIS Offices – 1700 hours

Agent Dobson gave specific instructions to the security personnel that no one was to have contact with McDougal and that his plane was to be considered a crime scene. He informed the MA to keep a log of everyone assigned to aircraft security and to secure all of McDougal's personal items as evidence. Dobson also wanted the name of the deputy who was at the gate with Trent's girlfriend, and he needed to know her whereabouts.

Trent was alone in the office when Agent Dobson returned. "Strip," Dobson said, throwing him a set of blue fatigues.

"What's going on?"

"I have new orders." Dobson turned around and informed the security guard that no one was to enter, and then he closed the door.

"So you aren't going to let me leave?" Trent asked. "Can I call an attorney?"

"No. Shut up and get changed."

"You're making a huge mistake. I've done nothing wrong. I'm not the bad guy here. If I was abducted by aliens, I told you that I won't tell anyone."

"I suggest you stow this shit about being abducted by aliens."

"How do you explain the fact that I've been gone for weeks? If it isn't a secret government experiment that went wrong, what else could it be?"

Dobson closed his eyes and quietly counted to five, then opened them. "Mr. McDougal, you have been classified as a national security threat."

"That's ridiculous."

"Before you say anything else, let me finish. I'm not in charge of the investigation. Someone else is pulling the strings."

"Okay. Who?"

Dobson rubbed the knotted muscles at the base of his neck. "I don't know. My interviewing you has landed me in hot water with my boss. I have been ordered not to have any further conversations with you."

"Sorry to hear that I got you in trouble."

Dobson stepped toward Trent. "For what it's worth, I believe your story. I have a feeling my career will be tied to whatever happens to you. So let me give you my best advice. Stay quiet until asked to respond. Are we clear?"

"We are. What about Alexa? Has she been arrested because she knows I'm here?"

Dobson shook his head. "She has not been arrested. But she did make quite a scene at the main gate trying to see you. She left after a local deputy escorted her and some of her friends away."

"What will happen to her and my friends?"

"I honestly don't know. They know you're here, thanks to you texting and talking to her. The agency that takes point on this investigation will want to question them. To what extent they will be interviewed, or held, I really don't know."

"Then I guess it would be better for everyone if I didn't say anything more."

Dobson smiled. "Now you got it."

NAS Key West — 1845 hours

Marvin watched as a large, gray C-17 Globemaster III turned on final to land on the runway. The seven-thousand-foot runway was almost twice as long as the plane needed for landing. The plane looked abnormally large with its four, forty-thousand-pound-thrust engines and its tall vertical stabilizer. It was making its approach from the west, and Marvin could see another C-17 following behind it. No other transport aircraft had landed at the base since he'd been watching. Alexa was right. This wasn't a coincidence. He was certain they were here to retrieve Trent and his plane. The C-17 could handle a heavy payload. A 2,500-pound Cessna 172 wouldn't cause a weight problem, but they would have to take the wings off to get it into the cargo bay. A good team could dismantle the plane in an hour, especially if they didn't care if the aircraft flew again. Marvin called Alexa. She answered on the third ring.

"What's up?"

"Two C-17s are landing at Boca Chica. I'm willing to wager they're here for Trent."

"Can you get the tail numbers?" Alexa asked.

"I'll try. The sun has set, so I'm losing light."

"I had a feeling they would fly him out."

"Anything else you want me to do?"

"Take as many photographs of the aircraft as you can. Note the times of arrival and departure, then let me know if the base opens again after the aircraft depart."

"Okay. I hope I can get a clear view of the aircraft once they land."

"Do the best that you can. Trent is going to be taken somewhere far away from here. I called a friend to see if she could track any aircraft that leave NAS Key West, which is why I really need the tail numbers."

"Do I even want to know who this friend is?"

"No. She owes me a big favor. It may be a long shot, but it's the best chance I have to find out where he's being taken."

"I'll get the numbers."

"I'm sure you will." Alexa hung up.

One thing Marvin knew about Alexa was that she had a tenacious, unrelenting, bulldog attitude. She would get to the bottom of the mystery and get Trent back—or die trying.

F O U R

Key West NAS — February 02 — 1850 hours

Marvin watched through his binoculars as two large aircraft taxied to a stop next to each other in front of a huge hangar. The tall vertical stabilizers extended above the buildings. Neither aircraft bore a designation as to their military affiliation. He copied down the tail numbers of both aircraft, but something told him they wouldn't shed much light on the matter. The aircraft numbers were probably classified, and anyone querying them would be flagged. He called Alexa with the information.

When Agent Dobson heard the jet engines spooling down, he walked to a window. The two C-17s were parked, and the base commander, Capt. Joseph Barker, was waiting in a car on the tarmac. Several of his staff officers stood by the front of his car. *Whoever these people in the aircraft were, they carried enough clout to get the captain to greet them personally,* Dobson thought.

A large group of men and women in camouflage fatigues disembarked from one C-17 and immediately walked toward the hangar where Trent's Cessna was secured. Another team of four people greeted the captain.

Captain Barker pointed in his direction. The small group walked toward his office building, leaving the captain and his entourage behind.

The first man through the door was dressed in graphite-colored fatigues. Dobson noted the Space Force patch on his shoulder and the embroidered star on his collar. A general. The second man through the door was muscular and as tall as the general and was dressed in similar fatigues. An Asian-looking woman, he guessed was Japanese, followed him. She was petite and was dwarfed by the two men standing in front of her. She had an embroidered medical insignia on her uniform. Dobson noted she was a colonel. The final person to enter the room sported a full brown and gray beard. Although he was dressed in Space Force fatigues, his uniform displayed no rank insignia, and he looked about as military as a hippie at a polo match. As they approached, Dobson knew this was no ordinary team.

"Agent Dobson, I presume. I'm General John Starke, United State Space Force. Allow me to introduce everyone. This is Col. Melissa Endo, Major Frank Striker, and Dr. Arnold Sanderson."

"Welcome to NAS Key West, but I'm sure Captain Barker already welcomed you," Dobson said. "Perhaps you can enlighten me as to what I have stepped into here. My SAIC wasn't happy to hear I had interviewed Mr. McDougal."

The general smiled. "I'm sure he wouldn't have liked that. He was given explicit orders forbidding anyone from speaking with Mr. McDougal. But communications being what they are sometimes, things get overlooked."

Dobson waited for him to answer his question, but the general didn't. "I imagine you would like to speak with Mr. McDougal."

"Yes, we would, so if you would be so kind as to show us where he's confined," General Starke said.

Dobson pointed at the locked door where a security officer stood guard. "He's right in there."

Major Striker walked past him, acknowledge the security officer, and opened the door. Col. Endo and Dr. Sanderson followed Striker into the room. The door closed behind them.

Dobson expected General Starke to follow them, but he didn't. At six-five, Dobson was two inches taller than the general, although he weighed less. General Starke appeared to be a man who always got want he wanted.

"Is there anything else you need, General Starke?" Dobson asked.

"Yes, there is actually. Let's you and I have a chat. Do you have a private office?"

Dobson's stomach turned over. He had a bad feeling about the direction the conversation was going to take.

"Yes, sir, right this way." Dobson turned and walked down the corridor to his office. The general followed him in and closed the door.

Dobson said, "What would you like to chat about, General Starke?"

General Starke made himself at home in the chair behind Dobson's desk. "Have a seat, Agent Dobson."

Dobson looked at the general and decided now was not the time to play alpha dog, even though this was his domain. He chose a chair next to his desk rather than the one in front of it. General Starke had to turn in order to look at Dobson.

"We have a bit of a containment problem, and I'm going to need your cooperation."

Dobson shifted in his chair. "Certainly, how can I be of service?"

"Well, the first thing for you to know is that I'm in charge. This is no longer an NCIS investigation. In light of the fact you have debriefed Mr. McDougal, you're now under my command. SAIC Sullivan has been informed that neither the NCIS nor the Navy will have further involvement. They have been directed by the highest authority to cooperate fully in *my* investigation. Do you understand what that means?"

"Yes, sir. But . . ."

The general raised his hand and cut him off.

"Before you tell me that you only take orders from your chain of command, I'm telling you that you now report to me, as required by a presidential directive. So unless you are prepared to terminate your employment with the federal government, you will listen to what I have to say, and you will follow orders."

Dobson clenched his jaw. It was worse than he thought. "I'm listening."

"Good. Now tell me everything Mr. McDougal has told you. I also need to know the identities and location of everyone else who knows he's alive and what they've been told, seen, or suspect."

Dobson briefed him on the conversation he'd had with Trent. He also told him that Trent's girlfriend and some of her friends were aware he was here. He told him about the deputy sheriff, but couldn't say how much the deputy knew about Trent. As to how many others they had told, he couldn't say. He added, "The gate security personnel, the security detail assigned to guard the NCIS office, and the hangar team know Trent landed here. I don't believe they've had any discussions with him."

The general nodded. "We're off to a good start. First, you are not to discuss anything you've seen or heard here with anyone. Secondly, you will sign a non-disclosure agreement that carries a very stiff legal penalty should you disclose anything you learn over the course of your involvement in my investigation. Are we clear?"

"Yes, sir."

"Excellent. You're going to get a bump in your security clearance. Consider everything about this event above the TK level."

Dobson felt a tingle crawl up his spine. He knew he was involved in something that was seriously classified. "Yes, sir."

"Agent Dobson, I need you to contact the deputy that was involved and determine what he knows about Trent McDougal. Find out if he's told anyone else about what has occurred here. Then I need you to track down McDougal's friends and determine who they told about his returning from the dead. You'll need to use your powers of persuasion to convince all of them that it is in their best interest to return to the base with you, immediately, including the deputy."

"General, you know how news travels, especially this kind of story on such a small island. I'm actually surprised that the media hasn't been calling."

"If they do, the cover story is that a small plane made an emergency landing. Nothing else."

"I already spun that story and denied he was here. But Trent called his girlfriend, Alexa, before security could secure his cell phone."

"So I heard. That's why I need you to find them and bring them back here. I'll take care of them once they're in custody."

Dobson didn't like the emphasis the general had used when he said, *take care of them.* "Tracking down all of the people involved will take some time and I'm a little short of resources."

"That's your problem. How you get everyone involved back to this base is your responsibility. I want them here within the next hour. I will deal with the base personnel."

"Yes, sir. Anything else?" Dobson knew the assignment was impossible to accomplish in such a short time, but he decided not to argue with the general.

"No." General Starke handed him a Space Force business card with a cell phone number on it. "Call me at that number with an update on your progress every twenty minutes. We will be wheels up at 2030 hours. Don't be late, and don't disappoint me." General Starke stood and added, "I hope you like cold weather."

Dobson frowned. "Why would you say that?"

"Because you'll be coming with us, and where we are going, it's cold. Contact anyone you need to and let them know you're being deployed to an undisclosed location for a while." General Starke walked past him and was out the door before Dobson could respond.

"Shit!" Dobson said. Then he called his wife, Candice. She wasn't pleased to hear this news, but after twenty years of marriage and numerous extended deployments, she understood.

Dobson called his boss next. SAIC Gordon Sullivan asked him if he'd like to resign. He declined, and Sullivan wished him well. It was obvious that Sullivan had received his orders and had probably gotten his ass chewed for his handling of the incident. The situation had gone from bad to worse, and his gut was telling him it was going to get even worse and more complicated before this was over.

His next call was to the Monroe County Sheriff's Office. He needed to find the deputy who was at the gate and determine where Trent's friends were staying.

National Security Agency, Fort Meade, Maryland – 1920 hours

Autumn Hudson, an NSA intelligence analyst, was working behind closed doors in her small office. A headset covered her short, brown, thinning hair, and wire-rimmed glasses sat low on a narrow nose. Autumn was forty, short, overweight, and had never married, and because of her work she had no social life. She was urgently trying to find the information Alexa had requested a few minutes earlier. Autumn couldn't refuse. Alexa had saved her life—and her career.

Five years ago she'd been compromised by a man she'd met at a hotel bar. He'd had a seductive Latin accent, and he'd taken an interest in her. Introducing himself as Carlos, he had offered to buy her a drink. Unaccustomed to any male attention, she'd gladly accepted. It was the last thing she remembered until she awoke in an ambulance.

She remembered Alexa holding her hand in the ambulance. She later learned that the drug she'd ingested would have killed her if Alexa hadn't followed her into the bathroom. Alexa had been having a drink with a friend at the same hotel bar, and noticed her stagger away and Carlos leave in a hurry.

A week after her encounter with Carlos, Autumn was still recovering in the hospital. Alexa had stopped by and told her that she'd identified the man at the bar from the security video footage. He was Carlos Santiago, a known member of a drug cartel. Alexa had told her that she'd called a friend at the FBI and that they'd tracked Carlos down and arrested him. Alexa had been allowed to sit in on the interrogation.

Alexa had explained that Carlos was unusually cooperative, and had admitted he was looking for a government insider to compromise to gain access to narcotics trafficking intelligence. Carlos knew the bar was a local hangout for federal employees and that she looked like an easy mark. After her reaction to the drug he'd slipped her, he knew that he'd be detained if he didn't flee. The good news was that she hadn't revealed any information other than she was an NSA analyst. Autumn was shocked at learning she'd even disclosed that much information. Telling a stranger she was with the NSA was a major violation.

After briefing her boss about what had happened, Autumn was relieved of duty while the agency conducted an internal investigation. A week later, she was cleared of any wrongdoing, thanks in part to Alexa's testimony and investigative work in identifying Carlos. Autumn felt deeply indebted to Alexa, and after hearing about Trent disappearing, she was determined to help.

Monroe County Sheriff's Office – 1920 hours

Deputy Griffin was about to leave for home when his department cell phone rang. "This is Deputy Griffin."

"Griff, there's an NCIS Agent Anthony Dobson here to see you. He says its important." The front desk deputy was a fishing buddy and knew that Griffin was about to leave for the day. His twelve-hour shift had ended twenty-five minutes ago.

Griffin had already completed his report documenting Alexa's statement concerning Trent and the information he'd received from the NTSB investigator. He'd flagged the report so that it would be held in the queue until the following afternoon so he could review it again before it was filed. His sergeant had already left for the day, so he planned to brief her in the morning. He wanted to see if she'd allow him to pursue the case further. Griffin hoped something else would turn up before he put his part of the investigation to bed. Maybe the NCIS agent could shed some new light on the subject.

"I'll be right there," Griffin said, with a little excitement in his voice.

Three minutes later, Agent Dobson was seated across a table from him.

"I was hoping you could help us in an investigation," Dobson began. "I'm on a tight time schedule, and I understand that you were the deputy who responded to the disturbance at the NAS front gate."

"That's correct. Alexa Padget and her friends believed her boyfriend, Trent McDougal, was being held on the base."

"So you interviewed Alexa and her friends?"

"I did."

"What did they say?"

Griffin started to get the feeling Dobson's intention was to tie up loose ends. If this was a cover-up, he was getting sucked into it, and that didn't sit well with him. "Ms. Padget told me she'd received a text from Trent. She said she called his cell phone and spoke with him. Mr. McDougal claimed he was at the base, but she couldn't get any additional information because their conversation was cut short. She didn't know why he would be on a Navy base or where he'd been."

"Anything else?"

"She told me that Mr. McDougal sounded calm for someone who had been lost for three weeks. She and her friends went to the base to find out what was happening. I was dispatched to the base after Alexa refused to leave. She insisted that she be allowed on the base to see Trent."

"Did Trent tell her where he'd been?"

"I don't believe so. Alexa seemed to think Trent was unaware he'd been missing. Damn strange if you ask me. Is Mr. McDougal alive and being held at the base?" Griffin asked. "I really need to know for my investigation. I'm sure the Sheriff is going to want an explanation. Actually, there are a lot of people that want to know what happened."

Dobson stared at him for a moment. "What do you think happened?"

"What I think doesn't matter. I just need to know if Trent McDougal is on the base so we can close our investigation. It's already cost the taxpayers a substantial amount of money for our search and rescue efforts. I imagine the Coast Guard and the other agencies that have been involved will want to close the case. If this is some kind of a hoax, I believe my department will want to seek reimbursement from McDougal. If I'm the one to close this investigation, it will give me some bragging rights."

"You think he's alive, don't you?"

"I do. I also think he's being held on the base. The NTSB investigator I spoke to has been ordered not to conduct any further investigation."

"Did you write a report?"

"Yes."

Dobson sighed. "I need to speak with Alexa and her friends. Where are they staying?"

"At a hotel not far from here."

"I also need to know the name of the NTSB investigator."

"It's John Garland."

"What's the name of the hotel?"

"They're at the Marriott, just over the bridge."

"I also need to see your report, and then you'll need to delete it from your system."

"I can't delete my report once it's in the system. My supervisor has to approve it before I can provide an official copy. Under Florida law, once it's in the system, it's a public record, and there are guidelines that have to be followed in order to purge a report."

"I suggest you not play this game with me," Dobson said forcefully. "I need to locate these people so I can speak with them. This is a federal matter, and it is way above your pay grade. I want that report deleted, and I don't care what you have to do to get it done. If I have to, I'll get a federal judge to seal it within the hour."

"What's going on?"

"None of your business. I also need your field notes."

Griffin smiled. "It's always a pleasure working with federal law enforcement. It never fails to be a one-way street." Griffin pulled out his notepad. He took his time flipping through it, starting at the first page. He could tell Dobson was getting angry.

"Give that to me." Dobson held his hand out.

"I have information in this notepad that I need in order to complete my other reports. Actually, this notebook is also a public record. You're going to need to get that judge to issue an order for it as well. However, I'll be happy to make you a copy."

"Deputy Griffin, we are wasting valuable time. Every minute is critical, and you're obstructing a national security investigation. Give me the notes from your interview. Now!"

Griffin leaned back and crossed his arms. "I'm a patriot, agent Dobson, and I will do whatever I need to do to defend our country and the rights of our citizens. I did one tour in Iraq and one in Afghanistan. If you will tell me what's going on, maybe I can assist you better. Your heavy-handed approach isn't going to get the job done."

Dobson clenched his jaw. "I appreciate your service to our country. However, you aren't cleared to know the details of the investigation, and I don't think you'd want to be included if you knew what was happening. So stop stalling me and do what's right. I'm going to take a chance and give you a tidbit in the spirit of cooperation." Dobson leaned across the table.

"We do have Trent McDougal, and we have recovered his plane. What you don't know is what's at stake here. I'd like you to take me to Alexa and her friends and get them to cooperate. I will ask permission to read you in, and I'll need you to come back to the base with me."

Griffin smelled a trap. "I think I'll stay here. If you guys can muzzle the NTSB, I think I'll stay out of this investigation. Besides, I'm not sure they'll be at the hotel, and there's nothing I can do to help you with there anyway."

"Deputy Griffin, I must inform you that you are involved already, and you will have to accompany me to the Marriott. I also need to advise you that you are not to discuss what you know about this incident with anyone from here on out, and that includes your supervisors. Any questions will be directed to me." Dobson handed Griffin his card. "Are we clear?"

"Crystal. But I don't have to accompany you anywhere."

"You do and you will, one way or another."

"That sounds like a threat."

"It's a promise. Under an obscure article in the Patriot Act, I can compel law enforcement to aid me in any investigation deemed critical to an imminent national security threat. If you choose to fight me on this, I will be forced to have you arrested. I'd prefer that you offer your assistance—willingly."

Griffin knew that this was a losing battle, and he really did want to find out what was going on. "Okay. You win. But I want to see that provision in the Act when we're done."

"Did you record your interview?" Dobson asked.

"No."

"You really don't have access to that report?"

"I really don't. It's already in the queue, and until my sergeant looks at it, I can't touch it. I can only add supplements."

"Let's go find Alexa and her friends," Dobson said. "I still need your notes."

"Since you made it clear that I'm going with you, I'll keep them for now. I'll help you find them. I really don't expect that you're going to tell me what's going on."

Dobson said, "Let's get going."

Griffin followed Dobson out to the parking lot.

"I'm in the black Tahoe," Dobson said. "You can follow me to the Marriott."

Griffin grunted and walked to his cruiser. He hoped Alexa and her friends weren't there.

The Marriott wasn't far from his office. Nothing was very far away in Key West. Dobson pulled into the parking lot and parked in front of the lobby door. Griffin parked behind him.

"I'll check with the clerk to get their room numbers," Dobson said. "Keep an eye out for them."

Griffin nodded and sat back down in his cruiser. A few minutes later Dobson walked out of the lobby.

"They're on different floors," Dobson said. "This is Alexa's room number. You go get her and bring her down to the lobby. I'll get the other two."

"Will do." Griffin had decided to take a side. Cover-ups and hurting innocent people wasn't what he stood for, and he wasn't going to let Alexa and her friends get ambushed. When Griffin got to Alexa's room, he stood there for a moment wondering what he should say. He knocked, and Alexa cracked open the door.

"Hello, there," Alexa said. "I didn't expect to see you again. Did you learn something new?"

Griffin touched a finger to his lips as he stood blocking the doorway. "I'm here with an NCIS agent. His name is Anthony Dobson. He wants to interview you and your friends at the base. I think he wants to do more than just talk. He sent me to get you while he went to get your friends. I think it best if I tell him you weren't here."

Alexa nodded. "Got it. I owe you."

He was sure she knew the risk he was taking. "He confirmed that Trent is on the base. He seems to have a deadline, so he recruited me to help him. Alexa, there is more going on here than meets the eye. He claims it's national security. But I agree with you. They're trying to cover something up. I can't just sit back and watch." Griffin backed away from the door as if no one had answered.

"I understand, and thank you." Alexa closed the door.

As Griffin walked toward the elevator, it chimed, and Dobson got off.

"I checked Alexa's room. No answer."

"Let me try. Maybe she was in the shower." Dobson brushed past him.

"I thought you were checking on the others."

"So did I, but then I got a feeling you might need my help convincing Ms. Padget to join us." Dobson banged on the door. "Alexa Padget, federal agents."

No reply. Dobson pounded on the door again.

Griffin sighed. "Like I told you, no one there. Maybe she's in one of her friend's rooms."

Dobson put his ear to the door, then tried looking through the peep hole. "I don't see or hear any movement. Let's go."

Their next stop was at Sue Calder's room. Griffin hoped Alexa had managed to call Marvin and Sue so they wouldn't answer the door.

Dobson knocked and listened. "Someone's home." The door opened a second later.

"Hi, Ms. Calder?" Dobson asked.

"Yes."

"I'm NCIS agent Anthony Dobson. I believe you already know Deputy Griffin."

"Yes, I do. I hope this means good news about Trent."

"It does," Dobson replied. "I need you to accompany me back to the base. I also need to find Alexa and Marvin. Alexa didn't answer her door."

Sue's room phone rang. "Come on in. That's probably her now." Sue walked toward the phone.

Dobson put his hand on Griffin's chest. "Stay outside and shout if either Marvin or Alexa show up."

Griffin nodded, and the door closed.

"Hello," Sue answered. When she turned, she was startled to see Dobson standing beside her.

"Don't answer your door," Alexa said.

"Why?"

"Just don't. Get out of there and go home. I already called Marvin."

"Uh-huh. Well that's interesting," Sue replied, then looked at Dobson, hoping he couldn't hear Alexa. "It's Marvin, a friend of ours. Marvin, there's an NCIS agent here right now."

"Shit!" Alexa said in a low voice. "Sue, listen very carefully. He will probably want you to go with him. Find a way to get away from him and hide. Make up any excuse, but don't go anywhere with him. I'll call your cell in twenty minutes, and we'll work out an escape plan."

"Twenty minutes. Got it, Marvin. Well, maybe we could meet you there. I think he has good news for us."

Dobson smiled and nodded at her.

"He says he does. He wants us to go back to the base with him."

"Don't do that under any circumstances," Alexa said.

"What's that? Okay, I'll ask him. Marvin wants to know if we can meet them at Schooners. Alexa is on her way there. Is that okay?"

"Deputy Griffin will take you to the base. I'll go pick them up. I'll be there in ten minutes. Have them wait outside."

"Marvin, Agent Dobson will pick you guys up in ten minutes. He says that you need to be waiting outside for him. Deputy Griffin is taking me to the base."

"Understood. You can trust Griffin. I'll find you later."

"Okay then. I'll see you both at the base." Sue paused, then added, "He hasn't said so, but I think they're going to let us see Trent." Sue looked at Dobson and said, "We're going to meet Trent, right?"

"Yes," Dobson replied. "He's fine. We had a few questions for him, and until we got some answers, we weren't going to let him go anywhere. I'm sure you can understand. He's confessed to this being a hoax."

"Marvin, Agent Dobson says Trent told them this was a hoax," Sue said. "I don't understand."

"Just hang up," Alexa said.

"Okay, see you then." She hung up and turned to face Dobson. "This was all a hoax? Alexa has been worried sick. Trent will wish he *was* dead after she's done with him."

"I'd probably feel the same way. Why don't we get going?" Dobson walked to the door and opened it.

Sue grabbed her purse, then put it down. "Oh, I need to change clothes. I can't go out like this. Give me a second to change."

Dobson sighed. "Griffin, you stay with her. I'm headed for Schooners to meet Alexa and Marvin. Take her back to the base. I'll leave word at the security gate that you're to be escorted to my office."

Griffin said, "What am I going to do with her at your office?"

"Just wait for me there. Make sure she's comfortable until we arrive. Some people there will help you." Dobson smiled at Sue, then said, "Ms. Calder, you're in good hands. See you soon."

"Okay, bye now."

When Dobson was gone, Griffin walked into Sue's room and closed the door. "That was Alexa on the phone, wasn't it?"

"Yes, it was. She said I could trust you. Can I?"

"You can, but this just got a whole lot more complicated. Call Alexa and tell her Dobson is on his way to Schooners. We won't have much time after he figures out he's been duped."

"I think she knows where he's headed." Sue called Alexa anyway, and a minute later she was in Sue's room.

Griffin thought the look on Alexa's face said it all. She was ready to go to war.

"Alexa, Dobson has the power to arrest all of you, and me, and keep you at the base. When he doesn't find you at Schooners, he'll probably shut down US 1. It's the only road to the mainland, and it isn't hard to block. The airport isn't going to be of much help. I hope you have a plan for getting off the island, because I need to leave here with Sue."

Alexa smiled at him. "I always have a plan. I have a motor yacht waiting for us at the marina. I called Marvin, and he's already on his way to the dock. Deputy Griffin, you will escort Sue down to your car. I want you to be seen on the security cameras just doing your job."

"I think at this point you should start calling me Griff. What do I do with Sue once she's in my cruiser?"

"I need you to drive out of the hotel parking lot. Sue needs to be in the front seat. At the first traffic light, Sue will jump out of the cruiser."

"I can do that," Sue replied, sounding energized.

"I'll be waiting a few cars behind you. Griff, Sue isn't a fast runner, so I'll need you to fake a stumble as you exit your cruiser, then give chase. Pretend you injured your ankle and limp so she has enough time to reach my car. I'll take off. Then you call Dobson."

"What do you want me to tell him?"

"Tell him you were taken by surprise, slipped and fell and injured your ankle. That you chased Sue on foot and saw her get in my car. The last time you saw us, we were headed north. Tell him you think we're trying to get out of Key West."

"Wouldn't he expect me to chase you?"

"I'm sure he would. Tell him that you're hobbling back to your cruiser, but you don't think you will be able to catch up to us."

"You should ask him to set up a roadblock at the entrance to the base," Sue said. "We'd have to go right by it to leave the island."

"That's perfect," Alexa said.

"See, I told you I could help."

"This sounds too simple," Griffin said.

"Simple is always better," Alexa replied. "I'll drive toward the bridge, then double back to the marina. You can run lights and siren to the base as if you're chasing me."

"That might work. Dobson wants me to go to the base with him, anyway. I have a feeling I won't be leaving there."

Alexa hugged him, then gave him a kiss on the cheek. "Thank you. Stick to the plan and the story. It'll all work out."

FIVE

Naval Air Station Key West — 2000 hours

Agent Dobson didn't want to call General Starke with the news. He knew that the general would go ballistic. Griffin had just called him and told him what had happened. Obviously, Alexa and Marvin wouldn't be at Schooners. He wondered if Griffin had tipped them off. Griffin had told him he was going to put out a BOLO for Alexa's rental car. The roadblock was good idea, but he didn't think it would net any results. He knew that the trio wouldn't get far before being apprehended. The problem was that he wouldn't have them all back to the base by Starke's deadline. He ordered Griffin to report to the base. He dialed the general's number.

"What do you mean they're on the run," Starke bellowed.

"Just what I said," Dobson replied. "Deputy Griffin was transporting Sue Calder back to the base when she made a run for it. Padget and Calder had to have communicated after I left for the bar where they were supposed to meet me. I think Calder called Padget on her cell phone when Griffin wasn't watching. We'll find them. It's a small island."

"I give you a simple task and you're outwitted by three civilians. What kind of a bumbling agent are you?"

"General, Alexa Padget is former Secret Service. She knows Trent's being held on the base. She'd figure out that anyone who knew Trent was alive would be corralled."

"Probably, which is why you should have anticipated her moves."

After a moment of silence, Dobson asked the question he really didn't want to ask. "General Starke, how do you want me to proceed? With Griffin issuing a BOLO for Padget's rental, we're going to become visible."

"Like you said, it's a small island. I'll have Major Striker assemble a team to start his own search and establish a roadblock. Call me back in two minutes."

Dobson drove back to the Marriott, searched the immediate area, parked, and called Starke as directed.

"Where are you now?" Starke asked.

"I'm back at the Marriott. No sign of them or the rental."

"Get your ass to the base. McDougal's plane has been dismantled and is already aboard a C-17. Colonel Endo has done her preliminary medical evaluation of McDougal, and Dr. Sanderson has begun questioning him. I hope your dragnet catches the fugitives in the next thirty minutes because we *will* be airborne in an hour. I sincerely hope that we have all parties aboard. I'm already behind schedule. Do you think you can handle getting the deputy to the base by then?"

"He should already be at the front gate. I told him he had to work with us under a provision in the Patriot Act."

"Good. If he's at the gate, I'll have Striker show him to your office."

"Do you still plan on taking me with you if we haven't found the others? I might be of better use looking for Padgett and her friends. I know the islands better than Major Striker."

"You and Deputy Griffin will accompany us. If the others aren't found in the next thirty minutes, Major Striker will stay behind to clean up your mess."

"I didn't make a mess, General Starke. Whatever caused McDougal's disappearance created the problem. When am I going to be fully briefed?"

"When I think you need to know."

The line went dead.

Forty-five minutes later, Dobson scrambled aboard a C-17 with his ready-go bag in tow and stopped at the top of the ramp. There had been no sign of Alexa or the others. He turned around as a Navy patrol car pulled up behind the plane. Deputy Griffin got out of the passenger side. He was dressed in fatigues, carrying a small overnight bag. He didn't look happy as he walked up the ramp. Another loose end had been contained. The plane ride would give him the opportunity to see if Griffin had tipped off the trio. He hadn't shared his suspicions with the general, but if he learned that was true, it could give him a way to save face.

"Nice to see you again, Deputy Griffin," Dobson said. "I was wondering why you weren't in my office."

"Blow it out your ass," Griffin replied, tossing his carry-on into a small storage compartment next to the row of seats.

Dobson didn't blame him for being pissed off. "Hey, I was involuntarily drafted for this assignment as well. Nice carry-on and attire."

"Base exchange purchase courtesy of the Navy. I can't believe I've been dragged into this situation. Where the hell are we going?"

"I haven't been told yet," Dobson replied.

Griffin nodded toward the officer standing at the foot of the ramp. "You going to tell me why a Space Force general is running the show? I thought this was an NCIS investigation."

"I'm afraid we've both found ourselves in the middle of some intrigue, wrapped in a national security blanket. I wasn't lying when I told you this was a matter of national security."

"I can see that. I assume that I'm supposed to forget everything I hear and see."

"That would be smart," Dobson replied, watching another car pull up and park behind the plane. "I think we'll both want to forget what we see and hear. Believe it or not, we're on the same team."

Col. Melissa Endo exited the front passenger seat of the car that had just arrived. Trent had to be helped out of the backseat by Dr. Sanderson. Major Striker drove up in another car and got out. Dobson watched as Dr. Sanderson made animated gestures in front of Starke and Melissa. Dobson couldn't hear what was being said, but Sanderson was obviously displeased about something. General Starke put his hands up, then pointed at the ramp. Sanderson shook his head, but he took Trent's arm and with

Melissa walked up the ramp and into the plane. He noted that Trent was handcuffed, and he wasn't very steady on his feet. A minute later, Major Striker saluted the general and left in the car. Then the general boarded the plane, and the ramp closed behind him.

"Deputy Griffin, let me introduce you to everyone," General Starke said.

After the introductions were made, Griffin said, "Where are we going? I have duty tomorrow."

"No, you don't," Starke said. "Sit down and buckle up."

Griffin didn't move. "Not until you tell me where I'm being taken."

The general walked over and stood inches from Griffin. "Are you good at geography, Deputy Griffin?"

"Yes, sir."

"Then keep an eye out the window and you'll know where you are when you get there." The general walked away and sat down.

Griffin looked around the cavernous aircraft. The seats all faced inward. There were no windows. Griffin's face flushed.

Melissa led Trent past Dobson and helped him into a seat next to where Dr. Sanderson had planted himself. Dobson noticed a bandage taped to the crook of McDougal's left arm. It appeared they'd taken a blood sample or drugged him, maybe both. He didn't want to know what other probing they'd done.

"We better take a seat," Dobson said to Griffin. "It's too late to run, and it wouldn't do any good."

"It doesn't look like I have much choice," Griffin replied. "I wonder if the general told my sheriff that I was going on this trip."

"I imagine Major Striker will brief him. Another mysterious disappearance wouldn't sit well with anyone. I think since technically we're hunting for three fugitives that pose a national security threat, your sheriff will understand."

"Let's sit on this side of the aircraft away from them," Griffin said. "You said that you'd read me in when we got back to the base. So what's this all about?"

"I lied to you. I can't tell you anything until the general says you're cleared to know. Remember that the less you know the less you have to forget." Dobson gave Griffin a crooked grin.

"I figured you wouldn't keep your promise."

The plane's giant engines came to life. A minute later, the plane taxied away from the buildings and rolled out onto the runway. The four Pratt & Whitney turbo-fan engines spun up to full power, and then they were airborne.

South of Key West – 2100 hours

A motor yacht drifted just south of the end of the Boca Chica runway. Alexa stood at the stern of the thirty-six-foot Hatteras peering through binoculars. Sue stood beside her. Marvin was at the helm. Alexa watched the C-17 take off and climb into the darkening sky.

"That's the second C-17 to depart," Alexa said.

"Yup," Marvin replied.

"Do you think Trent was on that one?" Sue asked Alexa.

"I imagine," she replied. "Marvin, let's head for Naples. I'll call my friend and have her start tracking those planes."

"It'll take us a few hours to get there," Marvin said.

"I know that, Marvin," she snapped. "I'm sorry. I don't mean to be short, but I'm tired, and I think this adventure is just beginning."

"Apology accepted. I hope your *friend* can give us some answers."

"She's very good at what she does. If anyone can find out where Trent is going, she can."

Ft. Meade, Maryland – NSA Headquarters – 2300 hours

Sitting alone in her small office, Autumn Hudson monitored the FAA flight database and the secure Space Force High Frequency Global Communications System. Since getting the call from Alexa, she'd loaded a special program that allowed her to monitor radar traffic and aircraft communications nationwide. She'd been able to track the two aircraft that had left Key West, but it hadn't been easy. The aircrafts' projected flight paths weren't available, but the periodic pings on the flight radar indicated that both planes were headed in the same general direction. The second aircraft to leave Key West was now approaching the Texas coast. The other C-17 was about an hour ahead and northwest of the other plane. Based on what Alexa had said, Trent was probably on the trailing C-17.

Autumn intercepted a radio check-in from the lead aircraft. The pilot confirmed a two-hour ETA at Mountain Home AFB, just south of Boise, Idaho. "That's a lucky break," she whispered. She knew that Alexa would be happy to know the destination of at least one of the planes. She pulled up information on the Mountain Home base on her laptop and learned that it was the home of the 580th Air Resupply Command and the 366th Fighter Wing. The things that caught her eye were that the 569th Strategic Missile Command and a specialized medical group were also based there. *Probably the perfect place to take Trent,* she thought. She decided to see what she could find out about the base and the medical group.

After about twenty minutes of research in a classified data base, she'd discovered only one tidbit that wasn't on the public website. About six hours ago, the base had been put on alert and was closed to the public. She did another check of recorded radio transmissions and confirmed the second C-17 was also going to land at Mountain Home AFB. She shut down the tracking program and left her office. After exiting through a security checkpoint, she walked to her car in the parking lot. She couldn't risk making calls from within the building.

Naples, Florida — 2330 hours EST

Alexa answered the burner phone after the first ring. "This is Alexa."

"It's me," Autumn said, not using her name. "Your friend is headed for Mountain Home AFB in Idaho. The lead plane will be on the ground at 2300 hours MST. Your friend's plane will land around midnight."

"Excellent work. Anything special about the base?"

"Not particularly," Autumn replied. "But, the base was put on alert and secured about six hours ago."

"Any indication as to why?"

"None."

"Hmmm. Is there another facility near the base?"

"Nope, just mountains. The base is southeast of Boise. I can tell you that there's a larger than normal percentage of medical personnel assigned there. Nearly double what's found on bases with twice the personnel."

"That's interesting. The medical aspect could be related to this operation."

"The base also serves as a resupply and fighter command location. Oh, and there's a strategic missile component there, too."

"I wonder why they would take him there. They could have taken him to a base a lot closer than Idaho."

"True, but you said he'd been missing for a while before he reappeared. Maybe they have special medical specialists at that base for these types of cases."

"Is there any way you can dig deeper into the medical group?" Alexa asked.

"If it's linked to black ops, any inquiry will be flagged."

Alexa leaned back against the boat railing. "Let's not push it for now. We're getting ready to dock at a marina. Can you call me back in thirty minutes?"

"Sure thing."

"Thanks for the update. I'll see what I can dig up on my end." Alexa hung up.

She told Marvin and Sue where Trent was headed, then used her burner phone to call another friend in Utah.

Salt Lake City, Utah — 2140 hours MST

Dan Mitchell had just turned into the driveway of his home when his cell phone rang. "Hello."

"It's me," Alexa said. "I'm on a burner and need some information."

Dan knew Alexa well. They'd worked together on the same protection team at the Secret Service for over two years. He'd heard about Trent's disappearance and thought her call might be related. He'd called Alexa just after Trent went missing and had offered to help in the search, but she'd declined. If Alexa was using a burner phone, then she wasn't calling just to chat. There had to be a problem. "How can I help?"

"Trent resurfaced earlier today at the Key West Naval Air Station. He's being flown on a military transport to an airbase in Idaho, and—"

"What? Wait, this isn't a secure line. Are you sure you want to proceed?"

"Yes, time is critical. I spoke to Trent briefly. He told me where he was, then he was detained and communication was severed. I attempted to gain access to the base to see him, but was barred."

"That's an interesting development. It's good to hear that he's alive."

"Very much so. What do you know about Mountain Home AFB?"

"Nothing."

"That's where he's going."

"That seems like a bit of a hike from Key West."

"Unknown military and an NCIS agent tried to have me and two of my friends detained. We managed to elude them. They're trying to keep the information from being released. You know what that means."

"Someone wants to keep Trent's reappearance quiet. What do you need from me?"

"I was hoping you'd offer your assistance, but are you sure you want to get involved? This may get ugly."

"I've been leading a boring life of late. This may get the blood pumping again."

"I'd use my own people, but I'm afraid they'll be monitored. They don't know you or your security staff. I'll cover salary and expenses."

"You can owe me. I'm sure I'll need some help in Florida sometime."

"Can you get a surveillance team to Boise? I'm in Naples, and I doubt that I'll be able to get up there until late tomorrow. He's on a C-17 which is landing at the base in a little over two hours."

"I'll get a team on the way. It'll be about six hours before I can have eyes on the base. I've got a buddy who works in Boise. Maybe he knows something about the base and can do me a favor and keep an eye out until my team gets there."

"The base is on alert and has been locked down. I don't know for how long, but it has to be related to Trent. They'll be actively looking for anyone snooping around."

"You must still be well connected to have this intel already."

"I am. Listen, I don't want to hazard anyone unnecessarily."

Dan laughed. "But you can hazard me?"

"You're used to it," Alexa teased. "Six hours is good. I'm not even sure what your team can do there, but I'll feel better knowing someone is near Trent."

"I'll call you when I'm in place. Are you contemplating an extraction?"

"I really don't know yet. If I do, I won't involve you or your team."

"We can still help with support and surveillance."

"Thanks, Dan."

"See you soon." After he disconnected, he called two of his surveillance specialists, gave them a quick brief, and got them rolling with the surveillance van and equipment.

Dan Mitchell was the president of Westcoast Security. Like Alexa, he specialized in VIP protection and security assessments for private companies. His company also provided security for a major communications defense contractor near Hill AFB, just south of Ogden, Utah.

Dan thought the world of Alexa, and he was sorry to hear that she'd left the Secret Service. She'd had a promising career. She was one of the good ones. But he couldn't blame her for seeking a more lucrative profession in the private sector.

He walked through the front door of his house and saw that his wife, Peggy, was just putting his dinner on the table. His two daughters were nowhere to be seen.

"You're late," Peggy said. "Tough day?"

"And going to get tougher. I need to pack a bag and drive up to Boise."

"You mean now?"

"Afraid so. I don't know how long I'll be gone. Are the girls upstairs?"

Peggy frowned and said, "I thought all this short-notice travel was over when you left the Secret Service. Don't you have a team you can send?"

"I do, and they are en route. You remember Alexa Padget?"

"Yes. Her boyfriend disappeared a few weeks ago. Does this have anything to do with that?"

"Yes. She sounded in desperate need of assistance."

Peggy bit her lip. "I know you two worked closely together, but what can you do for her in Boise?"

"Trent's alive. He's being flown to Idaho by the government."

"He's alive? That's wonderful. Why's he being taken there?"

"It's a long story, and I don't have time to explain everything. Don't tell anyone he's been located. I need to get going."

"You'll eat dinner first. You can wait fifteen more minutes, and then I'll help you pack."

"Thanks."

"Give Alexa a hug for me."

Thirty minutes later, Dan was headed north.

SIX

Over Utah — February 02 — 2330 hours MST

Colonel Endo and General Starke were speaking with one of the pilots near the front of the aircraft's massive cargo area. A minute later, the pilot went back into the cockpit and the general and Melissa walked back to the rest of the group.

"I've been told the outside air temperature at touchdown will be a balmy eighteen degrees," General Starke said. "I've asked the pilot to keep the engines turning until winter coats can be delivered."

"How thoughtful," Griffin said sarcastically. "I figure we're somewhere in the northwest."

"Correct," Starke said. "This will be a bit of a change for you."

"Exactly where are we?" Griffin asked.

General Starke smiled, then replied, "We'll be landing in Idaho in a few minutes."

"Idaho?" Dobson said.

"At Mountain Home Air Force Base," Starke added. "Not that it matters. We won't be staying there very long."

"Then where are we going?" Griffin asked.

"Someplace you'll never be able to talk about."

"I still don't know why I'm here," Griffin said.

"Because I felt you needed to be here," the general answered. "Colonel, you will ride with Dr. Sanderson and McDougal to the base hospital. I know that you want to do the preliminary screening before we transfer McDougal to Sawtooth. Dobson and the deputy will ride with me."

"Yes, sir," Melissa replied.

"This is nuts," Dr. Sanderson said. "We could've conducted all the tests at Boca Chica. Now we're involving more personnel and compromising the entire operation." He glanced at Dobson and Griffin. "Those two know more than they needed to know."

"Relax, Arnie," Starke said. "They won't tell anyone anything, and we couldn't have stayed in Key West with McDougal. Also, McDougal has a determined girlfriend and sympathetic friends searching for him. We didn't need the media making inquiries. Isn't that right, Deputy Griffin?"

"She does have lots of friends on the island, and she's resourceful. I still don't know why I need to be here. Even Dr. Sanderson is questioning that decision. I would've kept my mouth shut."

General Starke stared at him for a moment. "I don't think that Alexa Padget is all that resourceful. To be blunt, I don't trust you. I think you let Padget and the others get away. In order to stop you from running interference, I decided to take you out of the equation. Major Striker won't be as sympathetic to anyone else he finds that knows McDougal has returned from the dead." Starke paused. "I know that you believed you were doing the right thing. You felt sorry for Padget. The information you got from John Garland at the NTSB convinced you to take a side, and you decided to help Padget and her friends."

"How did you know about that call?" Griffin asked.

"Agent Dobson told me," Starke said. "You're a nosy deputy, which is usually an admirable trait for a law enforcement officer. However, in this case, you stuck your nose where it didn't belong. You should've just escorted Padget from the base, wrote a report about a disturbance, and called it a day. Now you'll be our guest until our investigation is complete."

"Then what?" Griffin asked.

"Then, you and Agent Dobson will be returned to Key West. If you say anything about this adventure, it will be met with the severest sanctions imaginable. Am I clear?"

"Yes, sir." Griffin answered. "I've been hearing that a lot."

"Good. Now give me your cell phones."

"Why mine?" Dobson asked.

Starke gave him a hard stare, then said, "Because I don't trust you, either."

Griffin and Dobson handed over their phones, and then Starke said, "I'm sure Ms. Padget has many friends who are still with the Secret Service. I wouldn't be surprised if she could find someone to help her track your phones. I should have taken them from you earlier." Starke pulled the batteries out of both phones. "You'll get them back when you leave."

Dobson glared at Griffin, then said, "Did you help them?"

Griffin only smiled.

"Damn, I knew it," Dobson snapped. "I ought to charge you with obstructing a federal investigation."

"Agent Dobson, there won't be any charges filed," Starke said. "That will only bring an unwanted investigation by all of Griffin's buddies at the Sheriff's Office. Isn't that right?"

"Yes," Griffin answered smugly. "General, you know that this could have been handled a lot better. All you had to do was let Alexa and her friends onto the base and reunite them. You would've had all the players in one place, and they'd have been waiting for you."

Starke said, "Deputy Griffin, you're absolutely right." He faced Dobson and said, "Agent Dobson, why didn't you do that?"

"Don't you dare try to blame this mess on me. I was in the dark until I spoke to Trent, and then you arrived."

"And talking to him is what got you here. If you hadn't started asking questions, you'd be at home now."

"I wasn't told not to question McDougal," Dobson said.

"That's a moot point now."

"So, am I officially your prisoner?" Griffin asked.

"Not at all. If you were a prisoner, we'd have you shackled and handcuffed."

"But I'm not free to leave."

"That's correct," Starke replied. "Consider yourself administratively detained."

"That's an interesting way to put it," Griffin said.

"Interfere again and your status *will* change, and Agent Dobson will get his wish, and you will be charged."

"Got it," Griffin said.

February 03 — Naples — 0215 hours

While Alexa checked in with Autumn at the NSA, she had Marvin call Karen, one of the volunteers who had helped search for Trent, to determine what was happening back in Key West. When she finished her call, Alexa joined Marvin and Sue on the aft deck.

"Marvin, what'd Karen have to say?" Alexa asked.

"I woke her up, but she had some interesting info. She said that there's a Space Force major by the name of Frank Striker asking a lot of questions about us. He claimed that wreckage from Trent's plane has been found. He told her that Trent was involved in a drug-smuggling operation and that he crashed while flying in restricted airspace."

"Did she buy that load of crap?" Alexa asked.

"No, and you'll like this even more. Striker is claiming that we're involved. Karen said she heard that Striker's spreading the same story to others who were involved in the search. He's also threatened a couple of them."

"How did he threaten them?" Sue asked.

"He's telling people that if they know where we are and don't disclose our whereabouts, it would make them accessories after the fact and he'll arrest them. Karen said that people don't believe a Space Force major is involved in a drug-trafficking investigation."

"Anything else?"

"A deputy that Karen knows said that Deputy Griffin has been temporarily reassigned to assist the military in finding us. None of his buddies have seen him since yesterday evening."

"Another mouth silenced," Alexa said. "It's a good thing we disabled our cell phones."

"Does this mean I can't go home?" Sue asked, sounding alarmed. "Can they arrest us?"

"Not arrested in the way you're thinking," Alexa replied.

"What does that mean?"

"I'm certain we'd be detained. Then they'd threaten us with incarceration if we ever disclosed anything about Trent being alive."

"I'm already frightened," Sue said.

"I know." Alexa put a hand on her shoulder. "I just spoke to my friend at the NSA. Trent's plane landed at Mountain Home AFB in Idaho a few minutes ago. She'll continue to monitor it and see if it takes off again."

"If it does leave," Marvin said, "it doesn't mean that Trent is still onboard."

"True, but I think that's the area where we'll find Trent. I don't think they'll keep him on the base. I'm thinking that they'll move him to a remote site."

Marvin said, "Makes sense. How soon until Dan's team is in position?"

"I don't know exactly. He'll contact me when he and his team are eyes-on. Sue, what have you found for us in the way of transportation out of Naples?"

"Not much yet. Since we're fugitives, I'm sure we can't travel by commercial air. What am I going to tell my family?"

"Call them and tell them Trent's alive, but the government is pursuing us in order to keep it quiet."

"Seriously?" Sue cried.

"No," Alexa said. "Just tell them there's been a development and that you're going to stay with me for a while longer. We don't want any more people involved. Based on what Karen said, I'd say their next step will be to go public. They'll say that Trent is dead and that he crashed trying to smuggle dope into Key West. They'll try to discredit us and turn people against us so they turn us in.

"Sue, tell your family that investigators will be contacting them. Let them know that they'll spread a story about us being drug smugglers. When questioned, and they will be eventually, all they know is that you called and that you're still in Key West with me. Make sure that they know you're safe and that you'll be back in touch when you can."

Sue nodded. "I guess I should call them now. I'll have my sister call my boss in the morning. No one will believe that I'm a smuggler."

"What about your partner, Linda?" Marvin asked.

"We broke up just before I came to help you guys."

"I didn't know that," Alexa said. "I was so absorbed in finding Trent that I didn't even think to ask how you were doing."

"Not a big deal. She found someone else, and I threw her out of my house."

"So I guess you don't need to call her," Marvin joked.

"Not a chance. Let her think whatever."

Alexa stood and stretched. "Let's get a few hours of sleep. We'll start fresh in the morning."

"You know we're going to have to operate on a cash basis," Marvin said.

"Yes. I still have the cash I took from my business account when we started searching for Trent."

"How much is left?" Sue asked.

"Just under a hundred thousand," Alexa said without batting an eye.

"You've had that kind of money with you all this time?" Sue asked. "Where is it now?"

"In my backpack. It should be enough to rent a private jet to Boise in the morning."

"Providing we aren't on a watch list by then," Marvin said.

"We won't be, at least not yet. They just want us driven to ground for the time being. They know we didn't leave Key West by vehicle. And if they think we left by boat, they'll search the lower Keys first."

"Alexa, a change of identity is in order," Marvin said.

"That would help."

"I know a guy in Miami that can provide us with false ID's." Marvin offered. "It may cost us a few grand, but you're rich."

Alexa grinned, then said, "Not as rich as I was once. Make the call. We'll need them fast."

"For the right amount of money, he'll get them to us by noon at the latest."

"I'll call the boat's owner in a few hours and let him know where we've docked."

"He won't mind that you took his boat to Naples?" Sue asked.

"Nope." Alexa held up a finger. "Don't ask."

Marvin grinned. "I'm always amazed by the depth of your contacts, boss."

Alexa smiled.

Mountain Home AFB — 0110 hours MST

"You're certain, Colonel?" General Starke asked.

"Very certain," Melissa replied.

"So he's a bona-fide abductee?"

"Based on the physical evidence we just discovered in his left tibia, he is indeed," Dr. Sanderson said.

"I guess it was a good idea to bring him here then, wasn't it?" Starke said.

"Don't rub it in," Sanderson replied. "I've investigated so many false abduction claims that I've grown cynical."

Melissa stepped over to the console table and typed a command. "General, if you'll look at this image." A wall-mounted monitor came to life. "This is Trent's left tibia. Dr. Sanderson, can you point out the implant for the general?"

Dr. Sanderson walked to the screen and pointed to a slight distortion in the image. "This is it."

General Starke took a closer look at the image. "Is it the same size as the one we removed from our guest?"

"It's exactly the same," Sanderson replied. "It's five millimeters long and has the same corkscrew shape. It's undetectable by a routine X-ray or CT scan. Only our advanced MRI can detect it, and then you have to know what to look for."

Melissa said, "By the looks of the depth of the implant, it was placed there when Trent was a small boy. The bone has grown around it."

"It's also located in the exact same place as our other guest," Sanderson said. "The size and shape of the scar are the same, too."

"Colonel, do you still think it's a monitoring device?" Starke asked.

"Yes, sir. As you're aware, when we removed the artifact from Taylor's leg two years ago, it dissolved as soon as it was exposed to the air. She hasn't experienced any more abductions since then."

"They used it to find her and probably to monitor her health," Sanderson added.

Starke said, "Taylor was also abducted several times. Do you think Trent is a repeat abductee and he just doesn't remember?"

"Possibly," Melissa replied. "I think it would be best if we don't try to remove the implant in Trent's leg, at least for now. I have some new equipment at the facility that may help us better understand its functionality, but there is a risk."

Starke nodded, then said, "Whoever planted it will know where to find Trent, which is what I'm hoping will happen."

"They didn't come looking for Taylor before we removed her implant," Sanderson said.

"That we know of," Melissa added. "They may have thought she'd died."

General Starke looked back at the image of the implant, then said, "Package him up, and let's get him transported. Is he still claiming that he has no idea what happened to him?"

"Yes, sir," Sanderson replied. "I've used a truth agent and dug deep. He has no recollection. All he remembers is a bright light, then feeling disoriented, and then he was back flying his airplane."

"I wonder if this is the only implant," Starke said, looking at Melissa.

She glanced at Sanderson, then replied, "It's the only one that we've found. We've examined Taylor thoroughly over the last two years, and her implant was the only one in her body. We saw no evidence of any new scar tissue."

"Sanderson, you said Trent remembers being abducted as a child," Starke said. "What exactly did he tell you occurred?"

Dr. Sanderson gave them all the details of what Trent had said.

Starke nodded, then said, "Colonel, scan Trent completely before we leave. I want to know if he has anything else in his body that isn't from Earth."

"Yes, sir," Melissa replied. "I doubt we'll find anything with the equipment they have here."

"I understand that, but I want it done anyway. Let me know when you're finished."

Medical Center — 0200 hours MST

Trent felt drained. He'd been drugged, probed, X-rayed, and scanned. He still didn't know where he'd been for three weeks. Everyone wanted answers, but he didn't have any to give them.

Col. Melissa Endo walked through the door. "We need to do some more medical tests."

Trent found her to be direct and clinical. "Any chance I could get some sleep and food first? I'm starving. I don't even remember the last time I ate."

"Mr. McDougal, we'll try to get you something once the tests are complete. Right now it's important that we not introduce anything into your body."

"Can you tell me what's really going on?"

"You've asked me that question many times. My answer is still the same. I ask the questions."

Trent actually liked her, even though she and the other doctor had taken enough blood to start their own blood bank. "I really need some food. Whatever you're serving in the IV drip isn't satisfying my stomach."

Melissa stopped what she was doing and smiled at him. "I know it isn't. The IV drip is only saline. I can appreciate you wanting to eat." Her brows furrowed as she looked at him. "When did you first feel hungry?"

Trent thought that was an odd question. "After landing, when I was with the NCIS agent."

Melissa put the computer tablet down and sat on the bed next to him. "I believe you have been truthful in all of your responses." She took his hand. "Trent, we need to find Alexa and her friends, so if you have any information that might help us locate her, I'd appreciate you sharing it now."

Trent thought this was a different approach. Up until now, the colonel had been all business. She was an attractive woman with short brown hair and brown eyes. He wondered if her change in demeanor was supposed to soften him up. But since he didn't know where they were, her charm was being wasted. "I understand you want to find them. But I have no idea where they could be, and no matter how nice you are to me, I can't tell you anything. Can I have my hand back?"

Melissa smiled and let go of his hand. "Humor is a good sign. If you think of anything, please let me know."

"Since I'm cooperating, can I call Alexa?"

"No."

"Ever?"

Melissa smiled, then said, "Dr. Sanderson told me that you were abducted as a child."

"I don't remember talking to him about that."

"You were drugged during the questioning. A side effect of the drug is that you won't recall what you've said. The small triangular scar on your left tibia is from an alien implant being surgically inserted into your bone. Tell me about the day you got it."

Trent looked down at his leg. An image of his mom and the old house sprang to mind. He remembered the day he'd seen the alien craft and the small creatures that had taken him away a few months later. He looked at Melissa. "I was seven or eight…" Trent told her everything he could remember.

"I'm sure the two abductions are related," Melissa said. "Tell me what you saw when the light took you away this time."

"I don't remember being taken anywhere. I recall only shadows in a foggy mist, and that was only for a brief time. I could have been seeing my instrument panel in the light, or maybe I just imagined it."

Melissa nodded. "Any shapes?"

"No. More like dark smudges. Has this happened to others?"

"Yes," Melissa replied.

Trent studied her face. It seemed as if she was thinking about whether she should tell him something else. "What is it? Maybe if you're honest with me, it will trigger something in my memory."

"You're only the second abduction case we've seen that's indisputable. The additional scans and tests we want to perform will tell us if there's anything else in your body that's alien. The other abductee had only the one implant in the same place as yours. We removed it."

"I don't think you'll find anything else. This is the only wound I remember getting, but scan away. Thank you for being honest with me."

"You deserved to know the truth."

Trent's room — 0430 hours MST

Two hours later, Trent awoke as Melissa and General Starke entered his room. Melissa turned on the lights. She held a food tray.

"That food smells good," Trent said. "What is it?"

"Two eggs, bacon, and biscuits with jelly," she answered.

"Thank you."

Melissa put the tray on the overbed table and unfastened his restraints.

"This can't be good if you're both here," Trent said. He didn't wait for an answer as he took a bite of the eggs. No one said anything as the eggs disappeared in three large bites.

"Slow down," Melissa said. "You don't want to choke."

"Sorry. This is really good." He took a bite of bacon, then stuffed half of a biscuit his mouth, leaned back, patted his belly, and moaned while he chewed.

"Your latest MRI scan proved interesting," Melissa said.

He stopped in mid-chew. "How?" he mumbled.

"We found another implant. It's in your brain. We'll need to get a better image of it at a facility with more advanced imaging equipment. It's quite small and a very different in shape from the one in your leg."

Trent swallowed and put the rest of the biscuit on his plate. "What exactly is it?"

Melissa smiled. "We don't know for sure. The neural implant has two tapered, thin, wirelike tendrils that are slightly larger than the width of a hair. They're joined at one end."

"Where in my brain is it located?"

"Both tendrils are woven into the cortex covering your frontal lobe."

"That doesn't sound good. I don't have any other scars. How'd they get it in my brain without leaving some sign?"

"I don't know. But from what I can tell, the device was implanted within the last few weeks."

Trent stared at her. "You mean it was done when I went missing? Is it deadly?"

"The answer to your first question is yes. We don't believe so to the second. We can remove the one from your leg, but we are inclined not to do so. I'm not sure about the one in your brain."

"Why don't you want to remove the one from my leg?"

General Stark said, "Because we removed one once and it dissolved when it was exposed to air. We think it could be a monitoring device."

"And the one in my head would require a more delicate procedure?"

"Yes, that one would require the skill of a neurosurgeon," Melissa answered. "I'm concerned that the cure may be worse than leaving it in there."

Trent looked at the general, then back at Melissa. "I think the real reason you don't want to remove the implants is that you want to study me."

"Yes," General Starke replied. "We believe that they put a monitoring device in your leg as a child and used it to find you again as an adult."

"Like we tag animals in the wild to study their behavior," Melissa added.

"I see. What about the thing in my brain? Is that like the wires we put in animal brains in the lab? Are they reading my thoughts? Are they going to stimulate my nerve centers to see what I do?"

"Like I said, I don't know what it's there to do," Melissa answered. "The cortex is the outer covering of your brain. It's called the bark of the tree. It's responsible for your memory, personality, motor skills, and visual perception. It's also the area responsible for critical thinking. The frontal lobe controls your abstract reasoning, judgement, planning, and organization skills."

"Enough with the anatomy lessons, Colonel Endo," Starke said. "Trent, we're going to study you for a while. If the beings who put this device in your head do start *stimulating* you, as you put it, we want to see your reaction."

Trent stared at Starke. "How long do you plan to study me?"

"Until we know what the aliens want with you and whether they're going to turn you into a weapon," Starke replied.

"So basically what you're saying is that I won't be going home any time soon."

"That's correct," Melissa answered.

Trent settled back onto the bed and closed his eyes. "What if I asked you to remove both of the devices? I don't care about the risk. I'd rather be dead than have to live like a zoo animal."

"We need time to study you," Melissa said. "I know you were about to get engaged, but how would you feel if the beings ordered you to attack your girlfriend? We don't know what you're capable of doing under their control. Staying with us is better for everyone."

Trent opened his eyes and nodded. "You're right. Can I at least call Alexa and tell her what's happening?"

General Starke said, "You could if we knew where she was. She's gone rogue, along with her friends."

"She's hiding?"

"Yes," Starke said.

"Why?"

"I think she got the wrong impression about why we wanted to talk to her," Starke replied. "We were going to bring her here so she could be with you while we sorted all of this out."

Trent smiled. "Alexa can be a handful."

"Apparently so," Starke replied.

"I can call her and explain to her what's happening. Otherwise, you won't find her."

"She's disabled her phone," Starke said. "I promise that *when* we find her, we'll let you talk to her."

"Go easy if you make contact. She's protective. Think of her as a cornered she-bear. She has teeth and claws, and she's not afraid to use them."

"I'm sure," Melissa said. "We have no intention of taking any aggressive action with her."

"Trent, we know all about her," Starke said. "We plan to give her some time to cool down before we bring her in. It was our mistake to try to corral her and her friends."

Trent said, "It'll be safer for everyone if you reason with her rather than trying to apprehend her."

"I agree," Starke said.

"Trent, we'd like to conduct some tests to determine if the implant is interfering with any of your neurological functions," Melissa said. "It would be much easier if we could trust that you won't try to escape."

Trent sighed, then said, "Considering I have an alien thing in my head and leg, you can count on my cooperation."

"General Starke, I'd like permission to release Trent from his restraints."

Starke nodded. "Permission granted."

"Thank you, sir. Can Trent be allowed to speak with Agent Dobson and Deputy Griffin?"

"I don't see why not."

"What about introducing Trent to Taylor?" Melissa asked.

"Who's Taylor?" Trent asked.

"Taylor Graham is another abductee," Starke said. "She came to our attention two years ago. We removed an implant from her leg."

"Is that the implant that dissolved?" Trent asked.

"Yes," Starke replied.

"And she's still here?"

Melissa chuckled, then said, "No. She was with us for only a few days. After we removed the implant from her leg, she hasn't been abducted again. She chose to live near the base just in case something else happened. She felt safer here. General, Taylor could help Trent adjust and explain what to expect over the next few days."

"That's a good idea. Make it happen. Ask her to join us at the facility."

"Yes, sir."

General Starke left the room, and for the first time the door was left open.

"What facility?" Trent asked Melissa.

"We're going to be moving you to a facility that's not far from here. It's a more secure site. It's also equipped with specialized medical equipment and personnel for this type of event."

"More secure than a military base?"

Melissa nodded. "Yes. We want to keep you protected from any harm and from being abducted again."

Trent thought for a moment and decided to play along. *What could it hurt?* "I think I'd like to meet Taylor Graham."

"Good," Melissa said. "I'll go make the arrangements."

SEVEN

Naples Municipal Marina — 0700 hours EST

Alexa had spoken to Dan Mitchell and learned that his team was in place around Mountain Home AFB. He'd reported there was very little traffic at the main gate. It appeared the base was still locked down. Dan believed Trent was still there, and the two C-17s with the tail numbers she'd given him remained on the tarmac.

Alexa had been pleased to learn that Sue had secured a private charter out of the Naples Jet Center to take them to Idaho, with few questions asked. She'd even arranged a cash payment for the flight. Their Embraer Phenom 100 executive jet would depart at noon. The jet could carry four passengers, which was perfect for them. It was a little slower than she'd hoped for, cruising at 390 knots, and its range was limited. They would have to make at least one stop on the way to Boise. It would take over six hours to get to Idaho, but it was the best they could do.

"Shit!" Alexa said as she watched two Naples police cruisers pull into the marina parking lot. "Marvin, what's the status on our taxi?"

"It should be here in a few minutes."

"Of course."

"What's wrong?" Marvin asked. He stood at the back door of the bait shop, so he hadn't seen the cruisers yet.

"We have company. Where's Sue?"

"She went for a walk on the docks. She should be back any minute."

Alexa walked to the back door and stood next to Marvin. She saw Sue walking up the dock toward the bait shop. She hesitated for a moment, then continued.

"She's seen the cruisers," Alexa said. "She's doing a good job of playing it cool." As soon as she was off the dock, Sue walked around the back of the Harbor Master's office next to the bait shop, then hurried to join them.

Alexa stepped to the front of the bait shop and watched as the two cruisers parked in front of the Harbor Master's office. Two officers got out. One of them headed for the office. The other waited by the cruisers. Alexa hurried out the back door, and ran to the rear of the Harbor Master's office, and slipped inside.

"Hey," Alexa whispered to a bald, gray-bearded man who was working behind a desk in a small office.

"Hey, yourself," the man replied.

"I need a favor. A police officer is going to come through the front door in a second."

"They come in to get coffee every once in a while. You in trouble with the law?"

"No, I used to be the law. It's a long story. The guy that's going to come in is my ex. We had a bad breakup, and he's been stalking me ever since."

"What? The cop is a stalker?"

"Let's just say he's very obsessed with me and prone to violence." She handed the old man three hundred dollars. "Will you tell him I'm not here?"

The crusty old salt took the money and stuffed it into his stained shirt pocket. "Hell, for that much money, I'll tell him anything you want."

"Thanks. He's going to claim that I'm a drug dealer."

"You don't look like one to me."

"I'm not. If he shows you my picture or pictures of my friends, just tell him we left about an hour ago with a guy in a red sedan."

"You got it. Now you better git."

Alexa rushed out the back and found Sue and Marvin hiding behind a smelly dumpster.

"Our ride should be here any minute now," Marvin said. "We can't just run to the cab. The cops will see us for sure."

"I paid the guy behind the counter to lie for us," Alexa said. "Let's hope he and the other cop just check the dock and leave. They can't see us if we stay on this side of the buildings."

A few minutes later, Alexa took a quick peek around the dumpster and saw both officers strolling down the dock.

"Ride's here," Marvin said.

"Perfect timing," Alexa said.

As a taxi pulled up next to the building, Alexa, Marvin, and Sue walked to the cab as quickly as they could without looking suspicious, piled in, and told the driver to head for the airport.

Alexa looked back as the taxi pulled on to the main road. She didn't see either officer. "Want to grab breakfast?" Alexa asked.

"I could eat," Marvin said.

"Me, too. I'm starved," Sue added.

"There's an IHOP on US 41," Marvin said.

"I don't want to know how you know that, but let's go," Alexa said. Marvin gave the driver the new destination as she checked again to see if anyone was following. "We're clear," she whispered in Marvin's ear.

"Good."

Alexa's cell phone rang. "Yes?" she answered.

"It's me," Autumn said.

"You're back at the office already?"

"No. I stayed home sick today. I haven't even been to bed yet."

Alexa didn't like the idea of her not being at the office. "What is it?"

"I have some interesting news. I got lucky. I called a friend of mine who used to work in Utah for the Comprehensive National Security Initiative. She's back in Maryland now, and she's been trying to get me to come to work with her."

"Autumn, please get to the point," Alexa said.

"Sorry. I asked her if she knew of any national security concerns or of any special interest in Mountain Home, AFB."

"And?" Alexa was growing impatient. Lack of sleep made her cranky.

"She said there wasn't anything concerning Mountain Home, but she knew of a secret military instillation hidden, or more accurately stated, buried near Greylock Mountain. It's codenamed Sawtooth. I presume that's after the national park where it's located. It's northeast of the base."

"What kind of installation is it?"

"She didn't know, and I haven't been able to discover anything further. It may be a secret facility that has actually remained secret."

"How did your friend find out about it?"

"Because she was tasked to monitor signals traffic for any reference to either the name of the facility or its location. It may be nothing, but the proximity to the base made it sound interesting."

"Thank you. I really appreciate your help. I think you've connected the dots for us."

"What are friends for? I'll call if I find out anything else, but it won't be until late tomorrow at the earliest."

"You know where we'll be. Thanks again." Alexa disconnected.

"Good news?" Marvin asked.

"Very," Alexa replied. "I'll tell you later."

It turned out that the IHOP was within walking distance of the airport. Marvin's cell phone rang just as they got out of the cab.

"It's my contact." Marvin walked away from the taxi.

Alexa paid the driver.

Marvin said, "He's come through for us. He'll meet us at the airport before noon with our new IDs."

"Excellent," Alexa said.

They walked into the restaurant and took a booth near the back. They all ordered pancakes.

"Sue, I never asked, but what name did you give to hold the plane?" Alexa asked. "And how did you get them to book a charter without a credit card?"

Sue smiled. "I told them I was part of a security team that needed to go to Boise. That a sheik's daughter was traveling there to look at property and that you didn't want to be seen."

"So I'm gonna be a princess?"

"Yup. I told the guy that everything related to your travels had to be handled in cash to ensure your safety."

"And the guy bought that line of crap?" Marvin asked.

"I can be very convincing. Offering him a thousand-dollar tip also helped. The princess can afford it."

Alexa smiled and said, "Sue, you are a resourceful fugitive. Especially when it comes to spending my money."

"I thought it was an inspired performance."

"I'll ask, again, what name did you give him?"

"I told him my name was Sue and that you were Princess Tamar."

"You really used your real first name?" Marvin said.

"I did. I told the guy it wasn't my real name and yours wasn't either."

"Let's hope our pursuers don't ask if a Sue chartered a plane," Marvin said.

"I hope you can pull off the Saudi princess role," Sue said. "I figured whatever ID Marvin came up with, it would work."

"I hope I can, too," Alexa said.

"If those cops were checking out the marina, somebody in Key West must have given us up," Marvin said.

"When I borrowed the boat, I didn't tell my friend to keep it quiet," Alexa said. "It's better for him if he stays in the dark. He doesn't know anything about Trent returning."

"If they find out that we're in Naples, they'll start canvassing the airport for us," Marvin said. "We should have gone farther up the coast."

"Maybe," Alexa said. "Our flight doesn't leave for three hours, and it's not leaving from the main terminal. Where's your buddy going to meet us?"

"Outside the FBO at the airport."

"At the what?" Sue asked.

"FBO means fixed-base operator. It's a private terminal for charters."

"I see."

"I figured I'd walk over to the Jet Center first," Marvin said. "If no federal agents swoop in after ten minutes or so, you two can follow."

"You mean that Princess Tamar won't be arriving in a limo?" Alexa said.

"It broke down at the IHOP, and you didn't want to wait for another one," Marvin said.

"That sounds good," Sue said. "Let's hope that if the authorities are checking the area, they're done before we get there."

"Let's hope so," Alexa added.

Mountain Home AFB — 0520 hours MST

"Is Trent going to cooperate?" Starke asked as Melissa entered his temporary office.

She sat down across from him and replied, "I think so. In any case, we need to get Taylor to play nice if we're going to pull this off. I ordered another neurological imaging test for Taylor."

"Taylor doesn't have any choice but to cooperate. Have you been to see her lately?"

"Not for a few months. All of her psych reports indicate that she's still waiting for the aliens to return. She's been traumatized for so many years by her abductions that I'm not sure our continuing to hold her at the facility hasn't contributed to her inability to recover."

"We both know she can't be turned loose, at least not yet. The aliens wouldn't be able to find her anyway."

"Not while she's at the facility, unless. . ."

"Unless what?"

"Trent leads them to her."

Starke smiled, then said, "I hope that will happen." His pad chirped, and he opened an email from Major Striker. "It seems Trent's girlfriend is in Naples, Florida."

"How did she get there?"

"By boat. Major Striker overheard a conversation a man was having with a group of people on the docks behind Schooners Reef Bar early this morning. It's the restaurant and bar where Alexa and her friends spent a great deal of time when they weren't out searching for Trent. Alexa's name was mentioned. When Striker inquired about her, the man clammed up."

"So Striker went into his usual intimidation mode," Melissa quipped.

"In a manner of speaking. Striker managed to find out that Alexa had borrowed the man's Hatteras."

"How did he know Alexa was in Naples?"

"Alexa called the owner of the boat and told him where it was located. She told him that she'd explain everything later and that it was best he didn't know anything else."

"That was nice of her."

"Striker said she'd used a burner phone. He got the number and tried to GPS it, but he was unsuccessful."

"She probably ditched it."

"Striker said that the guy didn't know she was on the run. He thought she was going out to search for Trent again. He wasn't pleased to learn his boat was used by a group of fugitives."

"So he claims," Melissa said. "Does Striker know what marina it's docked at?"

"Yes. The local police found the boat and checked the area. They were gone. The police reported finding an envelope lying on the dinette with a thousand dollars in it and a note apologizing for the inconvenience. Striker and a few men he's recruited are flying to the Naples airport as we speak."

"Maybe we'll get lucky," Melissa said.

"We can hope. In the meantime, I'll meet with Taylor and get her prepped. We need to leave here no later than 0800 hours."

"Yes, sir. I'll have Trent ready to travel. I thought some new clothes might make him feel more comfortable."

General Starke said, "Good idea." He paused. "I'd like your opinion on something."

"Certainly."

"Do you think we still need Sanderson assigned to the project?"

Melissa frowned. "I know he can be a pain at times, but he's very capable. It wouldn't hurt to keep him around for a while longer."

Starke nodded. "That's your call."

"What are we going to do with Trent's plane?"

"I was going to send it to Wright-Patterson, but I've decided to have it stripped down and examined at the facility. I'm flying in some specialists to take it apart. Is there anything else that we need to discuss?"

"No, sir."

"You're dismissed."

Mountain Home AFB Medical Center — 0630 hours MST

Trent's IV had been removed and he'd been given civilian attire. He'd just finished dressing when Melissa entered his room.

"Everything okay?" she asked.

"I'm good. When do I meet Taylor?"

"Soon. General Starke has sent a car to get her."

"She didn't mind the early wakeup?"

"Not at all. She's very much in our debt. You'll come to understand that we're going to be your best friends."

"How many times has she been abducted?"

"I'll let her tell you the story," Melissa replied. "I heard that Agent Dobson and Deputy Griffin are having breakfast. Let's join them. I'm sure they'll have some questions for you. Don't answer them unless I give you my approval. Understood?"

"Yes."

A few minutes later, Melissa and Trent found them eating in the small dining room. Trent sat down across from the two men. Melissa took a seat next to Trent.

"I believe all of you are acquainted," Melissa said.

"I know Agent Dobson," Trent said. "I only saw Deputy Griffin on the plane."

Deputy Griffin nodded at him, then said, "You have interesting friends. I interviewed them. Alexa was very concerned about you."

"You talked to them?" Trent asked excitedly.

"Yes, I spoke with her, Marvin, and Sue."

"So Alexa knows what's happened to me?" Trent asked Griffin.

"Not entirely. I really don't know what happened to you."

"So no one knows about the alien abduction?" Trent asked.

Melissa glared at Trent. "I thought we had an understanding."

"I figured it would be something like that," Griffin said. "Where did they take you? What did they look like?"

"That's enough," Melissa said. "We're all going to a secure facility in a few hours. You will not disclose anything you see or hear there. Understood?"

"Yes," Dobson answered. "I know the drill."

Griffin said, "I won't say anything. Colonel, how do I fit into all of this going forward?"

"We're still looking for Alexa and her friends. You may be of use in persuading them to join us. They trust you."

"I see," Griffin said. "So once they're found, you'll take me back to Key West?"

"That's up to General Starke. Gentlemen, let's eat and enjoy the day ahead. No more questions."

"I'm already sorry that I know what I do," Griffin replied.

"So you still can't find Alexa?" Trent asked Melissa.

"She's gone off the grid. As we told you earlier, she believes that we're out to arrest her and your friends." Melissa stared at Dobson, then added, "But we aren't. Isn't that right Agent Dobson?"

"I just needed to find them and bring them back to the air station for questioning," Dobson replied.

"Trent, we only want to debrief them and swear them to secrecy. That's why I thought Deputy Griffin may be helpful. The sooner we find them, the better for everyone involved. Trent, do you know anyone in Naples?"

"Florida or Italy?" Trent asked with a grin.

"Florida. She and your friends went there this morning."

"None that come to mind," Trent answered honestly. "You must have scared the crap out of her to make her go dark." Griffin gave him a look that confirmed his suspicions.

Melissa said, "I told Trent earlier that Dobson's and our approach were a bit heavy-handed. Deputy Griffin will attest to that. This is regrettable, but Trent, you must look at it from our perspective. We didn't know for sure that you'd been abducted. Standard protocol is to lock everything down until we know what we're dealing with and determine how much we need to contain."

Trent nodded. "I can understand that. But I'm still not buying that you need Deputy Griffin to persuade Alexa to join me. I can do that."

Melissa smiled. "I agree, but we have containment protocols to follow. Right now, he needs to stay with us. Besides, Alexa may think that you're just telling her to come in because you're under duress or drugged. She'll be less suspicious if Deputy Griffin speaks to her, too. I think you will all see the bigger picture later today."

"Where's my plane?" Trent asked.

"It's here," Melissa replied. "We had to take the wings off to get it on the C-17. It will be examined, but don't worry, we'll put it back together for you."

"That would be nice," Trent said.
"We'll make sure that it's airworthy again."
"I hope so. I'd like to fly it home."
Melissa smiled.

PART TWO

"Ye Gods! Annihilate but space and time.

And make two lovers happy."

ALEXANDER POPE

EIGHT

A black, ten-passenger van idled at the entrance of the medical center when Trent walked out. Snow covered the ground. The chilly air felt good. He climbed into the van and sat by a window.

"Where's General Starke?" Agent Dobson asked.

"He's gone on ahead," Melissa replied. "Please get aboard."

Deputy Griffin followed Dobson into the van.

"How far away is the facility?" Dobson asked.

"It's not far," Melissa replied. "Sit back and enjoy the scenic drive."

Trent looked out the window as the van made its way to the main gate. He wondered what the future held for him. How long would they hold him? And what about Alexa? He wanted to jump out of the van and make a break for it, but he knew that wouldn't solve anything. The neural implant would still be in his head. He'd have to wait.

Sawtooth Facility — 0810 hours

General Starke sat across the table from Taylor Graham. Her long, auburn hair hung loosely over her shoulders. Her pale complexion and smooth skin made her a perfect picture of a classic Irish lass. She was fairer now than when she arrived. Since her escape attempt a year ago, she hadn't been permitted to go outside the facility. Today he had allowed her to wear blue jeans and a white, long-sleeve pullover instead of the usual tan uniform BDU pants and blue polo shirt. After hearing what General Starke had just told her, she couldn't help but stare at him in disbelief.

"So will you help us?" General Starke asked for the second time.

"I've been held here for two years, and now you want *me* to help you convince this guy, Trent, that he won't suffer the same fate? Now I understand why you let me put on civilian clothes. I guess it wouldn't look believable if you presented me in my uniform."

"Yes. Taylor, you have been here a while. You know that it's been for your own protection. You're lucky you're alive after your last abduction."

"I don't need protection," Taylor responded with disdain. "You told me that after Melissa removed the alien implant from my leg that I wouldn't be abducted again."

"And you haven't been, have you? Taylor, we just want to make sure that you're safe. I believe that you are now. Over the last two years, there have been many alien abduction claims. Some credible, but not verifiable, and none of them had an implant."

"And you said Trent has an implant?"

"Yes, exactly like the one you had removed."

"So if I can convince Trent to cooperate with you, you'll release me?"

"Conditionally. You'll also need to get him to believe that you live off campus with your family, and that you want to help him. I know it's a bit of a stretch, but I think you can pull it off."

Taylor shook her head. "Why should I believe you? You've lied to me so many times."

"I know, but it was for your own good. I'm telling you the truth. I understand that you think of your time here as being held prisoner."

"I *have* been held prisoner."

"Taylor, think of your husband and daughter. What would have happened if they had been abducted with you?"

"Don't go there! If I agree, can I at least call my family?"

Starke rocked his jaw, then said, "We believe it will be best if you don't make contact with them just yet. They may not understand how you've suddenly reappeared."

"What do you mean? You told me a year ago that I could talk to them again if I promised not to cause trouble. Haven't I done everything you've asked of me?"

"Yes. You must understand how hard it would be for them if you just showed up on their doorstep. We'll need to do this slowly and with a good cover story. They can never know where you've been. We knew that this project would be long-term. We told you that from the beginning."

"You didn't tell me it would be two years."

"We did what we thought was best for everyone, so they could move on with their lives," Starke said.

"You told them I was dead, didn't you?"

Starke nodded. "It was necessary. Rick and Emma, are doing well. They've adjusted. By believing that you're dead, they have moved on."

Taylor felt stunned. "All this time you've been lying to me, making promises that you didn't intend to keep. You just convinced me that I shouldn't help you anymore."

"What other option do you have for getting out of here? Think about it. If you don't help us, I guarantee you that you won't be going anywhere for a long time."

Taylor sat back in her chair and bit her lower lip. "You said if I cooperate that I'll get to leave. Now you threaten me, and you expect me to sucker some other poor soul into this nightmare?"

"I will release you. When is up to you."

"Yeah, I'm sure I'll get out of here, eventually," Taylor said sardonically. "Probably after I'm really dead."

"Taylor, telling your husband and daughter that you were dead was best for them. This way your family could find closure. I'm offering you a chance to start over. A new life without fear."

Taylor wiped the tears from her cheeks. "What did you tell them happened to me?"

"The truth. That you had been abducted and disappeared."

"Rick wouldn't let it go at that. He's still looking for me, isn't he?"

"No. You're buried in Green Lawn Cemetery in your hometown."

"What?"

General Starke leaned forward. "Rick was displaying suicidal tendencies. He didn't know what had happened to you. He felt guilty because he hadn't been able to protect you. The guilt and grief were eating him up. Emma was acting out, getting in trouble at school, and she was starting to run around with the wrong group of teens."

"Drugs?"

Starke nodded. "She was headed down that path. We didn't want your family to suffer. A year ago, we leaked information about some skeletal remains that had been found in the woods near your home in Indiana. We made a copy of your wedding ring and left it near the remains. The clothes we found you in were treated to make them appear as if they'd been exposed to the elements for a year. Your remains were positively identified from DNA."

"How did you pull that off?"

"We had your blood and bone samples from when we removed the implant. With a little help from a forensic pathologist and a computer coder that we have on staff, the DNA from the skeletal remains taken from another woman were identified as yours."

"Who was the other woman?"

"A Jane Doe who had died about the same time you disappeared. We didn't kill her if that's what you're thinking."

"You're a bastard," Taylor snapped.

"We do what we must to protect our country. You were a victim of circumstance."

"I'm also your victim. At least the aliens had the decency to return me."

"How can you still defend them after all this time? They abducted you, multiple times since you were a child, performed very *intimate* tests on you, and put an alien device in your body. We were there to pick up the pieces. We monitored your family and made sure that they remained safe, and we provided the support they needed."

"I recall your medical staff getting pretty intimate," Taylor said. "Are you still monitoring them?"

"Twenty-four hours a day. We're still concerned about Emma. If the aliens were interested in you, we thought they might be interested in your daughter. So far they haven't paid her a visit. We never let Rick and Emma out of our sight. That's how we kept Emma from turning to drugs and Rick from killing himself with the Beretta he keeps in the nightstand."

Taylor nodded and wiped her wet cheeks again. "Tell me more about Trent."

"He's a good man. Like you, he was abducted as a child, then again a few weeks ago. We got involved when he resurfaced. He can't remember the second abduction, except for a bright light that engulfed his small plane. The memories he related about his first abduction are similar to your childhood experiences, right down to the short, flat-headed aliens. They carried him from his bedroom just like they did with you."

"What about after? You know, when I was in the ship."

"The light and the encounter with the brownish-gray creatures are identical, as is the triangular scar on his left tibia."

Taylor shook her head. "Why is he so special?"

"Why are you? Trent is your age, and he was abducted at about the same age and time."

"What do I need to do?" Taylor asked.

"Since you've been abducted numerous times, we need you to help him remember what happened during his second abduction. I want you to compare his experiences to your abductions. I'm hoping that talking about your experiences will trigger something he's blocked."

"Why not use regression therapy? It worked on me."

"Colonel Endo and Dr. Sanderson think you may be able to break through faster than months of hypnosis."

"Or the memories could lay dormant for many years before they surface," Taylor said.

"Possibly."

"What if he doesn't remember anything about his lost time?"

"We'll decide what other options we have once you've tried all other approaches."

Taylor thought about that for a moment, then sighed. "Okay. I'll do it. I'm going to tell him the truth about me, and I *will* rejoin my family when this is over. I don't care what line of shit you have to come up with to make it happen. Tell them I was lost on a deserted island or you made a mistake with the DNA identification. I really don't care what story you spin."

"You can tell Trent whatever you want, except that you've been our guest for the last two years. He needs to believe there's a light at the end of the tunnel. As for being reunited with Rick and Emma, I'm not sure what story we could come up with that they'd believe. I'll see what we can do *if* this goes well."

Taylor said, "I know you're lying to me, but like you said, I don't really have a choice."

"We'll give you a backstory. Read it, memorize it, and stick to it." Starke glanced at his watch. "They should be here in less than an hour. I want you to observe Trent from the booth during his orientation."

"You may want to throw in some quick acting lessons."

Starke smiled. "That won't be necessary. I know you'll do just fine. You've kept up with current events. He won't have any reason not to believe you haven't been living off-site. We'll have some new clothes put in your apartment. You should mention that you saw the newscasts of his disappearance and that you empathize with what he's been through."

Taylor held up her left hand. Around her wrist was a plastic band. "You may want to take this off and give me a visitor's badge or something. He won't believe I'm not being held here with this on my wrist."

Starke nodded. "I forgot you still wore one of those."

"I haven't." She pulled her hair back. "What did you say his girlfriend's name was?"

"Alexa."

"Talking about her may build trust."

"That's good. Tell him about your husband and daughter and say how grateful you are to have been cared for here after your abduction. Lay it on as thick as you feel is necessary. Now, let's get you ready."

"One more thing," Taylor said, as Starke summoned a technician to remove her wristband.

"What is it?"

"Why did the medical unit run another brain imaging scan on me this morning?"

"Because I requested it be done. Trent has a neural implant in his brain. Our scanning technology has improved over the last year. We wanted to make sure we hadn't missed anything."

"So, do I have something in my brain?"

"No."

Mountain Home AFB — 0815 hours MST

Dan Mitchell watched a black van leave the base through his high-powered binoculars. A minute later, when the van drove past him, he was able to positively identify Trent. Norman Childers, one of the men on Dan's surveillance team, was asleep on the short cot by the rear doors of their white surveillance van.

"Wake up, Norm," Dan shouted as he pushed through the security curtains and sat in the driver's seat. Norm took the passenger seat.

"Which vehicle?" Norm asked as he phoned Steve O'Malley, another member of the team.

"The black van in the right lane," Dan replied. "Tell O'Malley to get ready to take the eyeball."

When O'Malley answered, Norm said, "Target is active. We're northbound from the base. Black passenger van. Dan wants you to take the eyeball. I'll call the parallels. Let me know when you're ready."

"On the move," O'Malley replied.

"Norm, check the map of the area on your IPad and see if O'Malley's GPS tracker is on-line," Dan said. The live tracking system Dan had purchased allowed everyone on the team to locate the others' vehicles.

"Steve, I think if you stay on the road you're on, and punch it, you can get ahead of the target in about a minute," Norm said.

"Roger," O'Malley replied. "I have you on the box. How far ahead of you is the target?"

"Less than a quarter mile. Traffic is light, so we're hanging back."

Norm ran his fingers across his dyed black mustache, which he often did out of habit. He was a small man in his forties, and what few wisps of hair he had left on the sides of his head were also dyed black. Norm had been with Dan since he started the company, serving as Dan's electronic and audio surveillance specialist. Norm had worked narcotics for years at the Salt Lake PD, but he was forced to retire early because of an on-the-job injury. He'd been left with a permanent knee injury after he was struck by a fleeing suspect vehicle. He was lucky he wasn't killed.

"Can you set up the laser mike on the back of the van?" Dan asked.

"Repositioning as we speak," Norm replied.

The surveillance van had a state-of-the-art laser microphone concealed in a special compartment on the roof. Once pointed at a window, the infrared laser beam enabled them to monitor conversations.

"We're locked on the target," Norm said, adjusting the volume so both of them could hear the audio.

"That sounds like electronic interference," Dan said. "Can you clean it up?"

"Working on it. I think we're being jammed. Could their van be equipped with electronic dampeners?"

"Anything's possible," Dan replied. "It looks like they're going to drive through the town of Mountain Home."

"Perfect for the intercept. O'Malley, get ready to take the eyeball."

"Tell O'Malley to go to radio communication."

"You there?" O'Malley said on the radio.

"We got you," Norm replied. "It looks like you're in position to intercept."

"I have the target," O'Malley said.

Dan saw O'Malley's car pull out behind the van. Minutes later, they were northbound on Interstate 84.

"Are they headed for Boise?" Norm asked.

"In that general direction," Dan replied. "Traffic is picking up. Tell O'Malley that we're going to drop back a bit to avoid getting burned. We're not getting any comms from the van anyway."

Norm relayed the message.

Ten minutes later, O'Malley radioed, "They're getting off the interstate. Turning east on twenty-one. There's not much traffic to hide behind on the two-lane road."

"Stay with them," Dan said. "When we get close, break off, and we'll pick them up."

"Roger, but be advised there isn't much out this way," O'Malley replied.

A few minutes later, the target turned on to a spur road and headed south. There was no other traffic. O'Malley drove past the spot where the target had left the highway. "They left the road," O'Malley radioed. "According to my map, they're on an old dirt road to nowhere."

Dan slowed as he approached the obscure road. Based on the depth of the ruts on the gravel road, it appeared to be well-traveled. "O'Malley, turn around and hold to the west of the spur road," Dan radioed.

"Roger."

"Norm, check the satellite image of the area and tell me what's out that way."

"I have it up already. According to our expensive mapping program the spur road they're taking is labeled three-twelve. Looks like it meanders along the west base of Greylock Mountain, then turns into a dirt trail. This image isn't very clear."

"Guess that SatMap app was a waste of money," Dan said, finding a place to pull off the road so he could look at it himself.

"There's a creek to the south," Norm said, pointing at the map. "Nothing out that way except a little airport off China Basin Road. It's too small for any serious aircraft traffic. Satellite shows a few lakes with lots of snow and trees."

"Thank you, Norm, but I can see that myself." He looked at the satellite image for a few minutes. "Why would they go overland in a bulky van?"

"To hide the bodies?" Norm offered.

Dan turned toward him. "That's not funny, but it's possible. Trent didn't look very happy."

"Do we charge in and rescue him?"

Dan didn't answer. "Play back the recording of when the van drove past us. Maybe I missed something."

They climbed into the back of the van and played the recording.

"There's Trent," Dan said. "He doesn't look distressed, just resigned. There's two guys sitting in front of him in civilian clothes. Can we clean up these images? Maybe we can get the others in the van identified."

"I can try," Norm said. "The driver is in uniform, and so is the woman in the passenger seat. Doesn't look like a hit team to me." A moment later, Norm said, "I've got it."

Dan sighed. "You got what?"

"They're headed to a secret base out in the middle of nowhere."

Dan sat back and said, "Really?"

"It's the perfect location for a secret facility."

Dan snorted. "If the van comes back, there's only two directions it can take. Let's set up to the east."

Forty minutes later, O'Malley radioed. "I have the target. No passengers. Same driver as before."

"Stay with the van," Dan ordered. "See if it goes back to the base. Norm and I are going to go off-roading."

"We are?" Norm said. "Aren't we going to be a bit conspicuous?"

"Probably. If we get stopped, we'll tell them that we're looking for a secluded campsite. You can bat your eyelashes at them."

"Cute."

Naples Municipal Airport – 1125 hours EST

Alexa, Marvin, and Sue huddled in a back office inside the FBO. Marvin's acquaintance was showing them their new IDs.

Alexa frowned as she looked at her new Texas driver's license. "Not very original. My name is Alexa Storm, and where did you get this photo?"

"I gave it to him," Marvin said. "It was the only one I had on my phone to send him. As for the name, you can blame me for that too. Rule one in undercover work is to use your real first name in case someone recognizes you."

"And the choice for the last name?"

"As I see it, we're headed into turbulent times."

"Who are you?" Alexa asked.

Marvin showed her his Michigan license. "I'm Marvin Roosevelt."

"Well, at least your picture looks good. Sue, who are you?"

"I'm Sue Templeton from South Carolina," Sue replied with a slight southern accent.

"She's in character already," Marvin said. "Alexa, I thought you'd be happy with your new ID. I took some years off both yours and Sue's real age."

Alexa looked at the DOB. Marvin had kept the same birthday, but she was now thirty-three. "That I like."

"Me, too," Sue echoed.

"Can I get paid now?" the forger asked.

"You did good, Mr. Smith," Marvin said. "Alexa, pay the man."

"Do you do passports?" Alexa asked.

"I can, but they require more time to prepare," Mr. Smith answered.

"You think we're going to need to go global?" Marvin asked.

"It doesn't hurt to be prepared."

"I'll need passport-quality photos," Smith said.

"We can email them to you," Alexa said. "How much for three passports?"

Mr. Smith rubbed his chin, then gave her a Cheshire cat smile.

"Well?" she asked.

"For Marvin, I'll cut you a deal. Let's say five thousand for the package."

Alexa nodded. "Sounds fair considering the circumstances. How soon on the passports?"

"Once I have the photos, I can have them ready in a day. Delivery may take longer if you aren't local."

Alexa handed over the five grand, then said, "Thank you. We'll be in touch." She would have paid twice as much for them.

"Remember, I know where you live, Mr. Smith," Marvin said. "Not a word to anyone. We'll call with a forwarding address."

"I know how to keep my mouth shut," Smith replied.

After Smith had left, Alexa asked, "Do you trust him?"

"I do," Marvin said.

"Then let's board the plane."

"Don't forget that you are Princess Tamar," Sue said.

"How could I forget?"

They left the office and walked next door to the Jet Center. Alexa saw several police cars parked in front of the regular terminal. "Let's hope they don't come this way. We need to get aboard the plane as soon as we can."

"I agree," Marvin said. "Sue, you go in ahead of us. I'll stay with Alexa and pretend I'm her bodyguard. Wave us in when you're sure it's safe."

Alexa opened her backpack and handed Sue the money for the airfare and the thousand-dollar tip.

Alexa watched as Sue went into the Jet Center.

"Can I help you?" the uniformed receptionist asked.

"My name is, Sue. I have a reservation for a twelve o'clock charter flight."

The receptionist looked at the schedule. "Here it is. Party of three going to Boise. I'll let the captain know you're here. No bags?"

"We sent them ahead. We like to travel light."

"Where's the rest of your party?"

"Just outside. I don't know if you've been informed, but the other woman passenger is trying to stay off the radar. She's royalty, and she doesn't want to be noticed. I was told that cash was acceptable." Sue handed the woman the fare and the tip. "The extra is for the gentleman who made this happen."

"I understand. I'll see that he gets it. I see by the comments that she's a Saudi princess."

"Shhh! No fanfare and no finger-pointing or telling your friends. This needs to stay secret. If anyone asks about the princess, we were never here. That's why we're paying extra." Sue handed the receptionist two hundred dollars. "This is for you. Are we good?"

"Certainly. I understand."

Sue walked back to the front doors and waved to Marvin and Alexa.

Fifteen minutes later, they were all aboard the Embraer jet.

Alexa's cell phone buzzed. She fished it out of her backpack put it on speaker. "Hello, Dan."

"I have news. Trent left the base in a van. We followed him out into the boonies. He was with two men in civilian clothes and two people in uniform, a woman officer and an airman."

"Where is he now?"

"They vanished into a wooded area west of Greylock Mountain. When the van returned from their off-road excursion, only the driver was in it. I have one of my team following it. From the last report, it's headed back to the base."

"That fits," Alexa said.

"What fits?"

"I'm sorry, I should have told you earlier. I was informed that there's a secret military base under Greylock Mountain."

"Really? Yeah, that information would have been helpful. What kind of base?"

"Unknown," Alexa replied. "Can you reacquire Trent and the others?"

"I don't know. We're following an old, rutted road now. Let me text you the pictures we took of the people in the van as they left the base. Maybe you'll recognize some of the players."

A minute later, Alexa was scrolling through the pictures. "Definitely Trent. He looks miserable. The man in front of him by the window is Deputy Griffin from the Monroe County Sheriff's Office. He's the one that helped us back in Key West. Sue, do you recognize this guy?" She pointed at Dobson's photo.

Sue looked at it and said, "He's the NCIS agent that wanted to arrest us."

"NCIS?" Dan muttered. "Why are they involved?"

"Unknown," Alexa replied. "We don't know the military folks."

"And why would a deputy sheriff from Key West be here?" Dan asked.

"I think the military or whoever are tying up loose ends. Where are you exactly?"

"Right now I'm a mile off of Route twenty-one, just north of Idaho City."

"Not helping," Alexa said.

"Northeast of Boise. Greylock Mountain is just east of us. There are lots of places where a person could get lost. Norm thought there was a secret base out here. I guess he was right."

"I knew it!" Norm shouted.

"Who was that?"

"Norm. What do you want us to do?"

"Maintain surveillance and wait for us. We're leaving Naples in a few minutes. We should be in Boise in around six hours. Any chance someone from your team could pick us up at the airport? We'll be at the FBO."

"I'll come get you. I'm going to move the surveillance van back to the main road for a while. We'll keep an eye out for any changes. Give me a call when you're thirty minutes out. If anything changes on my end, I'll give you a shout."

"Sounds good. Great job, Dan."

"As always."

NINE

Trent sat in a type of vehicle that he'd never seen before. It was long and had a low profile. It had no windows in the passenger compartment and only two doors, one on the right side between the oversized tires, and the other was a ramp at the rear. The camouflage was unlike anything he'd ever seen. The outer hull of the armored vehicle reflected the terrain from all angles, making it virtually invisible.

The compartment where he was seated was sealed off from the driver. Trent hadn't heard any engine noise when they left, so he wondered if it was an electric vehicle. Melissa sat across from him, next to Deputy Griffin. Agent Dobson sat beside him. The seats were quite comfortable, and the ride was smooth, even though he knew they were traveling on an unpaved road. He couldn't tell how fast they were going, but they'd been in the vehicle for over thirty minutes.

"How much longer?" Trent asked Melissa.

She looked at her watch, then said, "Not much longer."

"You always seem hard-pressed to give a definitive answer," Griffin said. "Why is that?"

"I guess it's because of the nature of the work."

"I'm guessing we're going to a secret military complex," Griffin said.

"Yes," Melissa replied.

"This is an awfully futuristic-looking vehicle," Dobson said. "What is it?"

"It's an ST-4," Melissa replied. "Only a handful have been made."

"It's a nice vehicle, but I don't see a restroom, and I'm going to need to use one pretty soon," Griffin said.

"We'll be there shortly," Melissa said.

Twenty minutes later, the vehicle stopped abruptly. "Did we just hit something?" Trent asked.

"No," Melissa replied.

The side door of the vehicle slid open, and Melissa motioned for Trent to get out. As he exited, he was amazed to see where he was. "What is this place?" Trent asked.

"Your home for a while," Melissa said. "You're in a facility under Greylock Mountain."

The size of the hangar was incredible. The ceiling had to be at least a hundred feet high. Two Blackhawk helicopters sat nearby. There were four more of the specially designed vehicles like the one he'd just stepped out of parked next to two buses. There were two M1 Abrams tanks and several other armored personnel carriers parked near a large, closed door. At least twenty Marines in mountain camouflage uniforms milled around, watching them, all holding automatic weapons.

"Wow, this place is a real fortress," Griffin said.

"Yes it is," Melissa replied, then walked past him to greet General Starke.

Trent thought the general swaggered a little. He could tell the facility was something the general was proud of but seldom got to show off.

"You know," Griffin whispered to Dobson, nodding toward the general, "I don't like that guy."

"Me either," Dobson said.

"That makes three of us," Trent added. "I don't trust him either."

"Welcome to Sawtooth," Starke exclaimed, his booming voice reverberating in the vast space.

"Now we know the name of this place, at least," Griffin muttered.

Starke said, "It's seldom that we receive visitors, so forgive everyone for staring at you."

"What exactly is this place?" Trent asked.

"A very unique facility designed for advanced research," Starke replied.

"You mean it was designed for dealing with extraterrestrial contact, don't you?" Trent said.

"Correct."

"I really don't want to hear any of this," Griffin said.

"Me either," Dodson said.

"Then you didn't," General Starke said. "Come this way. Let me show you around."

"General, Deputy Griffin needs a restroom," Melissa said.

The general waved a Marine over to them. Griffin was escorted to an unmarked door on one of the walls.

As Trent looked around he remembered an old Eagles song, "Hotel California," and he wondered if any of them would ever check out.

The general said, "This is the hangar. It's the primary access to the facility. We're deep beneath Greylock Mountain, and we are impervious to any type of attack, including nuclear. This facility is better protected than Cheyenne Mountain."

"It's enormous," Trent said.

"And this is just a small part of the facility."

"Must've cost a fortune to build," Trent said.

"It did," Starke replied. "Billions more than Area 51 and many other bases combined, but it was a necessary expenditure to keep our country safe. The work we do here is more important than most people could imagine."

Trent saw his Cessna, or what was left of it, piled up in a corner. "Hey, that's my plane." He walked toward it. "Why did you do this?"

"We had to disassemble it for testing purposes," Starke said.

"Like I told you before, we'll put it all back together and make it better than new when we're done," Melissa said.

When he reached the plane, Trent stared at the jagged cuts in the aluminum wings. The engine was in pieces. The tips of the propeller blades were gone, and so were all of the electronics and gauges. He turned to Melissa and said, "I don't think it can be put back together. Look at the damage to the metal."

Starke said, "We needed to test the molecular structure of all the components and metals to see if they had been altered in any way. To test the different components, we had to dismantle it and take samples. We'll make it whole again, and if we can't, we'll buy you a replacement."

Trent had to force himself to turn away. He knew his plane would never fly again. He glared at Starke. "You will definitely buy me a new plane. There's no way it can be repaired. Damn, I loved that plane."

Griffin walked up to them and said, "Trent, if that's your plane, it's totaled."

"Yeah. I know."

"This way, please," Melissa said.

Once out of the hangar, they walked through a hallway to a large, steel double door. Trent noted the rubber seals around the frame. Two armed Marines stood guard. After passing through the doorway, he was amazed to see an atrium that extended upward for several hundred feet. Trent wasn't sure how many floors there were. Each floor was painted a different color, and enormous windows covered most of one wall. Two more armed Marines stood next to the elevator doors.

"This is an incredible structure," Trent said in awe.

"Yes, it is," Starke said. "This is the Altair annex."

Griffin snorted.

"What?" Starke asked, stopping and facing him.

"Altair in Latin means bird. In Arabic it means flyer. I just found it humorous that a building buried under a mountain would be thought of as a flyer."

"Maybe it was given that name because our visitors fly around the stars," Starke said.

"Seems like a lot of wasted space," Dobson said.

"This area was part of a giant cave system," Starke said. "We also have room for expansion."

"What's that?" Trent asked, pointing to four Marines standing by another steel door.

"Good question, Trent. I'll show you. Colonel, please escort Deputy Griffin and Agent Dobson to the Altair cafeteria while I show Trent the Nova annex."

"There's another annex like this one?" Trent asked.

"Yes," Starke replied.

"Don't we get to see it?" Dobson asked.

"No," Starke replied. "You've seen enough already."

"This way, gentlemen," Melissa said. "The food in the cafeteria is quite good." She walked toward the elevator with Dobson and Griffin.

Trent didn't want to leave the other two men. He didn't really know them, but they were the closest thing to allies that he had at the moment. "Why can't we stay together?"

"Because they aren't invited, and I need to show you something," Starke replied.

Trent followed the general to the door where the four Marines stood guard. The Marines snapped to attention as the general approached. One of the Marines turned, placed his hand on a biometric lock, then placed his right eye in front of an optical scanner. An audible alert tone sounded, followed by the double doors slowly opening outward.

"Quickly, don't dawdle. The doors will start to close again as soon as they reach maximum extension," Starke said, "and they aren't like an elevator. They don't stop if they hit you."

Trent hurried through the doorway.

He walked with Starke down a long corridor, passing many closed doors, each with a different-colored placard affixed to the outside. Several of the placards had radiological and biohazard symbols on them.

"What are these rooms?" Trent asked.

"These are labs," Starke replied, without any further explanation.

When they turned a corner, Trent saw two more Marines waiting by another door.

"This reminds me of a prison," Trent said.

"We have the highest level of security of any facility in the world."

They went through the same procedure as before, and the doors swung open. Trent passed through quickly.

He found himself in another cavernous area. This one had a circular atrium that extended upward like the one in the other annex. Each level was also color-coded. The concrete floor in the atrium was painted green, just like the passageways and the floors in the Altair atrium. He remembered that the floor in the hangar had been painted gray.

"This is the Nova annex," Starke said.

"Is each floor used for a different purpose? The color bands for each level are the same in both annexes."

"Yes. Nova is a more secure area. The first level where we're standing houses the Marines and security personnel." Starke pointed at the next level. "The orange level is our medical wing. The red above that is the medical isolation area. It has a positive pressure area, and there are over fifty sealed decontamination and medical examination rooms on that floor. Each room is connected to a central hub where the medical staff can enter biohazard suits to gain access to treat patients. We have a rather large medical staff."

"Why? I thought I was the only patient."

"We don't know if you'll remain the only patient. We have planned for all possible contingencies." Starke again pointed up at the structure.

"The blue and purple levels are classified because they relate to specific alien research. The gold area is where you will be housed for the time being. That's where the apartments are located for visitors such as yourself. The pink level is a common area with three restaurants, a cafeteria, a gym, and a coffee shop. There's also a game room and computer center there."

"I would have thought the common area would be near the bottom of the structure," Trent said.

"Why?"

"Because you'd want to keep it close to the troops."

"We wanted it centralized so it would be easily accessable to all personnel from any level. Medical personnel are housed on the orange and red level. The black, white, and brown levels are for staff housing and offices. Each color level corresponds to a specialty."

"Efficient," Trent said.

"Electromagnetic, physics, astrophysics, and general science personnel live on the black level. I guess you could call that our black hole."

"Funny," Trent said.

"Facility maintenance, mechanical, kitchen workers, and assorted other odd jobs that are needed to keep the place running are on the white level. The brown level is reserved for command staff. It has the fewest living quarters, but it has the most meeting rooms and additional storage space."

Trent smiled and said, "I guess brown is a humorous way of indicating that the feces flows downhill from there."

"Ha! I hadn't thought of that, but in a way, it's accurate. I'll have to ask the facility designer if that was his intent. As you can see, there are large plate-glass windows overlooking the atrium. The two windows in the center of the brown floor are my office and Colonel Endo's office. Any questions?"

"I'll just need to remember which color means what. One question. You said there was a computer center. Are there any computer terminals I can use?"

"We don't allow anyone to have a personal computer. All public-use computers are connected to a central quantum computer that's buried in the sub-basement. All personal correspondence is reviewed and censored, as needed, before transmission. All incoming emails are also reviewed."

"You mean there's more levels below us?" Trent asked.

"Yes. The sub-basements go down two hundred feet. Some of those levels are for mechanical, electrical, and environmental. Our mainframe computer and communications equipment are down there, as well as another gym and additional housing for our IT staff. You won't be going anywhere near the sub-basement, so don't worry about it. We affectionately refer to all of the sub-basement as 'Oz', and I'm the wizard who knows what's behind the curtain. We have additional clean rooms and quarantine areas in case our patient load on red level is exceeded or compromised."

"Where are Griffin and Dobson staying?"

"The visitors' quarters, gold level, in Altair."

"Why aren't they going to stay here?"

"They don't need to be here," Starke replied.

"Will I see them, again?"

"Yes, but later. First thing we need to do is get you settled in your room. Then we need to get your access badge and biometrics logged. It will give you access to the areas of the facility where you've been cleared." Starke paused, then asked, "What level are you going to be housed on?"

"Testing me? I'm on gold level."

"Good, you remembered."

"I'm not obtuse," Trent said.

"You haven't gotten very far," Melissa said, walking toward them.

"I was about to show Trent his quarters. Please join us."

General Starke swiped his key card through the elevator electronic lock, placed his hand on the palm reader, and peered into the optical scanner. One of the three elevator doors opened, and they boarded.

"Notice that the elevator buttons and floor indicator lights are color-coded, too," Starke said.

When they reached Gold level, Trent followed Melissa out of the elevator. The corridor walls were painted gold. Trent was astounded to see that the corridor was twenty feet across and extended for several hundred feet. Evenly spaced doors ran down both sides of the hallway.

"Is there another annex on the other side of Nova?" Trent asked.

"No," Starke replied. "Nova annex is larger than Altair. There's nothing beyond the end of the hallway except mountain. This corridor connects to other corridors, but they all circle back to the elevators or the stairs located here. The only way on to or off the floor is through the security checkpoint, so don't get any ideas."

They'd walked nearly halfway down the corridor when Starke stopped at a door that had the number two stenciled on the front of it. The door number was out of sequence with the rest. When Starke used the palm scanner, Trent heard a distinctive click as it unlocked.

"Go on in," Starke said. "This will be your quarters for a while."

Trent entered the apartment and walked around. It was nicer than he'd expected. It had two bedrooms and two bathrooms, a living room area with a sofa, two dark leather recliners, a wall-mounted television, and a large kitchen and dining area. He opened the pantry and found that it was fully stocked. All the walls were painted a warm, beige. A floor-to-ceiling screen covered one wall in the living room. *Alexa would approve,* he thought. *She must be going nuts not knowing where I am.* As expected, there were no windows. "Are all of the apartments this nice?"

"Not all," Melissa answered. "This room is reserved for special guests. It's important that our guests feel at home, regardless of their length of stay."

Starke took a step toward him and said, "Honestly, Trent, you may be here a while, so we want you to be comfortable. We need to figure out what has happened to you and why."

"What's with the large screen on the living room wall?"

Melissa walked over to a control panel that was next to it and pushed a few keys. The screen came to life with a scene of woods, and the sound of wind blowing through the trees filled the room. Melissa scrolled through several scenes. One was a beach sunset with waves crashing ashore. She faced him and said, "Since there aren't any windows, this helps change the ambiance in the room. Feel free to scroll through the different scenes. There are twenty of them."

"That's quite nice. Any word about finding Alexa and our friends?" Trent hoped to catch the general off guard. He saw his hesitation.

"No," Starke replied.

"Any leads?"

"No. I want you to meet Taylor Graham, but first, I need to run you through orientation. Colonel, please take Trent down to the orientation room on Purple Level and get him set up."

"Yes, sir."

"General, I have another question."

"Yes?"

"How did you get my plane in here?"

"There's a helicopter pad on top of the mountain. You must not have seen the large freight elevator in the hangar. It runs up to the landing pad."

"So why did we drive here? You could have airlifted us." Trent could tell the general wasn't used to being questioned.

"We use the landing pad sparingly so as not to draw attention. Two helicopters flying over the mountain on the same day would have drawn scrutiny. Do you have any other questions?" Starke sounded annoyed.

"No, sir."

Purple Level – Observation Room – 1140 MST

Melissa and two Marines escorted Trent to a room for orientation. When he entered he saw a rectangular mirror on one wall. Trent knew it was a two-way mirror. A round table and three chairs stood in the middle of the room. One was occupied by Dr. Sanderson. Melissa sat down in another one. He had no choice but to sit down facing the mirror.

"Lovely interrogation room," Trent said sarcastically. "And how are you today, Dr. Sanderson?"

"I'm fine, Trent. Let's get started."

"Who's behind the glass?" Trent asked.

Melissa said, "I don't even notice that anymore. I don't believe anyone is there."

"Yeah, right. I'm starting to feel like an animal in a zoo."

Dr. Sanderson said, "Trent, let me have your left arm." He was holding a wristband.

Trent extended his arm. "That's isn't just a key card, is it? You can track me with it, too, right?"

"Yes," Melissa replied. "Over the next few days we'll be conducting tests on you, so we'll need to know where to find you."

Dr. Sanderson secured the rubber wristband, then handed him a large Manilla envelope. "This is your orientation packet. It lists the areas where you are permitted to go. You will note that access to certain areas is restricted. They are highlighted for you."

Trent pulled out the packet. He glanced over the material and saw that he had access to most of the gold and pink levels in both the Altair and Nova annexes. He was allowed in part of the hangar if he had a security escort. The rest of the facility was off limits. "Not many places I can go."

"This is a top-secret military facility," Dr. Sanderson said. "We can't let you just roam around. There are some dangerous areas."

"I imagine. Am I allowed to talk to other people?"

"Certainly," Sanderson answered. "But don't take it personally if they don't answer your questions. Personnel in the facility have been briefed on who you are, so you may get some wary looks. If you have any issues, contact me immediately by using any white phone. My extension is in the packet."

"I'm assuming the phones are for internal use only?"

Melissa chuckled. "That's correct. The only phones and communication equipment for external access are in secure areas on the brown and green levels. Both are heavily guarded at all times."

"Guess I won't be ordering a pizza," Trent said. "Anything else I need to know?"

"You may feel disoriented for a while," Dr. Sanderson said. "You'll need to establish a routine as soon as you can. Scheduled medical tests will be posted on the TV screen in your room."

"What medical tests are left? You've taken *lots* of blood, scanned my entire body twice, examined me from head to toe, and know all about my alien encounter. I don't know what else you could discover."

"We plan to observe your behavior closely and test your brain activity at different times of the day using the AMRS, the AMEG, an fMRI, and a Dynamic MRI scanner, just to name a few," Melissa said.

Trent shook his head. "I've heard of an MRI, but not the others."

"The AMRS is an Advanced Magnetic Resonance Spectroscopy. It will paint a picture of your brain's activity patterns. The fMRI produces images faster than a regular MRI. The Dynamic MRI involves using a contrast dye. An IV is required for that."

"Great, more needles," Trent said.

"The MEG is a Magnetoencephalography," Melissa said. "It scans and measures the magnetic fields created by your nerve cells. We will also run EEG's, EKG's, perform more blood tests, and check your immune system periodically to determine if there have been any changes from the baseline. Your dexterity and mobility will be tested, as well as your cognitive and mental acuity. We will have you solving puzzles to determine how your brain is processing what you're seeing and how you are thinking. It will show us what area of your brain is most active. We will also be checking the implant daily to look for any anomalies."

"What do you mean by *anomalies?*"

"We need to make sure the implant isn't affecting you and remains stable," Melissa answered.

"You mean it could become unstable?"

"We don't know. That's why we're going to check it periodically. Trent, we don't know what it does or how it operates. We want to see if it grows larger or changes positions. You've experienced no seizures or other loss of brain function, which is a good sign. We've detected no reduction in your physical or mental abilities so far. Your long-term and short-term memory appear normal. The only memory loss is the three weeks during your alien encounter."

"That's all good news," Trent said. "I don't feel any different from how I was before my flight. What I'm missing never existed for me."

"We know, and that's what's so interesting," Dr. Sanderson said. "Your sequential memory resumed uninterrupted from exactly where you had your encounter."

"Trent," Melissa said, "Your hippocampus, which essentially controls your memory function, is normal. You have no lesions, tumors, or anything else that would account for your lost time. You should be able to remember what happened to you, but for some reason the memory is being blocked."

"You think the implant is responsible?"

"That makes the most sense," Melissa answered. "We need to determine if the implant is some type of BCI, a brain-computer interface."

"And if it is?"

"That's why you're here," Sanderson said. "We will need to monitor your activity, watch for any behavioral or physical changes."

"Isn't that special. There's no way you can remove it?"

"Not now. We need to understand it. Trying to remove it could cause permanent brain damage or death. The brain is resilient, but also fragile. I know that sounds incongruous, but if we damage the wrong neurons, you could be left with irreparable damage. It could impact your judgement, personality, and inhibitions. I could list a number of other possible side effects—all things you wouldn't want to have happen to you. Until we understand its purpose, we have to wait and watch you for changes. You're in a secure environment. Think of this as the best medical care you could possibly imagine."

Trent nodded. "I get it. I'm not happy about it, but I do get it. Is it possible that what I'm experiencing, my thoughts, are being transmitted to the beings that put the implant in my head?"

"That's a possibility," Dr. Sanderson answered.

"So they would know what I see and feel?"

"Again, that's possible," Melissa said. "Now you should understand why we've gone to the lengths that we have to keep this secret."

"Am I the only one in the world with a neural implant?"

"That we know of," Melissa replied.

Trent leaned back in his chair and looked at his image in the glass. "So Taylor doesn't have one?"

"No."

"When do I meet Taylor?"

"Soon."

The Observation Booth

Taylor had been observing Trent since he'd been escorted into the room. The way he'd just looked at the mirrored glass made her feel as if he knew she was sitting there. General Starke was the only other person in the observation booth with her. Multiple recording devices had started the moment Trent entered the room. She knew that everything Trent said and did would be analyzed. She thought back to the day that she'd been brought into that room for the first time. The atmosphere had been far different and far less cordial then.

"You gave him permission to walk around the facility?" Taylor asked.

"Yes," Starke replied.

"How do you plan to keep us from bumping into each other? Do you plan on putting me back in isolation?"

"No. We actually want you to interact with him as much as possible. His apartment is next to yours. I want you to make him feel at ease. Tell him you come here periodically for tests, and that you have your own place to stay while you're here. You'll need to convey your concern and understanding of what he's going through."

Taylor faced the general and said, "That won't be easy, seeing how he's being given the red carpet treatment, while you caged me like an animal."

"Taylor, you'll tell him that you're staying in the facility while he's here to make him feel more comfortable."

"I read the script, or should I say the crap, you want me to tell him. I'm supposed to mentor him and earn his trust so you can screw him over." She pulled the chain around her neck, where her new identification card hung. Her wristband had been removed.

"We are not here to screw anyone over," Starke said. "You both have been selected by an alien species. The reason is unclear. I hope Trent will help us find out the reason so that you both can leave here."

"I want to have that in writing."

Starke smiled. "What do you say we go introduce you to him?"

TEN

General Starke knocked, entered the room, and said, "Is this a good time?"

"Perfect timing," Melissa replied. "Hello, Taylor. Nice of you to come by."

"No problem. I'm always willing to help, and I'm really very grateful for all that you've done for me."

Trent thought Taylor's delivery sounded a bit overly dramatic, and he noticed that General Starke was glaring at her. He wondered why. He stood and said, "It's a pleasure to meet you, Taylor. I hear we have something in common."

He took her hand and felt a connection to her immediately. He could tell by her reaction that she'd felt something, too. It made him feel as if they'd met before.

"It's nice to meet you, Trent," Taylor said, squeezing his hand tightly, then letting go. "I've been asked to help acclimate you to your new home and to see if I can help you recover some repressed memories."

"General, why don't we let them get started?" Dr. Sanderson said.

"Excellent idea," Starke replied. "Colonel, do you agree?"

"Yes, sir. We'll leave you two alone to talk."

Trent motioned for Taylor to sit, then said, "How do we get started?"

Taylor sat in the same chair that Melissa had taken earlier so that her back was to the mirrored glass. "I think the best place to start is to compare experiences," Taylor said. "When I was brought here, I'd just returned from an abduction."

"I was told that was two years ago."

"Yes. I'm surprised they told you."

"They said you had an implant in your leg, like the one I have, and that after it was removed you were medically cleared and that you and your family chose to live nearby for follow-up medical visits."

Taylor nodded. "My husband, Rick, and my daughter, Emma, are at home. I've chosen to stay in the facility for a while to help you adjust. I know how important it is to have someone around who's experienced what you're going through. I wish I'd had someone there for me."

"How old is your daughter?"

"She's fourteen. I've been told you have a girlfriend and that you were on your way to propose to her when you were abducted."

"You're well briefed. Her name is Alexa. I'd really like to call her. Our last conversation was cut short." He looked over her shoulder at the mirrored glass, then said, "They're watching us, aren't they?"

Taylor smiled and nodded. "We're being recorded as well." She gave him a wink and a little head nod toward a hidden camera.

"I figured as much." Trent gave her a serious look. "Are you really an abductee, or are you just on their payroll?"

"I was really abducted." Taylor pulled up her left pants leg and showed him the scar. "Let me see yours."

Trent showed her, then said, "Your scar is bigger and not as triangular as mine. How do I know that your scar wasn't caused by an accident?"

"Paranoia is healthy. I like that. The scar I had originally looked exactly like yours, both in shape and the color it turned the skin. After they removed the implant, I was left with what you see. I also have a small scar behind my ear. I don't know how I got that one. They said that you have an implant in your brain. Since I was coming here, they decided to run another imaging test of my brain. It appears that I'm clean." She turned and pulled her hair back to show him the mark behind her ear.

Trent stared at the scar for a moment. His mind raced when a memory flashed in his head. When she faced him again, he looked carefully at her face and her dazzling blue eyes. He leaned in closer.

"Is there something wrong?" she asked. "You look as if you're examining me."

"I'm sorry. I didn't mean to be rude. I just feel as if we've met before. I remember a girl from my childhood who had a scar just like that behind her ear. Where were you raised?"

"In Indiana, Newburgh. It's near Evansville."

"I know where it is. I have family there."

Melissa saw the general smile when he heard Trent's last comment.

"Interesting," Starke said. "Colonel, why didn't we know he had family there?"

"I will find out, sir," Melissa said.

"While you're at it, cross-check everything again. I want to know every place both of them have been since birth. See if there's a connection between their ancestors, vacations, schools, interests—anything at all."

"That may be tough to do since we don't have everything on Trent's history yet."

Dr. Sanderson cleared his throat. "Do you think it's possible they knew each other as children?"

"Perhaps they met during an abduction when they were kids," Starke said. "Wouldn't that be interesting."

"Interesting?" Sanderson said. "That would make sense. Neither can recall their exact age when they were first abducted. We know they were both seven or eight years old. They are the same age, and they were both born in the same month."

"It couldn't be that easy, could it?" Melissa said.

"Anything is possible," Starke replied. "We know that the aliens have made repeated abductions of Taylor to harvest her ova. Maybe they didn't need Trent again until now."

"You think they need him to fertilize her ova?" Melissa asked.

"Possibly," Starke replied.

"Maybe they couldn't find Taylor, so they tracked down a person she may have known," Sanderson said.

Melissa sat back and listened to Trent and Taylor talking about family, life at the facility, and the things they remembered during their abductions. She tried to tune out Sanderson and Starke as they continued to speculate. She knew that Taylor and Trent were connected somehow. Now she wondered if bringing them together had been the right thing to do. Would the aliens come for Trent, as she hoped? And what would happen if they found both of them together? Would the electronic field that surrounded the Nova annex be strong enough to repel the light that Trent described? Would the containment vessel trap the aliens as designed? There were too many variables, too many unknowns.

"General, perhaps we should discuss the containment protocols in case the aliens do come for Trent," Melissa said.

"Why?"

"We haven't discussed how to keep both subjects safe simultaneously. What if they want both of them, and they're in separate areas of the facility when they arrive? It will be difficult to maintain control. If the electronic dampers can't prevent transmission from Trent's implant, the aliens may already know Taylor is here."

"Signals intercept hasn't detected any electromagnetic flux from Trent's implants," Sanderson said.

Starke said, "The electronic communication dampers around the facility should prevent any electronic signature from being broadcast."

"Possibly, but we haven't isolated his neural implant or run any tests to determine if there is a signal," Melissa said. "And if he *is* transmitting a signal, we may not detect it."

"I see your point," Starke said.

"General, I'm positive that we'd detect anything being broadcast," Sanderson said. "When we're ready for them to receive Trent's signal, we'll turn off the dampers and follow our preplanned protocols."

"That's all well and good," Melissa said. "But Trent wasn't dampened on his way here. If they were tracking him, they know the place where he disappeared. And they know where Taylor's implant was last transmitting."

Starke said, "We discussed this already. We *want* the aliens to investigate."

"Yes, eventually and under controlled conditions," Melissa said. "I think we should house Taylor and Trent in the same apartment."

"Why?" Starke asked. "Her apartment is next door to his. The area is secure."

"Look at Trent," Melissa said. "He's reacting to her, and we already learned something we didn't know. I believe putting them together will increase the chance that Trent will remember what happened to him. I also think if the aliens return, having Taylor with him will narrow our containment response."

Starke sighed, then said, "There are two bedrooms and two bathrooms for privacy. Even so, Taylor may not agree to the plan."

"She'll have to go along," Melissa said.

"I agree," Sanderson said. "I can enhance the containment field around Trent's room for added security. That will reduce the area we need to monitor—at least most of the time."

Melissa watched Trent and Taylor closely. It certainly did seem as if they knew each other. They looked . . . comfortable. If Trent could remember what happened to him, maybe they would be able to release Taylor, provided she didn't say or do anything careless. Taylor could be hard to handle—was stubborn and free-willed sometimes. Usually when it was least expected.

Trent felt more at ease with Taylor by the minute, as if he had known her for a long time.

"Tell me everything about your first abduction," Taylor said. "They gave me a synopsis, but I want to hear all of the details."

"I'm surprised they didn't tell you everything. Alright, I was seven or eight years old," Trent began, recalling what had led up to the abduction. "My mom and I were living in St. Petersburg, Florida."

"Where is your mother now?"

"She passed away a few years ago."

"I'm sorry."

"Thanks." Trent looked up at the ceiling. "There were two events that happened fairly close together. It was late summer, and I remember it was hot out. The windows were open because the air conditioner was broken. I saw something in the sky that I didn't recognize. It was a strange-looking craft, and it was flying over the bay headed slowly toward the Gulf of Mexico. I knew it wasn't a plane. It wasn't making a sound, and it was moving too slowly. When I told my mom about what I'd seen, she insisted that I'd seen a blimp, but I knew it wasn't."

"What exactly did it look like?" Taylor asked.

"Like a long, shiny cigar. I remember a blue-white aura surrounded the craft and a flash of light blinding me for a moment, like a laser beam had been pointed at me. Then the craft was gone."

"Then what happened?"

"Nothing for a couple of months. Then one night I was awakened by a strange noise in the house. At first I thought it was my mother doing something in the kitchen, but then an otherworldly blue light illuminated my bedroom. I wanted to cry out, but I couldn't. I was frozen in my bed, only able to move my head from side to side."

"I know the feeling of being paralyzed. It's happened to me several times. Very scary."

"That's for sure, but what was more frightening were the creatures. At first I only saw their shadows on the wall, and then several small, flat-headed beings appeared by the foot of my bed. I was so scared I wet myself."

"I've done that, too." Taylor said, without a hint of embarrassment.

"I couldn't see the creatures' faces clearly, but I knew they weren't human. They had dark, matted hair covering their shoulders. They lifted me into the air, but I didn't feel them touching me. I floated past my mother's open bedroom door, and I couldn't believe that she didn't wake up. I tried to call out, but couldn't." Trent took a deep breath. "I still feel that terror."

"Do you want to take a break?"

"No, I'm alright." He glanced at the mirror. "I know that they're comparing this story to the one I told them earlier."

Taylor leaned closer and whispered, "You're going to be telling them about your experiences many, many times. When I first arrived, I went over my abductions so many times, with so many people, that I lost count. What happened next?"

"I was floated across the small living room of our house and out into the night. I don't think they opened the front door. It was as if I'd passed through it. Then I rose toward a huge ship, and then I lost consciousness.

"When I woke up, I was in a large, darkened room. The place reeked of something I'd never smelled before, a horrible rotten smell. When I looked to my right, I saw a creature sitting there. It didn't look anything like the ones that had taken me. This one was very big and had a large head. Its body was covered with grayish-brown, leathery skin. It didn't look anything like the aliens in the science fiction movies or television shows."

"No, they don't," Taylor said.

"I remember the creature's dark, penetrating eyes. They weren't predatory. They looked more inquisitive. The creature leaned toward me to examine me more closely. Then one of its long fingers moved toward my cheek, and I watched in terror as the creature wiped my tears away. Its skin felt hard, almost callused."

Taylor's eyes welled up. "I understand the fear you experienced. I've seen that creature before and felt its touch."

"This is upsetting you, isn't it?" Trent said.

"A little, but you need to continue."

"I remember screaming for it to leave me alone and tried to pull away, but couldn't. I closed my eyes, hoping the thing would leave. When I opened my eyes again, a man was standing next to the table I was on. He placed a clear mask over my face."

"A man?" Taylor asked.

"It wasn't really a man, but its physique seemed more manlike than a woman. His eyes and facial features were odd-looking, his movements slow and deliberate, like a robot. The gas I smelled in the mask was worse than the other odor in the room. Then I went to sleep."

"I remember seeing a humanoid being," Taylor said. "It was always the one that did my examinations."

"It sounds like we were taken by the same aliens."

"Yes, it does. What happened after you woke up?"

"I was in my bed. I ran and told my mom what had happened. Even after I showed her the wound on my leg, she still didn't believe me. She said it was just a bad dream."

"My family didn't believe me either," Taylor said. She told him about her first abduction.

Trent noted that she was choosing her words carefully. She seemed to be hiding something. "Tell me what you remember about your last abduction."

Taylor shifted uneasily in her chair. "I remember a bright light surrounding me. It was intense. I wondered why Rick didn't wake up. The shadows cast by the aliens appeared on the bedroom wall, and I knew it was happening again. My body was frozen in place. I thought about Emma. I didn't want them to touch her like they'd touched me. Then came a calming, blue light, and I was taken into the ship."

"Do you remember any details of the ship?"

"Not really. I know it was a gray metallic color, and it seemed to be long and narrow, like the one you described. I only saw the bottom of the craft. I was taken through a translucent portal. It felt as if I passed through an electronic field. My nightgown felt cold, and my skin was tingling. The next thing I remember is being placed on an examination table, and my nightgown was removed."

Her eyes became less focused, as if she was gazing at something in the distance. She was reliving the event. Trent had no doubt that she was an abductee.

Taylor said, "The strange thing is that I wasn't embarrassed by being naked. It was a clinical setting, and I'd been there before. The humanoid being you described stood over me, and it touched my face. I felt as if it cared about me. Then I felt pressure in my abdomin. Somehow, I knew what it was doing."

"What was it doing?" Trent asked.

"It was harvesting ova from me. When the pressure stopped, I saw a small medical-looking device retract into a dark ceiling. I glared at the being standing over me. It had intense dark, reddish eyes. It put a mask over my face. There was a foul odor, and then everything went black."

"I remember the red eyes," Trent said. "Were you returned home?"

"Not this time, which was strange. I was left in the woods near a military base in Utah. I awoke to find that I was dusted with a light covering of snow. I had no idea where I was, but I knew I wasn't in Indiana. I was freezing, and the lower part of my nightgown was covered with blood. I was bleeding vaginally. I remember staggering to the base entrance and collapsing at the gate."

"And you ended up here?"

"Not right away. I woke up in a military hospital. They must have thought I was a dependent, so they admitted me. A gynecologist told me that I'd had a miscarriage."

"I'm sorry," Trent said.

"Me, too. I explained to the doctors what I'd been through. No one seemed to believe me. The next day General Starke and Colonel Endo arrived. They recommended I be transferred to a better medical facility. They told me that they believed my story about being abducted by alien beings and that they needed to better understand what had occurred so they could treat me properly. The general explained how important it was to keep what had happened to me a secret.

"They brought me here, and the medical team performed a number of additional tests. That's when they found the implant in my leg, and Colonel Endo removed it. The thing dissolved as soon as it was exposed to the air."

"How long were you here before they let you leave?"

She broke eye contact. "It was . . . about a week."

"Do you think your pregnancy was deliberately terminated?"

Her eyes suddenly brimmed with tears. "I'm sorry." Taylor looked down at the table and wiped her tears away, then said, "Yes, I do."

"I'm sorry if talking about this is upsetting you."

Taylor took a deep breath. "It is, but maybe it'll help you remember what happened the last time you were abducted."

"I know that everyone wants me to remember that experience, but I'm blanking. How soon was it before you were reunited with your family?"

"When I was discharged. They'd flown Rick and Emma out here, and after I explained what had happened, we decided to stay close to the base. I felt safer here. Of course Rick felt guilty about not protecting me. Even now when I wake up from my nightmares, I see the fear in his eyes, not knowing if I've been abducted again. But thanks to General Starke and Colonel Endo, I haven't been."

"That's good. I imagine your family feels safer, too."

Taylor bit her lower lip. "Enough about me. I saw the news about your disappearance. You were flying when they snatched you this time. General Starke told me that three weeks later you were returned to the exact same place, and you were still in flight. That had to be strange. So what happened?"

"Like I've told everyone, I don't know."

"I think it'll all come back to you eventually. That's why I'm here. I know that the sooner the repressed memories work their way to the surface, the quicker you can move on with your life."

"Taylor, how many times were you abducted?"

"Four. The two I told you about, then once as a teenager and again when I was pregnant with Emma."

When the airtight seal on the door was broken, it made a hissing sound, and air rushed into the room. Starke and Melissa entered. They were both smiling. Trent took that as a good sign.

"So how's it going?" Starke asked.

"You tell us." Trent cocked his head toward the mirrored glass.

"Yes, Trent, we were listening," Melissa said. "It sounds like you are getting to know each other, and it seems as if both of you were taken by the same beings. Trent, I think Taylor will be able to help you remember what happened this last time. The trauma and length of your abduction could be blocking your memory."

Starke said, "Trent, I know you're anxious to get back to your old life and get back to Alexa and your friends."

"But," Trent said. He noticed Taylor tense up.

"We've come up with an idea that may expedite the process—if you both agree," Starke replied.

"I'm listening," Trent said.

"It's a bit unorthodox. We'd like Taylor to move into your apartment."

"What?" Taylor cried. "That's not a part of the deal."

"What deal?" Trent asked. Melissa glanced at Starke. Now he knew for certain. "So this was all a sham." He waited for an answer, but no one spoke.

"General, perhaps we should tell Trent the truth," Melissa said.

"Perhaps. Trent, Taylor has been our guest for nearly two years."

Trent stared at Taylor, then said, "You lied to me. All of this is a lie. I knew something didn't feel right. Your answers were too pat."

Taylor glared at Starke. "The deal was that I get him to remember so that I could rejoin Rick and Emma." She turned to Trent and said, "I'm sorry. I'd say or do just about anything to get out of here and go back to my family. You must understand that. What I told you about my abductions was true."

"I could tell that was sincere," Trent said calmly. "General Starke, you have no intention of letting either of us go, do you?"

"I'm done playing this game," Starke said. "I *will* let both of you go once I understand why you two were selected for abduction out of the billions of other people on this planet. We have to know what these creatures want with you and what they have planned."

"What about Agent Dobson and Deputy Griffin?" Trent asked. "Will they be given an apartment and forced to stay until you have your answers?"

"Listen and listen good," Starke said, taking an aggressive step toward Trent. "Your job is to remember what happened to you. Taylor's job is to help you do that. Then, and only then, will we discuss releasing anyone. Are we clear?"

"Crystal," Trent replied, standing to face Starke. "I figured that was what was in store for me, and I knew that you were an asshole from the first time we met. But you really went deep into the cesspool when you victimize Taylor again. I hope that Alexa continues to elude your grasp and causes you many sleepless nights."

The general's face flushed. Taylor smirked, then gave Trent a little nod of approval.

"If I may," Melissa said, stepping between the two men. "We must work together to get to the bottom of this mystery. General, Trent isn't going to cooperate if he feels he's being manipulated, and we need him. Taylor is trying to help. Maybe it's time we work together instead of threatening them."

"You're out of line, Colonel," Starke said.

"General, this is a unique situation. We need to allow for some flexibility."

"What do you have in mind?"

"We go forward with our plan. Trent and Taylor move in together. We drop the electronic dampers and see if we get the aliens to bite."

"You want to use us as bait?" Trent asked.

"In a manner of speaking," Melissa said. "Taylor's implant was removed at this facility. I think the aliens will be curious about why two specimens have been brought to the same location. I'm certain that they'll investigate. That'll give us an opportunity to make contact or capture them."

"Specimens?" Trent said.

Starke ignored that comment. "Once we have our answers, Colonel Endo will remove the implant in your leg and I'll release you both."

"You have a history of breaking promises," Trent said.

Melissa said, "Trent, you have my word. The general and I have already discussed this. He's telling you the truth. We've held Taylor far too long already."

Trent looked at Taylor to see her reaction. Her blank expression told him she knew this was just another hollow promise. "What about the thing in my head?"

"Like I said, we need to study it, then try to find a way to remove it without causing any neural damage," Melissa replied.

"That doesn't sound very reassuring," Trent said.

"Enough!" Starke shouted. "The two of you will live together, and you will do whatever is required to make this a successful operation."

"So much for flexibility," Taylor said. "General, I'll agree to stay in Trent's apartment, but I'm not going to sleep with him."

Trent didn't know how to react. Surely, they didn't plan on them sharing a bed.

"Taylor, we aren't asking you to," Melissa said. "There are two bedrooms. I hope that your close proximity will help expedite Trent recovering his memory. That's all."

"Damn straight, that's all," Taylor said.

"It sounds like you've had a plan for this scenario since before I was abducted, haven't you?" Trent asked.

"Not for you specifically, but yes, there was a scenario that we considered," Melissa said. "We develop scenarios daily for every possible encounter we can think of and then design plans and protocols to deal with them."

"Is there a scenario where Taylor and I are abducted together?"

"Yes," Melissa replied.

"And you'd let them take us if you couldn't capture them, right?" Trent asked.

"Yes. We hope to capture one of them before that occurs. If not during your abduction, then upon your return."

Starke said, "As you know, they're interested in Taylor's reproductive system. We want to know why and what role you play in all of this."

"Wait a minute," Trent said, raising his voice. "Neither of us are going to engage in reproduction."

"That may not be your choice," Melissa said. "They may have already taken samples from you and joined them with her ova."

"I knew it!" Taylor cried.

Trent felt stunned. Was that really what this was all about? He'd seen programs about ancient aliens and abductions, and some of those involved creating hybrid beings. Was that why they'd been taken?

"It's not what you think," Melissa said.

"I know exactly what this is all about," Taylor said.

Trent looked at Starke and said, "Finding out why they'd want to use us for reproductive purposes is only one consideration, but it's not the most important issue, is it? What you really want us to do is establish contact with these beings and convince them that it's time to meet."

"We prefer that option over capturing them," Starke said. "It'd be more civilized."

Taylor paced around the room. She stopped in front of Starke and said, "I will do whatever it takes to regain my life. I have no problem living with Trent. But just so you know, if I get an opportunity to kill one of those creatures, I will. They killed my baby."

"I don't believe that will be possible," Starke said.

Taylor turned to Melissa. "Can we talk outside?" She looked at Trent. "We *will* discover what happened to you during your abduction. I need to speak to Melissa, and then we'll talk—privately."

"Okay," Trent said. *Were there two good cops and one bad cop?* he wondered.

Melissa and Taylor left the room while Starke took a seat. "Sit down."

Trent sat down and stared at him. Taylor had either given the best theatrical performance of her life, or she was really desperate to leave. Trent decided it was the latter.

"General, how do you live with yourself?" Trent asked.

Starke leaned forward, putting his hands flat on the table. "You have no idea what sacrifices I've made to protect this country. I will do whatever I have to do to ensure our way of life."

"I wonder if you'd feel the same way if you were in our shoes."

"Knowing what I know, I wouldn't hesitate to do anything I could to help."

"Yeah, I'm sure that's true if you volunteered. But what if you had no choice? What if you were the one being held in captivity, deprived of being able to speak to your family? Have you thought about what Taylor has been through?"

"Every. Single. Day. I get no pleasure from having to do this, but it's necessary."

"Is it?"

Trent closed his eyes and thought about Alexa and their friends. He hoped they could evade Starke. He didn't know how he would cope if they were brought here and used as pawns against him. He couldn't blame Taylor for her deception. That was all on Starke.

Why did he feel like he knew Taylor? Why did he feel attracted to her? There was something about her that he couldn't quite grasp, a memory that hadn't coalesced to form a clear picture. He knew only that she was special to him.

ELEVEN

Boise, Idaho Airport – 1730 hours MST

Alexa, Marvin, and Sue walked out of the airport FBO. Alexa shivered when a biting blast of winter wind greeted her. She hadn't been in snow for years and had grown accustomed to the warm Florida climate. The snow fluttered down from the gunmetal clouds. She was glad that the pilot had recommended buying cold-weather clothing when they'd stopped to refuel in Texas.

Alexa spotted Dan standing next to an SUV in the parking lot. He nodded at her, then got into a gray SUV and started the engine.

"Let's go get warm," Alexa said.

"Sounds good to me," Marvin replied.

"My word, it's freezing out here," Sue said.

They walked across the road to Dan's rented Toyota Highlander. Alexa jumped in the front passenger seat. Sue and Marvin jumped in the back.

"It's good to see you, Dan," Alexa said.

"Likewise."

"Everything good?"

"It's all good. Let's get away from the security cameras."

"I appreciate everything you've done," Alexa said, as they pulled out of the parking lot.

"You'd do the same for me. I rented two rooms at the Marriott Residence Inn and this vehicle for us. I figured we may need another surveillance vehicle. You and Sue will have to share a room. Marvin gets the bachelor pad. All the rooms have kitchens in case we're here for a while."

Marvin said, "Can you crank up the heat?"

"It's already on high. Weather report says this area will get more snow tomorrow—about ten inches."

"How far away are we from where Trent disappeared?" Alexa asked.

"From the hotel, about fifteen minutes. O'Malley and Norm are monitoring the only access road. The trail road is covered with fresh snow. If we drive down it now, we'll leave tracks. I'm hoping the military makes another run out there so we can use their tracks as cover."

"So we wait," Alexa said.

"That's all we can do for now. I've made you a map of the area." Dan pointed to the glove box.

Alexa opened it and removed a large envelope.

"I included satellite and topographic sectionals in the packet. You'll find that Greylock Mountain and most of the area around here is challenging for conducting surveillance operations. There's not much traffic out that way, and our vehicles will stand out after a few days. The trail road where we lost Trent is surrounded by lots of trees, and the terrain off the road is very rough."

"That could actually work in our favor," Alexa said. "Makes it harder for people to see us if we go in on foot. Any unusual activity in the area?"

"No, nothing. No other vehicles since the van carrying Trent and the others used the road."

Marvin said, "We need to find the base."

"Finding it is one thing, finding a way into it is a whole different thing," Dan said. "It's well hidden. We can't follow the military van down the road to see where they stop because the road is one lane. We'd be spotted in a second."

"With the fresh snow, we can follow their tracks until they end," Alexa said.

"That's a good idea if they come back," Dan replied.

Alexa opened the envelope and looked at the satellite images and ground photos Dan had taken. "From what I see here, the road you marked doesn't go anywhere. It just meanders up toward the mountaintop and then back down. Looks like there's another spur that goes south toward a small airport."

"Yeah, that's China Basin. No activity there. There's a bunch of hiking and fire trails that intersect with the spur roads, but nothing we saw leads anywhere."

"Some of the trails look like they could be cross-country ski trails. I don't see anything that looks unusual. No clearings for helicopter operations except one that's near the peak of one of the ridges, but there's no road around it."

"So where did everyone go, and how do we find the entrance to your secret military facility?" Dan asked.

"Any ideas, Marvin?" Alexa said.

"Yeah, but you won't like it."

Alexa turned toward him, then said, "You want to go for a hike in a snowstorm, don't you?"

"That would cover our tracks," Marvin replied. "A heavy snowfall will also disrupt any optical or motion sensors. If we're lucky, we can reconnoiter most of the western base of the mountain in a day."

"And if we're discovered?"

"We show them our fake IDs and claim that we're doing some cross-country training while hunting."

"I'm not much of a winter outdoorsy kind of person," Sue said.

"No problem," Alexa said. "I think Dan will have something you can help him with while we're gone."

"We can always use another pair of eyes," Dan said. "Sounds like you're going hiking. You'll need supplies."

"We're going to need weapons, snow gear, climbing and camping gear, and cross-country skis," Alexa said. "Do you know where we can find everything we need?"

"There's an outdoorsman store not far from here. Let's get you checked in at the hotel, and then we'll go shopping."

"Sounds good," Alexa replied.

"How about we eat, too?" Sue said.

"There's a good Italian restaurant near the hotel," Dan said. "I'll get some takeout for O'Malley and Norm."

"Sounds like a plan," Alexa said.

Sawtooth Facility – Nova Annex – Pink Level – 1730 hours MST

Trent and Taylor sat next to each other at a dining table, with Starke and Melissa sitting across from them. Their table was in a reserved portion of the dining room. They were the only ones there. They'd picked up the menus on their way to the private dining room, and Trent noted the diverse selection being offered. The cafeteria was also busy, as was the common area. A steady clamor of noise echoed off the concrete floors and walls.

"Are Deputy Griffin and Agent Dobson dining elsewhere?" Trent asked.

"It's best they stay segregated for now," Starke said, just as a server came to the table.

"I'm hungry," Taylor announced. "Trent, the food's pretty good. I recommend the steak. That's what I'm having, and I'd like it well-done with a side of carrots and rice."

"I'll have the same," Trent said.

Melissa and Starke ordered the steak, too.

After the server left, Starke said, "We'll drop the security dampers tomorrow. I think it best that after dinner you two retire to your private quarters and get to know each other better."

"You make it sound like we're on a date," Taylor said.

"Not the way I meant it. I want both of you to understand that it's imperative that you share anything you discover about any commonalities. If you do, bring it to Colonel Endo's or my attention immediately. There's a reason you were selected by these beings."

"I believe we've already covered all the relevant commonalities that I can remember," Trent said.

"Trent, our lives are intertwined," Taylor said. "I'd like to get this figured out sooner rather than later. Then we'll see if Melissa and the general keep their promise."

"Enough," Starke said. "I'd like you both out of here tomorrow, but that isn't going to happen unless your alien friends snatch you. The reality is that even if we make contact and everything goes according to plan, we may still need your help in the future."

"I don't remember that being discussed earlier," Trent said.

"They change the rules to suit their needs," Taylor said, rolling her eyes at him.

Starke glared at her. "Defiant, as always."

Melissa said, "Trent, unless we're able to find the answers we seek, we'll still need to monitor you and Taylor even after you're released. Any children you and Alexa have will need to be monitored, just as we're keeping an eye on Taylor's husband and daughter."

"So we'll never be free of you?" Trent asked.

"Probably not," Melissa replied.

"You plan on keeping Deputy Griffin and Agent Dobson around until we receive a visit?"

"We're not sure," Starke said. "There are unresolved issues with them. One of which is how Alexa and your friends eluded them."

Trent smiled. "Learn anything new from the tests you did on my plane?"

"Yes, the molecular structure of the aircraft's outer aluminum skin isn't the same as the aluminum in the interior sections," Starke replied. "It's still aluminum, but it has been fused with an unknown element that allows it, and the paint, to withstand a higher surface temperature before melting. The engine and denser metals have not been altered. The plastics and fabric materials in the interior and instrumentation are also unchanged. The Hobbs meter and engine time recorder confirm that the engine wasn't operated except while you were in flight."

"How do you know the engine time is correct?" Trent asked.

"We found your log books. You keep excellent records."

"What about the fuel?" Trent asked.

"Based on you having topped off the tanks prior to leaving for Key West, you used the exact amount that you should have used for the trip."

"I wonder why only the aluminum exterior portions of the aircraft changed?" Trent said.

"Our forensic engineers think the structure was exposed to an extreme ionization event and that the element was somehow fused at a molecular level. My guess is that the aliens knew they would damage your plane if they didn't strengthen it."

"I wish I could remember what happened."

"So do we," Melissa said.

The food arrived, and they ate dinner without any further discussion concerning the abductions.

"Trent, you look tired," Melissa said.

"I am. Any chance I can head up to the apartment?"

"Certainly," Melissa replied. "Taylor, why don't you take Trent up. Gather what you need for the night from your place, then you two should retire."

Trent looked at Taylor and said, "You alright with that?"

"I'm fine with that."

Trent's Apartment — 1930 hours MST

Trent had taken a shower while Taylor went to get her personal belongings. He felt more like himself than he had since the ordeal had begun. He dressed in a pair of jeans and rugby shirt that someone had left for him in the closet next to a uniform. Both were his size. When he entered the living room, Taylor was sitting on a sofa, watching television.

"That was fast," Trent said.

"I travel light."

"Anything good on the TV?" Trent asked.

"Same old stuff. At least they provide primetime cable." She turned the volume up, then patted the spot next to her.

Trent sat down beside her. Taylor leaned toward him. He thought she was going to kiss him and pulled back.

Taylor cocked her head. "I want to ask you something." Then she leaned in again and whispered in his ear. "Do you feel it?"

"Feel what?"

"That we've been together before."

"Like I told you earlier, I remember seeing a girl with a scar behind her ear like yours. I also remember seeing your blue eyes."

"I think we're connected to something bigger and much more encompassing than what Starke and Melissa can imagine."

"What could be bigger than interacting and being examined by an alien being?"

Taylor scooted closer. Their hips and thighs touched, and she rested her head on his shoulder. Trent liked the way her hair smelled, and he could feel his heart beating faster. He wasn't sure if it was because he felt something for her or because he felt guilty about being so close to Taylor—and liking it.

"This feels right," Taylor said. "I don't know why, but I'm attracted to you. Not in a sexual way, but in a comfortable way. Like we've been friends for years."

Trent put his arm around her shoulder and squeezed her arm. A dim memory tugged at him. "I feel it, too. Perhaps this is simply a reaction to us having shared similar experiences that no one else could ever understand."

She looked up at him. "It's not just that. I remember seeing you when we were kids. I didn't want to say anything around the brass. But I'm nearly certain now."

"What did I look like?"

"I remember you had long hair, and it was wet." She turned slightly toward him. "You kept pushing it away from your face, and you were shivering."

Trent nodded. A memory sparked in his mind as he stared into her eyes. "You were missing one of your front teeth."

"That's right. We were huddled together, like we are now. You said something to me. It was comforting." Taylor turned her face away. "There was an awful odor in the air. I can still remember that distinctive smell."

"I didn't want to let go of you when they came for you." Trent started to sweat. He could see an alien being in his mind. A long-forgotten memory made him feel the fear again. "A humanoid-looking creature came for you." He began to tremble as Taylor trembled against him. They were both reliving the event.

"As they took me away, I saw you run after me," Taylor said. "The little brown creatures restrained you, but you fought against them until . . ."

"Until, what?"

"Until they injected you with something. Then the little brown beings took you away. When I was taken again at fourteen, I looked for you, but you weren't there. No one was with me then, or at any of the other times."

Trent thought about his flight to Key West. He remembered descending, then seeing the light. He relived the encounter until there was nothing. "I really want to remember what happened this last time, but it's a blank canvas after the light and feeling disoriented. I was gone for weeks, not hours, so something should be there."

She looked up at him. "It'll come in time. Mine did. Every now and then I remembered something I'd blocked out. Our brains protect us from the terror and trauma we experience. At least for a while."

Trent took a deep breath. "We need to get some sleep."

"That's when they always came for me. I haven't felt that frightened in a long time, and it was usually before they took me away. Do you think they will come tonight?"

"You're safe. It's just bad memories playing with your emotions." Trent smiled at her.

"Will you sleep with me tonight?" Taylor asked.

"When you say sleep, you just mean sleep, right?"

"Yes. Nothing sexual. Just for comfort."

"That will be fine. Strength in numbers."

Trent followed her into the bedroom and watched her get under the covers. He took a deep breath and climbed into bed, fully clothed. Taylor snuggled up against him. Sleep came quickly.

The Marriott – Alexa's Room – 2300 hours MST

Alexa, Sue, and Marvin sat at a small dinette. Two pairs of skis stood in the corner by the door, and backpacks and gear littered the couch.

"Do you think we have enough bottled water and MREs?" Alexa asked.

"We're good for several days," Marvin replied. "It's a shame we couldn't get the rifles we wanted."

"They would've slowed us down," Alexa said. "The handguns Dan gave us will be enough for this scouting mission. If caught, we are just doing some cross-country skiing."

"Still, I'd prefer to reach out and touch someone, or a mountain lion, at a distance," Marvin said. "Did you see the warning posters at the store?"

"I saw them," Alexa replied. She finished packing the ready-to-eat meals. "What do you think Trent is doing now?"

"Probably sleeping," Marvin replied. "I'm sure that they've been interrogating him and doing their best to scare the crap out of him. Who knows, maybe he'll call us to say they're releasing him. But with our luck, they'll probably put him on a plane and fly him to Key West while we're freezing in the mountains."

"Trent doesn't have any of our new cell phone numbers."

"Maybe he's called your office already," Sue said.

"I can't call my office," Alexa said. "I'm sure they've got all the lines tapped."

"Good point," Sue replied.

"Marvin, we should be at the drop site before sunrise. The sooner we can get up into the mountains the better. I'll call Dan and tell him we'll be ready at 0500 hours."

"I'm still on Florida time, so that works out to 0700 hours on my body clock," Marvin said. "I can work with that."

Alexa looked at her two friends. They'd been there for her all these weeks, and the road ahead was only going to get harder. "If things get dicey, I want you both to play it safe. No heroics, understood?"

"When have you ever known me to do anything heroic?" Sue asked.

Marriott hotel — February 04 — 0500 hours MST

Alexa helped Marvin load the gear into Dan's SUV. The bitter cold morning seemed worse than the day before. Heavy snow was falling. Alexa smelled the coffee before she saw Dan walking toward her with several cups.

"You're a lifesaver," Alexa said.

"Sue sleeping in?" Dan asked.

"No, she'll be down soon. She went back to the room to add another layer of clothing."

"Did you get any sleep?" Marvin asked Dan.

"I did. Listen, once I drop you, I'm going to let the team go back to their motel in Idaho City for some rest. Sue and I can cover the road."

"Your teams not staying here?"

"No. I decided to post them closer to the trail-road cutoff. It's a few minutes faster to reach the road from there." Dan handed Alexa a two-way radio. "This has a thirty-mile range. It'll work better than cell phones once you're in the mountains."

Alexa hugged Dan. "How will I ever repay you?"

"Just bring Trent back. Then we'll discuss my bill."

They all laughed.

"What's so funny?" Sue asked as she joined them.

"Nothing," Alexa replied. "You feel warmer now?"

"I'm a Florida girl," Sue said. "I don't like cold weather."

"I can relate," Marvin said. "Let's get going."

They drove to the cutoff road. Surprisingly, the main roads had been plowed. Dan parked the SUV a half mile from the trail road, and then he called O'Malley and Norm on the radio and had them stand down.

Dan said, "You're going to need those skis. Head southwest and you'll intersect with the trail road."

"It's dark as hell out here," Marvin said. "I'm glad I brought a compass."

"It'll be light soon," Alexa said. "We'll parallel the trail road once the sun comes up. Let's get going."

"You stay safe," Sue said. "You too, Marvin."

They skied around the various pine trees without much difficulty. The snow was only a few inches thick. The exertion kept them warm.

"It's not so bad," Alexa said. "I haven't been skiing in years." She looked back along the path they'd taken. Even in the darkness, she saw that they were leaving a trail, but that was inevitable.

Thirty minutes later, they stopped for a break. Alexa saw that their tracks were beginning to be covered by the snow.

"Even in the insulated packs, the water's nearly frozen," Marvin said, handing her a bottle. "My thermometer says it's only three degrees."

"It's really starting to come down. We need to drink a bottle every thirty minutes to stay hydrated."

"I'm the one with arctic survival training," Marvin said. "Hated it then, and I'm not liking it now."

"I want you to take the lead," Alexa said, sounding serious. "Let me have the heavy pack. It'll start getting light soon, but we won't see the sun for a while. We'll be in the mountain's shadow for a few hours. I think we're well past where Dan said they turned around. We haven't seen anything that looks like security monitoring equipment."

"Not yet. Motion sensors are probably buried in the snow. They could be using thermal, but in this stuff, we'd never see it."

"What kind of range on the thermal?"

"It depends."

"What about audio sensors?"

"Possible, but again, the snow will interfere. We should be okay if we talk quietly."

"Just in case, let's limit our conversations. You have the lead."

Marvin pulled his goggles down over his eyes. "Tallyho!"

Trent's Room — 0700 hours MST

Trent cried out, then jerked up in bed.

"You're okay," Taylor whispered.

"What time is it?"

"It's seven."

"We better get up," Trent said, getting out of bed. "I'll start breakfast. I saw some eggs in the fridge." He couldn't help but notice how beautiful Taylor looked. Her auburn hair, even mussed, seemed perfect to him. She stared at him with her blue eyes. His heart skipped a beat.

She smiled, then said, "Eggs sounds good to me." She rolled out of bed and stepped past him saying she was going to her room.

Trent brushed his teeth and checked to make sure he didn't have bed-head. He needed a shave, but that could wait. He went to the kitchen and started the eggs. Except for the bad dream that had awakened him, he'd slept well. He heard the toilet in the other bathroom flush, then heard the water running. *Thin walls*, he thought, and decided he'd better change his shirt. He turned down the heat on the eggs and hurried back to his bedroom.

When he returned, Taylor was in the kitchen. She had two types of bread sitting on the counter.

"Do you like whole wheat or plain?" she asked.

"Wheat is fine. I saw some orange juice in the fridge. Do you want some?"

"None for me."

Trent couldn't help but feel as if they were an old married couple. "Taylor, I had a dream or maybe it was a flash of a memory this morning. It woke me up."

"Yeah, something got to you." Taylor opened the pantry door. "Your choice of coffee is French roast. Is that okay?"

"That's fine."

"Trent, I have dreams about my abductions, too. They feel very real, and they're disturbing. I had a dream last night, too. What did you dream?"

"I was in a place that I didn't recognize. There was red-colored sand covering the bottom half of a floor-to-ceiling window, and the sky had a reddish tint. I was sitting at a desk. There was an older woman—a teacher, I think. She was telling me to pay attention to the lesson. But I'd heard something hit the window."

Taylor asked, "Was the woman older, white-haired, and wearing a blue dress?"

The hair stood up on Trent's arms. "Yes. How did you know?"

"I had that same dream last night. I was sitting at a desk in a classroom with a bunch of other students." She went silent for a moment, then said, "A boy was sitting by a window looking out." Taylor looked at him. "I was sitting two seats over from *you.*"

Trent smelled the eggs starting to burn. "The eggs!"

Taylor spun around and took the skillet off the burner. "I think they're done. So what was it about the dream that woke you up?" She checked on the coffee.

"The glass had started to crack, alarms were sounding, and then I was running away from the window. I know that I wasn't on Earth." He pulled two plates out of the cupboard and set them on the kitchen counter next to the coffee maker. He'd expected a reaction from her, but there was only silence. "You okay?" Trent asked.

"Yes." She fiddled with the eggs in the skillet.

"What are you thinking?"

She looked up and said, "I'm thinking about our dream. They're the same one. I remember I tripped and fell trying to get out of the room. Kids screaming and running past me kept knocking me down. Then the door to the classroom began to close. I knew that if I couldn't get through the door before it sealed that I was going to die."

"I helped you up," Trent muttered, as images flooded his mind. "I yelled for someone to help us, but we were the only ones left in the classroom. Finally, after I got you to your feet, we bolted for the door. I tried to stop the door from closing so you could get by me. I remember pushing against the door, but I couldn't stop it. I wasn't strong enough. But then you ran past me into a hallway, and you were safe. I don't remember what happened after that."

Taylor stared at him. She was pale. "I grabbed your arm and pulled you through just as the door sealed. It nearly trapped your hand. Then we hugged."

"Well, either we somehow experienced the same dream or we lived the same event." Trent brushed past Taylor, and put the eggs and toast on their plates. "I think there's some jelly in the fridge."

"I'll pour the coffee," Taylor said. "Do you want sugar or cream?"

"Just sugar, thanks." As Taylor approached him with the coffee mugs in hand, he had a desperate urge to take her in his arms. He didn't understand what he was feeling.

He was in love with Alexa, but there was something about Taylor that transcended love. It was more of a primal need, like breathing. She filled a part of his being that had been missing until now.

When he looked up, she was staring at him. Her blue eyes melted his willpower. He tried to fight off his desire to pull her close and kiss her. She put the mugs on the table, walked to him, and hugged him. He felt the heat of her body against his, and a deep yearning for her cascaded over him.

"You feel it, too?" Taylor said.

"Yes," Trent answered, his voice cracking. "Taylor, I'm in love with Alexa, but I have a powerful attraction to you."

"I know. I love my husband. But it feels as if we are destined to be together. Like we were together in another life." She took his face in her hands gently.

Trent closed his eyes, trying to drive his desire away. He opened his eyes and saw the yearning on her face. She wanted him as badly as he wanted her. They leaned closer and when their lips touched, he felt more at home than with any other person in his life. Her lips parted, and they kissed deeply, passionately. She pulled back after a minute. He thought it was a good thing that she'd found the willpower to break away. He knew it wasn't in him to let go of her.

"That felt so right, yet so wrong," Taylor said.

"I know what you mean."

"They say people that are thrown together in a crisis share a bond," Taylor said. "They need to be close emotionally, to do things they wouldn't do under normal circumstances."

"I've heard that before. I think what we've experienced puts us in a class of our own. We need to explore why we had the same dream, or whatever it was that we experienced together."

Taylor nodded, then said, "The eggs are getting cold. We should eat."

Trent sat down across from her. Her leg brushed his as she pulled her chair to the table. His stomach felt like a big knot.

They ate in silence, both lost in their thoughts. Just as they finished, there was knock at the door.

"I'll get it," Trent said.

"Morning," Melissa said. "May I come in?"

"It's your house." He stepped aside, and Melissa entered.

"Good morning, Taylor," Melissa said. "I see you've both eaten."

"We were hungry," Taylor said.

Trent positioned himself in front of Taylor.

"Can I get you something to eat, Melissa?" Taylor asked.

"Interesting," Melissa said.

"What's interesting about me asking if you wanted something to eat?"

"Not that. I sensed a protective response from Trent. He went out of his way to stand between us." Melissa smiled knowingly. "You did it without even thinking about it."

"I think you're reading too much into it, Colonel," Trent said defensively.

Melissa shook her head, then said, "I'm not hungry, thank you." She walked into the living room, looked around, then went into both bedrooms.

"What are you looking for?" Trent asked her.

"She's trying to determine if we slept together," Taylor said.

"Did you?" Melissa asked.

"Yes," Taylor replied. "But it wasn't sexual. We felt the need to be close."

"Hmmm. Did you learn anything about each other?"

"Yes," Taylor replied. "Something very weird actually. Trent and I had the same dream."

Melissa sat down on the sofa. "I don't know how that could happen. Tell me about it."

Trent told her what they'd experienced.

Melissa nodded. "Now that's interesting. It sounds to me like it was more than a dream. I think you both lived it. Perhaps during an abduction when you were younger."

Trent shook his head. "It wasn't from an abduction. We were in a school classroom."

"You said you saw a red sky and reddish-brown sand outside," Melissa mused. "That sounds like Mars. We need to explore this dream further, but that will have to wait. I've scheduled you both for some tests. Get dressed. I'll wait for you outside."

After the door closed, Trent looked at Taylor and said, "Should we have told her about the dream? You know she's on the phone to Starke now."

"I think it's important to tell them anything that will help us get out of here. Thank you for omitting our moment of weakness."

Trent grabbed her by the hand and pulled her against him. "I would never do anything that would make you feel uncomfortable or cause you any harm." He hugged her tightly, and she threw her arms around him. "We better get dressed. The colonel is waiting." She kissed him gently on the lips.

T W E L V E

Alexa felt fatigued. "Marvin, let's take a break for a few minutes."

"Happy to hear you say that."

Alexa shrugged off her backpack, and just as she dropped it in the snow, the radio crackled.

"Creeper, this is Babysitter. Do you copy?" Dan asked.

"We copy," Alexa answered.

"You guys staying warm?"

"The exercise is keeping the blood circulating. It looks like the snow is letting up."

"Latest weather advisory indicates a change in the forecast. It's supposed to stop snowing by noon. The front pushed through faster than expected."

"Thanks for the update. Visibility has improved. No sign of any prey. We'll start our ascent in another hour and cover our tracks."

"Copy that. Check back in two hours."

"Roger."

Alexa put the radio into her backpack. "What do you think?"

"I think we stay off anything that even vaguely looks like a trail," Marvin said. "Without the snow covering our tracks, we'll be easy to locate." He pointed up the mountain. "I think we should head for that notch. Keep using the trees as cover in case they're able to use drones."

The peak was covered by a cloud, but the notch was visible. "That looks like a good spot to take a long breather and eat. How long do you think to reach it?"

"About two hours. That's at least a thousand-foot climb, and it's a good two miles away. The snow is going to get deeper. The skis will be useless."

Alexa pulled out the hiking guidebook she'd bought at the store. "It says Greylock's summit is just over nine thousand feet. No high-altitude issues."

"Easy for you to say. Air is still thinner up there than in Florida. I doubt we'll run into anyone else hiking except a military patrol. The guy at the outdoorsman store said it's well past hiking and climbing season."

"Which means we'll know anyone we see is probably with the government." Alexa used the binoculars to look at the notch. "Where could they hide a base out here? In the summer and fall, this place has to be crawling with hunters, hikers, and campers. It's like an outdoor enthusiasts' mecca."

"It'll be buried and well camouflaged," Marvin replied. "If a van can reach it, there has to be another access road somewhere."

"That's what I was thinking. Do you think we're too far north?"

"I don't know. Let's stick to the plan. I'll take the heavy pack for the climb."

"We'll leave the skis here for the return hike," Alexa said. "I'll mark the location on the handheld GPS."

"You ready?"

"I'm good. I'll lead for a while. You can tell me if I start to stray."

Alexa and Marvin had nearly reached the notch when the radio crackled. Dan told them he'd seen an increase in traffic on the main road, but so far no one had turned on to the trail road. Alexa thanked him for the update and told him that they were already ascending the mountain.

Thirty minutes later, they reached the notch. Alexa found a snow-covered stump and dropped her pack. The climb had been more physically draining than she'd expected.

"Looks like there are a number of peaks surrounding the area," Alexa said.

Marvin dropped his pack beside hers and sat down on the stump. "Phew! I must be getting old. GPS confirms that we are where we wanted to be. You set a good course."

"Thanks. What do you think our elevation is?"

"Almost six thousand feet. Greylock is that peak over there." He pointed at the highest peak.

"That looks a long way off," Alexa said. "Maybe we should have come in through China Basin."

"If the military is using the access road Dan saw them use, then it's the easiest way to get to the base."

Alexa scanned the area for a few minutes with the binoculars. "Marvin, look over there." She handed him the binoculars and pointed.

"I'm not sure what you want me to see. All I see are rocks just below the tree line."

"What don't you see?"

"Ahh—. Those rocks aren't covered with snow."

"With all the snow we've had, why don't they have any snow on them?"

"A camouflaged heated air vent or an exhaust vent?"

"Exactly. Either one would have to be kept free of snow and ice."

"That's a big area for a vent," Marvin said.

"Maybe it's a big base. I think that should be our next objective. How long of a hike to get there?"

"We'll have to descend, then work our way over to that plateau. There's a frozen lake next to the tree line. We can set up camp on the other side near that ridgeline."

"Marvin, I asked how long?"

"Grumpy, grumpy. You're tired, aren't you?"

"And I'm hungry. How long?"

"At least six hours," Marvin replied. "It's farther than it looks."

Alexa pulled the topographic map and the satellite photos from her pack. "The lake isn't visible on the recent satellite photos. The map indicates that it's at least a hundred yards across. Plenty of room to land a chopper on during the winter, if the ice was thick enough."

"Maybe, but the military wouldn't use it as a primary landing zone. There has to be another LZ nearby."

"Let's get started."

"You may want to let Dan know where we're going. We may lose comms down in that valley."

Alexa nodded. "Babysitter, this is Creeper."

"Creeper, your signal is weak, but I read you," Dan replied.

"We're going down into a shallow valley for a few hours. I think we have a lead on the prey's den. We may be out of radio contact while in the valley. I'll check in when we reach higher ground. Do you copy?"

"Affirmative," Dan replied. "Stay safe, and good hunting."

"Thanks. We'll do our best. If we acquire, we'll need an alternative mode of extraction. I'm not sure the prey will be able to move very far under these conditions. Area south of us looks easier to traverse."

"I already have several places in mind to the south. If you want, I can get a chopper for an airlift. Let me know what you bag."

"Roger. Out."

"I'll lead," Marvin said.

"Thanks."

Trent's Room — 1330 hours

Taylor and Trent sat on the sofa in the apartment. They'd spent most of the morning explaining their dream to a number of specialists and to General Starke. Each mental health expert had a different theory as to why both of them had seen the same thing. One of the psychologists claimed that the dream was a release of repressed lust. The psychologist said that the sand and the window represented what was forbidden. The crack in the window meant that Trent and Taylor both wanted to escape their bonds or succumb to their latent desires. Trent figured the psychologist was a bit too Freudian, but in this case, it was a pretty accurate diagnosis. Neither of them had said anything about their attraction to each other. They'd agreed to keep that secret.

Some of the specialists wanted to know how thick the window that cracked was. Another thought the older woman in the classroom was a projection of a mother figure. The other children in the room that kept knocking Taylor down was her way of being punished. Trent saving her was his atonement for feeling responsible for breaking a window. Trent thought all of this was crap. No one had said how they both could have had the same dream.

Trent had been hooked up to an MEG scanner when he told his story. Melissa said she wanted to monitor his brain activity. Trent had no idea why. Taylor had undergone the same test. Now he was just glad to be back in the apartment.

"I'm really tired of this," Trent said. "Is this how it's been for you these last two years?"

"Not at all," Taylor replied. She put her head on his shoulder.

Her soft her hair brushed against his ear and neck. He leaned against her. "Do you think it's a good idea, I mean our getting this close?"

"Trent, something extraordinary is happening to us. I'm having the same dreams as you are at the same time. That isn't normal."

"It feels as if a repressed part of us is waking up."

"Exactly. What did they say about your scan?"

"They didn't," Trent replied. "I have to wait for the brain trust to form an opinion. Either Starke or Melissa will tell us the results." Trent took her hand. "How about your scan?"

"Same."

"Is it possible we were taken together as children and that we imprinted, for lack of a better word, on each other?" Trent asked.

"I don't have a clue. I wonder if they implanted those memories during an abduction."

"Maybe they wanted us to see the same thing."

"But why a classroom on Mars?" Taylor asked. "If that's really where it happened."

Trent leaned over and kissed her. He could feel their connection again.

"What was that for?"

"Research," Trent said. "As things grow more intense between us, I feel different."

"In what way?"

"Like I need to experience your touch. That somehow it's important." Trent thought for a moment. "I going to say something, and it's going to sound a bit crazy."

"Yeah, like that'll be a change."

Trent smiled and kissed her forehead. "What if we were programmed? Maybe the implants sent information into us that we were supposed to remember."

"Possibly, but mine has been removed. How could I see what you did last night?"

"Is it possible that we were taken to another world, we met, we were friends, and who knows what else? That time was somehow altered. What seemed like a few hours or weeks was really much longer. When we were returned to our homes, we became who we were once again, and we didn't remember what we'd experienced."

Taylor sat quietly for a minute. "You mean like a time warp?"

"I'm don't know if there is such a thing. Einstein thought time could be folded over. What if we lived in another time and were. . . lovers—soul mates? Is it possible we lived an entirely different life together? Then, when we died in that time period, they returned us to the point in time when we were taken in this reality."

She looked up at him. "I think anything is possible. I also know that my head hurts."

"Do you get headaches often?"

"Hardly ever. Ever since I met you I've been experiencing them more often. No offense."

Melissa entered the apartment without knocking. Trent and Taylor jumped up as if they'd been caught doing something wrong. They were still holding hands.

"How dare you just walk into our home without knocking!" Trent shouted.

"The protector role again," Melissa said. "I thought you'd both like to know the results of the tests and the experts' conclusions."

Trent moved toward Melissa. He was angrier than he'd been in long time. "We may be just specimens to you, but we still need our privacy."

"Noted," Melissa replied. "Anyway, all of your test results were inconclusive, except for one."

"Which one?" Taylor asked.

"The tentacles of Trent's neural implant have grown."

"How have they grown?" Taylor asked, sounding concerned.

"The tentacles have wound deeper into the prefrontal lobe. It's not a significant amount of growth, less than a millimeter, but I'm glad we drew the baseline when we did."

"Do you think they will continue to grow?" Trent asked.

"We don't know. Do you feel any different?"

"No. Just tired."

"That's to be expected," Melissa said. "How are you feeling, Taylor?"

"I'm fine."

"She has a headache," Trent said.

"How bad?"

"It's nothing," Taylor said. "Feels like sinus, but Trent is worried it may have something to do with him."

Melissa looked from Taylor to Trent. "We have another idea about how the two of you are seeing the same vision."

"We're listening," Taylor said.

"Trent may be unknowingly transmitting his thoughts to you through the implant."

"How would that be possible?"

"We don't know. It was just one idea that we want to investigate. I can tell that the two of you are growing closer, and much faster, than I expected, considering your significant others. I think that it's important that you explore how deep your feelings are toward each other."

"Why?" Trent asked.

Melissa cleared her throat. "I believe you're linked by more than your abductions. So does Dr. Sanderson. We have another theory, but we need to wait to see if we can prove it."

"What's that theory?" Taylor asked.

"I don't want to say right now. Just know that we think you need some time together—alone. I've cancelled all of your tests for the rest of the day. I suggest you both take a walk around the annex. Taylor, let me know if your headache doesn't go away. I'll be back to see you both at 0800 hours tomorrow." She turned and left.

Trent turned to Taylor. "I'm sorry if I'm sending you signals that are causing you to get headaches. I don't want to do anything that would hurt you."

"It's not you. If it's anything, it's the neural implant." She smiled and kissed him. "I don't think it was a dream. I believe that we experienced the event together. We need to see where all of this takes us. Let's take that walk."

"Good idea."

Taylor walked past him toward the door. The way her hair swung across her shoulders was intoxicating. An image flashed through his mind. He was standing in a white corridor. There were bubblelike windows along the walls spaced about twenty feet apart. Taylor was in front of him, looking out one of the windows. He joined her and gazed at the reddish landscape.

"Stop!" Trent shouted.

Taylor spun around. "What is it?"

"I'm not sure." He focused on the vision. He could still see Taylor smiling at him while they stood in front of a convex window. She was only a little younger than she was now. Then the vision faded.

Trent felt Taylor's hand on his shoulder. He was sitting on the floor, holding the sides of his head. He didn't know how he'd gotten there.

"Trent, are you okay?"

He couldn't respond. Another vision pierced his mind. Taylor was lying naked on powder-blue sheets. She had a small mole on her left breast and another one just below her navel. Her skin was as white as fresh snow. There were no tan lines on her body. She was. . . beautiful.

"Trent, talk to me!" Taylor yelled.

He heard Taylor calling him from afar. How could she be yelling at him and still be lying there? Her lips weren't moving. Suddenly he felt a sharp pain on the side of his face, and the vision faded. He looked around. He was back in the apartment with Taylor.

"Trent, I called Melissa. A medical team is on the way."

"What happened?"

"You collapsed."

A moment later, the apartment door burst open, and Melissa rushed in and knelt next to him. "How long was he out?"

"He wasn't totally out," Taylor said. "He slid down the wall gradually and just sat there, unresponsive. He was mumbling, incoherently."

Melissa took Trent's pulse and checked his pupils. "His pulse is rapid, but not fast enough to worry me. His pupils are responsive. I don't think it was a seizure."

Trent asked, "Taylor, did you hit me? The side of my face feels like I've been punched."

"I was trying to get you to wake up. I'm sorry if I hurt you."

Trent tried to stand, but Melissa held him down. "You're not going anywhere, except to medical."

"I'm fine. I had another vision."

"You did?" Melissa asked.

"I don't know if they're visions or memories, but I was someplace else. Taylor, I need to ask you something personal. Is that okay?"

"Yes."

"Do you have a small mole on the underside of your left breast and another one below your navel?"

Her eyes widened. "How do you know that?"

"I saw them."

"You *what?*" Taylor exclaimed. "When?"

"I don't mean here. We were someplace else." Trent described their encounter in the hallway, the landscape, and their time in the bedroom. "I think it was your hair swinging back and forth as you walked away from me that triggered the event. Your hair fell over your shoulder the same way as when you motioned for me to come look through a window."

"What did you see outside?" Melissa asked.

"Reddish sky and soil. Large boulders and mountain peaks in the distance." Trent slumped back against the wall. He was back in the other world. He saw the white walls of the corridor again. Taylor was at the window, but her name wasn't Taylor.

"Trent!" Melissa yelled.

"I'm here . . . and there," he said quietly, as if in a trance. "It's just a different reality. We live in both worlds."

"How can we be in both places?" Taylor asked.

"We just are. It's not Earth. I can tell by the landscape that it's got to be Mars. We're happy there."

Just then, the trauma team arrived. "Let's get him to medical," Melissa ordered. "Taylor, I want you to hold his hand, talk to him. Keep him awake."

Trent felt her squeeze his hand as he was lifted onto the gurney. "That feels good, Shona. You know I love you."

His head dropped back onto the pillow. His mind took him back to another world.

"What did he just call you?" Melissa asked.

"He called me Shona. I have no idea who he's talking about."

Medical — Purple Containment - 1800 hours

Trent gasped. "Air," he mumbled. "The airlock malfunctioned."

Taylor was still holding his hand. "Trent, what airlock?"

"The lower crater airlock. It didn't seal. Maya was sucked out."

Taylor turned to Melissa and Dr. Sanderson. "What's he talking about? Who's Maya?"

"Let's get him in the AMRS," Sanderson directed.

Two medical technicians sitting at a console behind thick glass began setting up the machine.

"Three headsets—now!" Melissa ordered. A technician standing behind her ran to the cabinet and retrieved them, then hurried back.

Melissa placed one headset over Trent's ears and handed Taylor one, then said, "You and I are staying with him. Put this on."

Dr. Sanderson left the area with the technicians.

"He's mumbling something," Taylor said. "I can't understand him with the headset on."

"Once the AMRS starts, we won't hear him anyway," Melissa said.

They carried Trent to the machine. As soon as the machine started, Taylor couldn't hear anything except the clamor of the AMRS. She stood away from the machine and watched. Trent didn't move during the procedure.

"Well?" Taylor asked when the machine finally went silent.

Melissa leaned over Trent. "Trent, can you hear me? Taylor is here."

Trent opened his eyes, exhaled quickly, then took a deep breath.

"Is he holding his breath?" Taylor asked.

"It appears that way," Melissa replied. "I don't understand why."

A moment later, Trent exhaled and said, "Maya's okay. I got to her in time. She'll have some bruises from the impact with the outer door, but she'll be okay." Trent looked around the room. "Where am I?"

"Trent, you're okay," Taylor said, touching his arm.

Trent clasped the front of his head, grimaced with pain, and said, "I guess I decompressed more than I thought. Wait, what'd you call me?" He looked at Melissa. "And who are you?"

"Col. Melissa Endo. One of your doctors. She called you Trent. Don't you remember your name?"

He blinked. "That's not my name. I'm Aiden Cooper. What the hell happened? What is this place?"

Dr. Sanderson burst into the room. "We got it. It's unbelievable. Melissa, you need to see these images immediately."

"Taylor, stay with him," Melissa ordered.

Trent said, "Why did she call you Taylor?"

"Because that's my name. Don't you recognize me?"

"Of course I do. But your name isn't Taylor." Trent looked around, then said, "This is a medical lab, but I don't recognize it. Where's Maya?"

She wasn't sure how to answer. The name *Maya* meant something important to him, so if she told him she didn't know he may have an adverse reaction. She didn't want to lie to him. "You need to rest. You've had a bad experience."

"I know that, but where's our daughter? She should be here, not me. Shona, tell me she's alright."

"Everyone is okay. Do you know what day it is?"

Trent closed his eyes. "It's . . . I don't know what sol it is. Why did you ask me what day it was? Has everyone gone crazy?"

"Do you know where you live?"

"Hecates Tholus Station, sublevel seven, Aldrin wing, white area."

Taylor gasped, then hesitated before she said, "What year is it?"

"Two-one-seven-seven," Trent said, enunciating each number. "I'm a little confused. I guess that's just a side effect of going into atmosphere without my pressure suit. I couldn't have been outside for more than twenty seconds. Well within the acceptable range of external atmospheric exposure. I don't understand why I'm so confused."

Taylor said, "Who am I to you?"

Trent cocked his head when Melissa joined them. "Shona, you're my wife, and we have a daughter, Maya. She's ten, and she likes creating holographic maps. See, I'm fine. Please tell me what's going on."

Taylor couldn't believe what she was hearing. She looked at Melissa. Melissa nodded at her, then said, "Do you know what planet you're on?"

"What kind of question is that?" Trent replied.

"Please answer my question."

"We're on Mars."

"Tell us about yourself," Melissa said.

"Checking my memory, huh? Shona and I attended Ares prep school, and then we went to Elysium College for our undergrad and graduate work. We are native-born Martians."

"What do you do on Mars?" Melissa asked.

"I'm an astrophysicist. Shona works in botanical bioengineering." Trent smiled. "She's the best we have. Currently, she's working on a method to grow more plants in our thin atmosphere, and her work has been groundbreaking. Like I said, I'm fine. Now let me get up so I can give Maya a hug."

Taylor was stunned by his answers. "What did the scan show, Melissa?"

"There was an increase in brain activity around the neural implant. I'll skip the detailed scientific explanation. Let me just say that his overall brain activity was off the chart. I've never seen anything like it before."

"What are you talking about?" Trent asked. "What neural implant?"

"I think we should tell him," Taylor said.

Melissa nodded and said, "I agree."

Taylor took his hand. "You're not my husband, we're not on Mars, and we don't have a daughter." His brow furrowed as Taylor continued. "We're on Earth in a government facility in Idaho. We're here because we are both alien abductees."

"Is this a joke?" Trent tried to sit up.

Melissa pushed him back down and said, "This isn't a joke. Your name is Trent McDougal, and you have two alien implants—one in your leg and one in your brain. I can take you outside to prove what I'm telling you. You'll see trees, clouds, and snow."

Trent gaped at her, then looked at Taylor. "I know you're Shona Cooper. We grew up together. Your maiden name is Price. Our parents live in Hecates Tholus Station, sublevel seven, Collins wing."

"I can't believe this," Taylor said. "What's wrong with him?"

"It could be a dissociated identity disorder," Melissa said. "His mind or the implant could have created an alternate reality, or the aliens could be sending him a different reality through the implant."

Taylor looked at Trent and said, "You're not Aiden, at least not here. I'm Taylor Graham. I have a husband, Rick, and a daughter, Emma. Does that sound familiar?"

"What the hell are you two talking about?" Trent cried. "I know exactly who I am, where I live, and Shona, you *are* my wife."

"Okay, maybe the best thing we can do now is to shock him back to reality," Melissa said.

"You're not going to shock me with anything!" Trent said.

"Not an electrical shock," Melissa said. "I want to prove to you that you're not on Mars. The psychological shock may bring you back to us. Taylor, help me get him up."

As they walked through the complex, Taylor held his hand. His palm became sweaty as they approached the hangar.

Trent said, "What is this place? This is all very strange to me."

"It's a research center for alien encounters," Melissa replied. She nodded to a Marine who was standing by the outside exit door. "Open the door."

Trent froze as the Marine pulled the door open, and then he collapsed.

The Camp — 1945 hours

The hike had taken a lot longer than six hours. The terrain had been more rugged than expected, forcing them to create their own trail through deep snow and brush. Crossing the frozen surface of the lake had also been a challenge. They'd been blocked twice by unforeseen rock cliffs that were too icy to climb. The clouds had rolled in again, blocking what little sun they'd seen earlier. After sunset, the darkness was complete under the trees.

"I can barely see my hand," Alexa said, waving her hand in front of her face.

"This looks like a great place to camp," Marvin said. "We have good cover here."

"I don't think anyone could see us in this darkness without night-vision goggles."

"We need to set up the tent."

"I haven't put up a tent since I was a teenager, and that was in daylight," Alexa said. "My feet hurt, I smell like a yak, and I have to pee like one, too."

"I'll help you with the tent. Keep your boots on. You don't want frostbite. You're on your own for the other things."

They broke out the blue-lensed, shielded flashlights. Thirty minutes later, their tent was anchored, Alexa had found a place to relieve herself, and they'd settled down to eat their MRE's.

"The beef stew isn't bad," Alexa said. "Or maybe it tastes better than it should because I'm hungry."

"Yeah, it's pretty good. Alexa, I'm not keen on making the ascent to the vent in the dark."

"I agree. We need some rest anyway. We'll wait for daylight." Alexa tried to reach Dan by radio and by cell, without success.

"Let's get some sleep," Marvin said after dinner. He pulled two thermal blankets out of a pack. "Wrap yourself up in one of these. Leave only a hole the size of a football for air. Cover your head and all the parts of your body."

"You want me to cocoon?"

"Exactly. Without exertion, your core temperature will drop. I don't want you becoming hypothermic."

Alexa followed Marvin's instructions and was asleep within minutes.

Purple Level - Containment Conference Room — 1945 hours MST

"What were you thinking?" General Starke asked as he sat down at the conference table.

"Trent needed to be shocked back to reality," Melissa replied. "I thought if he saw that he wasn't on Mars, he'd snap back to the present. We don't want real memories being supplanted by false ones."

"I agree with her decision," Dr. Sanderson said.

"You do, huh?" Starke said.

"Yes, I do. I believe Trent created Maya in response to learning about Taylor's daughter, Emma. I think he took Rick's place as her husband. The facility he imagined is a projection of what he's experiencing here. The airlock is the door you took him through when he passed through security. The pressure suit is a reflection of him changing into the clothing you provided. He feels that he can't leave, thus the lack of atmosphere outside. His earlier psych evaluation points to stress-induced delusions."

"Then why does he think Taylor is Shona and that he's Aiden Cooper? That seems like a pretty elaborate delusion."

"It's possible his abduction triggered a dissociated identity disorder," Melissa replied. "Or . . ."

"Or what," Starke asked.

"The neural implant could be creating a false reality. I'm leaning toward identity disorder. Severe trauma, such as multiple alien abductions, could cause that. He drifts into a different identity as a coping mechanism to shut off, or dissociate from, the trauma he's experienced. We've been pushing him to remember his last abduction. This could be a manifestation of his attempt to remember."

"Is this a common reaction?" Starke asked. "Does Trent have a history of mental illness?"

"No, to both questions," Melissa replied.

"Shona and Maya are not common names," Starke said. "We know from our background research that he doesn't associate with anyone by those names. He also doesn't have any connection to anyone by the name of Aiden Cooper."

"That's true, but that doesn't mean he doesn't know someone by those names, or he could have just made them up," Sanderson said.

"I'm not buying the psychobabble," Starke said. He leaned back in his chair. "There was an increase in brain activity around the implant when this occurred. I think the aliens are sending him these visions, and I want to know why."

"At this point I don't know how we could determine anything they may be doing to him," Melissa said.

Starke smiled. "What if Trent *is* on Mars in the year 2177?"

"You mean you think he was taken into the future during his last abduction?" Melissa asked. "How could that have happened? And what about Taylor? She's never had any recollection of being on Mars in any of her abductions. Her only account of Mars was in her dream last night."

"Don't be ridiculous," Sanderson said. "There's no such thing as time travel."

Starke waved at the man who had just walked into the room.

"That's not entirely correct," the older, white-haired man said in a deep voice.

Melissa and Sanderson turned to face the newcomer as his escort left the room.

"General Starke, is this a good time?" he asked.

Starke replied, "Perfect. This is Dr. Harold Maxwell. He's on loan from a special project that only a handful of people know about. He used to be a professor of astrophysics at MIT. Hank, this is Col. Melissa Endo and Dr. Arnold Sanderson."

"Pleased to make your acquaintance," Maxwell said. "I heard your comment on time travel as I came in. Is this a classified briefing?"

"Yes, but you're cleared," Starke said.

Melissa glanced at Sanderson, then looked at Starke and said, "I'm sorry, but I've never heard of Dr. Maxwell."

"I would hope not," Starke said. He didn't offer anything else.

"Alright, I'll bite," Sanderson said. "How can you travel through time?"

"I don't think there's enough time left in the day for me to explain it thoroughly. Let's just say it has to do with time dilation."

"I'm familiar with time dilation, Dr. Maxwell," Melissa said. "What exactly is your area of expertise?"

"Direct and to the point. I like that," Maxwell said. "Most of my work is classified. Before I left MIT, I changed my field of research from astrophysics to quantum mechanics. I wanted to bridge the two fields as they relate to gravitational time dilation."

"Your two areas of study are not exactly complimentary," Melissa said.

"My work has shown me that they are more similar than you might imagine. We can discuss all of this later." Maxwell took a seat next to Sanderson.

"I don't recall reading anything that you've published," Melissa said. "General, does he know about our two subjects?"

"Yes. The professor was one of the original founding members of a special team, code named Bright Light. It was started twenty years ago, and he has been operationally black ever since then. I've been sending him updates, and he offered to help, so I asked him to join us. I thought Hank might be able to provide additional reasons for the time Trent lost."

"Which is why you mentioned time travel," Melissa said.

Starke nodded.

"Any addition to the team is welcome," Sanderson said. "But we need to keep it real, not science fiction. As I was explaining to General Starke, I believe Trent manufactured his trip into the future."

Maxwell grinned, then said, "I'd like to meet the abductees and hear about this trip to the future. I've received everything up until noon today, so I'm not sure what you're referring to, Dr. Sanderson."

"Colonel, will you introduce Dr. Maxwell to Trent and Taylor?" Starke asked. "He's to be given full access to all of our research data and anything else relevant to what we're facing. Is that clear?"

"Yes, sir. With your permission, I'd like to check on Trent before I take Dr. Maxwell in to see him."

"Granted."

"How should we address you?" Melissa asked Maxwell.

"Hank is fine. I'm not big on titles."

"I hope you don't mind waiting in the hall for a few minutes when we get to medical," Sanderson said.

"No problem," Maxwell said. "General, is there anything you wish to discuss with me before I take my leave?"

"No." General Starke's computer notepad chirped. It was a flash message from the Space Force Command with attached satellite images from the National Reconnaissance Office. "Hold on a minute." He opened the ultrasecret communique and saw the photo files that were attached. "It seems we have another one."

"Another abduction?" Melissa asked.

"Yes. Another plane disappeared in midair. This one occurred a little over four hours ago, twenty miles east of Fort Pierce, Florida. The aircraft disappeared from radar after crossing the ADIZ."

"The what?" Sanderson asked.

"The Air Defense Identification Zone. Aircraft flying into U.S. airspace have to file a flight plan and notify an FAA control center before they penetrate the zone. The plane reappeared three hours after disappearing in the exact same place."

"That sounds familiar," Melissa said.

"The pilot is one of ours. An Air Force Missileer based at Malmstrom AFB, in Montana."

"Where's the pilot now?" Sanderson asked.

Starke continued reading the brief. "She landed in Ft. Pierce and had the good sense not to say anything to anyone about being abducted. After she landed, she immediately contacted her commander at Malmstrom AFB. He in turn contacted the base commander at Patrick AFB. She was cleared by customs and escorted to Patrick for debriefing."

"So the plane is still at Ft. Pierce airport?" Sanderson asked.

"It is. Sanderson, I want you on a plane to Ft. Pierce immediately. Bring the aircraft back here. Let's see if there's any molecular change in the metal like what we found on Trent's aircraft."

"What about the missileer?" Melissa asked.

"She will be brought back as well. Her name is Capt. Tai Su." Starke rubbed the back of his neck as he read further. "There's more. She had a passenger, also military. Capt. Kimberly Wood, who's an Air Force pilot. She's assigned to the 920th Rescue Wing at Patrick."

"Two at once?" Melissa said. "That doesn't fit the pattern."

Starke read on. "Captain Wood was flying the plane in the left seat. According to Su, they were enveloped in a white light. When the light disappeared, Wood was gone, and Su was left to fly the plane. Fortunately, Su's also a pilot."

"Captain Wood is still missing?" Melissa asked.

"She is. Su radioed Miami Center and told the controller Wood had fallen out of the aircraft. She didn't know that three hours had passed. The Coast Guard is searching for Wood now."

Sanderson said, "We need all of the recordings from the FAA and the name of the controller, and we need to call off the search. We know she didn't fall out of the plane."

"I'll take care of all that," Starke said. "You all aren't going to believe it, but the controller was the same guy who was on duty when Trent disappeared and reappeared."

"Brett Stone?" Melissa asked.

"Yes," Starke replied. "I think it might be prudent to bring him here. I don't like the fact that the same controller worked during both disappearances. It may be a coincidence, but let's be sure. Sanderson, I'll have him transported to Patrick. He'll be there by the time you land."

"Is it wise to bring another civilian here?" Melissa asked.

"At this point I'd like to have everyone that's involved in one place."

"I think I'm going to be busy," Sanderson said. "I'll try to be back in twelve hours. I'll have a team retrieve the plane and put it in the hangar next to Trent's plane. What type of plane is it?"

"The report says it's an older Cessna 182, 1977 version," Starke replied. "I'll make sure the plane is sequestered and available for you at the Ft. Pierce airport. I'll have a C-17 ready and waiting at Mountain Home AFB by the time you get there. We were conspicuous enough in Key West. We don't need a repeat. Understood?"

"Yes, sir," Sanderson replied.

Starke looked at the satellite images that had been attached. "Good God!" He could hardly believe what he was seeing. The NRO had captured the moment when the aircraft was caught in the light. In the next image both the light and the plane were gone.

"What is it?" Melissa asked.

"Documented proof of the light taking the aircraft," Starke said. He showed them the images. "Any doubt that's what grabbed Trent's aircraft?"

No one said anything.

"Sanderson, get moving," Starke ordered. "If anything else develops, I'll contact you."

"Yes, sir," Sanderson said.

Starke looked across the table at Melissa and Maxwell. "Colonel, I want everyone involved in these disappearances, except Griffin, Dobson, and Stone, in quarters on Gold Level in the Nova annex. Make sure we have adequate security there. Captain Su will be brought here to Red Level, then confined to Purple Level until we sort all of this out."

"What about Trent and Taylor?"

"Keep them together. Start work on Su as soon as she arrives. Bring in additional staff if needed. Once cleared, she's to be moved to Gold Level."

"General, I've been told that Griffin and Dobson have been trying to engage staff in conversation in the common areas in the Altair annex. It's possible Trent will run across them."

"I'm aware of that. I don't think they'll be too inquisitive. They both just want to get the hell out of here. I'm sure the controller isn't going to be happy about being forced to come here. He'll need to be debriefed as soon as he arrives. Set secure times on chow and recreation for all three men. Isolate them as much as possible from everyone else in the Altair annex." Starke looked at the photos again. "I'll send you the photo file of the abduction. Show it to Trent and Taylor when you think it's appropriate."

"That might shake something loose," Melissa said. "Any progress on finding Alexa and the others in Florida?"

"Not yet. If we get lucky, Striker will have them corralled before Sanderson gets there, and they can all fly back together."

"General, what do you want me to start working on?" Maxwell asked.

"I'd like you to get with the NRO and see if there's any additional satellite images of the abduction. I'd like to hear what you think caused the light. Then you can sit in on the interview with Captain Su. She may have information that would make sense to you."

"I'll try to be of some help."

"Colonel, I'll have Intel start cross-checking everything. Trent's a pilot like our other two abductees. I can't help but wonder if the events are related."

"There has to be some kind of a link," Melissa said. "If not, then the extraterrestrials are trying something new to get our attention."

"Two aerial abductions in daylight within a hundred miles of each other has certainly gotten my attention," Starke said.

"Do you have any particulars on Su or Wood?" Melissa asked. "That information may be useful to us when we speak to Trent."

Starke opened another attached file. "Capt. Tai Su was commissioned seven years ago. She went through OTS hoping to become a pilot. She had a medical issue after being commissioned, so she was assigned to missiles. Her evaluations are all excellent, as are her psych evaluations and fitness reports." He went to the next page.

"She's career-oriented. Enjoys working as a member of the combat missile crew. By all accounts, she's very squared away. She's been a private pilot since she was nineteen. Unmarried. She's of Viet-Chinese ancestry. Grandfather immigrated to America in 1960 from China. Her grandmother was Vietnamese. Su is American-born, raised in California, graduated from Stanford . . ." He looked at Maxwell. "You'll like this. She double-majored in math and physics."

"I like her already," Maxwell said.

"Capt. Kimberly Wood is also an OTS graduate," Starke continued. "Same class as Su. She had her commercial, multiengine rating at twenty-one. After graduating from flight school, she did a tour in Korea. Then she was assigned to Patrick AFB and has flown C-130s for the 920th Rescue Wing for the past three years there. Excellent evaluations, also unmarried, and a graduate of Florida State University. She majored in Political Science. Excellent flight evaluations, and she, too, is career-oriented. The plane that disappeared is owned by Wood. That may be significant."

"Are Su and Wood just friends or in a relationship?" Melissa asked.

"Unknown."

"Where were they coming from?" Melissa asked.

"They'd flown to Treasure Cay, Bahamas, three days ago. That's all that's in the file. I'll forward any additional updates as I receive them."

"I wonder if either of them have met Trent at a fly-in or have mutual pilot friends," Melissa said.

"Ask him if he knows either of the women."

"I intend to," Melissa replied.

"Plans change quickly around here," Maxwell said.

"Yes, they do," Starke said. "You stay with the colonel."

Sawtooth Security Communication Center – 2000 hours

The signal had been faint, but it was there. Gunnery Sergeant Willis Radley sat at the console, waiting for a repeat transmission. He adjusted his headset. Nothing. "Play that radio transmission again," he ordered.

"Yes, Gunny."

Radley listened to the transmission. It sounded military— "Creeper to Babysitter"—but the oscillation indicated the transmitter was very weak, not up to military specs, and there'd been no response.

"Corporal, issue an alert. The transmission originated northwest of the base. I want two patrols on the back side of the mountain ASAP. Post two spotter teams with thermal and night vision. Whoever it is hasn't triggered any motion sensors at the perimeter, but I want to be ready to intercept if they do. No one else goes out in this weather unless they have a purpose."

"If we spot them, do we engage?"

"No. Find, report, and surveil. Let's see what they're up to. I'll advise the lieutenant."

THIRTEEN

Taylor sat in a chair next to Trent's bed. The positive-pressure door hissed as it opened. Melissa and an older, thin man entered.

"Any change?" Melissa asked.

"No."

"Taylor, this is Dr. Hank Maxwell. He's here to help us."

"Good," Taylor replied. "Trent looks pale."

Melissa examined Trent, then said, "His heart and lungs are good. I'll order another blood panel and a scan of his implant." She used her computer tablet to make the request.

"He's probably anemic from all the blood you've already taken from him." Taylor joked. She stared at Maxwell for a moment. "What kind of doctor are you?"

"I'm a physicist."

"We're exploring all of our options for treating Trent," Melissa said.

"How long has he been unconscious this time?" Maxwell asked.

"A little over an hour."

"Can I see a picture of the implant?"

"Certainly." Melissa pulled up three images to her tablet screen. "This is what the implant looked like when we did the first scan. And this is the second one when he says he was on Mars." She clicked on the third image. "This was the last image before he woke up."

"Wow."

"Can I see them?" Taylor asked.

"Sure."

When she saw the implant, her heart began to race. "You're sure there isn't one of those in my head?"

"Positive," Melissa replied.

"I don't know how I got the scar that's behind my ear. Could something have been removed from my brain?"

"I looked for signs of tissue damage on your last scan. I didn't detect anything abnormal."

Taylor nodded, then said, "Melissa, is it possible that what Trent and I experienced in our dream was real? Could we be living on Mars in a different time?"

"I'm still leaning toward a psychiatric explanation, until proven otherwise. Dr. Maxwell is here to help us determine if it could have been a real event. He's exploring theoretical time displacement—time travel."

"This might sound crazy, but I think Trent was recalling something that happened to him while on Mars. I would've had to be there with him. He knew things that he shouldn't have known about me."

"You mean about your moles?" Melissa asked.

"Exactly. How could he know about them?" Taylor glanced at Maxwell. "Does he know about what Trent has claimed?"

"Yes," Melissa replied.

Feeling embarrassed, Taylor said, "There's something else I haven't told you. I'm attracted to Trent. I feel as if we've known each other for years."

"Taylor, you haven't had any male companionship for quite a while. You and Trent have had similar experiences. It's only natural that you'd feel something for him."

"It's more than that, Melissa. I love him."

"You just think you do. Yesterday the only thing you wanted was to get back to your family."

"I know. That's why it feels so strange." Taylor heard the sheets rustle and turned. Trent was awake.

"How long have I been out?" Trent asked.

"Quite a while," Taylor answered.

"Do you know where you are?" Melissa asked.

Trent looked around the room. "Yeah. I'm in medical."

"Who are you?" Taylor asked.

"What? I'm Trent McDougal."

"Good. What do you remember about this last event?" Taylor asked.

Trent closed his eyes. "I was standing in the hallway of the apartment, watching Taylor walk toward the door, when I had a vision." He opened his eyes. "Then I felt a pain in my skull. Melissa arrived, and I felt like I was in two worlds at the same time."

"Do you remember asking about Maya?" Taylor asked.

"No. Who's that?"

"How about Shona?" Melissa asked.

Trent jerked upright and said, "Shona is on Mars, and she's pregnant with Maya." He shook his head. "Wait . . . What did I just say?"

"Interesting," Melissa said.

"I don't understand," Trent said, rubbing his forehead.

"When you came to a little while ago, you said I was Shona Cooper and you were Aiden Cooper. We lived on Mars with our daughter, Maya. Does that sound familiar?"

"Maya?" Trent replied. "I remember an airlock malfunctioned."

"Yes," Melissa said. "Do you remember anything else?"

"I'm not sure. I remember I was concerned about a little girl."

"That's a good start," Melissa said.

"Who are you?" Trent asked Maxwell.

"Dr. Hank Maxwell. I'm here to see if I can help in any way."

"He's a physicist," Taylor quickly added.

"You don't remember anything else about the visions?" Melissa asked.

"Taylor looked younger. I remember the landscape."

"What was the last thing you said to me in the apartment?" Taylor asked.

Trent smiled at her. "That I do remember. I told you I loved you."

"That's right."

"Colonel, may I ask Trent some questions?" Maxwell asked.

"Certainly."

"Trent, describe the place where you saw Taylor pregnant."

Trent closed his eyes. "There's a long, wide corridor. The walls are white, and they curve into an arch at the ceiling. The window she was standing in front of was circular and convex."

"Tell me about the landscape you saw outside the window."

"Desolate, like a desert with a reddish-brown surface. Boulders were scattered across a plateau, and there were mountains in the distance."

"What color was the sky?"

"Crimson."

"Did you have a sense of time?"

"It was light outside, but I can't say what time it was exactly."

"Just one more question. Was it today?"

Trent opened his eyes. "I don't understand."

"Were you there today, or was this at a different time?"

"It felt like it was today. But if I was here, it couldn't have been, could it?" Trent looked at Melissa. "Could the neural implant be creating these visions?"

"It's possible. I'm wondering if your knowledge of Taylor's moles was provided by the aliens. They've examined her."

Trent nodded, looking confused. "Maya," he muttered. "If these are visions from the aliens, why would they want us to have a daughter?"

"Good question, and I don't have an answer," Melissa replied.

"The aliens must want us to be together," Taylor said. "Providing us with a daughter cements our union."

"Unlikely," Melissa said.

"Professor, you said you were a physicist," Taylor said. "What exactly do you study besides time?"

"I specialize in quantum mechanics."

"What does that have to do with time displacement?"

"More than you could imagine."

Trent said, "Any chance I can get something to eat? I'm starving."

"I want to run another AMRS before you eat," Melissa said. "You up for a walk?"

"Sure," Trent replied, sitting up.

"Trent, before we run the test, I have another question," Melissa said. "Do either of you know anyone named of Tai Su or Kimberly Wood?"

Trent shook his head. "No. Who are they?"

"Never heard of them," Taylor replied.

"Tai Su is an Air Force missileer. She and Captain Wood were abducted today while flying off the east coast of Florida."

"Are you kidding me?" Trent cried.

"I'm very serious. Dr. Sanderson is on his way to Ft. Pierce as we speak. Captain Su returned in a small plane three hours after disappearing. Captain Wood wasn't with her. She's still missing. All of this was happening while you were having your visions."

Trent said, "What kind of plane were they in?"

"A Cessna 182. Why does that matter?"

"Small aircraft. They were the only people aboard?"

"Yes," Melissa replied.

"Are you bringing Captain Su and her plane here?" Trent asked.

"Yes. I'd like for you and Taylor to talk to her and make her feel welcome. Her plane, like yours, will be examined."

"Does Captain Su remember what happened?" Taylor asked.

"We'll know more tomorrow. She'll be here early in the morning. Taylor, will you and Dr. Maxwell walk Trent to the imaging center? I need to let the general know that our patient is awake."

"Any chance we can go back to our apartment?" Taylor asked.

"As soon as the test is completed. One other thing." Melissa pulled up the NRO photo of the light on her tablet. "Trent, does this look like what you saw?"

Trent peered at the image of the light surrounding a plane. "The one I saw was larger, but the color and intensity of the light is the same. Is that what took the other plane today?"

"Yes. I'll have you look at it in more detail later."

"How did you get that photo?" Taylor asked.

"NRO satellite."

"But they didn't capture my plane being taken."

"No."

Security Command Center — February 5 — 0000 hours MST

"To sum up, we've found no sign of intruders in or around the perimeter," Radley told Gunnery Sergeant Brian Falconi, his duty relief. "Lieutenant

Davis has been notified. He wants you to call him if any of the team makes contact." He paused, then said, "Don't give me that look."

"What look?" Falconi asked.

"The look you always have when you think we're walking into a stinky swamp."

Falconi smirked, then said with a strong Bronx accent, "You mean like the last time we spent three days in the bush only to discover that you'd had us chasing what turned out to be a bear? Then there was the time you heard a repetitive tapping noise. That only wasted two days of hunting for the source, which turned out to be water dripping from a tree branch onto a sensor. Don't worry, Radley, we'll find the source of your phantom radio call, like we always do."

"I know what I heard, Falconi."

"No one is questioning your hearing. In fact, it might be too good."

Radley went back to business. "Since thermal and audio have been negative since the first radio intercept, I think I'll join my team in the search."

"I figured you would, and I'll be waiting to hear what you find."

Radley left the center. When he opened the exterior security door, the drop in temperature took his breath away. He did a radio check with Falconi, then checked in with Falconi's team, which were already in the field. He decided to reconnoiter the area around the lake. He didn't think he'd find anyone. No one in their right mind would be camping in this weather, but he needed to eliminate this area from the search grid.

The Camp — February 05 — 0100 hours

When Alexa felt the nudge, she jolted awake and rolled over, the thermal blanket making a crinkling sound. In the blue glow of Marvin's flashlight, she saw him put a finger to his lips. Then he pointed toward the lake and turned off the light. The sky had cleared a little. The moon and stars peeked between the fast-moving clouds. She saw a lone figure walking slowly along the shoreline as if looking for tracks. She also saw the outline of an M4 rifle.

Marvin whispered, "He has night vision goggles. Stay under the thermal blanket. Where there's one soldier, others will be nearby."

"You're sure it's a guy?"

"Yes. Movement, gait, and physique are male, and I got a glimpse of his face in the moonlight."

"We could follow him back to the entrance," Alexa whispered.

"Maybe. Make sure all your stuff is turned off. I recommend we hunker down. The base entrance must be close."

Alexa watched the soldier move in and out of the shadows as he walked farther away. Moving silently, he looked like a professional. He stopped near the shoreline, knelt, and turned his head from side to side. He picked up something near where they'd left the ice to set up camp.

Then her world exploded. Her pupils contracted so fast that it drove a spike of pain through her head. An intense white light enveloped the area. She knew it wasn't from an ordinary searchlight. She struggled to see through the glare. The soldier knelt, then moved slowly toward some boulders. He dropped flat behind a bolder and peered around it. He wore arctic fatigues. Suddenly, the light winked out.

"I can't see shit," Alexa whispered. "My night vision's gone."

Marvin replied, "Just make like a rock until we can see again."

Alexa closed her eyes, hoping to regain her night vision faster. The ball of light must have been at least fifty feet in diameter. "What the hell was that?"

"I really don't know. Now be quiet."

SCC — February 05 — 0105 hours MST

When the light disappeared, radio chatter broke the silence. Radley scanned the lake from behind a boulder.

He heard his name being called on the radio. It was Falconi.

"Radley, do you read?"

"Falconi, go to condition red. I repeat, go to condition red!"

"What the hell is going on out there?" Falconi asked.

"Possible alien contact. Intense light over the lake for a few seconds, now nothing."

"Are you messing with me?" Falconi asked.

"No. I'm serious. Sound the alarm. Radley to all teams, take up defensive positions between the lake and the facility entrances. Report any contact or movement." Radley activated his homing beacon, then broadcast that the other team members to do the same. Falconi would know exactly where all of the blue team members were positioned.

"Blue Six, Gunny, I'm three hundred meters above and to your west. I saw you when the light appeared."

"Blue Three, in position at the back door."

"Blue Two, I'm south of the lake. What the hell was that?"

"Knock off the chatter," Radley ordered.

"Blue Spirit Maker One, I'm east of you. I'm painting one thermal target on the ice through the scope. It's near where the light was most intense."

"Is it moving?" Radley asked.

"Affirmative. Appears to be crawling. It could be injured."

Radley moved away from his cover. He had recovered enough of his night vision to see a figure on the ice. "Spirit Maker, I have visual on your target. It's stationary and balled up. Falconi, do you copy?"

"Affirmative. The nest is humming."

"I need three more squads deployed, now! I want them to set perimeter around my position. I also want a biomedical response team. Make sure medical has containment capability. Call in the Hawk. I want air support and a shitload more firepower down here."

"Understood. Lieutenant Davis is en route with the additional squads. He should be with you in five."

"Copy," Radley replied. "Spirit Maker, anything else out there?"

"I'm only painting the one target. I'll check wide."

Thirty seconds later, Radley's radio crackled. "Spirit Maker has no other targets in the area. I'm back on the target."

"It looks like the target is trying to stand," Radley said.

"Spirit Maker confirms. It's on its knees and appears to be looking around. Wait one."

"Stay with the target," Radley ordered.

"Affirmative. Target appears human, and judging by the shape, I'd say female."

Radley couldn't tell if the being was male or female from his position. "I can't make out any detail," Radley said. "Confirm it's female."

"It appears to be a human female," Spirit Maker replied. "Very unstable on her feet. She's down!"

"Is she armed?" Radley asked.

"Nothing visible. She's trying to get up again."

"Radley, this is Davis. We'll be with you in three. Maintain visual. Do not approach the subject. Biohazard team and containment unit will be with us in ten. I repeat, do not approach the subject. Maintain defensive perimeter, but do not engage."

"I copy," Radley replied. "Radley to all teams, you heard the LT. Maintain observation positions. Do not engage. Weapons cold." The team members acknowledged.

"Subject is on her knees again," Spirit Maker said. "Looks like she's really cold. She has her arms wrapped tightly around her body."

"Stay on her," Radley encouraged.

"I got her. She's crawling toward the shoreline."

Three minutes later, Lieutenant Davis was kneeling beside Radley, breathing hard from exertion. Two eight-man teams had taken flanking positions on each side of them, as another team fanned out behind them.

"Subject is at the shoreline," Spirit Maker radioed.

"We can see her," Radley said. "She's not dressed for cold weather. Looks like jeans and a light-colored, short-sleeve shirt. She's unarmed and is trying to stand again."

"Davis to bioteam. How soon?"

"This is Colonel Endo. We copy your transmissions. We'll be there in less than one."

Radley heard the medical staff crashing through the brush, then crunching sounds in the snow behind him. He turned and saw the colonel and several others in full biohazard suits. As the colonel approached, her pace slowed.

"I want close support as we advance," Melissa ordered over the radio. "Have a thermal blanket ready. Alert medical for a hypothermia case. Containment vessel forward."

"Radley, you're with me," Davis said. "Spirit Maker, stay sharp, fire only if I order it. You copy?"

"Yes, sir," Spirit Maker replied.

"Colonel, we're ready when you are," Davis said.

"Let's move," Melissa ordered.

They broke from rocky cover and slowly advanced on the woman. The woman extended a hand toward them.

"Stand down. No weapon," Radley radioed. He wanted to make sure none of the team members took the woman's outstretched gesture as an aggressive action.

"Confirming—no weapon visible," Spirit Maker radioed.

Radley stood back as Colonel Endo and her team reached the woman. She was shivering uncontrollably and barely speaking above a whisper. As they wrapped her in the thermal blanket, the area once again was bathed in light, but not as intense as earlier.

"Identify the source of that light!" Radley ordered over the radio. Then he heard the sound of the helicopter rotors as it circled overhead.

"It's ours," Davis said.

A biohazard team placed a stretcher next to the woman. She was helped onto it, then she was cocooned in a portable, clear plastic, biohazard containment vessel. They attached hoses to the vessel, and Radley could hear the sound of the oxygen and carbon dioxide scrubbers working. When positive pressure was established, the biohazard team lifted the containment vessel, and carried her slowly away.

"Lieutenant Davis, I want this place kept secured," Melissa ordered over the radio. "I want a perimeter two hundred meters in all directions from where she appeared. I want the scene kept pristine. None of your men are to go out on the ice-covered lake."

"Understood," Davis replied.

"My contact specialist team will be here shortly to check for radiation and to gather any evidence that may have been left behind. They may need some of your men to help cut through the ice. We'll be taking samples of everything in the area that was exposed."

"Some of my men were exposed to the light," Lieutenant Davis said. "Radley was closest to it."

"All personnel that were exposed to the light must report to Nova Red Level quarantine and stay there until they're screened and cleared. They must not have contact with anyone else."

"What about those of us who came into contact with those exposed?" Davis asked.

"Lieutenant, I hate to do this to you, but I'll need you and any of your personnel that were in *close* contact with those exposed to report to quarantine and remain there until cleared."

"I understand. Radley, you heard the colonel."

"Yes, sir."

The Camp — 0130 hours

Marines and assorted personnel combed the area around them. A biohazard team carrying a woman in an enclosed chamber had passed within fifty feet of their position.

"Marvin, they're going to step on us if we stay here," Alexa whispered.

"They certainly have a lot of people assigned to this facility."

"Do you think we can work our way to the vent without being seen?"

"Did you hear what that colonel said? We're in a contamination area."

"Are you saying that we should give up?" Alexa asked.

"I don't want to, but if we were exposed to something toxic, we don't want to die either. You saw those hazmat suits and heard the order that all personnel exposed are to report to Red Level. Whatever that is."

"Marvin, we were, for the most part, covered by the blankets and the tent. Our exposure would be minimal."

"I don't think these thermal blankets would help much if it's biological."

"I bet that light was the same thing that took Trent."

"Could be. No one at this facility was expecting that light to appear, that's for sure. They were surprised and scared. Whoever the woman was that was left behind didn't belong here. Alexa, our answers are in there." Marvin pointed back toward the mountain.

Alexa sighed. "You want to walk in with the others and just tell them who we are?"

"I think it's our best option."

"And we were so close."

"Then you agree?" Marvin asked.

"Reluctantly. I think you're right. With as many people as they have searching the area, we both know that sooner or later they're going to stumble over us. The tent is well camouflaged, but not that good. They'll find us. Trent's in there. Hopefully, they'll lock us up with him."

"We can't reach Sue or Dan from here," Marvin said. "They won't know what's happened to us."

"Knowing Dan like I do, he'll figure out that we've been caught," Alexa said.

"Don't count on it. I think we need to be medically cleared like the others."

"I guess we just need to show ourselves." Alexa unwrapped herself from the thermal blanket and stowed it in her pack.

"Securing all the gear is stupid, they're just going to tear it apart," Marvin said.

"True. Are you ready?"

"Let's get it over with."

They walked out of the trees, and within thirty seconds, Alexa heard the rapidly approaching Marines.

"We're in the contamination zone and were present when the light landed," Alexa shouted. "Stay back. I recommend you recall the biohazard team."

"Identify yourself," someone yelled.

"Alexa Padgett and Marvin Thanos. We're armed, but our weapons are secure."

"Are you the only ones out here?"

"Yes. You've been searching for us since we left Key West. My boyfriend is Trent McDougal. He's being held inside the facility."

"Stay where you are. Do not move."

It seemed like forever before anyone called out to her again. She could hear the muffled conversations and the accompanying movement as they were surrounded.

"Alexa Padget," a voice called out.

"I'm still here."

"We have a biohazard team coming to you."

"We have gear and weapons that I'm sure you'll want to secure."

"Copy."

She could hear bits and pieces of conversations. A few minutes later, two people dressed in biohazard suits walked up to them.

"You'll need to put these on over your clothes," a woman said. "I'll walk you through how to work the air, and I'll make sure you're sealed in."

"I've used these before," Alexa said. "Who's in charge?"

"All in due time," the woman replied.

"You're holding my boyfriend, Trent McDougal. I want to see him."

"That will be arranged after you're cleared and debriefed."

Nova Annex — Red Level — 0215 hours

Twenty minutes later, dressed in biohazard suits, Alexa and Marvin walked into the facility and were escorted to Red Level. Their gear was put in quarantine containers. Alexa knew it would be thoroughly checked. The room they entered was sparse, with only a couple of chairs, a table, and what looked like sealed lockers. The door closed behind them and was sealed. One of the technicians remained in the room with them.

Alexa stared at a mirrored window on the far side of the room as a technician sprayed their biohazard suits with decontaminant. The liquid swirled around a drain that was in the middle of the floor.

"Extend your arms to the side and move your legs apart," the technician instructed.

Alexa and Marvin complied.

A moment later, a violet light filled the room for several seconds, followed by a red light, and then a heavy, oily mist.

"They certainly know how to decontaminate a person," Marvin said.

"That they do."

A high-powered vent fan turned on, and the mist cleared, but droplets remained on their facemasks.

"Alexa Padget, you are a difficult person to pin down," a male voice boomed over the intercom.

"Sorry if we caused you any trouble," Alexa replied sarcastically. "Who are you, and where are we?"

"I'm General John Starke. My adjutant, Major Striker, is still in Florida looking for you. He won't be happy to hear that you were found hiding outside our facility. I must say, the Secret Service trained you well."

"We weren't found," Alexa said. "We allowed you to find us in *light* of the alien event. I see you've done a little homework."

"We did. I'm sure Marvin's Marine training was helpful in getting you close to the facility without being seen."

"It was helpful," Marvin replied. "In fact, I could help you hide this place a little better if you'd like to hire us."

"Funny," Starke replied. "I'm amazed that you found us. Very impressive sleuthing. I'm going to want to hear all about how you did that."

"I'm sure that you'd like to know, but first, where's Trent?"

"He's safe three floors above us. Where is Sue Calder?"

"Safe," Alexa replied. "She's staying with a friend."

"I see that you still want to play games, but I can assure you that this game is over," Starke said with an edge in his tone. "Once you two are cleared, we'll talk in person."

"Looking forward to it," Alexa said.

FOURTEEN

Melissa was running on caffeine. She couldn't remember the last time she'd had eight hours of sleep. Capt. Kimberly Wood wasn't recovering as expected. She'd already resuscitated Wood twice since her arrival in medical. Performing CPR on her while sealed in a positive-pressure suit was challenging. Wood's body temperature was still dangerously low, which was unexplainable considering the short time that she was outside. Their efforts to elevate her core temperature had failed. Something else was contributing to her hypothermia. Melissa suspected Wood's hypothalamus was to blame. Something was interfering with its function, and she suspected a neural implant. She'd check on it after Wood was stable. She'd already found a triangular scar on Wood's left tibia, identical to the scars on Taylor and Trent. She speculated that Wood was also abducted as a child.

The doctor standing next to Melissa said, "Colonel, you look beat. I'll stay with her and advise you if her condition changes."

Melissa nodded. "Thanks. I need to check on the others who were exposed to the alien light. I'll leave her in your care."

Melissa walked backward to the wall. When she reached the access portal, she leaned back, grabbed the overhead support bar, and pulled herself free of the one-piece Biological Safety Level 4 suit. The suit's weighted feet and hard composite material allowed the suit to stand upright. The wall-mounted BSL-4 suits provided a closed system, allowing the wearer to forgo decontamination before and after entering the room.

The BSL-4 medical rooms were the highest level of biohazard containment in the facility, and they had their own air supply and decontamination system.

Melissa left the containment access room and pulled up the latest information on her tablet concerning the Marines that had been quarantined. She noted that none of their clothing had tested positive for contaminants or radiation, which was a good start. Every one of the men would be put through a comprehensive physical exam over the next several hours, but she didn't expect to find anything. Neither Trent, Taylor, or Su had presented with any foreign microbes. Wood, having been dropped on their doorstep, along with being unresponsive, was enough reason for Melissa to require the heightened level of precautionary protocols. She wanted to be absolutely certain that Wood wasn't contaminated with an alien pathogen.

The last time the facility was on Alert One, the highest status, was during a drill a year ago. They had planned for every conceivable possibility over the years, including an alien intrusion, but this event had made it all too real. Trent was supposed to have been the lure for alien contact, but on their terms. The electronic dampers hadn't been turned off. She believed that the aliens were sending a message that they knew where Trent and Taylor were being held. She had no doubt that the aliens could take them anytime they wanted. There wasn't any possibility that the containment field they'd designed would hold the aliens. *How did we ever think we could capture them?* Melissa thought.

She needed to check on the two newest arrivals. She had a feeling that Alexa Padget was going to be a handful. *It will be interesting to see how Trent reacts when Alexa and Taylor meet,* she mused.

She walked past the quarantine area where the Marines were being examined. Alexa and Marvin were being held and screened in a separate containment area. She found General Starke standing at the window in the observation room. She looked past him and saw Alexa seated a table, dressed in military fatigues, and she was staring at the mirrored glass.

"Have you spoken with her?" Melissa asked.

"Briefly," Starke replied. "I'm waiting for Marvin Thanos to be cleared and dressed to join her."

Melissa's tablet chirped. She read through the report, then said, "Neither of them show any sign of exposure to anything harmful."

Just then Marvin was escorted into the room. He sat down next to Alexa and didn't say anything.

"Good, we won't have to suit up to interview them," Starke said. "Let's go talk to them."

"I wonder how many others know where they are," Melissa said.

"That's what I intend to find out. Shall we go formally introduce ourselves?"

Red Level – Observation Room – 0400 hours

Alexa heard the door hiss as it opened. A general entered, followed by an Asian woman—a Space Force colonel by the looks of the uniform and rank insignia. Two Marine guards followed them in and stood against the wall on each side of the door.

"Got tired of watching us, huh?" Alexa asked.

General Starke smiled and said, "I'm General Starke, and this is Col. Melissa Endo. She's been treating Trent."

"It's nice to meet you," Melissa said.

"You were the one that met us in the biohazard suit," Marvin said.

"Yes. It was smart of you to turn yourselves in. Good news, all of your tests are negative."

Alexa asked, "Was the light we saw out there responsible for Trent's disappearance?"

"We think so," Melissa replied.

Alexa noted the glance Melissa gave Starke and his little nod of approval. She turned to face the Marines at the door and said, "Please wait outside."

The Marines left.

"Alexa, Marvin, Trent was abducted by an alien species, just like the woman you saw that was left outside," Melissa said. "We trust that neither of you will disclose what you saw or what I'm going to tell you."

Alexa looked from Melissa to Starke. "You know that I held a high security clearance while in the Secret Service. Marvin is a former Marine. We know how to keep secrets."

"First of all, we need to build some trust."

"Colonel, I've been trained in interrogation tactics," Alexa said. "You'll have to do better than using the old build trust routine."

"I see," Melissa replied. She sat down across from them.

"So we're definitely talking alien encounters?" Marvin said.

"Obviously," Melissa said. "That's why we ran the tests on both of you. We needed to make sure that you hadn't been exposed to an alien pathogen."

"Who was the person the aliens returned?" Marvin asked.

"What we're dealing with is very complicated," Starke answered before Melissa could respond. "That's the reason we needed to find and talk to all of you. Where can we find Sue Calder?"

Alexa didn't reply. Marvin just stared at the general.

"We need to examine everyone that was in physical proximity to Deputy Griffin and Agent Dobson," Melissa said. "Although Trent doesn't show any signs of an invasive pathogen, it's only prudent that we screen her."

Silence.

"Don't be stupid," Starke said. "We've brought everyone here that had direct contact with Dobson. We need to evaluate Miss Calder before she comes in contact with too many more people."

Melissa said, "It's precautionary. Anyone you were in contact with will need to be screened and so on. The longer we wait to contain and evaluate those exposed, the larger the pool of people we will need to contact trace."

"No one is sick," Marvin said. "I imagine you both spoke to Trent, and you look healthy."

"That's true," Melissa replied. "But we're under strict quarantine pro-tocols until we're certain. We can't risk a pandemic, especially one caused by an alien pathogen."

"What a load of crap," Alexa said. "The van you used to bring Trent out here was seen leaving the area, and it went straight back to the base. Are you going to tell me the driver was medically screened, as were all of the Mountain Home base personnel and the people on the C-17 that brought Trent here?"

"You had us under surveillance?" Starke said, sounding surprised.

"Yes," Marvin answered.

"How did you know we were coming here?" Starke asked, taking a seat. "And who else knows about the facility?"

"Is Trent alright?" Alexa asked Melissa, not answering the general.

"Yes," Melissa replied. "Physically, he's fine. There are some things that we're still monitoring."

"Look, we're not buying the secondary exposure claim," Alexa said. "You want to know who we've told about Trent. Scaring people into keeping quiet usually works the best, unless of course something occurs to prevent it. And you know as well as I do that cover-ups are a bitch to contain once they've been leaked."

"Has our involvement been leaked?" Starke asked.

"What do think?" Alexa replied.

"Don't play games with me," Starke said.

Alexa didn't respond.

"We really do need to speak to Sue," Melissa insisted.

Alexa said, "You only want to scare her and the rest of us so we don't say anything about the aliens. Rest assured we have no intention of doing that—at least for now."

Starke bristled and took a deep breath. "If any of your friends go public with any information about Trent or reveals the location of this facility, there will be severe repercussions."

"I understand," Alexa said. "And I'm sure you don't want to have another Area 51 problem. Especially with aliens landing outside."

"You're on thin ice," Starke said forcefully.

"I'll put your mind at ease before you blow a gasket," Alexa said. "We won't say anything." Alexa leaned forward in her chair and put her elbows on the steel table. "I can understand your need to debrief Trent and the need to contain the information about what happened to him. The deputy sheriff and the NCIS agent are here to limit the number of people who can expose what's going on here."

Melissa nodded. "You are correct. Deputy Griffin and Agent Dobson are here for security reasons."

"Can we see them?"

"Not now," Starke said. "They're being housed in the Altair annex next door. Alexa, I know you aren't operating on your own. Miss Calder needs to be debriefed. We can do it away from the facility, and I'll assure you that she will be free to leave once I'm convinced that she'll keep her mouth shut."

"If you want us to trust you, release us now, and we'll go get Sue."

"Not happening," Starke said. "I'll give you access to a phone. You will call her and tell her and whoever else is helping you to keep their mouths shut. Everyone will need to be personally interviewed. I promise not to detain them for very long. We have too many other pressing matters to deal with right now. Can I assume that she and your confederates are nearby?"

Alexa stared at him for a moment, then said, "Sue's in a safe place, and she won't say anything to anyone so long as I check in with her. Otherwise, you'll have to find a new hiding place."

"Your cell phones are being analyzed," Starke said. "We're already tracking the phone numbers you've called. We'll find her and whoever else is involved, one way or another. But, as a sign of good faith, I'll let you call Miss Calder. You will tell her that we'll be in touch, and in the meantime, if one word of this leaks, you, Marvin, and Miss Calder will be spending the rest of your lives in a very small, confined space."

"If I call Sue and convey your message, will I be able to see Trent?"

"Yes," Melissa said before Starke disagreed. "I'll escort both of you to see him."

Alexa looked at Marvin, and he nodded. "Very well. I'll call her. I'll need a phone."

"We'll make that happen," Starke said. "I have another question for you. How did you get here?"

"By private jet," Alexa answered, knowing that the general would find out anyway.

"How were you able to track our aircraft?"

Alexa didn't answer.

"You're going to make this difficult, aren't you?" Starke said.

"Only until I get to see Trent. Can I use my cell phone to call Sue now?"

"No. Your cell phone won't work within the facility."

"General, if my call comes from an unknown number, Sue won't answer."

"We'll clone your cell number, and then you can make the call. I'll need to know who tracked our aircraft."

"I can't tell you that, general."

"We'll discuss this again later." Starke rose and left the room.

Looking at her computer tablet, Melissa said, "Alexa, I don't see anything in your medical file that indicates you have a scar on either leg."

Alexa didn't know why Melissa would ask her about scars. She replied, "I don't have any scars on my legs."

"Marvin, do you have any unexplained scars?" Melissa asked.

"No. I can tell you how I got every one of mine."

"Alexa, did Trent ever discuss his childhood abduction with you?"

Alexa sat back and crossed her arms. She felt stunned. "Are you telling me this isn't the first time Trent's been abducted?"

"Correct. He told us that he was abducted when he was a child."

"Are you being straight with me?"

"Yes. There are some things you both need to know about Trent. Some of them will be shocking, so I have to know that you won't do something rash."

"Did he grow a third eye or turn into a lizard or something?" Marvin asked jokingly.

Alexa smiled. Marvin always had a way to lighten the mood. He'd kept her from lashing out on more than one occasion. "Well, did he?" Alexa asked Melissa.

Starke walked back into the room and said, "Did he what?"

"I'm glad to see you both haven't lost your sense of humor," Melissa replied. "They want to know if Trent is part alien."

Starke placed a sophisticated-looking phone on the table and said, "Well answer the question, Colonel Endo."

"No, Trent isn't an alien. However, he does have an alien implant in his left tibia, which was inserted during his abduction as a child. You've probably seen the scar."

"Yes, I've seen it," Alexa replied, believing that what Melissa had told her about his abduction was true.

"We found the same scar, in the same location, on the woman that was left outside the facility earlier."

"And there's another woman who had that same mark that's staying with us," Starke added. "Her name is Taylor."

Melissa said, "It, too, was placed there during a childhood abduction. It's possible Taylor and Trent met then."

Alexa didn't know what to say.

"Are there more people here who've been abducted?" Marvin asked.

"We'll get to that later," Starke said.

"You think Trent knows Taylor from his previous abduction?" Alexa asked.

"Yes," Starke said. "Has Trent ever mentioned anyone named Taylor?"

"I've never heard him talk about anyone by that name," Marvin said.

"Me either," Alexa said.

"How about the names *Aiden* or *Shona Cooper?*" Melissa asked.

Alexa's mouth went dry. She knew the name, *Shona*. She licked her lips. "Yes, he once mentioned a Shona."

Melissa asked, "How does he know her?"

"I don't know. Trent had a nightmare just before I left for Key West. I had to shake him hard to get him to wake up. It was like he was stuck in a dream state. He kept shouting Shona!"

"What else?" Melissa said.

"Nothing. He finally woke up. I thought Shona might be an old girl-friend. When I asked him who Shona was, he said he had no idea. He didn't even remember having a dream."

"Interesting," Starke said. "Has he told you about any of his previous relationships?"

"No. We agreed not to dwell on failed relationships."

"So he could know a Shona, but lied about it to protect your feelings," Starke said.

Alexa's anger surged. "General, Trent and I don't lie to each other. If there was a Shona in his past, he would have told me about her when I asked."

Starke said, "I think Shona and Trent are . . . more than old friends."

"What are you implying, General Starke?" Alexa asked, knowing that he was baiting her. She felt Marvin's hand touch her leg. He'd done that in the past to keep her from lashing out or jumping to unfounded conclusions.

"That they are or were intimate," Starke said.

"You're telling me that Trent's been cheating on me? Not a chance."

"Alexa," Melissa said, "let's not get off track. Did Trent ever mention anyone named Maya?"

"No. Is that another woman he's supposed to know?" Alexa felt as if she might explode.

"I know this is hard for you," Melissa said in a soothing voice, "but I'm afraid it's going to get harder. Trent had an . . . I'm not sure where to begin."

"Trent may have had a dissociative event," Starke said.

"You mean he had an emotional meltdown?" Alexa asked.

Melissa answered, "In a manner of speaking. It might be related to a neural implant that we discovered."

Alexa shot to her feet, knocking over her chair. "He has something in his brain!" Alexa cried.

Marvin stood, took her by the shoulders, and said, "Alexa, let her finish." He picked up the chair and she sat back down.

Melissa said, "Trent claims that he and Shona live on Mars together as a married couple, but his name there is Aiden Cooper. He told us that they have a daughter, Maya, who's ten."

"A daughter?" Alexa said, trying to grasp what Melissa was telling her. "You think he's delusional?"

"Honestly, we're not sure," Melissa said.

"Taylor and Trent have an unusual attraction to each other," Starke said.

"What do you mean?" Alexa asked.

"This is going to be hard for you," Melissa said. "I think it might be best if we let them explain it to you."

"Them?" Alexa snarled.

"Yes, them," Starke said. "They share an apartment. You need to be prepared that the Trent you know may not be the Trent you'll meet now."

"How do you mean?" Alexa's voice cracked. "He sounded normal when I spoke to him in Key West."

"Your relationship will be different from now on," Melissa said. "He's asked about you several times. He told me that he was going to ask you to marry him in Key West. He had a ring with him, which is now in safekeeping. It's quite lovely." Melissa glanced at the general. "Like the general said, Trent and Taylor share a strong bond, and his being near her has brought back memories, perhaps visions—. We're not sure what they are, but Trent believes the events he's described have occurred. It's very complicated."

Tears welled up in Alexa's eyes. "I figured he was going to ask me to marry him. He told me he had something special planned."

"Is the brain implant recent?" Marvin asked.

"We aren't sure. We do know that it's grown since his arrival and that it was most active when Trent was having an episode."

"What kind of episode?" Alexa asked. "You mean like a seizure?"

"No. He enters an unconscious state. When he awakens, he tells us about what he saw on Mars."

"I'm not believing this," Marvin muttered.

"We have several theories as to what's happening to Trent," Melissa said. "Trent has provided incredible detail from his visions."

"We haven't completely ruled out a trauma-induced psychosis caused by his meeting Taylor again," Starke said.

Melissa said, "We're dealing with something that is difficult to define."

Alexa wiped the tears away and said, "I want to talk to Trent. I want to see him."

"Call your friend and we'll make that happen," Starke said, pushing the communication pack over to her. "Put it on speaker."

"I want to see him first."

"No way," Starke said.

Alexa knew she needed to tell Sue where they were. She also knew Starke wasn't going to give in until she called her. She dialed Sue's number, and Dan answered.

"Put Sue on," Alexa said, hoping Dan wouldn't say anything.

"She's asleep."

"Wake her up," Alexa demanded.

"Hang on."

Alexa could hear him moving around.

"It's Alexa," Dan said, and then there was a moment of silence. Alexa knew that Dan was telling her to keep it short so they couldn't track their location.

"Alexa, are you and Marvin alright?" Sue asked.

"We're fine. I'll be seeing Trent in a few minutes, but there are some conditions."

"Someone else is there with you, isn't there? Is it that NCIS agent?"

"No, Sue. You're on speaker, and there are some people from the government listening to us." She could picture Dan's reaction to hearing that.

"Sue, this is General Starke, United States Space Force. I'm here with Alexa, Marvin, and Trent. Deputy Griffin and Agent Dobson are also here. We want you to join us."

"Not a chance," Sue replied.

"I figured that would be your response. Alexa has assured me that you're smart enough to keep your mouth shut. Is she right?"

"That all depends," Sue replied.

"Sue, it's okay," Alexa said, hoping she'd just go along and not let her fiery temper get the better of her. "I explained that you're in a safe place. No one knows where you are. Things have happened that have changed my original premise. I want you to cooperate, but you do not need to meet anyone." She glared at Starke.

He nodded his approval.

Alexa heard shuffling sounds, then a door thudded shut.

"Sue, are you still there?" Starke asked.

"Yes."

"Are you in a car?" Starke asked.

Silence.

"I don't know who you're with, but they'll need to be debriefed," Starke said.

"Alexa, what am I supposed to do?" Sue asked.

"Talk to no one and you'll be safe. I'll explain more later."

"Sue, who else is there with you?" Starke asked, raising a finger at Alexa as a warning.

"A friend," Dan answered. "I won't say anything either. You have my word. Alexa, I expect that you'll contact us again, soon."

"When permitted."

"Can I at least have your first name?" Starke asked.

"Jack. We'll wait to hear from you, but don't make it too long. If we don't hear from Alexa within a few hours, we'll broadcast your location and tell the media everything we know."

Alexa grimaced, then said, "Jack, you're not helping. Just keep a low profile. No threats or media contacts. General, may I call him again in six hours?"

"Yes," Starke said.

"Jack, are we clear on a no interference protocol?"

"Yes," Dan replied. "We'll stay quiet as a ghost."

Alexa knew that meant Dan was going to remain nearby and that he knew his phone was being pinged. He'd disappear before anyone got to him. "Thank you, Jack," Alexa said.

Starke said, "Jack, lives hang in the balance. *Am I clear?*"

"Yes, General Starke. I look forward to hearing from you all again. Alexa, use the alternate line. This one is burned."

The line went dead.

"I love it when people play secret agent," Starke said. "Stupid, but always entertaining. We'll know the new number as soon as you call him back. Alright, let's go see how Trent reacts to seeing you."

Alexa thought that there was a sadistic bite in Starke's voice.

"General, I'd like to run another scan on both of them first," Melissa said. "It'll only take thirty minutes."

Alexa glared at Melissa. "That wasn't what we agreed to."

"I want to make sure that you don't have an alien neural implant. Trent didn't know he had one in his head until we found it. It's important this be done."

"What kind of scan?" Marvin asked.

"An advanced MRI. It doesn't hurt. Please, I'm really trying to help. If either of you have an implant, we need to know. We haven't put two implanted people together before, and I don't want any surprises."

"I thought you said Taylor has one?" Alexa said.

"Had," Starke said. "We removed the one from her leg long before Trent arrived. She doesn't have one in her brain either."

"How long ago did you remove the one from Taylor's leg?"

"Almost two years now."

"She's been here the entire time?" Alexa asked.

"Yes," Starke replied. "Mostly for her own safety."

"You plan on keeping Trent that long?"

"I don't think so," Starke replied.

"Let's get this over with," Alexa said. She realized that this was going to be a prolonged struggle.

FIFTEEN

Trent's Room — February 05, 0545 hours

Trent awoke with a start and was momentarily disoriented. When he rolled over, he was disappointed that Taylor wasn't lying next to him. He checked the time on the clock that was on the nightstand. He wasn't feeling motivated to start the day. He got up and went into the living room and found Taylor asleep on the sofa. The TV was on with the sound turned down. Her auburn hair hung over the edge of her pillow. She was beautiful even in her gray sweatpants and white T-shirt. "Why am I so attracted to you?" he whispered.

He rubbed his face and ran his hand through his hair. Even though he'd gotten some sleep, he was emotionally drained. So many things had happened that he didn't understand.

Trent shuffled into the kitchen, turned on the coffee maker and opened the refrigerator. As he reached for the orange juice, he heard Taylor moan. He turned and saw her stretching her arms. She gave him a look that melted his heart. *I'm so in trouble*, he thought.

"Morning," Taylor said.

"Sorry. I didn't mean to wake you."

"It's okay." Taylor got up and walked into the kitchen. "You feeling any better?"

"Tired, but I'm good. Why did you sleep on the sofa?"

"The Marine bed check woke me up. I moved out to the sofa about two-thirty."

"I must have been out of it. I didn't hear a thing. Has security ever checked on you before?"

"Only twice in two years. Both times I was told it was a drill. The last time was about a year ago."

There was a knock on the door. "Trent, Taylor, it's Melissa."

"Well, at least she knocked this time," Taylor said. She opened the door to find not only Melissa standing there but Starke and two other people.

"May we come in?" Melissa asked.

"Why so formal?" She turned and walked back into the kitchen and stood next to Trent. "Is this about the *drill* last night?"

Melissa entered the room, followed by Starke, then Alexa and Marvin.

Trent froze when he saw Alexa. Then he thought about how wonderful it was to see her. A wave of emotions cascaded over him as he wondered what Alexa must be thinking with Taylor by his side.

Alexa ran to him and threw her arms around his neck, then kissed him. She wiped the tears from her cheeks. "I've missed you so much."

"Alexa, it's good to see you, too," Trent said, sounding too formal and without much enthusiasm. He was certain his lackluster response wasn't lost on her. "How did you get here?"

Alexa released him and took a step back. "You don't seem very excited to see me."

"I'm excited," Trent said. Again without much emotion. "It's just such a surprise."

Alexa glanced at Taylor, then locked her gaze on Trent. "Are we interrupting something?"

"No. We just got up. Marvin, it's good to see you, but you guys didn't need to come here."

"Good to see you, too," Marvin said.

Alexa cocked her head, then said, "What do you mean we didn't have to come? They snatched you and then began hunting us. I wanted to know that you were alright. We tracked you here."

"Alexa, I'm fine. So much has happened."

"So I've heard," Alexa said. "You must be Taylor."

"I am. It's nice to meet you. Trent's told me a lot about you. But I don't think he mentioned Marvin."

Marvin said, "I'm a friend of theirs."

"Now that the introductions are complete," Starke said, "why don't we all sit and get down to business."

"Let me put something else on," Taylor said. She grabbed her pillow and blanket from the sofa and left the room.

Trent closed his eyes when he felt a sharp pain in his head.

"Trent, are you alright? Alexa asked.

He didn't respond.

"Trent," Melissa said, taking a step toward him.

"I'm okay. Let me get changed." He hurried into his bedroom and closed the door. He needed a minute to sort things out. As glad as he was to see Alexa, he felt as if something was missing. He was thankful Taylor had the good sense to return to her bedroom.

The pain in his head subsided. He walked into the bathroom and noticed Taylor's toothbrush on the countertop. He turned and saw her clothes on the floor by the bed. If Alexa came in now—, it wouldn't be good. He gathered up Taylor's things and stuffed them into a drawer, then straightened up the bed.

Trent went back into the bathroom and looked in the mirror. He needed a shave. He put Taylor's toothbrush in a drawer, brushed his teeth, and shaved. He found a clean blue polo with the Space Force logo on the front hanging in the closet. He was about to put it on when he heard the bedroom door open and close. He turned to find Alexa standing there. Guilt overwhelmed him. He pulled the polo over his head so he could delay looking into her eyes.

"You want to tell me about it?" Alexa asked quietly.

He wouldn't hide the truth from her. "First, you have to know that I love you."

"And?"

"And that I'm emotionally conflicted by everything that's happened." He motioned toward the bed. "Please sit down."

"I'll stand."

He took a pair of tan BDU pants off their hangar and closed the closet door.

"There seems to be a pillow missing, and you don't have auburn hair." She picked up a strand of Taylor's hair from his pillow and held it up. Her lower lip began to quiver. "Are you sleeping with her?"

Trent slipped his pants on and shook his head. "It's not what you think."

Alexa shoved him backward. "Answer me!"

"Yes, and no."

"Well, which is it?"

"We shared a bed last night, but we didn't have sex. We just cuddled for a while."

"I risked my damn life, and spent a fucking fortune trying to save you," Alexa shouted. "And you're 'cuddling' with *her*. Melissa explained some things to me, but I didn't think it would be like this. Do you love her?"

Trent took a deep breath. "I do, but not in the way I love you."

"A sisterly love?"

"No, not like that either. It's confusing." He rubbed the knot at the back of his neck. "Alexa, I know Taylor. We have a life together in a different . . . I don't know how to explain it."

"A life with Taylor or Shona?"

Trent felt as if he'd been gut-punched. "They told you about Shona?"

"Yes. I told them that you had a nightmare about her before I left for Key West."

"I'd forgotten about that. I don't remember what I dreamed."

The door opened and Melissa entered. "Everything alright? We heard loud voices."

"Yes, everything's fine," Trent answered. "Please give us a minute."

"Alexa, I can see that you're upset," Melissa said, ignoring Trent. "We told you that Trent may seem different."

"You didn't tell me he was sleeping with Taylor."

"Come back into the living room, please."

Alexa glared at Trent, then walked quickly out of the bedroom. Trent knew that Alexa was furious, and he couldn't blame her. He was mad at himself for having kissed Taylor. He followed Melissa back into the living room just as Taylor emerged from her bedroom. She was dressed in the same uniform as Trent's.

Alexa rounded on Taylor. "Trent tells me he loves you. Do you love him?"

"I do. But let me add that I love my husband and my daughter, too." Taylor walked up to Alexa. "I can't explain my attraction to Trent. I don't think he understands his attraction to me. But we're connected, and we hope that connection will help him remember what happened to him. That's why they put us together in this apartment. We're trying to figure it all out."

"Connected, as in romantically?"

"Yes, Alexa. I have strong feelings for him, and I know he has strong feelings for me. But his feelings toward you, and my feelings toward my family, haven't changed. It's confusing."

"I'm hearing that a lot," Alexa said. "Either you're romantically in love with someone—exclusively—or you aren't. You can't be in love with two people at the same time. At least I can't."

"I understand how you must feel," Taylor said. "I'd feel the same way."

"Marvin, I think we made this trip for nothing," Alexa said. "Trent, I can't marry you, so don't bother asking me. Give the ring to Taylor."

"Alexa, please," Trent pleaded. "Try to grasp what we're experiencing here. Somehow our lives have become entangled. I know her in a different time and place." He paused, then said, "Wait, how do you know about the ring?"

"I told her," Melissa said. "Please, everyone, sit down."

After a few moments of tense silence, Alexa plopped down next to Marvin on the sofa. She crossed her arms and glared at Trent.

"Trent, tell Alexa and Marvin what you've experienced and what you know about Taylor," Starke said. "Taylor, then you tell them about your experiences."

Trent took a chair at the dining room table. Taylor walked over and sat down next to him. He didn't miss Alexa locking her jaw.

"Tell her," Taylor said. "Tell her everything."

Hanford, Washington — February 5 — 0545 hours PST

Dr. Charles "Chuck" Andrews sat at his desk, studying the data he'd received hours earlier from the LIGO-affiliated research labs at MIT and Caltech. Being the newest astrophysicist assigned to the Hanford

Laser Interferometer Gravitational-Wave Observatory, he was relegated to working the flex shift. The rotating hours were hard on him, but he was gaining invaluable experience, especially in light of what had been occurring over the last month.

The Hanford LIGO facility is one of two interferometer detection sites in the United States. The Hanford and the Livingston LIGO detector in Louisiana work in tandem to detect gravitational waves that originate in violent cosmic events. Each location consists of L-shaped detection arms that are two and a half miles long. The research centers at the California Institute of Technology and the Massachusetts Institute of Technology provide analysis and verification of the gravitational wave detection. Three other gravitational wave detectors, located around the world, are integrated with LIGO, providing around-the-clock GW detection capability.

Chuck had earned his doctoral degree from Caltech. His groundbreaking work in advanced interferometry had opened the door for him to take the position on the National Science Foundation-funded project. Part of his job entailed monitoring equipment and working with engineers to find ways to improve the sensitivity of the detectors. Usually his work was uneventful, but over the last few weeks, four gravitational waves had been detected. The last one had occurred just hours before, and if the information he was looking at was correct, it had been centered only three hundred miles from where he was standing.

He thought the data had to be wrong. The detectors must have malfunctioned, but he knew the odds of all five detectors failing at the same time was nearly impossible. Gravitational wave generation within Earth's atmosphere was unexplainable.

The first in-atmosphere anomaly occurred on January 10, near South Florida. Then, three weeks later, two more waves struck within two days of each other in the same general area. The detectors in Italy, Germany, and Japan had provided additional source location confirmation. So far, the research labs hadn't been able to disprove the events. Something was definitely happening, and it had all of the scientists on the project very concerned.

Gravitational waves are ripples in spacetime caused by the acceleration of massive galactic systems, usually originating billions of light years from Earth. Until three weeks ago, black holes colliding, supernovae, and neutron stars had been the only known sources of a GW.

Scientists feared that the magnitude of the gravitational waves detected in Earth's atmosphere was the beginning of a cataclysmic event that could spell the end of the planet.

Chuck scrolled through the data. All of the GW bursts had been short-lived, intense, and very powerfully focused energy. So far, none of the waves had been destructive, which was odd considering they originated in the atmosphere. His colleagues hypothesized that the events were spontaneous energy bursts of nanoparticles of extreme mass and energy on a quantum level. But, that hadn't been proven yet.

All of the analysis of the events had been forwarded to the Pentagon for military interpretation. Some officials speculated that the Russians or the Chinese were experimenting with a new weapon. Conspiracy theories circulated at the highest level of government. Some scientists suggested that experiments at the CERN supercollider in Switzerland were responsible. Everyone wanted answers, including his boss's boss, the mysterious Dr. Harold Maxwell. No one knew who Maxwell reported to, only that somehow he was affiliated with the NSF and military.

The phone chirped. Chuck answered it. "Andrews."

"Dr. Andrews, this is Dr. Maxwell."

"Yes, sir."

"Have you confirmed a point source for the last GW burst?"

"Yes, sir. Near Idaho City in the northern part of Greylock Mountain."

"What was the intensity?"

"Preliminary analysis indicates the same strength as the last three waves."

"Thanks for the update."

"Sir, what do you think is causing these waves?" Chuck asked tentatively.

"I don't have enough information to provide an opinion. If you detect another wave, call me directly." Maxwell gave him a number at the facility. "If I'm not available, leave your callback information with the duty officer. I want to know the time and place of any other event immediately."

"Is this your cell phone number?"

"No. Just call that number, it's a secure line. Don't ask any questions."

"Yes, sir. I'm staying at the facility, so if anything happens, I'll see to it that you are notified right away."

"Thank you."

Chuck spent the next few minutes notifying the other team members of Maxwell's request. There was something odd about the way the waves just materialized. He had an idea that needed exploring before he shared his thoughts with anyone else. He didn't want his credibility getting trashed before his career got off the ground.

Trent's and Taylor's apartment — 0650 hours MST

Alexa didn't know what to say after Trent and Taylor had explained all that had happened to them, including the visions.

"Strange, isn't it?" Trent said.

"Extremely," Alexa replied.

Melissa turned her tablet around so Alexa could see the screen. "These are the images of the implants, and this is a photo of the one that we removed from Taylor's leg before it vaporized."

Alexa examined the implants, then asked, "Why are you sharing all of this information with us?"

"It may be important for Trent to have you nearby and so that you will be able to understand what he's experiencing. We aren't sure what will happen next."

"And Marvin?"

Melissa pursed her lips, then said, "I don't think that he'll be of any value to us, but you may need a friend."

Alexa nodded.

"Dr. Maxwell has offered another theory as to what may be occurring—time dilation," Starke said.

"Time dilation?" Alexa said.

Trent said, "He's proposing that my visions are really memories from another time."

"Let's table that discussion for the moment," Starke said. "He can explain it better than I can."

"So you believe that Trent and Taylor lived, or will live together in another time?" Alexa asked Melissa. "Why didn't you mention that earlier instead of telling me he was having dissociative events?"

"I told you that there could be a number of reasons for Trent's behavior."

"I don't understand why the aliens would want Trent and Taylor to learn about their living in a different time together, and why now?" Alexa said.

Starke replied, "Good question, but I don't have an answer. I think all of these abductions are connected. I believe that the aliens have been experimenting with human subjects for decades, if not centuries. This could be an experiment of some kind to see how we react."

"Trent and Taylor are being used as lab rats?" Alexa asked.

"Maybe," Melissa said. "If Dr. Maxwell is correct, Trent and Taylor may exist as a couple in a different universe within the multiverse. You two may have never met in the other time."

"All of the possibilities lead us to more questions," Starke said. "I need to check in with Maxwell and tell him what we've discussed. I'm sure he'll want to talk to all of you."

"I feel like the odd man out," Marvin said. "I'm not sure what I can bring to the table."

"Just be there for me," Alexa said, taking his hand. She looked at the general. "Is there any place we can get a bite to eat?"

"There's food in the fridge," Taylor said. "I can make you something."

Starke said, "I think it would be better if the colonel took everyone up to Pink Level and got them acquainted with the mess area. I believe we're all on the same page now. Am I right?"

Everyone nodded in agreement.

"Alexa, do you want your own quarters?" Starke asked.

Alexa glance at Trent, then replied, "Yes. I need to get my head around all of this."

"Marvin, we'll set you up in quarters next to Alexa," Starke said. "Alexa, you and Marvin will go through a facility orientation later today. You'll be provided with passkeys to the areas that you're authorized to enter. Leaving the facility is not allowed unless escorted by either Colonel Endo or myself."

"We're going to be staying a while?" Marvin asked.

"A few days," Starke replied. "Alexa, either the colonel or I will have to be with you to make your check-in calls with Jack. This is a secure facility. Don't try and disappear on us."

"I wouldn't think of it."

"You may go wherever your passkeys allow," Starke said. "I think you're both smart enough to understand what we're facing. I *trust* that you both will behave. I'll have Maxwell join you in the dining hall."

Alexa stood and faced Taylor. "I'd like speak to Trent for a minute—alone."

"Certainly," Taylor said.

Alexa noticed the way Taylor glanced at Trent before she left. She could tell that Taylor didn't just love him—she was *in* love with him. She wanted to be angry with both of them, but after hearing their stories, she decided it wasn't their fault that they'd been thrown together.

Alexa wasn't sure how Trent felt about her, and sadly, she didn't know what she could do to change things or if she should even try. If Trent still wanted to marry her, she knew that Taylor would still be in his thoughts. The general and Melissa were right. This was complicated and confusing.

Alexa knew that Trent may never lead a normal life again, even if he was released from the facility. Could she handle living with the fear of him being abducted and not being able to help him? She'd have to give that some thought.

Alexa said, "Taylor, wait a minute." She turned to General Starke. "I think we all need some time to process what's happening."

"I expected that you would," Starke said. "I have other matters that need tending to, so I'll leave you with Colonel Endo."

"Trent, do you mind if we all go eat and talk later?" Alexa asked.

"I think it would be better if we all had a good breakfast," Trent replied.

Melissa said, "Follow me then."

Pink Level – 0715 hours

When Alexa walked into the private dining area, she noticed a man sitting alone. "Melissa, is that Dr. Maxwell?"

"Yes."

They walked to the table and sat down, and introductions were made.

"Melissa, when will Dr. Sanderson, Captain Su, and the FAA controller arrive?" Maxwell asked. "I'm anxious to ask Captain Su about her abduction experience."

"There's been another one?" Alexa said.

Melissa sighed, then said, "Yes, two women were aboard an aircraft. Both women are Air Force captains. Captain Wood was the one you witnessed returned last night. Capt. Tai Su will be flying in later."

"Where and when did it occur?" Marvin asked.

"Yesterday afternoon, between the Bahamas and the east coast of Florida."

"Why bring the FAA controller here?" Trent asked.

"Brett Stone was the same controller that spoke to you when you disappeared and when you returned. We need to debrief him fully."

"And you want him to understand how important it is to keep his mouth shut," Alexa said.

"That's part of it," Melissa replied.

"Have you determined if Captain Wood has a neural implant?" Trent asked.

"I haven't had the opportunity yet," Melissa replied.

"I'd like to speak with Captain Wood when she's alert," Maxwell said.

"I'll let you know as soon as she's conscious and can handle questions."

"How'd the aliens find the facility?" Marvin asked.

"They probably followed Trent here. Dr. Maxwell, why don't you fill them in on what it is that you do. I know everyone is curious."

"I'd be happy to. I'm an astrophysicist. I was a professor at MIT, but now I do research for the government. Quantum mechanics mostly. I'm exploring gravitational time dilation at the quantum level."

Trent said, "Please explain that further."

"Do you have a background in physics?" Maxwell asked.

"Basic stuff," Trent answered.

"Then I'll keep this simple. Einstein's special theory of relativity."

"Oh, good, the easy stuff," Trent joked.

Maxwell smiled, then said, "Let's just say that it deals with a relationship between space and time. Time dilation tells us that time moves slower when a person is moving, especially as we approach the speed of light." He spent the next several minutes explaining the difference of elapsed time between two events as measured by different observers.

"Is time different on a quantum scale?" Alexa asked.

"Good question. It depends on what time we're observing."

Melissa said, "Haven't many philosophers argued that the passage of time is associated with one's own reality?"

"That's true," Maxwell said. "Some philosophers have held that the past and future aren't real. Some postulated that the past is real, but it's different from what we'll believe is real in the future. The present is only dependent on one's point of view."

"That's deep," Marvin said.

Maxwell nodded, then said, "Yes, but fitting for our discussion. Studies using an atomic clock have been done that show the time kept aboard the International Space Station is actually different from the time recorded on Earth. It's an incredibly small difference, but it's detectable. In addition, the strength of a gravitational field can slow the passage of time when observed by someone outside of a field. For example, the gravitational field around a black hole is extraordinary, and we believe that it's strong enough to create time dilation."

Alexa rubbed her forehead, then said, "My understanding of black holes is that anything near an event horizon will be shredded by its gravity. Black holes eat stars and planets or anything else that falls into their gravitational grasp."

"Correct," Maxwell said. "Perhaps the aliens have developed a technology which allows them to create a gravitational field, enabling them to make small jumps in time. It's also possible that Trent and Taylor are living in a different multiverse. We have many questions that need to be answered."

"Okay, you've lost me," Marvin said. "I thought there was no such thing as time travel. Time is supposed to be linear and not reversible. Everything in the universe began after the Big Bang nearly fourteen billion years ago. The clock, so to speak, started running from zero and continues to move forward."

"In a relativistic context, that is true," Maxwell said. "It's known as the 'arrow of time.' It's supposed to point in only one direction and follow the Second Law of Thermodynamics. Entropy, or disorder, always increases in a closed system as a result of the system's entanglement with the environment. But on a quantum level, our understanding of time as it relates to entanglement and entropy is being altered. Time can't be separated from the other three dimensions of space, but recent experiments have shown that the arrow of time *can* be reversed on a quantum level. The phenomenon is called 'Quantum Arrow.' In addition, the results of some experiments I've conducted indicate that the phenomenon can be applied on a macro scale."

Maxwell leaned forward in his chair. "If we put our Euclidean symmetry way of thinking away, spacetime can be viewed by using a displacement vector. In any given spacetime, an event occurs at a specific point." Maxwell took out a pen, drew a straight line on his napkin, and slid it to the middle of the table.

"This line represents spacetime." He then drew dots along the line. "These points represent events. The unification of all these dots is linear along this spacetime path. But spacetime doesn't have to be linear. As I said, it's really the observer that chooses when the event occurs." He folded the napkin until two of the dots touched. "These events can occur at the same time, but in different spacetimes."

"I'm getting a headache," Marvin said.

"You asked," Maxwell said, then chuckled. "Think of it as a spacetime interval."

"Yeah, that really helps," Marvin said.

"In general relativity, spacetime is curved by matter, but it is also smooth and continuous. In special relativity, spacetime can be noncurved or flat, and as I explained, time slows as speed increases as seen from another reference point. This slowing is time dilation."

Trent said, "All you're saying is that the spacetime continuum is perceived differently by each observer depending on where they view the event and at what speed they are traveling relative to the event."

"Exactly. It also takes a great deal of energy to alter the spacetime continuum. The gravitational energy around a black hole can create time dilation. Anything within that field will be shifted in spacetime, and possibly dimensionally within the quantum field. Theoretically, a mass could move into a different multiverse, instead of being destroyed. Enough energy could even create a cosmic dilation that isn't spatial or temporal, possibly something we've never thought of or detected."

"By mass, do you mean people or things?" Taylor asked.

"Both."

"You're talking about M-theory, aren't you?" Trent said.

"To some extent," Maxwell replied. "In my research I've been exploring the geometry of spacetime while focusing on quantum gravity."

"So we're talking about things that are only theoretically possible," Alexa said.

"I can't go into that," Maxwell replied, then winked at her. "String theory predicts that there could be as many as twenty-six different dimensions, while M-theory limits that number to eleven—ten spatial and one temporal. Any more than four dimensions requires that we look for them at the subatomic level. If the energy field that captured Trent and the other abductees was created with the same amount of energy found around a singularity, time dilation could occur."

"But even if the aliens have the technology to create that kind of energy, how would anyone survive?" Marvin asked.

Maxwell said, "As long as a mass doesn't pass through the event horizon, it would be exposed to energy and gravity that could alter spacetime on a quantum level without being destroyed. It would be a fine line to control, but I can't help but wonder if the extraterrestrials are somehow tapping into the power of a quantum gravitational field. They could, in theory, move people through time or between universes within the multiverse. It's still conjecture, but based on current events, I have a feeling it's true."

"So we could be in two places at the same time?" Taylor said.

"I think it's more complicated than that," Maxwell said. "Just before breakfast, I received a call from a colleague at the Hanford LIGO station. Melissa, I haven't even told the general about the call. May I tell them what I know?"

"We should wait for the general to clear it," Melissa said.

"You've got to be kidding me!" Taylor cried. "We're so deep in classified shit now, anything else we hear isn't going to matter."

"Nevertheless, the general has the final authority," Melissa said. "Give me a moment." Melissa excused herself.

Alexa looked at everyone. "I don't know about you all, but I would like to eat. All this thinking is making me even hungrier."

Everyone laughed.

A server came to the table and took their orders.

"Professor, can you tell us what LIGO does, if it's not classified?" Alexa asked.

"It's not. LIGO stands for Laser Interferometer Gravitational-Wave Observatory. It measures gravity waves created by very large masses."

"We're back to black holes, aren't we?" Alexa said.

"Afraid so. Hopefully, I'll be able to tell you all about what I've learned. It may clarify some things for you."

Fifteen minutes later, General Starke and Melissa walked into the dining room just as breakfast arrived.

"Colonel, we ordered for you," Maxwell said. "Sorry, general, we didn't know you'd be joining us."

"I've eaten, thanks," Starke said. "Hank, the colonel tells me you have information you received earlier from LIGO. I see no reason not to disclose it to everyone."

Maxwell said, "Okay. A colleague at Hanford LIGO advised that at 0105 hours MST, they recorded a gravity wave that coincided with the event that took place here. I'm assuming that would be Captain Wood's arrival."

Starke nodded.

"LIGO has confirmed several events that have occurred over the last few weeks. Gravitational bursts, all within Earth's atmosphere, and they correspond to the times of the abductions and the returns." Maxwell took a bite of his toast.

"You think these beings can control that much energy?" Starke asked.

Maxwell swallowed and said, "I've been working on a project that could produce a gravitational wave on the same magnitude as a black hole. It could transport people along a quantum spacetime continuum."

The others at the table appeared stunned by his revelation.

"You've been busy," Starke said. "Tell us."

"The technical aspects are highly classified."

"What isn't?" Starke replied. "If it's relevant to our discussion, we need to know."

"Very well. Are you familiar with a white hole?"

Only Melissa indicated that she was.

Maxwell said, "Instead of pulling everything into a gravity well like a black hole, a white hole produces a focused burst of energy. On a quantum level, the gravitational field acts like a tiny black hole, and the white hole pushes mass away. In theory, both produce the energy needed to cause a spacetime dilation. In fact, some theoretical scientists believe that white holes are responsible for generating the expansion force in our universe."

"So the Big Bang was caused by a white hole?" Marvin asked.

"Possibly," Maxwell said. "There could be other reasons our universe exists. Perhaps quantum energy was generated from another dimension that broke through the fabric of space and time, which caused a cosmic blast." He took a sip of his coffee, then added, "I think the light that you all witnessed may have been an alien-generated quantum white hole."

General Starke tipped his head back as if in thought.

Alexa took a moment to reflect on what Maxwell had said. If Trent had been transported through time and had fallen in love with Taylor in a different time, she certainly couldn't fault him for loving her. Trent was an honest man—a good man—which was why she'd fallen in love with him. She imagined that he'd be the same person regardless of the time or dimension. If Trent and Taylor were destined to be together, or were together, there was nothing she could do to change it.

She looked across the table at Taylor. It was obvious that Taylor cared for Trent. Alexa decided her jealousy wasn't going to make any difference in what happened between them. They shared a strong connection.

Alexa said, "Trent, Taylor, I apologize for my behavior earlier. I'm sorry. There's an element at work here that's blurring the normal lines, and I'm having a hard time working through my feelings. Taylor, I know this has to be hard on you, considering you have a husband and child waiting at home. I'm not a psychologist, and I'm not sure one would be able to sort it all out anyway."

Taylor nodded, then said, "Trent, in this time, isn't mine, but I do have strong feelings for him. Like I said earlier, I also love my family. Are you willing to help us work through this together?"

"I'm willing to try," Alexa said.

"Happy to hear you've come to an understanding," Starke said. "If Hank is correct about the aliens being able to generate a type of focused energy comparable to that found around a black or white hole, we'll need to rethink our defenses. He turned to Melissa. "Wherever Trent, Taylor, and Wood are, I want security to be nearby at all times."

"I don't think any of our plans to deal with the aliens will work," Melissa said. "Our best hope is to establish contact through Trent and Taylor."

"What about Marvin and me?" Alexa asked.

"Your quarters are next to Trent and Taylor," Starke said. "Security will be outside your doors."

"Trent, I'm okay with Taylor sharing your bedroom, platonically," Alexa said. "From what I've heard, your shared closeness may help us find out what your visions mean. We still need to talk though."

Trent said, "Thanks for understanding, and we will talk. I need to figure out what's happening to me, and Taylor is the key."

"I'll try to keep my hands off of him," Taylor joked.

Alexa gave her a weak smile, then said, "Taylor, you know that I'm still in love with Trent. I want what's best for him. If it turns out that you're the one he needs, then so be it. I don't want to be loved out of a sense of guilt."

"Alexa, I want what's best for Trent as well. Somewhere out there we're together, and we have a child. We need to figure this out."

Starke said, "Enough. Wherever Trent goes in the facility, I want either Taylor or Alexa to be with him, along with a security detail. Sanderson should be back soon with Captain Su."

"Do we have any updates on Captain Su or the controller?" Melissa asked.

"Sanderson left word that they'd be back earlier than expected. Colonel, Trent's and Captain Wood's tests can be run by the medical teams. I want you to get some rest. That's an order."

"Yes, sir."

PART THREE

"There is no difference between time and any of the other three dimensions of space except that our consciousness moves along it."

H. G. WELLS

SIXTEEN

"The neural implant has grown even more?" Trent asked in dismay.

"Yes, one of the tentacles is slightly longer and it's shifted position," the technician replied.

"Shifted. It's still in the prefrontal cortex though, right?"

"Yes. It's still where it was, but one of the tentacles is at a different angle."

Alexa squeezed his hand. She and Taylor had been with him for his last series of tests. "What does that mean?" Alexa asked.

"I'm not sure," the technician replied. "Colonel Endo will need to determine what it means."

"What about Captain Wood?" Taylor asked. "Does she have a neural implant?"

"Yes. It's also in her prefrontal cortex," the technician replied. "It's positioned differently from Trent's, and the tentacles are farther apart."

"Is she still unconscious?" Trent asked.

"Yes, and we don't know why. All of her vitals are normal. Her EEG and AMRS indicate normal brain activity. It's very odd."

"Can we see her?" Trent asked. "Melissa asked me if I knew her. The name isn't familiar, but if I saw her, I'd know for sure."

"I'll check with General Starke, and if he approves, I'll make the arrangements."

"Thank you."

The technician left the room.

"At least we know you aren't the only one with a neural implant," Taylor said. She joined Alexa at Trent's bedside. "I wonder if I would have one if they had found me again."

"Probably," Trent replied. "Maybe we knew Captain Wood in another time. Maybe the aliens need us to make contact with her again for some cosmic reason."

"Why would they have returned Captain Su to the plane?" Alexa asked.

"She wasn't taken as a child like we were," Taylor said. "Maybe she doesn't have a role in the future and was just an unlucky bystander."

The technician returned and said, "General Starke gave permission for you to visit Captain Wood. We'll have to go down to Red Level to see her."

They entered the restricted medical area on Red Level and walked down the main corridor. Trent felt a tingling sensation creeping over his skin as they approached Captain Wood's room. Then all the hairs on his body stood up, as if he'd been statically charged. He stopped at the door and said, "Wait. Something's wrong."

"What's with your hair?" Alexa asked.

"No one move," the technician ordered. "I need to notify General Starke before we proceed." She ran to a wall phone and made the call. Just then the door to Captain Wood's room opened slowly, and a nurse backed out. She looked pale.

"Something weird is happening in there," the nurse said.

"What's wrong?" Trent asked.

"Captain Wood's forehead is glowing, and every hair on her body appears to be electrically charged." When she saw Trent, she backed away from him. "You have the same charge without the glowing forehead. What the hell is happening?"

The medical technician ran back and joined them. "General Starke is on his way. Colonel Endo has been notified. I was ordered not to let you into Captain Wood's room. And no one is to touch Trent."

A minute later, Trent heard the sound of someone running toward him. He turned and saw Starke. *For an old guy, he moves pretty good,* Trent thought.

"What do we have?" Starke asked as he gave Trent a once-over.

"Captain Wood's hair looks just like his, and her forehead is glowing," the nurse said.

"How do you feel?" Starke asked Trent.

"I feel fine." He saw Melissa walking briskly down the corridor with a video technician behind her. Melissa wore pajamas, her hair was a tangled mess, and she had dark smudges under her eyes.

"I ordered you to get some sleep," Starke said.

"I did sleep," Melissa replied. "Trent, are you okay? Tell me what you're feeling."

"Like I told the general, I'm fine. It's just my hair is standing on end like I'm in zero gravity."

"I can see that," Melissa replied.

The nurse told Melissa about Captain Wood's condition.

"Keep Trent out here," Melissa said. "In fact, I want Trent in another room." She pointed at the video technician and said, "You're with me."

The video technician was a small Asian man. Trent judged him to be in his thirties, and by the look on his face, he really didn't want to go into Wood's room. The nurse yelled down the corridor, saying she needed another room opened immediately. Additional medical staff hurried toward Captain Wood's room, one of them pushing an assortment of medical scanners. They all rushed through the doorway after Melissa.

When Melissa returned to the corridor, she said, "Trent, have you been in to see Captain Wood?"

"No."

A door snapped open several doorways down and on the other side of the corridor from Captain Wood's room. "Is that for us?" Trent asked, as Melissa circled around him slowly without touching him, examining him.

"Yes," Melissa replied. "Let's get you down there."

Melissa escorted Trent to his room. Alexa and Taylor followed. Another medical technician hurried toward him with another scanner. "More tests?" he asked.

"What do you think?" Melissa replied. "Taylor, you and Alexa stay out here."

Once in the room, Melissa had the technician begin Trent's scan.

"This imaging machine maps electromagnetic fields," Melissa said. "And judging by what I see, you're connected to a strong field. The question is, what's producing it?"

"I don't know how I could have created it," Trent said.

"Taylor, can you hear me?" Melissa called through the door.

"Yes," Taylor replied.

"Come in here."

After Taylor entered the room, Melissa had the technician scan her.

Afterward, Melissa said, "Nothing's going on with you."

There was a loud crack, and a force pulled Trent toward the door. He grabbed a bedrail next to where he was standing. "What the hell is going on?" he shouted.

Melissa picked up the electromagnetic scanner and pointed it at the doorway. A horizontal electrical tornado appeared on the screen. It spun into Trent's room from the hallway.

Melissa followed the charged particles. "It's growing stronger the closer I get to Wood's room. That's interesting. Trent, how strong of a pull are you feeling?"

"It's a healthy tug, but I don't feel as if I'm going to be sucked into a vortex. I can still maintain my balance."

"What's happening to Trent?" Alexa said, looking concerned.

"He's being pulled toward Wood's room by an electromagnetic field," Melissa replied. "From what I'm seeing, you and the general are standing in the middle of the electrical stream. Are either of you feeling anything?"

"I'm not," Alexa replied.

"Me either," Starke said.

"General, I suggest you move down the corridor, away from Wood's room," Melissa said. "Everyone else, clear the hall. Trent, follow me."

"It's getting stronger," Trent said as he exited his room.

"It certainly is," Melissa said.

As Trent entered Wood's room, he caught a glimpse of the screen on the monitor that Melissa was holding. Wood's room was ablaze with vivid colors that reached out to the tornado whirling between them.

"How you doing, Trent?" Melissa asked.

"Feeling the amps," Trent replied. "The force of the tug has stabilized."

"The field strength is increasing the closer you get to Captain Wood."

Trent took two more steps into the room. Wood's legs were covered by a sheet. He took another step and saw her face. He blinked and shook his head. He tried to focus, but a buzzing noise filled his ears, and he was becoming confused. "I better not get any closer. Something is happening to me."

"Stay right there," Melissa said. "Somebody send for Dr. Maxwell."

"I'm feeling very strange," Trent uttered weakly.

"What do you mean by strange?" Melissa asked.

"There's a buzzing in my head. I don't know how much longer I can take it. I feel nauseous."

"Hang in there," Melissa said. "Can you take two more steps toward Captain Wood?"

Trent moved slowly, his legs feeling as if they weighed a thousand pounds. After those two steps, the dizziness increased, and it felt as if ants were crawling over his body. "Feeling much dizzier. Body is tingling."

The video technician took up a position where he could get a clear shot of both Wood and Trent.

"Taylor, come in here," Melissa shouted. When Taylor entered the room, Melissa asked, "Do you feel anything?"

"No."

Captain Wood's forehead glowed a pale orange. Then she opened her arctic-blue eyes and stared at Trent. Then it hit him.

"I know her!" he shouted. "I know those eyes. She was on Mars, younger, and I think she was a student in one of my classes."

The electromagnetic field vanished, and the glow on Captain Wood's forehead disappeared.

"I'm feeling much better now," Trent said.

"Where am I?" Wood said with a raspy voice.

Melissa approached the bed and took her hand. "You're safe, Captain Wood."

Wood looked around the room, then said, "I don't know this place, and I'm not Captain Wood."

"You're going to be fine, Captain Wood," Melissa said with a reassuring voice.

"I just told you that I'm not Captain Wood. I'm Dr. Stefanie Morgan."

Trent stepped closer to her. "I know you."

Her eyes grew wide. "Aiden, is that you? What are you doing here? You should be at Hecates Tholus Station."

Melissa said to the technician, "Keep recording."

Trent edged closer to Wood. Images flashed into his mind. He became unsteady on his feet. Taylor grabbed his arm to steady him. "Thanks, I'm good now."

Wood said, "Shona, what are you doing at Hadley?"

Trent struggled to stay in the present. The present here, not on Mars. He could see both places at the same time. His mind was swimming. He turned to Taylor and said, "Keep me here in this time."

Taylor clutched his arm and told him Alexa was still in the hallway.

When he focused on Alexa, the images of Mars slowly faded. "Better," he said. He turned toward the door. Professor Maxwell and Starke stood there, staring at him. Trent walked toward the door, his mind clearing. Taylor had kept him grounded in this time and place.

"Shona, Aiden," Wood said, "Are you going to answer me? What's wrong with you two? Who are these people?"

Trent took a deep breath and asked Starke, "Should I tell her?"

"Yes," General Starke replied.

"Stefanie, you're not on Mars, and neither are we."

She looked puzzled. "Okay, then where am I?"

"I need to ask you something first," Melissa interrupted. "What year is it?"

"It's twenty-one seventy-seven."

"Where do you think you are?"

"Well, Aiden said I wasn't on Mars, so I have no idea. Are we space-bound? Am I injured?"

"No," Trent answered, empathizing with her confusion.

"Where do you think you should be?" Melissa asked.

"I should be in the operational control center at Hadley Station. We just sent a team out for a three-day exploration and mapping mission. I was monitoring their progress toward the crater rim when . . . I woke up here."

"Where is the crater rim?"

"Don't be daft. It's the southern edge of Elysium Planitia."

"What do you do on Mars?" Melissa asked.

"I'm the project leader and commander of the Colony Four Mars exploratory team. I'm also the developmental coordinator for the region."

"Dr. Morgan, do you know Capt. Tai Su?"

"No. Is that someone new to the Colony Four Mars team?"

"No," Trent said. "I'm sorry, Colonel, but I need to tell her. That may shock her back."

"Go ahead."

"Stefanie, you're on Earth. Shona and I live on Mars, but it's in another time. You were abducted by an alien species, just like Shona and I were. Here you are Capt. Kimberly Wood. Shona is Taylor, and I'm Trent."

"What?" Wood said, gaping at them. "Is this a joke?"

"Do you remember Maya?" Taylor asked.

"Of course. She's your daughter, and she was one of the first to be born in Colony Four." Wood suddenly passed out.

Melissa checked her vitals.

"Trent, do you know Kimberly on Mars?" Maxwell asked.

"Yes."

"Taylor, do you recognize her?"

"No."

"EEG activity in the prefrontal lobe spiked while she was awake," Melissa reported. "They're normal now."

"Hank, it would appear your work is no longer theoretical," Starke said. "I have no doubt that we're looking at time dilation. The question is, are these alien encounters a threat to our national security?"

"I think the alien species is trying to educate us," Maxwell said. "I think they're preparing us for formal contact. They're demonstrating their technology and using these people as proof of their capabilities. Trent and Wood might be here so we can establish contact with them."

"That's one hell of a supposition," Starke said.

"Yes, it is. General, if they want to invade our world and conquer our species, I'm sure that would have happened by now. They wouldn't start taking people so overtly and returning them. They're trying to send us a message, and they're using Trent and Wood to get our attention."

"So now what do we do?" Melissa asked.

"Keep studying our guests," Starke replied. "I'm going up to my office to make some calls."

Melissa nodded, then ordered the video technician to leave the room.

After they left, Trent said, "I don't remember Kimberly as an adult. I don't know what she was talking about, but I sensed that it was real."

"I think it is," Melissa said. "You said you knew her when she was younger?"

Alexa entered the room. "Mind if I join you? I was listening."

"Not at all," Melissa said. "Trent, go ahead."

"I don't know how old for sure. I remember she was seated in front of Taylor in a classroom. It could have been the same classroom that I remember from when the window cracked."

"You're sure?" Taylor asked.

"Yes, the image was clear."

"I don't remember her," Taylor said. "Why would he remember her and I can't? I remember Trent."

"Both Trent and Kimberly were given neural implants. They must trigger the connection to the future world."

"This is far beyond anything I could have ever imagined," Alexa said. "Captain Wood knew both of you, and your daughter."

Trent nodded. "We're linked."

"I have a theory, if anyone is interested in hearing it?" Alexa said.

"Go ahead," Melissa said.

"Trent, Taylor, and Wood have to have been taken for a particular reason. They must all possess an attribute the aliens wanted to study, needed, or found conducive to some function they could perform in the other time. Captain Su must not have that trait."

"You think we were taken because of a particular genetic trait?" Trent asked.

"Exactly," Alexa replied. "Melissa, do they have any common DNA or genetic connection?"

"We have their DNA on file, but I haven't run a cross-comparison for any specific genome."

"I think Alexa may be on to something," Maxwell said. "We need to look for genetic similarities and traits."

Melissa said, "I'll order a complete comparative analysis on all of them. I haven't spoken to Dr. Sanderson about Captain Su. I don't have any of her test results. But as long as I'm doing comparisons, I think I should include her."

"Trent, how many students do you remember in the class on Mars?" Maxwell asked.

"I can't say for sure. Ten, twelve, maybe fifteen. Wood and Taylor are the only two that I know for sure. Maybe if I see other faces, I'll remember them." Trent thought for a moment, then said, "I think there's one thing for certain—they want us to be together, here and now."

"That's what I think, too," Melissa said. "Professor, I can see the wheels turning. What are you thinking?"

"That we're just beginning this journey."

"Shit!" Alexa said. "What time is it?"

"Twelve thirty-five," Melissa answered.

"I need to check in with Sue. I should have done that two hours ago. I need a phone."

"Come with me," Melissa said. "Trent, do you want to say hello to your old friend?"

"That'd be great."

Melissa ordered a medical team to stay with Wood, and then they headed for the Green Level.

Idaho City — 1245 hours

Dan paced in his motel room. He was considering notifying the authorities and spearheading a rescue attempt when the phone rang. He answered it and put the phone on speaker so Sue could hear the conversation.

"Jack, it's Alexa."

"You're late," Dan said. "I was getting concerned."

"I know. Many things have happened over the last few hours. Everyone is fine. Trent would like to say hello."

"Trent, is that you?" Sue said, moving closer to the phone.

"Yes, it's me. I'm fine. We all are. I can't thank you enough for everything you did and for being there for Alexa."

"Alexa was a wreck," Sue said. "So where are you?"

"I'm not at liberty to say. Just know that we're all being well cared for. Here's Alexa."

"Sue, I don't have much time, so I'll make it brief," Alexa said. "I want you and Jack to pack your bags and go home. I'll call you when everything is resolved."

Dan said, "Alexa, are you sure?"

"Yes. We're all fine."

"So you've said."

"I mean it. There are some things that we need to sort out before we can leave, and it would be best for all of you to go home. I'll contact you in a few days. In the meantime, you guys get some well-deserved rest. Jack, we'll settle the bill when I get back."

"I'll take it easy on you. Sue and I will leave tomorrow morning. I think we'll drive to home plate and fly back from there." Dan hoped Alexa would understand he was taking Sue back to Salt Lake with him.

"That sounds good. Stay out of the sun."

Dan knew Alexa understood. "How are you, Marvin, and Trent going to get back to Florida?"

"I have a feeling the military will give all of us a lift back to Orlando or Key West. I have to go. You both stay safe, and thanks again, for everything."

SEVENTEEN

Melissa finished examining Captain Su, then had her escorted to an interview room. As a precaution, Su had been brought to the biohazard lab for screening and, as expected, she had no implants, and all of her tests were negative. She had no signs of contamination from her alien encounter and neither did Gunnery Sergeant Radley and his team.

Unlike the others, Su didn't like being confined and tested, and she voiced her anger about everything that had happened to her, including being forced to come to the Sawtooth facility. For a member of the military, Melissa thought Su had displayed an unreasonably negative attitude during her examination. Su didn't mention anything about the abduction.

Melissa entered the interview room. Dr. Sanderson sat across the table from Su. The look on his face told her that Su's attitude had not improved.

"Am I interrupting?" Melissa asked.

"Not at all," Sanderson replied. "The captain was just expressing her displeasure about my continuing to question her about what has happened to her."

"I'm tired of being questioned when I don't have any answers," Su said, looking angry. "Can someone tell me what's going on? I don't remember anything happening to me. I can't account for the three hours that are missing from my life or what happened to Kim."

"Dr. Sanderson hasn't briefed you?" Melissa said, feigning ignorance.

"No, Colonel Endo, he has not. He's been asking me the same questions since we met in Florida, and I keep telling him the same thing."

"I understand your frustration, but repetitive questioning sometimes elicits new information," Melissa said. "How are you feeling?"

"Like I told you earlier, I'm fine."

"Good. Captain, you aren't going to like this, but I need you to tell me everything you can remember about Captain Wood's disappearance, again."

Su huffed. "Yes, ma'am. Like I told Dr. Sanderson, we were flying back from Treasure Cay in the Bahamas. We'd just checked in with a controller and had gotten permission to penetrate the ADIZ. Kim was the pilot-in-command. She was sitting in the left seat. I was in the right seat. Luggage and personal items were stowed in the cargo area and on the back seat. Will I be getting my things back?"

"Yes," Melissa replied. She looked at Sanderson. His expression hadn't changed since she'd sat down. He was focused on Su's responses. "Continue, please," Melissa said.

"I was watching the instruments when a brilliant, white light enveloped the cockpit. I closed my eyes. At first I thought it was the sun reflecting off of the windscreen. It only lasted a few seconds. When I opened my eyes, I felt Kim's absence before I saw her empty seat."

"What was your first thought?" Melissa asked.

"That she'd fallen out of the plane."

"Was the door open?"

"No. The lock bar was secure. I looked out the windows. It was an incredibly strange feeling."

"How so?" Melissa asked.

"I was watching the instruments, and we were in level flight. Except for the light, everything was the same."

"Is that when you contacted Miami control?" Melissa asked.

"Correct. I was confused. I hadn't heard the sound of the door opening, and you can only push the locking bar down if you're in the aircraft. I detected no change in sound. If you've ever cracked a window or opened a door in a small plane, it gets real loud.

"I advised Miami Center about her disappearing from the aircraft and said I was going to reduce altitude and circle the area. I couldn't imagine what had happened to her."

Melissa turned to Sanderson and asked, "You haven't told her yet?"

"No," Sanderson replied.

"Told me what?" Su asked.

"Captain Wood is alive," Melissa said.

"Where is she?"

"I'll tell you in a moment," Melissa replied. "Let's continue the debrief. When did you learn that you'd disappeared for three hours?"

Su shifted uncomfortably in her chair. "The controller told me when I contacted him. He sounded perplexed."

"What did you think?"

"I thought he had confused our aircraft with another one. I checked my watch and then the Hobbs meter to verify that I wasn't crazy. The time on my watch was consistent with the time when we'd checked in a minute earlier. The Hobbs meter was right where it should have been, and so was the clock on the instrument panel. I told the controller he was mistaken."

"What was his response?" Melissa asked.

"He said that he wasn't and that I had to leave the area immediately. He gave me the vectors to Ft. Pierce. When I told the controller that I was going to stay on station until the Coast Guard arrived, he insisted that I follow his instructions."

"And you refused."

"I did, but only for a few minutes. My friend was missing, and I wasn't going to leave her there. As I circled I realized the sun was lower in the sky than it should have been according to the time on my watch. A few minutes later, I was advised the Coast Guard was on the way to my location, and they needed the airspace to conduct their search."

"And that was when you left the area?"

"Yes. I flew on to Ft. Pierce. After landing I was directed to a special area at the far end of the field. Several rescue vehicles, ICE, a military vehicle, and the airport police were waiting for me."

"Did you say anything to them?"

"No. An Air Force lieutenant in military fatigues stepped forward and ordered me to stay in the aircraft."

"Then what?" Melissa asked.

"I called my base commander at Malmstrom and explained what had happened and where I was being held. He ordered me not to talk to anyone until I was debriefed at Patrick. I didn't say anything to anyone until I arrived at Patrick."

"Who did you talk to at Patrick?"

"The base commander interviewed me. He told me Kim was still missing and informed me that foul play had not been ruled out. I couldn't believe that anyone would think I'd harm Kim. The base commander left for a while, and when he returned he said someone was flying in to question me further. My first thought was that I was going to be interrogated by OSI, the Office of Special Investigations, and then be arrested. Even I was having a hard time believing that Kim had just disappeared. Several hours later, Dr. Sanderson came into the office and started asking me these same questions."

"I know all of this seems redundant, but like I said, sometimes small things are remembered after going over a story several times," Melissa said. "What do you think happened on the plane?"

Su lowered her head and rubbed her neck. "With all of the secretiveness and military presence, I wondered if we'd flown through a military weapons test area and had been struck by a particle beam. But I kept coming back to Kim not being there. Then, and don't laugh, I thought maybe it was a Bermuda Triangle event."

"An interesting supposition," Melissa said. "Do you ever use drugs?"

"Never. May I ask a question?"

"Certainly."

"I know that I'm in a secret military instillation under a mountain somewhere in Idaho. There was a civilian onboard my C-17. I wasn't allowed to engage in conversation with him, but I could tell he was spooked. So what's going on, and where is Kim?"

"She's here," Melissa replied.

"How did she get here?"

Melissa ignored the question. "Dr. Sanderson, do you have any more questions?"

"Yes," Sanderson said. He leaned forward. "Captain, have you ever experienced any other unusual events in your life? Any other loss of time or strange encounters?"

"I already told you. No!"

Sanderson said, "Do you believe in alien life?"

"Yes. I believe there are other life forms in the cosmos. There's too many worlds for there not to be life out there. Where is this going?"

Melissa straightened, then said, "What if I told you that an alien life form was responsible for taking Captain Wood off of your plane?"

"Are you saying we were abducted by aliens? That's ridiculous."

Melissa knew that Su was a scientist at heart. Her math and physics background compelled her to demand proof. She watched Su's brown eyes dart back and forth between her and Dr. Sanderson. She was waiting for further explanation.

"This is some kind of a psychological test, isn't it?"

"Captain, did Kim ever tell you about being abducted by aliens when she was a child?" Melissa asked.

"No. Never."

"You're certain."

"Yes. I'd remember her telling me something like that. She'd probably lose her security clearance if she said that to the wrong person."

"Dr. Sanderson, is there anything else you'd like to ask the captain before I tell her what's going on?" Melissa asked.

"No. Her statements have been consistent."

"Captain, we have some additional medical tests that we want to run on you." Su opened her mouth to speak, but Melissa raised her hand to keep her from complaining. "Before you get belligerent, let me finish. These tests will give us additional baseline data. When I'm finished telling you what has happened, I'm certain that you'll want the tests done."

"You have my attention."

Melissa showed Su the images of their airplane surrounded by the light and told her that Captain Wood had been returned to the facility by the same light. She told her about Trent being abducted and his return, about the implants, and finally about Taylor's abduction history, Mars, and the time dilation theory.

"That's an incredible story. Kim thinks she's living on Mars sometime in the future or in another universe?"

"Yes," Melissa answered.

"All of this is hard to believe. I want to see her."

"Let's get your tests done, and then I'll take you to her."

Sanderson stood and said, "By the way, the civilian you saw on the aircraft is the air traffic controller you were communicating with at Miami Center. His name is Brett Stone. He was also the controller that was involved when Trent McDougal's plane disappeared and when it returned." He looked at Melissa and added, "After everything that's happened over the last eighteen hours, I'd say bringing him here wasn't necessary."

Melissa nodded. "I have to agree. I think we can start working on sending Deputy Griffin, Agent Dobson, and Stone back home. Have you told Stone why he's here?"

"Not entirely, but I'm sure he has a good idea. I need to give him his orientation."

"Will he be a problem if we keep him in the dark?"

"I don't think so," Sanderson said. "He's former military."

"Captain, you'll be staying with us for a while," Melissa said. "Your commanding officer will be informed that this was a black op. Your family, friends, and anyone else who learns that you've disappeared will be given a cover story. Everything you see here is classified. Clear?"

"Yes, ma'am. If what you're telling me is true, then I have a lot more questions. Will I have an opportunity to speak freely with you later?"

"Of course. We'll have lots of time to get to know each other."

Altair Annex — Pink Level — 1715 hours

"Mr. Stone, this is where you will eat," Dr. Sanderson said as they walked into the cafeteria. "It's open all day, and you can order anything on the menu."

"It's free?"

"Yes." Sanderson scanned the dining room for a table. "Oh, that's good timing. I see some people I'd like you to meet." They walked over to a table where Agent Dobson and Deputy Griffin were sitting. He introduced Brett Stone to the two men.

"Another volunteer?" Griffin asked.

"Yes," Sanderson replied. "I have pressing business. Can you gentlemen get Mr. Stone acclimated? He's staying on Gold Level. His room is next to both of yours."

"Certainly," Dobson said.

"Thank you." Sanderson walked away.

"Brett, have a seat," Griffin said. "How'd you get sucked into this mess?"

"I'm an air traffic controller from Miami. I had two planes mysteriously disappear from my radar and then reappear. I'm not completely sure why I was brought here."

Griffin said, "Two planes?"

"Yes. One was gone for three weeks, and another earlier today for a few hours."

"The one aircraft sounds like Trent McDougal's plane," Dobson said.

"It was Trent McDougal's plane," Stone said. "Is he here?"

"Yes," Dobson replied. "Tell us about the other plane."

Stone told them what he knew and about there being a woman on the plane with him.

"Interesting," Griffin said. "And since you were the primary controller when both aircraft disappeared, they needed to bring you here to impress upon you the need to stay quiet about what you know."

"Are we talking alien encounters?" Stone asked.

"What do you think?" Griffin replied.

"What's your involvement?" Stone asked.

"Nothing now," Griffin replied. "I interviewed McDougal's friends in Key West, and because I knew that Trent had returned, I was brought here."

Dobson said, "I was assigned to babysit McDougal when he landed in Key West and was sucked into this investigation."

"How long have you both been here?" Stone asked.

"Since the day that Trent reappeared," Dobson said. "We don't know much else. We've been cooped up in this annex since we arrived, and haven't been briefed on anything new. Your information about the second plane is interesting. Tell me about the other woman that was with you on the plane."

"I don't anything about her. We were put on the plane together and told not to talk. When we got here, she was taken someplace else. I presume she was the pilot I spoke to over the radio. On the radio, she kept insisting that her friend had fallen out of the plane."

"She's probably in the Nova annex," Dobson said.

"There's another facility like this one?" Stone said.

"Yes," Dobson replied. "We haven't been allowed in there."

"Did Dr. Sanderson give you any idea how long you'd be detained?" Griffin asked.

"No. He told me to keep my mouth shut."

"They say that a lot here," Griffin said.

"I'm assuming speaking to both of you is alright since he introduced us."

"I believe that's a correct assumption," Dobson said.

"What happens now?" Stone asked.

"We sit and wait," Dobson replied.

Captain Wood's room — 1730 hours

Melissa had just finished her medical scan of Su's brain when a medical technician contacted her. "Yes?"

"Captain Wood moved her arms and legs," the technician said.

"Excellent." Melissa decided to take Su with her to see Wood.

When they got to Wood's room, Melissa said, "Captain, please wait in the hallway until I call for you. You may listen to our conversation at the door if you like."

"Thanks. Were my tests alright?"

"Yes. You don't have any implants, and all of your other tests were negative."

"That's good to know."

Maxwell, Sanderson, and General Starke approached them. Su snapped to attention.

"Stand easy, Captain Su," Starke said, then introduced her to Maxwell.

"Colonel, how is Captain Su?" Starke asked.

"She's medically cleared," Melissa replied. "No implants, and she's been fully briefed. I thought it would be good to have her here. Captain Wood may recognize her and come back to reality. Professor Maxwell, you're aware that Captain Su graduated from Stanford with degrees in physics and math. I think she may have some questions for you. Would you mind waiting in the hallway with her?"

"Not at all," Maxwell replied.

"Let's see how the patient is doing," Dr. Sanderson said, sounding impatient. He walked into the room ahead of Melissa and Starke.

Melissa had just finished checking Wood's vitals and her latest EEG when Wood's eyes snapped open.

"Captain Wood, it's nice to have you back," Melissa said. "How are you feeling?"

"I feel more alert. I remember you. You're a doctor."

"Yes, I am. This is Dr. Sanderson, and the man behind me is General Starke."

Wood stared at each of them, then said, "I don't know anyone by the name of Wood except my great-great-grandfather. I've also never heard of Dr. Sanderson or General Starke. I'm Dr. Stefanie Morgan. Where's Aiden and Shona? I know they were here earlier, but they weren't making any sense."

Melissa nodded, then said, "Your latest EEG indicated normal brain activity, which I find interesting considering your neural implant."

"What are you talking about? What implant?"

"Dr. Morgan, I have some questions," Sanderson said. "Would you mind answering them after Colonel Endo finishes her examination?"

"That's fine. Tell me about the implant you claim I have in my head."

Melissa noted Wood's pupils responded to the light, and her blood pressure was only slightly elevated, which was understandable under the circumstances. She stood back and said, "The neural implant is located in the prefrontal cortex of your brain. There's another implant in your left tibia, which you received as a child during an alien abduction."

"What? I wasn't abducted by aliens."

"Captain Su, will you please join us?" Melissa said in a loud voice.

Su entered the room and walked to Wood's bedside. She looked concerned about Kim's reaction, or rather her lack of reaction.

"Say something to her," Sanderson instructed.

"Kim, I'm glad you're okay. I was really worried about you."

"Who are you?" Wood asked.

"It's me, Tai Su. We're friends. Don't you remember flying to Treasure Cay? We were flying back from the Bahamas when you disappeared."

Wood made no sign that she recognized Su.

"Don't you recognize your friend?" Melissa asked.

"No. Who are you people? This is crazy."

"This may be hard to believe, but you and Captain Su were abducted by extraterrestrials while flying back to Florida from the Bahamas," Melissa said. "They took you off your aircraft, then returned you to us here in Idaho."

"What the hell are you talking about? I've never been to the Bahamas, and I don't know this woman."

"You have no recollection of your abduction, not even your encounter with an intense light?" Sanderson asked.

"I don't know anything about an abduction," Wood replied. Her forehead began to glow a pale orange, and her blue eyes clouded over.

Melissa said, "I don't know what's happening. Send in the trauma techs."

"Is this what happened last time?" Sanderson asked.

"Not exactly. Unlike Trent, I don't think her mind can handle the shock of existing in two worlds at the same time."

A moment later, the glow on her forehead faded. Wood blinked rapidly several times, then shook her head as if she was trying to clear her mind. Melissa noted a spark of recognition when Wood saw Su.

"Tai, is that you?" Wood asked.

"Yes. You're safe, Kim." Su took her hand.

Wood looked at everyone in the room, then back at Su. "Did we crash?"

"No, Captain Wood, you didn't crash," Melissa said.

"I don't understand. Why am I in a hospital bed?"

Melissa saw that she was becoming anxious. "Kim, you are perfectly safe, and you're going to be fine. I'm Dr. Endo."

The glow returned to her forehead. "How many times do I have to repeat myself? My name is Stefanie."

Wood's heart monitor beeped rapidly. Her eyes darted back and forth, then locked on to Su. Her head tilted to the side, and the glow on her forehead grew brighter. Melissa could see the outline of Wood's brain through her skull. She didn't need an imaging machine to see the implant. It was glowing bright orange now, like a lightbulb filament. Suddenly it went dark, and Wood started convulsing. Then she coded. As alarms sounded, Melissa ordered everyone from the room.

"I'm not leaving her!" Su cried.

"You're in the way," Melissa said. "Get out!"

For the next thirty minutes Melissa and the medical team tried to resuscitate Wood, but it proved pointless. When the implant had darkened, her brain activity ceased. Melissa decided not to put her on life support. She hoped that Wood had found peace, at least in this life.

When Melissa left the room, she found Starke, Sanderson, and Su waiting for her. "Captain Wood is dead," Melissa said.

Su burst into tears.

"What happened?" Starke asked.

"I don't know. I'll perform an autopsy as soon as I can. I'm hoping to get a look at the brain implant before it dissolves. It may give me some answers about how to get the one out of Trent's head."

"Could this happen to Trent?" Starke asked.

"I don't think so," Melissa replied. "Trent appears stable. They had Wood for less than a day, then dropped her in a hostile environment. It's possible that the shock was too much for her body and mind to handle, or maybe the implant malfunctioned."

"Do we tell Trent what's happened?" Sanderson asked.

"We have to," Starke said. "He and Taylor were asking about her. Melissa, I'll deliver the news while you get started on the autopsy."

"What about Su?" Sanderson asked, gesturing toward the distraught woman, who had moved away from them and was leaning against a wall.

"After we tell everyone about Wood's death, she can join them," Starke replied. "She's an abductee. As I said before, billet her in the Nova annex, Gold Level, with the others."

Sanderson and Starke left. Melissa couldn't help but wonder if she had missed something. She stepped up to Su and said, "Would you like a moment with your friend?"

"Please," Su replied.

A few minutes later, Melissa returned to Wood's room and found Su holding Wood's hand. With her head bowed, Su chanted what sounded like a prayer in Chinese.

When Su was finished, Melissa said, "What did you say?"

Su looked back at her, tears streaming down her face. "It's an ancient Taoist saying. I said, 'returning to the source is stillness, which is the way of nature. The way of nature is unchanging.' I learned it when I was young."

"You're a Taoist?"

"My grandmother was Vietnamese, and she followed Buddhist teachings. My grandfather was Chinese, and he followed the Tao, the Way. I guess you could say I'm spiritual. I tend to blend Buddhism with Taoism. I felt that I should say something to help Kim on her journey."

"I'm sorry for your loss," Melissa said. "You and Kim must have been close friends."

"Yes. We were."

"I don't remember reading anything in your file that indicated you were fluent in Chinese."

Su wiped the tears from her cheeks. "I know a little of both Chinese and Vietnamese. I understand more than I can speak. What happens now?"

"Now I try to find out why Kim died. Do you know her family?"

"I met her father once. Parents are divorced. She never talked about them. We became friends at officer training school. We both loved to fly, and even though our career tracks took us in different directions, we stayed in touch. I will miss her very much."

"I know you will."

"What are you going to do with her body after the autopsy?"

"It will be kept here. I don't think General Starke will allow it to be released to the family, at least not for a while."

"What will you tell her family and friends?"

"The general will provide a cover story."

Red Level – Biohazard Containment – 1930 hours

Melissa tried to save both of Wood's implants for further examination, but without success. Even though the neural implant was removed in a vacuum chamber, it stayed intact for only a minute. Fortunately, she was able to get good images of the devices. The leg implant dissolved faster than the neural implant, but she did get a few X-rays of it. Now it would be up to the bioengineering specialists to figure out what made them work.

She ordered Wood's body to be placed in cold storage, then went to meet Starke on Pink Level to brief him and to grab a bite to eat.

Pink Level — 1950 hours

"Learn anything?" Starke asked bluntly as Melissa sat down in a dining room chair.

"Enough to know that we don't know enough to mess with Trent's neural implant," Melissa replied. "I got some good images before both of Wood's implants dissolved. Keeping them in vacuum didn't help. Where are the others?"

"They left a few minutes ago. So what did you learn from the autopsy?"

"As I suspected, the tissue around the implant in her prefrontal cortex was severely damaged. I don't know if it was because the implant was in a slightly different position than Trent's or if the implant fried her neural circuitry. I'll know more after the med techs complete the brain dissection and examine the tissue more closely."

"How long?"

"We should have something by midmorning. How did Trent and the others take the news?"

"Not well. I could tell by the way Trent kept touching his forehead that he was waiting for his brain to explode."

"Can't blame the guy," Melissa said. "I don't think he has anything to worry about. Everything I've seen on his scans indicate the tissue around the implant is healthy. Is Su with the others?"

"She went back to Trent's and Taylor's room. Trent questioned her about the aerial abduction over dinner, and he wanted to ask her some more questions. I don't think he'll learn anything, because Su doesn't remember being taken. Maxwell and Sanderson decided to go upstairs with them. It appears Alexa and Taylor are getting along."

"Do you think we should tell Taylor's family anything?" Melissa asked.

"I believe we've been down this road. Emma is at a terrible age and I don't think she'll keep her beak shut if her mom magically reappears and tells her that she was held at a secret military facility after being abducted by aliens. Besides, I heard Rick was dating again."

"When did all this happen?"

"It was in the weekly security brief. Rick had a woman come to the house. The meeting between Emma and the new friend didn't go well. The woman left right after Emma went into a tirade. The surveillance detail said they saw Emma standing at the front window giving her the finger as she drove away."

"All the more reason to tell them now," Melissa said.

"No. I have a feeling that would only further complicate what I think is going to happen between Trent and Taylor."

Melissa said, "I'm not convinced Trent will leave Alexa."

"I think he will. He's curious about what the future holds. Now he's worried about the implant, which means he'll go where he thinks he'll make contact with the aliens in order to insure it doesn't explode."

"Do you think Trent's in love with Taylor?"

"I think in one life he is. They share something that Alexa will never be able to understand. Alexa's a tough cookie, but she won't want to stay cooped up in this mountain if I decide to keep Trent here indefinitely. Plus, Taylor and Trent have a child in the other life."

"Yes, Maya. Wood clarified some things for us before her unfortunate demise."

Starke yawned. "Let's not forget that the aliens may have something to say about their relationship. I believe they want Taylor and Trent together for some reason."

"General, I'm going to get some rest. I'll be in my quarters."

"Let's get started early tomorrow. I'd like you in my office at 0700 hours."

EIGHTEEN

Hangar Bay — February 06 — 0325 hours

Light exploded across the vast hangar area with such intensity that the two technicians working on Captain Wood's plane were nearly blinded. When the light disappeared, neither technician could see clearly. But what they heard scared them more than losing their sight. A child's blood-curdling screams came from the center of the hangar. The wails echoed off the hangar bay walls. Then the child's shrieks were suddenly lost in the blaring sound of the intruder alarms.

Red Level — 0325 hours

A thin beam of light snaked toward a metal door in the biocontainment area. As if by magic, the door opened, and the light expanded until it was the size of a basketball. It hovered over Captain Wood's body for a few seconds. As it swelled, two small brown alien beings emerged. They lifted Wood's body gently into the light, and in a flash they were gone. The only witness to the event was a security camera.

Trent's Room — 0325 hours

The sound of the alarms jolted Trent awake. He jumped out of bed and ran into the living room wearing a T-shirt and sweatpants. Taylor opened her bedroom door and stared at him. He rubbed his eyes as the intrusion alarms wailed a few more seconds. Then came the announcement. As he listened to it the phone rang. He picked up.

"Trent, this is Melissa. We have a situation. Gold Level and your apartment are sealed. I'm calling Alexa and sending her to you. You can unlock your door by using the TV remote. Just type in four sevens. Stay in the apartment."

Before he could ask any questions, the line went dead. He looked at Taylor. She was beautiful. "That was Melissa." He told her what Melissa said.

"Great," Taylor replied, walking into the living room wearing her blue uniform polo shirt and panties.

Taylor's auburn hair was unbrushed. She looked as if she'd been tossing and turning in bed. "I think you should put some pants on," Trent said.

Taylor looked down at herself and shrugged. "What time is it?" she asked.

"Almost three-thirty."

"This could take a while," Taylor said, shuffling toward the kitchen. "I may as well make coffee."

"Taylor, get dressed. Please."

"Really? It's not like I'm naked."

"Please," Trent said again. "Alexa will be here any minute."

Taylor slowly shook her head, then ambled back to her bedroom. A few moments later, Taylor returned to the room wearing uniform pants. Her shirt remained untucked. "Better?"

"Yes, thank you." He turned on the television. The only thing on was an intrusion announcement scrolling across the screen. It kept flashing "Condition X-Ray" every few seconds. He turned off the television.

There was a knock on the door. Trent typed in the unlock code. The lock made a distinctive *click* sound as it released. Alexa entered and sat down on the sofa. She was wearing the same uniform that Taylor wore.

"How the hell did you unlock the door?" Taylor asked.

"Melissa gave me a code," Trent said.

"She gave me one too," Alexa said.

"I've been here two years, and I've never been given a code to override the door lock," Taylor said.

"It must be serious," Trent said. "We're not supposed to leave the apartment."

"Do you think the aliens have come for you and Taylor?" Alexa asked.

"I don't know," Trent replied. "I think if they wanted to take me from here, they'd just take me like they have before. Captain Wood's death has me a bit rattled. I really thought Melissa and Starke would be able to protect us. I'm not so sure now."

"I don't think she was supposed to die," Taylor said, as she walked out of the kitchen carrying a cup of coffee. "I think she was sent here for a purpose. Maybe to confirm that Trent and I are husband and wife on Mars."

The phone rang. Taylor set her coffee mug on the credenza and answered it.

Trent and Alexa waited quietly as Taylor nodded and the color drained from her face. Her expression made Trent's heart race.

"Okay, Melissa, we'll see you here in a few minutes," Taylor said. She slowly put the handset back on the cradle.

"What is it?" Trent asked.

"We need to go meet our daughter."

"What?" Trent and Alexa said at the same time.

"The intruder is our daughter, and she's in the hangar, scared out of her mind. Get dressed. Now!"

Trent ran to his bedroom, changed into his uniform, and returned to the living room in record time. Taylor had tucked in her shirt and put on her shoes.

"Trent, didn't Melissa say not to leave the apartment?" Alexa asked. "I thought she was coming here."

"She did, but I think we should get down there. I can't imagine what that little girl is going through."

A moment later the door opened, and Melissa and Starke stood there.

"Is she still in the hangar?" Taylor asked, her voice strident and etched with concern.

"Calm down," Melissa said. "Yes, and she's safe. Biohazard protocols are in place, so the hangar is sealed." Melissa frowned and tilted her head slightly. "Taylor, do you remember Maya?"

"No."

"Then why are you so upset?" Melissa asked with a hint of skepticism in her voice. "You're acting as if you have a motherly attachment."

Taylor glared at her.

"How do you know it's Maya?" Trent asked, hoping to give Taylor a moment to recover.

"She told the men in the hangar that her name was Maya Cooper," Melissa replied.

"We need to go," Taylor said. She grabbed Trent's hand and pulled him out of the apartment. Melissa hurried to catch up with them, leaving Alexa standing with Starke.

"Alexa, I know this is difficult, but we need to let it play out," Starke said. He motioned for her to follow him.

Alexa nodded, closed the apartment door, and walked beside Starke down the hallway.

Hangar Bay – 0340 hours

Taylor and Trent stood in front of the sealed steel door to the hangar. Melissa and Alexa were next to them. Starke had ordered the hangar security camera feed to be sent to the monitor next to the hangar door.

"Open the door!" Taylor demanded. She looked at the monitor. "Trent, is that our daughter?"

Trent looked carefully at the image. The child was sitting on the floor in the center of the hangar surrounded by several people wearing biohazard suits. "Can we get audio?" Trent asked. A moment later, the sound of Maya's sobs burst through the speaker. Trent clutched his head and squeezed his eyes shut, stunned by a spike of pain. An image of the child flashed in his mind. "Yes, that's Maya."

"Trent, are you alright?" Alexa asked, taking his arm.

"I don't know." He dropped to his knees.

"She has my auburn hair," Taylor said, her voice cracking. "Trent, open your eyes."

When he did, the pain diminish. Memories flooded his mind—or were they just dreams? He clenched his eyes shut again and let the images take him.

When he opened his eyes, he was on Mars. Maya was sitting next to him. He'd saved her from a certain death after the airlock malfunctioned. He could feel the pain and the heartache of almost losing her. When that sensation and the image faded away, he found himself sitting on the floor. Taylor and Alexa were kneeling next to him.

"What happened?" Alexa asked.

"I went back to Mars," Trent said. "Seeing Maya must have triggered something. I remember now. I remember everything." Trent stood and shouted, "Open the damn door! She's not a threat or a biohazard. It's cold in the hangar and she's not dressed for it. She's freezing!"

"How do you know she's not a biohazard threat?" Melissa asked.

"Because I do. There are no biohazards on Mars, except what was taken to the planet from Earth. There's been no indication that contact with the aliens is an issue."

"Trent, is Maya the same age as the last time you saw her?" Melissa asked.

Trent looked at the monitor, then said, "Yes. I was with her just a moment ago. She was sitting next to me. Now open the damn door!"

"In a minute." Melissa turned to Starke. "General, where was the girl found?"

"I just reviewed the security footage. The light appeared in the center of the hangar and only lasted a second. Then the child started screaming hysterically and hasn't moved since."

"She doesn't know where she is," Trent said. "She knows that she can't survive outside on Mars. The hangar looks like a work area, and some of those areas aren't pressurized."

"You're suddenly remembering all of those details?" Starke asked.

"Yes. From an early age, children are trained not to venture outside of the modules without an adult. All vacuum door release buttons are covered and locked, and they're located at least five feet above floor level."

"More details," Starke said.

"Can we go get our daughter?" Taylor asked.

"Is the area secure?" Starke yelled.

"Yes, sir," a Marine responded.

"Open the door."

A moment later, the door locks retracted, and Trent ran into the hangar.

"Daddy!" Maya cried when she saw him.

Trent was by her side just seconds before Taylor got there. He picked her up off the cold floor and held her tightly. Her sobs turned to sniffles as she hugged him. Then Maya jumped into Taylor's arms. She locked her legs around Taylor's waist.

"Mommy," Maya whispered. "Where are we?"

Taylor stroked Maya's auburn hair.

When Trent turned around, Alexa was standing there.

"We should get her inside where it's warm," Alexa said.

They walked back toward the hangar security door where Starke and Melissa were standing. Taylor repeatedly told Maya everything was okay. That she was safe. He hoped that was true.

When they reached the door, Melissa stepped out, along with two medical technicians pushing a biocontainment gurney.

"Is that really necessary?" Taylor asked.

"I'll carry her to medical," Trent said, taking her into his arms.

"Very well," Melissa said.

"Colonel, we should follow established protocols," Starke said.

"General, with all due respect, I believe Trent is correct. The child isn't a biohazard. No one's health has been compromised by any alien encounter. I think it's more important to get Maya to Red Level."

"Very well," Starke said. "Just the same, I want the annex atriums and passageways cleared of personnel."

The general grabbed a phone and made an announcement, and everyone who had been standing in a common area disappeared. All of the doors on their level closed and sealed. Trent and the others hurried toward the elevators in the Nova annex.

Maya looked around, wide-eyed. "Where are we?" she asked again. "I don't recognize this place."

"You're safe," Trent said, hugging her tightly.

"I remember an airlock malfunctioned," Maya said. "I couldn't breathe, and I was scared. I remember going to medical. Then somehow I ended up here."

Trent said, "Pumpkin, we're in a very special place. We need to get you checked by the doctors." He nodded at Melissa. "This is Melissa. She's going to examine you."

"I don't want doctors to examine me."

"Maya, you have to be examined," Taylor said. "You've been through something that we need to understand, and your dad and I want to make sure you weren't injured. Can you do that for us?"

"I guess so," she replied.

They rode the Nova elevator up to Red Level, where they were met by additional medical staff in biohazard suits. Then they walked briskly to one of the exam rooms.

"Her clothing looks futuristic," Melissa said. "The fabric is strong."

"It's designed for work in a vacuum," Trent said. "All of our clothing is designed for safety, comfort, and durability, and it can be worn for work in the thin Martian atmosphere."

"Get a gown for her," Melissa ordered a nurse. "Take her clothes for analysis. Prep the lab and send for imaging."

Trent could tell that Maya was on the edge of panic. "Pumpkin, listen to me," he said. "They need to do some tests. Things will look different to you than what we have back at home. Your mom and I will stay with you the whole time. They aren't going to hurt you."

"Okay," Maya answered, running the back of her hand across her running nose.

A vision hit Trent again. He pictured Maya wiping her nose like that whenever she cried. Most kids used their palm, but she'd always used the back of her hand. He couldn't remember her ever being sick or having allergies. Her nose ran only when she cried. Maya was born on Mars, just as Captain Wood had said. There was no disease there, so Maya wouldn't have immunity to any of the diseases on Earth. Fear suddenly gripped him. Then his focus returned to the room.

"Where'd you go, Trent?" Melissa asked.

"She's Martian by birth," Trent said. "There are no biohazards on Mars, so she has no immunity to the diseases we have here. Medical advancements put an end to all known viruses. She's never received any vaccinations."

Melissa nodded in understanding. "We'll keep her isolated. Maya, do you know where you were born?"

"I was born at the Hecates Tholus Station Maternity Center on January 14, 2167."

"Where do you live?"

"Is that a trick question?" Maya answered, casting her first smile across the room.

"No," Melissa replied. "I need to know where you live."

Maya rolled her eyes. "Hecates Tholus Station, sublevel seven, Aldrin wing, white area."

Melissa took a step back. "Trent, that's where you told us you lived."

"Yes. I remember." Trent glanced back at the mirrored glass. He knew Starke was watching them from the observation room.

"Taylor, does any of this make sense to you?" Melissa asked.

Trent knew she didn't want to reply in front of Maya. He said, "Let's focus on Maya,"

"Okay," Melissa said. "You're right."

"Dad, why did the doctor call you Trent and Mom Taylor?"

"We'll explain everything as soon as the doctor finishes."

Melissa began her exam. Taylor took Trent's hand and squeezed it.

A few minutes later, Melissa said, "I need to draw blood and scan her for implants. I'm also going to have a DNA panel run."

"You want to be sure Maya is ours?" Trent asked.

"Among other things."

Maya screamed.

"What is it, Pumpkin?" Trent asked. Then he saw the hypodermic needle. "They have to take a little blood to check you out. You'll feel a little stick, that's all."

"That's not what we use at home. Where are we?"

Trent looked to Melissa for guidance.

"Maya, you're back on Earth," Melissa told her.

"How can that be? I don't remember spacing. I would remember that because I've never done it before."

"It's a very complex story," Trent said. "Mom and I will tell you all about it when they're done running your tests." It felt natural to call Taylor Mom.

"Are Trent and Taylor your Earth names?"

"Yes, they are," Taylor replied.

"Why don't I have one?"

"Because you're special," Taylor said.

Observation Room — 0400 hours

General Starke, Alexa, and Dr. Maxwell sat in the observation room discussing Maya's sudden appearance, and watching her interact with Trent and Taylor.

There was a knock on the door. When it opened, a Marine said, "General, you have an urgent call."

Alexa looked at Maxwell. He was smiling at her. She didn't know what warranted a smile. Maybe it was nervous energy from knowing he'd be left alone with her. Alexa didn't completely trust the academic. He seemed aloof, as if he knew something no one else did. She could hear Starke talking on the phone just outside the door.

"What?" Starke said with an annoyed tone. "When? You're absolutely sure? Secure the area and begin a search. Dead bodies don't just get up and walk away. Send me the security footage." He slammed the receiver into its cradle and returned to the room.

"I take it Wood's body has disappeared," Alexa said.

"That's what I've been told. First, Maya is delivered inside the facility, and now Wood's body has been snatched right out from under our noses. What do you make of all this, Hank?"

"I'm not sure," Maxwell replied. "Let me make a call. LIGO may have some new information for us. Will you excuse me?" Maxwell left the room.

Alexa looked through the two-way mirror into the medical treatment room and listened to Taylor and Trent talking. They looked as natural a couple as she could imagine. Maya was their daughter. She didn't need to see the DNA results. She could tell by the way Trent spoke to Maya and by how intimate his conversations with Taylor were that they were a family, or would be in the future. That was destined. Alexa needed to come to grips with the fact that Taylor and Trent shared something that could not be denied.

"General," Alexa said. "I know Trent better than anyone. I can see he believes Maya is his daughter. Look at Maya's features and hair color. She resembles Taylor. I'm sure they'll want her to stay with them after Melissa finishes her exams. Maybe the aliens brought Maya here to bring Trent and Taylor together in this time."

"Alexa, I agree that there must be a purpose behind their bringing Maya here. I'm bothered by the fact that the aliens penetrated the Nova annex."

"Which means they can come and go as they please, so Trent, Maya, and Taylor really aren't safe from being taken again."

"Unfortunately, that's correct. None of our security measures can stop them."

"I've never seen Trent act so parental. He went straight to Maya, and she ran to him. They have a bond." A tear slipped down her cheek. She wiped it away.

"Maybe I should leave the facility and let them get on with their lives. Is that possible?"

"It's possible, but I think it best you stay put for a while. The aliens could be testing them, and us." He nodded toward the window. "Perhaps they want to see if Trent chooses Taylor over you."

"How would they know I exist?"

"They had Trent for three weeks. He has a neural implant that I'm sure is feeding them intel. If they were able to penetrate our facility, I doubt our electronic dampers are preventing them from knowing what's happening here. Trust me, they know about you."

"What happens if Trent decides to stay here with me? It's possible that the aliens won't let him."

The general sighed, then said, "True. We'll just have to wait and see. Alexa, do you think Deputy Griffin can be trusted to keep his mouth shut if I cut him loose?"

Alexa shrugged. "You're asking me? I only met him a few times."

"I trust your judgement of character."

Alexa looked into the room again. Maya was still holding Taylor's hand. They'd finished the blood draw and the DNA swabs. "General, we've all experienced something quite out of the ordinary. Deputy Griffin strikes me as being trustworthy. I think he'd stay quiet for fear that you'd have him brought back here."

Starke nodded. "And if he opened his mouth, I would."

"Why not send everyone involved home?" Alexa suggested. "It would make things easier for you."

"You've read my mind. What about your friend, Marvin?"

"He should go. He won't want to leave, but he will if I insist."

"I'll make arrangements for them to be transported back to Florida."

"Marvin will want to stay close to Sue."

"So she's nearby?"

"Yes."

The general smiled a knowing smile. "I think your friend Jack is former Secret Service, lives locally, and is probably in the same line of work as you."

"He is. He's an old friend that's always willing to offer a helping hand. None of them will say anything about what they've seen or know. They're all very good at keeping secrets. They know the drill."

"You ever going to tell me who Jack really is? I need to prepare the paperwork for him to sign."

"I'll call him and see if he's okay with that," Alexa said. "If he isn't, then you'll just have to trust my judgement. It looks like they're done."

The general and Alexa stepped out of the observation room and into the hallway. When Trent came out of the examination room, Alexa could tell he was more conflicted when he saw her. She'd wait a while before leaving Trent, but she knew she'd have to break off their romance sooner or later.

Purple Level — 0515 hours

"Mommy, why is that women always talking to Daddy?" Maya asked, after the AMRS test.

Alexa wondered how Taylor would field the question.

"Alexa's an old friend of your dad's here on Earth," Taylor replied.

"Oh. Mom, I'm really hungry. Can we get something to eat?"

"When did you last eat?" Melissa asked.

"I think I had breakfast before we had the airlock accident," Maya replied.

Alexa thought Maya was the sweetest kid she'd ever been around. The child was obviously smarter than most children her age. The schools in the future must be really good. From what she'd learned over the last hour, Maya was also a very inquisitive young lady and didn't miss much.

"Then you must be starved," Melissa said. "Let's get you something. What would you like?"

"A galaxy melt would be good—, wouldn't it, Mom?"

"I'm sorry, but I don't know what that is," Taylor replied.

"Sure you do. You make them all the time."

Taylor looked at Trent and said, "You want to help me out here?"

"Maya, we're on Earth. I'm not sure if they have those here."

Maya nodded. "We're really on Earth?"

"Yes," Taylor said.

"I'm sorry I behaved so childishly before," Maya said, sounding more mature. "I don't know how I got here. I was so scared. Nothing like that has ever happened to me, and I'm still not sure why I don't remember spacing."

"We're all a little confused," Taylor said. "It's early here, Pumpkin. Do you mind having breakfast again?"

"Do they have pancakes?" Maya asked.

"There's pancakes on Mars?" Alexa asked.

Maya huffed, then said, "Of course there are."

"I think we can get you some pancakes," Melissa said. "I need to check on your test results." Melissa stepped away to consult her computer tablet.

"How did you meet my mom and dad?" Maya asked Alexa.

"That's a long story that I think we need to save for later," Trent said before Alexa could answer.

"Was she your girlfriend before you met Mom?"

"Out of the mouth of babes, "Taylor said. "Yes, Maya, Alexa knew Trent before you were born."

Melissa rejoined them and said, "You are one very healthy young lady."

"I try to eat what I'm told," Maya said. "I don't care for peas though."

They all laughed.

"What about the DNA test?" Taylor asked.

"It'll be a few more hours before we have those results," Melissa replied.

"Any other issues?" Trent asked.

Melissa shook her head. "Nothing. Her brain activity is normal. She's perfectly healthy and without implants. Let's go get something to eat."

Green Level — 0530 hours

Doctor Maxwell was still waiting in the security communications center for a call from Chuck Andrews. He'd left word for Andrews to call him back over an hour ago. Knowing how Andrews was always prompt with returning his calls, the only conclusion he could come to was that something of great importance had occurred.

General Starke entered the center and said, "Anything?"

"Nothing yet. Andrews can't be that busy."

Just then the phone rang. A Marine duty officer answered, then nodded at Maxwell and said, "It's for you."

"Finally," Maxwell said, picking up the secure line.

"Professor, I apologize for the delay," Andrews said, "but all hell has broken loose here, and I couldn't be in two places at the same time."

"Tell me you've had additional gravity wave bursts."

"Yes, we did. There have been several in-atmosphere waves detected over the last four hours. How would you know that?"

"Lucky guess. How many is several?"

"Two in the area of Greylock Mountain in Idaho. The bursts were almost on top of each other. Total time separation was less than ten seconds apart. Slightly less intensity than any of the others recorded during the last few hours."

"How many others?"

"Five additional bursts scattered across the United States. We've had two in China, one in Russia, one each in England and Canada, and the strangest one was in the Virgin Islands. Interferometers in Italy, Germany, and Japan confirmed the location sources."

"So eleven total beside the two here?"

The general gave him a look of concern.

"You're near Greylock Mountain?" Andrews asked.

"Yes, but that's classified. Is that clear?" Maxwell looked at the general. He knew he'd screwed up.

"Yes, sir."

"What was the intensity and duration of the other bursts?"

"Comparable to the first five that we recorded. Professor, are you responsible for creating these waves?"

"No. I want to know the exact locations of all the bursts. Send me everything you have on them."

"Send them where?" Andrews asked.

Maxwell put his hand over the mouthpiece and said, "General, how do I receive messages here?"

Starke said, "He can send the information to me. He gave Maxwell his personal Space Force email address. He can't disclose that address to anyone."

Maxwell gave Andrews the address and the general's message.

"I'll have to send it in batches," Andrews said, "There's a lot of data."

"That'll be fine. How soon until I get the first batch?"

"I'll send it immediately."

"Keep monitoring, and I'll be in touch."

"Dr. Maxwell, can I have another minute?" Andrews asked.

"Go ahead."

"I've discovered an echo wave within the gravity waves. I theorized that there had to be one, and this last batch of data from Japan confirmed it."

"A what?" Maxwell asked.

"An echo wave. I asked Professor Tanaka in Japan to reset their interferometer calibration detection algorithm to look for a second wave burst within the first. It's a secondary wave that's produced by the original gravity burst within the atmosphere. I'm calling it an echo wave."

"Like an aftershock?"

"Yes. The bursts are being produced by something incredibly small. The gravitational field produces the initial wave when it appears. It's followed a light-second later by the echo wave. That's why I asked if you were creating the waves. These are not being produced by a natural phenomenon."

Maxwell understood the implication. "Did you detect anything other than the second wave?"

"No, sir. Just the initial burst followed by the echo wave. Both waves push out from the source in all directions on a subatomic level, and as best as we can determine, they dissipate quickly. It's bizarre. Professor, I have a theory, but I've been hesitant to tell anyone."

"I'm listening."

"I was wondering if the waves are being produced by subatomic white holes."

"That's a good guess. It's one of the source options I've been working on." He couldn't tell him what was really going on.

"I don't need to tell you that being this close to a gravity wave source of this magnitude, even on a subatomic level, should have been felt like a strong earthquake for hundreds of miles."

"Not if the wave is suppressed," Maxwell said.

"But how could anyone control that kind of energy?" Andrews asked. "Is this a new type of weapon?"

"I'll call you later, so be available this time." Maxwell hung up.

"So there have been additional events?" Starke said.

"Yes, eleven additional GW bursts worldwide, all within the last few hours." Maxwell gave him the locations.

There was a knock on the door, and a Marine entered. "General Starke, you have a call from Secretary of Defense Barrington. He says it's urgent."

"I'll take it here," Starke said. The phone chimed a few seconds later, and he answered. After the call ended, Starke said, "Well, things just got interesting. The SecDef is going to pay me a visit later today."

"When?"

"In about seven hours. He wants a firsthand accounting of what we're doing."

"What's happened that he needs to come here?"

"Thirty people on a cruise ship off St. Thomas in the Virgin Islands witnessed a passenger disappear in a ball of light. She was talking to her husband by a railing when a light materialized over the water. The light advanced on the ship, and something within the light pushed her husband out of the way. What looked like tiny hands reached out of the light and grabbed her. Then the light encapsulated her and vanished. Rescue operations are under way, but we both know what happened. The SecDef wants us to come up with an explanation to release to the media."

"Why do *we* need to explain anything to the media?"

"Because two of the ship's passengers recorded the event."

"That *will* be hard to explain to the public. How about using the ball lightning explanation?"

"Ball lightning won't fly this time. The woman that vanished was singled out. I'm sure the images of her abduction will be broadcast on every news channel in the world."

"Do you think the woman will be brought here like Wood and Maya?" Maxwell asked.

"I think that's a very good possibility. We'll need to be prepared. The president will want to squelch anything that suggests alien abductions."

"How do we do that? You said that people saw tiny hands in the light."

"I don't know what the SecDef has in mind, but I have a bad feeling that the president wants to offer us up as the culprits in an experiment gone wrong."

"Shit. More likely, you mean me, don't you?"

Starke shrugged, then said, "We need to find out if there are other missing people associated with the other bursts and if any of those incidents were recorded. If you'll check on that, I'll check with National Reconnaissance to see if they captured any of the events. We always have satellites pointed at Russia and China."

Pink Level – Dining room – 0600 hours

"How were those pancakes?" Melissa asked Maya.

"Delicious," Maya replied. "I really liked the blueberries. They were a lot juicier than the ones we get at home."

"I see," Melissa said. "Trent, do you agree?"

"Dad, doesn't eat blueberries," Maya said. "He likes strawberries on his pancakes."

"Yes, he does," Alexa said without thinking.

"How do you know how he likes his pancakes?" Maya asked.

"I've known your father for a long time."

Trent smiled at Alexa. "I do like my strawberries."

"Excuse me," Taylor said. She stood and walked away from the table.

"Mom's been acting strange ever since I got here," Maya said. "What's wrong with her?"

"She's just tired," Trent answered. "How about you and I take a walk. I'll show you around the complex."

"Will you explain how we got here and why I don't remember spacing?" Maya asked.

Trent looked at Melissa for help with what to say.

"I think that would be a good idea," Melissa said. "Trent, go ahead and tell her what's happening. I think she can handle it. Take her back to the apartment. I'll be up in a bit to see how it's going. It would be good to have Taylor with you."

"You're sure?" Trent asked.

"Kids have a way of figuring things out. I believe it's the right thing to do."

Trent and Maya left the dining room, holding hands. They found Taylor standing by the elevator, looking out at the concourse. Trent told her what they needed to do and asked her to join them.

Pink Level — 0630 hours

Alexa was worried about how Maya would take the news. At age ten she still had a lot of little girl left in her that could be damaged if Trent told her Taylor didn't remember her. She didn't understand why she was worried about Maya. She'd only just met her, but her maternal instincts were on edge.

General Starke and Dr. Maxwell joined them at the table.

"Where are Trent, Taylor, and Maya?" Starke asked.

"They ate and went back to the apartment," Melissa replied. "I told Trent he could tell Maya what was going on. She was asking questions."

"I hope it isn't too much for her to handle," Alexa said.

Starke said, "Alexa, I'm going to release Griffin, Dobson, Stone, and Marvin at noon today. I requested that they meet us here so I can better explain the conditions of their release."

"That's excellent news," Alexa said. "I'll need to convince Marvin to leave. He'll want to stay."

"If he decides to stay, I can live with that. He's already in the know. It'll be your call."

"Thanks. If I can get him to go, will you drop him someplace where Jack can pick him up without anyone watching?"

Starke smiled. "No problem. Jack's the least of my worries. Melissa, you'll need to prepare for an influx of abductees."

"What's happened?" Melissa asked.

"There's been eleven more abductions. One of them was witnessed by more than thirty people, and it was recorded."

"Eleven more," Alexa muttered in disbelief.

"Who recorded it?" Melissa asked. "Why couldn't the incident be contained?"

"Because a woman was taken off of a cruise ship, and I just learned about it. The ship is at sea, so there's no way to keep the recordings from being released. The Secretary of Defense will arrive here after lunch to talk with our returned abductees firsthand. The president's been briefed as well as the Joint Chiefs. They want a way for us to explain what's happened without saying it was an alien abduction."

"That's where I come in," Maxwell said. "Secret experiment gone wrong, and I'm to play the villain."

"It doesn't make sense for them to take so many people in plain sight," Melissa said. "And why now?"

"I don't know," Starke said.

"Even more strange is that all of those taken are women," Maxwell said.

"All women?" Alexa said. "Trent's the only male involved out of all of these abductions?"

"That appears to be the case," Maxwell said.

"I can tell you that there were six Americans, one Brit, one Canadian, two from China and one from Russia," Starke added.

"Who are they?" Melissa asked. "What are their occupations or professions? Are there any connections?"

"I don't have all the details yet," Starke replied.

"Where were the American women abducted from?" Alexa asked.

"Two were taken from Florida, one from Jacksonville, and the other was from Ft. Myers. The NRO captured some good images of those events. There was one from Texas, Maryland, Kansas, and another woman that was taken from the cruise ship. What I find interesting is that all of the American women are the same age as Trent and Taylor."

"Previous abductees?" Melissa asked.

"Unknown. I'll have the full bios on everyone shortly, including medical. I need you to begin working them for when they're returned to us here."

"You think all of them will be returned here?" Melissa said.

"I do," Starke said.

"I wonder if they were all taken as children, around the same time as Trent and Taylor." Alexa said.

"That's how I'm leaning," Starke said. "I'm wondering if they have a counterpart on Mars. Maybe this is the group from Trent's and Taylor's classroom."

"We'll be ready for them," Melissa said. "Hopefully, they won't all arrive at the same time."

Alexa saw Marvin walking toward her. He was followed by Dobson, Griffin, and Stone. None of them looked happy.

"Good morning, everyone," Alexa said.

"What's so good about it?" Marvin said.

Griffin said, "Marvin told us you were here, but he wouldn't tell us what's been going on. This annex looks nicer than where we've been staying."

"Would anyone care to enlighten us?" Dobson asked. "And who's this gentleman?"

"I'm Hank Maxwell. Nice to meet you all."

"What was all the intrusion alert stuff about last night?" Marvin asked. "I couldn't get out of my room."

"We had an event last night," Starke said. The men sat down around the table. "It's been resolved. I have good news for all of you. You're going home."

Dobson said, "Why the sudden change of heart?"

"Circumstances have changed. If you speak of your experience to anyone, you'll never see the light of day again."

"I won't say a damn word," Griffin said.

"They do say that a lot, don't they?" Stone said.

"Mr. Stone, you were a victim of circumstance. I apologize for any inconvenience, but we had an investigation to complete, and we now know that you weren't involved."

"I understand, General Starke," Stone replied. "It was actually nice to see snow again."

"Marvin, Alexa has vouched for you. Agent Dobson, we both know you won't say anything. After breakfast, you all need to gather your things and report to the hangar bay to exit clear and sign the NDAs."

"What about Alexa?" Marvin asked.

"She's staying behind, voluntarily."

"They can't release Trent, so I'm staying," Alexa added.

"Then I'm staying," Marvin said.

Alexa leaned across the table and said, "Marvin, I need you to find Sue and stay with her."

"I'm not leaving here without you," Marvin said.

Alexa sighed. "I told the general you wouldn't want to go, but Marvin, I really need you to keep Sue company. I also need you to check on our business. We've been away too long. You can stay nearby, and you know where I am." Marvin rocked his jaw back and forth. That usually meant he'd do what she asked of him, but he wasn't happy about it. "Marvin, I'm going to call Jack and find out where they're staying. You can coordinate with them once you're dropped off. The general has assured me that you won't be followed."

"I so swear, Marvin," Starke said.

A communication specialist walked into the dining room. "General, you may want to see what's being broadcast by a local news station."

"Thank you. Turn the monitor on," Starke ordered. "I imagine that it's being broadcast on every news channel. I'm surprised I haven't been summoned."

Just then another communication specialist entered the dining room. "I spoke too soon."

"General Starke, you're needed in communications, immediately," the second specialist said.

Starke stood. "Remember, get your stuff together and go to the hangar bay. The sooner you sign out, the sooner you're on your way. Duty calls."

"What's on every news channel?" Dobson asked as the monitor came to life. "What the hell?"

The recording of the light taking a woman from a cruise ship was playing. Then a second recording made from a different angle showed the abduction as well.

"That's the recording of an alien abduction that occurred last night in the Virgin Islands," Maxwell told them.

"If that's being broadcast worldwide, what difference does it make now if we know that Trent was abducted by aliens?" Dobson asked.

"The recorded evidence doesn't get any better than this," Stone said.

"You know the aliens are going to come back," Marvin said. "Or is that what happened last night?"

"Marvin, we aren't discussing what happened last night," Melissa said.

"Really?" Marvin said. "Can we talk about the little girl's voice I heard in Trent's room when I knocked, before I went to get these guys?"

"Need to know," Melissa replied.

"They came back, didn't they?" Marvin said.

"Marvin, I can't talk about it."

"And that's why you're staying, isn't it?" Marvin asked Alexa.

"Yes," Alexa answered. "Please, don't ask any more questions. It's very complicated. Let's not make this more difficult."

"Guess I better get packed up then," Marvin said, his voice strained. "The sooner the better, right?" He stood and headed for the door.

Alexa said, "I'll call you."

Marvin didn't acknowledge her.

"Speaking of calls, you need to call your friend Sue," Melissa said.

"Yes, I do."

"I'll walk down to the communication center with you," Melissa said. "The rest of you enjoy your breakfast. Don't ask Hank any questions."

Boise, Idaho — 0700 hours

The phone rang. Dan Mitchell didn't want to answer it. The abduction scene from the cruise ship was unbelievable. He turned down the volume on the television. "Hello."

"It's me," Alexa said. "Things have changed. Marvin will leave here shortly. I need you and Sue to pick him up."

"Does this have anything to do with the ball of light that plucked that woman off the cruise ship?"

"Yes. Marvin will call you in a few hours. Some of the others are also being released. I may need you and Sue to sign an NDA."

"What about you?" Dan asked.

"I'm staying. That's part of the new development. Trent and I are here on our own terms. It's important that we stay."

"Okay. I'm assuming that the light that snatched the woman was like the one that took Trent."

"Yes."

"The people that have been holding you are going to drop Marvin off?"

"Yes. Thank you again for everything. Marvin will take care of what we owe you. You know how I am about that."

"It sounds like you may not be leaving the mountain anytime soon."

"It could be months."

"I'll take care of your people, Alexa. You take care of yourself and Trent."

"I will. Give Sue my best."

NINETEEN

Trent and Taylor sat next to Maya on the sofa. Trent had reservations about telling Maya that her mother didn't know her, but he could tell that Maya was already wondering why her mother didn't seem herself.

"Maya, I need you to be a big girl for what we're about to tell you," Trent began. "You won't understand some of it, and I'm sure you'll have questions. We'll answer them."

Maya looked from Trent to Taylor. "Is one of you dying?"

"No, no one is dying," Taylor said.

"Good. I was worried. Mom, you don't look like yourself. You look older."

"Gee, thanks," Taylor replied.

"Maya, you already know that we're on Earth," Trent said. "but we're here in a different time than when we are on Mars. The date is 2030 here. You've been transported through time by an alien species. That's why you don't remember spacing."

"Aliens!" Maya exclaimed. Then she frowned and said, "I don't remember any aliens. I only remember seeing a light, and then I was here. How did I travel back in time? Did you see the aliens take me?"

"No," Trent replied.

"So when did you and Mom get here?"

"This is the hard part," Trent said, taking Maya's hand. "We're not sure that we've ever been on Mars, at least not in this lifetime."

"I don't understand."

"It's very difficult to explain. I have an alien implant in my brain that's allowing me to see bits and pieces of a life in another time. I know who you are. I remember what Mars looks like and where we live. But your mom doesn't have an implant. She only knows you because of what I've told her."

Maya looked at Taylor, her lower lip quivering. "You have to know me. You're my mother."

Taylor said, "The mom you know is in a different place. It's very confusing. I'm not sure I understand all of it."

"Both of you were born on Mars," Maya said. "I studied the records of our family lineage in school. Your name is Shona Price Cooper. Dad's name is Aiden James Cooper."

Trent squeezed her hand. "Pumpkin, we're still trying to figure this out ourselves. I have some memories of a life on Mars, but they are memories of things that I haven't done yet or may never do. Right now, I'm here in this time. When I was on Mars, I had no memory of this life, and up until a few days ago I didn't know anything about Mars or you."

He closed his eyes, trying to find the right words that would soften the shock of what he needed to tell her. But he couldn't think of an easy way to do that. "Your mother and I were abducted by an alien species when we were about your age. I was abducted again while flying my plane to Key West, Florida a few weeks ago." He pulled up his left pant leg. "See this scar?"

"Yeah."

"There's an alien device embedded in my bone. It was implanted during my abduction in 1998. Your mom had the same kind of implant, but it's been removed."

Taylor showed Maya her scar, then said, "Colonel Endo removed mine about two years ago. Since then, I haven't been abducted again. I've been living here for the last two years while they studied me."

Maya said, "I don't have any scars."

"We know that," Taylor said, "for which we are thankful. You were brought to us in this time period for a purpose. We just don't know why."

Trent said, "In this life, your mom has another family, another husband, and a daughter."

Maya's eyes grew large. "You aren't married?"

"No," Taylor said. "Like Trent, I only learned that you existed two days ago."

"Mom, where's your other family?"

Tears welled up in Taylor's eyes.

"They're here on Earth. My daughter's name is Emma. She's fourteen. My husband's name is Rick. We live in Indiana, or at least they do. I live here."

"Do you know where Indiana is?" Trent asked.

"Yes. We've studied the geography of Earth. It's in the middle of North America. Why isn't your other family here with you?"

"Because they can't be. My abductions made me unique, and they were told that I was dead after my last abduction."

"That's awful," Maya said.

"Yes, it is," Taylor said, then wiped a tear from her cheek. "Trent and I are still trying to put the pieces together, but we know that we're connected by our abduction experiences, and perhaps even by a future life on Mars that we don't yet understand. There's a reason Trent was abducted last month and given the memory or given the visions of a life on Mars with you and me."

"This is all so weird," Maya said.

"I know," Trent said. "But you being brought to us means the aliens want us to be together in this time. Maya, I get visions of the future, but I haven't been given all of Aiden's memories."

"Will I get to go back to my time?" Maya asked. "I want my real mom and dad back." Maya took a deep breath. "I mean you're like them and sound like them, but you aren't really them, are you? I don't want to be here anymore." Maya started to cry.

Maya's sobs melted Trent's heart, and he hugged her. "I don't know if you can go back. Maya, please understand that as hard as this is to grasp, we love you in this time."

"How can you love me?" Maya cried. "You're not my parents. You don't even know me."

"Listen to me," Trent said. "Up until a few days ago, I didn't know you or your mom existed. But I know that I love you both now."

Maya sniffled and wiped her nose with the back of her hand. "Does anyone back home know where I've gone? Are my parent's wondering what's happened to me?"

"I don't know," Trent said. "It's possible that we exist in both places at the same time."

"How?"

"That's a very good question and one that I can't answer," Trent said. "It's a time paradox. Maybe in order for you to exist here now, we must also exist in the future. It's also possible that we're living simultaneous lives in different dimensions, and we don't know this version of ourselves exists. Aiden and Shona may not even know that you're gone."

"I'm confused. I'm here, so I can't be there. They'd have to miss me."

"If you live in the linear future, you and your mom and dad haven't been born yet. They don't miss you because they don't exist."

"But I'm here, so I've been born."

Taylor said, "As Trent said, we could all be living simultaneous lives in different dimensions."

Maya shook her head. "I don't get it."

"I wish I could explain this better."

Maya stood up and looked at both of them, then said matter-of-factly, "I think we're a family no matter where we are."

Trent smiled and said, "Maya, in this time Alexa and I are together. I was on my way to ask her to marry me when I was abducted." Maya didn't respond. Trent gave her time to process what he'd just told her.

"But you said that you loved Mom."

Trent fought with his emotions, then said, "I love them both equally in different ways."

"So you love Mom on Mars, and Mom loves you there, too, but she also loves another family like you love Alexa here."

"That sums it up quite well," Taylor said.

Trent could see that Maya was struggling to comprehend the complexity of it all. "Maya, Alexa and our friends looked for me for three weeks when I was recently abducted. When I came back, I didn't even know I'd been gone until people starting telling me what had happened.

"It's possible I'm connected to that time because of the neural implant the aliens put in my brain. Although, before I disappeared, Alexa says I was calling out Shona's name during a dream that I don't remember. I guess I could have been connected to that time even before the neural implant. But it wasn't until after I returned that I saw and felt the other world the way I do now. Even when I see that world, I'm still physically here on Earth. My mind takes me to Mars. Does that make sense?"

"I'm trying to understand," Maya said. "I wonder if I'm just asleep on Mars."

"No, you're on Earth," Trent replied. "You don't have an implant, which makes your presence here all the more confusing."

"We're struggling with all of this as well," Taylor said. "We wanted you to know the truth. It's possible that you may be here for the rest of your life. It's also possible that you'll be taken from us and put back on Mars and never know that you were here."

Maya twisted a lock of her hair. "You may not remember me, but when I look at you I see my mom. I love her, so I must love you. Emma would be my sister, right?"

Taylor nodded. "Yes. She would be a half-sister."

"I always wanted a sister. I guess in our time she wouldn't be alive."

After a moment, Taylor said, "That's true. Maya, since you've never been on Earth, would you like to take a walk outside?"

"It would be nice to go outside without my TES."

"Your what?" Taylor asked.

"My terrestrial excursion suit."

"No, you won't need one of those," Trent said.

"What do I wear?"

"Well, it's really cold outside. It's winter in this hemisphere. There's snow on the ground. You'll need a heavy coat to stay warm."

"It'll be weird to breathe unfiltered air."

Trent stood. "I'll call Melissa and see if it's possible for us to go outside. Maya, do you have any questions?"

"Not right now, but I think I'll have some later."

"I'm sure you will," Trent replied.

Purple Level — 1000 hours

Melissa slid Trent out of the AMSR. He was glad the machine noise had stopped. "Melissa, how many of these can I be exposed to before it starts affecting my health?"

"They aren't like X-rays. You can have as many scans as we need."

"Not that it matters much anyway. I mean I do have an alien thing in my head that could explode and fry my brain."

"The implant remains unchanged from the last image. You're fine. How did Maya take the news?"

"Better than expected. She's confused, but who isn't? It's harder for Taylor."

"I'm sure it is. Just so you know, I asked General Starke if I could have Taylor's family brought here."

"I bet he said, no."

"Correct."

A medical technician walked into the room and handed Melissa a tablet. She quickly scanned the data, then said, "Have these been verified?"

"Yes," the technician replied. "We ran them twice."

"They have to be wrong. It's simply not possible."

"The results are correct, Colonel. The samples we used were collected from the patients after their arrival."

"I'll take new samples and run them again," Melissa said. "You're dismissed."

"Melissa, what is it?" Trent asked.

"Some of the DNA samples have been compromised." Melissa continued to study the results.

"Are those our DNA results?"

"Yes."

"What's wrong with them?"

"Get dressed. I only want to say this once."

Five minutes later, Trent, Taylor, and Maya sat around the table in front of Melissa's desk. There was a knock on the door.

"Come in," Melissa said.

"You wanted to see me?" Alexa asked.

"Yes, come in and have a seat."

"Why is she here?" Maya said.

"Maya, that's rude." Taylor said.

"I needed to see all of you," Melissa said. "I have the DNA results, but I need to run them again. I need additional samples from all of you, and I wanted to collect them myself."

"Does that mean I'm going to be stuck with a needle again?" Maya asked.

"No," Melissa replied. "I'm going to swab the inside of your cheek."

"What was wrong with the results?" Taylor asked, sounding concerned.

"There was problem with the collection or something in the lab. I need to run another panel. That's why I wanted all of you here at the same time and away from the medical area."

Trent could tell that Melissa was holding something back. He didn't want to speculate, but he was getting a funny feeling in the pit of his stomach. "How long until you get the results?"

"It'll take at least twelve hours."

After Melissa took each sample, she placed it in a clear, sterile tube and bagged, sealed, and labeled it. Then she placed each specimen bag into a plastic container and sealed and labeled it. Between each swab, she put on a new pair of gloves.

Melissa said, "I'll take these to the lab myself and make sure the equipment is operating properly. General Starke approved taking Maya outside. It looks like a beautiful day. Go out now and have some fun."

"Would anyone object if I tagged along?" Alexa asked.

"No," Maya answered quickly. "Mom and Dad told me about you."

"They did?"

Trent grinned, then said, "Yes, we did."

"We'd be happy to have you join us," Taylor said.

"Maya, I think you'll like your first walk in fresh outdoor air," Trent said.

The Woods — 1045 hours

It took some doing, but they finally found a coat for Maya to wear, although it was too big. The fully insulated parka made her look as if she weighed two hundred pounds.

"Are you ready, Maya?" Trent asked.

"It's weird not having a TES on, but I'm ready."

Trent, Taylor, Maya, and Alexa walked to the small exit door adjacent to the main hangar entrance. Trent held Maya's hand, and she squeezed his hand when the door opened. She also looked as if she was holding her breath. That practice was drummed into the kids on Mars, much like parents on Earth teach their children to hold their breath while learning to swim. The sky was crystal-clear, and no wind stirred the powdery snow.

"It's okay, Maya," Trent said. "The air is breathable."

Maya exhaled and took a tentative breath. "The air smells strange."

"That's because it's fresh, not filtered," Trent said.

"It's nice. Can I touch the snow?"

"Sure." Trent let go of her hand, and she walked off the heated walkway into the snow.

She took off one glove, bent over, and touched the snow. "Wow. It's really cold."

Taylor asked, "What did you expect it to feel like?"

"I'm not sure."

"Let me show you how to make a snowball," Taylor said.

"You don't need to." Maya formed a snowball and hurled it at Trent.

Trent laughed and said, "How did you know you could do that?"

"I watched it on a learning program in school. It looked like fun."

"You're in for it now," Taylor said, making a snowball.

For the next few minutes, they threw snowballs at one another until they were laughing so hard that none of them could stand up.

"That was fun," Maya cried. "Let's do it some more."

"I can't," Trent said.

"I'm done," Taylor said.

"Me, too," Alexa added, then said, "Maya, what do you think of Earth so far?"

"Why?" Maya asked.

"I was just wondering if you liked it here?"

"I haven't seen very much. I like not having to worry about monitoring my air supply. The trees and blue sky are pretty. Can I tell you what I think later?"

"Yes, you can," Alexa replied.

"Can we go exploring?" Maya asked.

"I think that would be okay," Trent said, "but I don't think they want us to go too far away."

"Let's walk down to the frozen lake," Alexa said. "It's just around that rock outcropping. That's where Marvin and I camped while trying to find an entry point to the facility."

"Lead us to it," Taylor said, taking Maya's hand.

General Starke's Office — 1100 hours

"These are the results from the first two DNA sequence runs," Melissa said. "For obvious reasons, I'm running another series."

"How long until we have the new results?" Starke asked.

"Twelve hours."

"That long?"

"The sequencing used to take twenty-four to twenty-six hours."

"What if the results are the same?"

"Let's hope they're not. That would mean we have some very difficult questions to answer."

"Trent and the others still outside?" Starke asked.

"Yes," Melissa replied. "According to security, they're down by the lake. Maya seems to be adapting to her new world. I wonder how long she'll be with us."

"Who knows? I still don't have a clear picture as to why Maya's here."

"I've been wondering about that myself. Wood confirmed that Trent and Taylor are living on Mars in the future."

"But by different names," Starke said. "Could they just look like them?"

"I think it's more than that. We may have the answer when we get the new DNA results."

"What did you find out from Wood's autopsy? You know Secretary Barrington is going to ask about that, so you should be ready to answer his questions."

"I'm ready. Captain Wood died from a malfunctioning alien implant. Why they came back and took her body is baffling."

"Maybe they wanted to find out what happened to her. Any chance Trent's implant will malfunction?"

"I think if it was going to, it would have by now. It hasn't changed since the last exam."

Starke nodded. "Colonel, when we talk to the SecDef, you may want to throw in some medical lingo as to Wood's cause of death. Barrington likes technical jargon, even though I don't think he understands most of it."

Melissa chuckled. "Will do. How about this? Her innate immune system detected tissue damage from the alien neural implant through her TLR synapse response mechanism, which initiated a pathophysiological ischemic event."

"That sounds good," Starke said. "What does it mean in English?"

"Just what I told you. The implant fried her prefrontal cortex. Why, I don't know."

Starke leaned back in his chair. "Which means the president and others may consider it a hostile act."

"I don't believe her death was an intentional act of aggression by the aliens. I believe it was an unanticipated event."

"Put that in writing."

"I already have," Melissa said. "General, I'm wondering why they chose to leave Captain Wood outside the facility. They obviously had the means to make entry."

"I'm sure that Barrington will ask me that same question, and I don't have a clue about what to tell him. If Captain Wood had been delivered inside and had not become hypothermic, would it have made a difference in her survival?"

"No."

"Perhaps they didn't want to risk that we would open fire on them or Captain Wood," Starke said. "They knocked on the door with Wood to tell us that they were around, then dropped Maya here after deciding that we weren't going to shoot at them."

"Maybe. What can we do to keep them from entering the facility and taking Trent and the others?"

"Nothing. That won't be what Barrington wants to hear, but it's the truth. I think if they'd wanted Trent back, they'd have taken him by now. They want him here with Maya for a reason."

"I agree. I just wish I knew why."

"Maxwell told me that the aliens' technology is so far ahead of ours that all of our countermeasures are useless. Even if we understand how they're able to penetrate the facility with that light, we still wouldn't be able to do anything to stop them. The security recording of Wood's body disappearing didn't give us anything to work with. There appeared to be something moving around within the light, just like what we saw on the cruise ship abduction videos."

"The images weren't very clear," Melissa said. "The light was too intense for the cameras."

"Maxwell thinks the aliens have found a way to harness a power equal to that of a white hole."

"I heard him discussing that earlier."

"Colonel, I'd like you back in my office at 1400 hours so we can meet Secretary Barrington together."

Melissa nodded. "I'm sure he'll want to see Trent and the others. I'll brief them on what to expect. Barrington will have many more questions after our first meeting with him."

"I'm sure he will."

The Hangar — 1200 hours

Alexa had lost track of the time when they were at the lake. She and Taylor walked back to the facility together while Trent stayed with Maya. Taylor had confided that she had conflicted feelings about Maya.

"Maya isn't my daughter in this time, but she still needs a mother," Taylor said. "Trent knew her, or at least of her, because of the implant. I don't have that knowledge."

"You're right, she needs her parents, but that isn't possible," Alexa said. "I'm actually surprised that she's adjusted so well. I think that's because you and Trent have shown her love."

"She likes you."

"I like her, too." Alexa was starting to admire Taylor for what she'd been through over the last two years. Separated from her family, imprisoned, subjected to medical tests over and over again, and now having to become a surrogate mother. Few people would have remained as strong as she had without true inner strength.

A Marine standing by the side entrance motioned for them to come back inside.

"It looks like we're wanted," Alexa said. She looked back and saw Trent and Maya racing toward them. She realized that was something else that kids couldn't do on Mars. If they fell and ruptured a suit there, it could be fatal. "Trent and Maya seem so natural together."

"They really do," Taylor said. "I can see Trent in her. Are you and Trent planning to have a family?"

Alexa nodded. "We discussed it. I'm not getting any younger. I'm forty."

"That's not too old."

"It is when you know that your child will be a teenager learning to drive when you're fifty-seven."

"I hadn't thought about it that way. Emma will be driving soon, and then she'll be married and having children of her own." Taylor bit her lower lip. "I had trouble getting pregnant with Emma."

"Really?"

"We went to a number of fertility clinics for years. We weren't given much hope. I was told that I had scar tissue around my ovaries. They weren't sure what that was from, but I know now. After giving up hope, it just happened."

"I'm happy for you," Alexa said. "I know you must miss your daughter very much."

"I do."

When Alexa and Taylor reached the entrance, the Marine said, "The general wants you to wait by the transport."

"Thank you," Alexa replied. Then she looked into the hangar and saw Marvin standing by a transport. His bags sat together on the hangar floor. It looked like he had all of the gear they'd taken with them on the trek to the mountain. It seemed so long ago that they'd started out to rescue Trent. She waved at him. He waved back.

She turned at the noise coming from the doorway and saw Trent carrying Maya. Taylor unzipped Maya's coat.

"Looks like they're getting ready to leave," Trent said, walking toward her.

"Do you all want to say goodbye to Marvin?" Alexa asked.

"Absolutely," Trent replied.

"Of course," Taylor said.

"Being outside is fun," Maya said excitedly. "Can we go out later and have another snowball fight?"

"We'll see, Pumpkin," Trent said.

They walked to the transport. Alexa gave Marvin a hug and said, "Thank you so much for everything you did to help me. You take care of yourself."

"I will," Marvin said. "You'll be back with us soon. I plan to stay at the hotel in Boise for a few days. You know, just in case you need to be rescued."

Alexa chuckled. "Let's hope not."

"Check in with us when you can."

"I will, but don't be concerned if I go dark for a few days. You know how communications are around here."

"No more than three days between check-ins."

"I think that's doable," Alexa said, hugging him again.

"Thanks for taking care of her, Marvin," Trent said.

"My pleasure. I'm just glad you didn't crash. Taylor, Maya, it was a pleasure meeting you both."

"Nice to meet you, too" Taylor said. Maya said nothing.

Alexa saw that Maya was focused on the open transport hatch. "Do you want to see inside?" Alexa asked.

"Can I?" Maya asked. "I've never been inside one of those."

"I don't see why not," Marvin said, taking her to the open hatch.

Maya climbed in and looked around. "This is nice," she said, then climbed back out. "It looks like one of the crawler-explorers."

"What's a crawler-explorer?" Alexa asked.

"It's what we use on the surface to travel from station to station or to explore different areas for potential settlements. I got to ride in one once."

"Was it fun?" Marvin asked.

"Yes."

General Starke, Dobson, Griffin, and Stone walked up to them.

"I guess everyone is ready to leave," Starke said.

"Very ready," Dobson said.

"Gentlemen, I wish you a safe journey home. Agent Dobson, I'll have Secretary Barrington contact the SecNav and tell him that you did a great job here."

"Thank you, General Starke," Dobson replied. "I didn't do much, but commendations are always appreciated. I hope you get all of this sorted out. Alexa, Trent, I hope to see you both back in Key West someday."

"We'll do our best to stop by and give you some trouble," Alexa said.

"I hope to see you there as well," Griffin said.

"Likewise," Alexa said. "We wouldn't have made it here without your help. You stay safe."

"Deputy Griffin and Mr. Stone," General Starke said, "I'll call your supervisors and give you glowing reports as well."

"Appreciate that," Stone said. "Trent, if you ever plan on flying into my airspace again, please let me know so I can take a vacation day."

Trent laughed and said, "I'll do that."

"Well, everyone, I want you all to forget about us," Starke said.

The four men went up the rear ramp into the transport, and the ramp closed behind them. As the transport left the hangar, the camouflage system came to life, and the transport disappeared from sight.

"I still can't get over how it does that," Trent said.

"It's the best money can buy," Starke said. "Why don't we all get back to the Nova annex?"

Alexa thought his tone sounded more like a command than a request. Maya took Trent's and Taylor's hand as they walked toward the door leading to the Green Level. Alexa glanced back as the huge hangar door locked into place. She thought that this facility must be something like what Maya experienced daily on Mars. She couldn't imagine living sealed inside a structure with an artificial atmosphere, where the view outside was the same every day. Red soil, rocks, and sandstorms. No wonder Maya enjoyed the scenery outside. Yet, somehow, she thought Maya would feel at home in either place.

Alexa hurried to catch up with them. "Maya, I have a very grown-up question to ask you."

"Okay," Maya replied.

"Not too grown-up, I hope," Taylor said.

"Maya, if you had a choice, would you rather live on Earth or on Mars?"

Maya appeared to think about the question, then said, "I think I'd like to live on Earth, but only if I was with my real mom and dad. I liked being outside. I liked feeling the air on my face and being able to touch things without gloves on. Smelling the fresh, cold air was really nice. I'd never seen my own breath like that before." Maya grew quiet for a while, then added, "I do like Mars, though. There are things there that you don't have here. So that's a difficult question to answer."

"I know it is, and that's a very grown-up response."

Maya's look turned serious, and then she looked at Trent. "If we lived here, we'd have to live through the dark times, wouldn't we?"

Alexa cocked her head to the side and looked at Trent. "What dark times?"

"I don't know," Trent replied.

"We learned about it in school," Maya said. "Everyone on Mars knows what happened. It's when the Earth became unlivable and half the people on the planet died. It followed the perfect geological tempest."

"What happened?" Alexa asked.

"A geomagnetic polar shift and a volcano in North America erupted around the same time. Then a violent energy burst of some kind came from deep space, and volcanos all over the world erupted. The ash clouds from the erupting volcanos blocked out the sun for decades."

Goosebumps prickled Alexa's skin. "When does all this happen?"

"I know that preparations were made so that humanity could survive before the tempest began. Mars was used as a sanctuary, and eventually as a place where food could be cultivated and then shipped back to Earth. It forced all the nations in the world to come together. Exploratory missions began before the dark times occurred."

"When?" Alexa pressed.

"I think the Mars colony missions began in 2045, a few years after everything happened. I know that on June 26th, 2051, our first colony became self-sustaining, and a few years later, food produced on Mars was being transported to Earth in massive cargo vessels."

"Maya, what I'm asking is, when does the geological tempest begin?"

"I don't remember the exact date. It's sometime in February 2037."

Alexa's blood ran cold. "Trent, do you know what she's talking about?"

"No."

"Everyone on Mars knows the history," Maya said. "That's why we're there. That's why my parent's jobs are so important."

"What does your mom do on Mars?" Alexa asked.

"She's a bioengineer. She works with plants."

"And what does your dad do there?"

"He's an astrophysicist."

Alexa couldn't believe what she was hearing.

"Trent told us what Shona and Aiden did on Mars before you arrived," Taylor said.

Trent said, "I'm working on how quantum gravitational waves can influence time dilation."

"You're doing what?" Alexa said.

Trent looked surprised. "I don't know where that came from, but I know that's what I'm working on."

"Okay, that's new information," Taylor said.

"Just like Professor Maxwell," Alexa said. "We need to talk to General Starke. Now!"

TWENTY

Brown Level — February 6 — 1245 hours

"How did we miss this?" Starke shouted at the group of scientists and abductees seated around the table. "No one interviewed Maya about the future. Cataclysmic events are looming, and the future Trent is working on a time dilation theory."

"Trent doesn't remember any details about his work," Melissa responded defensively.

"Trent, you sat through Maxwell's explanation about black holes and quantum gravity and never said a thing," Starke said.

"Because I don't know anything," Trent replied. "It's Aiden Cooper who's the astrophysicist. Knowing that Aiden is working on time dilation just popped into my head."

Alexa watched as the general clenched his fists repeatedly as if he wanted to hit something.

"Maya," Starke said, "Alexa said that you learned about these events in school. Are you sure about the date?"

Maya nodded, then said, "Yes."

"And you said that the first volcano to erupt was located in North America?"

"Yes."

Sanderson said, "General, Yellowstone has the only supervolcano in North America. The magma dome has been rising steadily for decades."

"That's it!" Maya shouted. "I remember it was in Wyoming. Sorry I didn't remember sooner."

"Hank, could a supereruption cause an extinction event?"

"Not likely," Maxwell replied. "If Yellowstone erupted, it would destroy a lot of the agriculture in the United States, but it wouldn't decimate the food production in the rest of the world. The largest immediate loss of life would occur near the eruption epicenter. Sulfur dioxide and ash would block the sun's rays, which would reflect solar radiation away from the atmosphere. This would cause the planet to cool. It's called the albedo effect."

"So we'd be facing a volcanic winter," Starke said. "For how long?"

"Hard to say. There have been many volcanic eruptions in the past that have caused volcanic winters, but those only lasted a year or two. From what Maya's described, I think it would last much longer."

Maya tapped Alexa's leg.

"Maya, is there something you want to say?" Alexa asked.

"Yes. The winter lasts for over twenty years."

"Good God!" Starke said. "Hank, what does that mean for our survival?"

"Well, Maya's here, so humanity must survive, or at least a version of it in another multiverse. There will be less food production, and it's conceivable that the competition for food will result in riots, military skirmishes, and maybe even all-out war. Maya, can you tell us more about the energy burst from space or what caused it?"

"No one knows," Maya said. "It's only been described as an exotic matter burst."

Maxwell said, "Numerous volcanic eruptions would require massive tectonic plate movement on a global scale, which would create massive earthquakes and floods that would cause incredible damage."

"Any estimate for the loss of life?" Starke asked.

"Hard to say," Maxwell replied.

"How many will die from starvation?" Sanderson asked.

"Depending on how well prepared we are to deal with the loss of crops, it could be hundreds of millions."

Maya said, "Four billion people died during the dark times."

"That's over half of the earth's population!" Starke exclaimed.

"That's what we were taught in school," Maya said. "The majority of the people who survived the dark times stayed in underground shelters that were built before the tempest began." Maya sat up straighter. "Mars had to be turned into a food production center."

"How could Mars become a food production center?" Sanderson asked. "There's no atmosphere on Mars."

"Our scientists are working on that," Maya said.

"Mars is being terraformed?" Maxwell said with a look of disbelief. "How is that possible? It would take centuries to complete."

Maya pursed her lips, then said, "My real mom and dad are part of the team that's working to create an atmosphere."

"I thought your dad was an astrophysicist?" Starke said.

"He is, but both my mom and dad have several jobs. Everyone on Mars does."

"What about the polar shift?" Starke asked. "What will that do? When does that occur?"

"The geomagnetic polar shift began in February, 2037, around the time of the Yellowstone eruption," Maya replied.

"You're certain?" Maxwell asked.

"Absolutely. I got an A on that exam. I usually get an A on all of my exams."

"I think Maya was sent here to warn us," Alexa said. "I also think that Trent was taken and returned with enough evidence to confirm not only the existence of alien life but to give credibility to Maya's warning."

"You think all of these abductions occurred just so the aliens could send us a warning?" Starke said. "We can't even be sure anything will occur. There could be a lot of other reasons why the aliens are abducting people. And why haven't the aliens just told Trent to tell us what's going to happen? Since Trent's visions come in short bursts of information, you'd think the aliens could tell him about the end of the world."

"I have to agree with the general," Maxwell said. "Trent, why haven't the aliens provided that information?"

"I have no idea," Trent replied.

"What Maya has described doesn't seem possible," Sanderson said. "Especially a cosmic energy burst of exotic matter. What evidence is there that any of this will occur?"

"I believe Maya," Alexa said. "Perhaps there's more to it than just telling us about the dark times. Maybe Trent will receive the technological insights we'll need to survive in the future or learn how we can succeed in getting all nations to cooperate. It's possible that the aliens don't want us knowing certain things until the last minute. Perhaps the future is shaped by our actions or omissions today. What if we can't know about something too far ahead of time, because if we did, we'd react differently and that would change a future event that the aliens know has to happen?"

"Interesting point," Maxwell said. "What's occurring now, and the manner in which we are receiving information and responding to it, is known, and our actions have to match precisely the way it did in the future's past."

"That's what I'm thinking," Alexa replied.

Starke said, "Maya, do you remember reading anything about Trent McDougal in any of your history lessons?"

"No."

"So much for that theory," Sanderson said.

"If the aliens wanted to use Trent and Maya to warn us, why would they need to take Captain Wood and the others?" Melissa asked.

"Exactly," Starke said. "If a cataclysmic event is looming, why not land and tell us? Their presence would be proof enough."

"Maybe they can't land," Alexa replied. "Has anyone ever seen a ship land and take a person?"

"Another good point," Maxwell said. "All of the abductees are carried aloft or taken in a ball of light."

"General, it's also possible they know how we would react to seeing an alien craft sitting on the White House lawn. These beings must understand human nature. When threatened, whether real or just perceived, humans usually resort to a forceful response. Maybe this is their way of giving us the information we need to those who can make a difference without causing pandemonium."

"Seems like a very hard way to make a point," Starke said.

"Would you have believed Maya was from Mars if Wood hadn't confirmed that?" Alexa asked.

"Honestly, no," Starke replied.

"Trent, have you had any other visions about your working on quantum gravity or time dilation?" Maxwell asked.

"No. I've had brief flashes from time to time of complex equations, but they didn't mean anything to me. My most vivid visions are of Shona and Maya, and even those are just snippets."

"Colonel, do you have any objection to me showing Trent my work?" Maxwell asked. "He might react to something."

"I have no objection."

"I'm not sure I'll be of much help, but I'm willing to try," Trent said.

"If Maya's warning is accurate, is there anything we can do to prevent this geological disaster?" Starke asked Maxwell.

"No. We can't stop volcanic eruptions, a magnetic polar shift, or a gamma ray burst."

"How often do magnetic polar shifts occur?" Starke asked.

"It varies," Maxwell replied. "Magnetic field reversals have occurred many times on Earth. We know that one is coming because the magnetic field has been weakening for some time now. Give me a second." Maxwell began typing on his tablet.

"Was anything learned from the examination of Kim's plane?" Su asked.

"Nothing we hadn't seen before on Trent's plane," Sanderson said. "It had the same molecular changes in the same areas."

"General, what role do you think the other eleven people abducted play in this?" Su asked. "They were all taken within hours of each other, from all around the world, but none have been returned."

"I don't know," Starke admitted. "Government leaders are demanding answers, which is why the Secretary of Defense is paying us a visit today. I'd like to have some answers for him."

"I found it!" Maxwell cried.

"Found what?" Starke asked.

"The last *major* magnetic-field reversal occurred about eight hundred thousand years ago. During a reversal, the magnetic field weakens and exposes Earth to higher doses of ultraviolet light."

"What would cause the field to reverse?" Trent asked.

"It's caused by fluctuations in the liquid iron core, which in turn disrupts the main dipolar magnetic field," Maxwell explained. "A geomagnetic field extends from the earth's interior out into space, and protects the planet from solar winds and radiation. It's also responsible for biomagnetism."

"What's biomagnetism have to do with anything?" Starke asked.

"Certain animals can detect the Earth's magnetic field. Birds and sea turtles, for instance, use it for navigation. Deer and cows tend to stand with their body aligned north-south when they're resting."

"I didn't know that," Taylor said. "That doesn't sound all that important."

"But it is," Maxwell said. "A disruption in the biomagnetism will have devastating effects on the ecosystem. Animals and plants will die. Combined with a volcanic winter, food will be very scarce."

"How long do polar shifts last?" Starke asked.

"It depends on the abruptness of the shift. Maya, you said it began in February 2037. Do you know if it's still shifting?"

"No, it's not. The shift was very fast. I don't remember the exact time it took, but I know that it caused a lot of problems."

"Hank, how long could the effects last?" Starke asked.

"They could last for several hundred years. A reversal in the magnetic field usually takes centuries, sometimes tens of thousands of years. During that time, the planet would be exposed to higher doses of radiation. Earth's oxygen levels would also decrease, and the lower temperatures would persist for many decades. If the shift was rapid, that could increase the speed of recovery."

Trent gripped his head.

"Trent, are you alright?" Melissa asked.

"Yes." He took a deep breath and said, "I just had a vision."

"Of what?" Starke asked.

"I know that people lived and farmed underground in preparation for the dark times, but that wasn't enough. Too many didn't believe it would happen. That's why so many people died. People needed food, and just as Maya said, Mars and the colony missions were needed to produce food at an accelerated rate. The food sent to Earth supplemented what humanity couldn't grow underground. There are stations at the poles on Mars working to create a magnetic field so that Mars can develop its own atmosphere."

"Really?" Starke said. "You just learned that?"

"Yes."

"I'd love to hear more about how the magnetic fields are being created," Maxwell said.

"I don't know how it's being done or anything about the technology needed," Trent replied. "I just know that it's being done."

"Is there a water source on Mars?" Sanderson asked.

"Yes," Maya said. "We've developed methods to mine and synthesize water."

Starke said, "Perhaps between Maya's memories and Trent's visions we can learn more about Mars and what we need to do to prepare ourselves."

Silence filled the room.

Then Maya said, "I have a question. Where are the other people that were taken?"

"We don't know, Pumpkin," Trent answered.

Alexa saw that Maya was thinking hard about something. "Do you have another question?"

Maya looked at her and said, "Not right now."

"Back to the main issue then," Maxwell said. "*Why* are we being told about future events in this way, and is Alexa's theory correct? Maya only knows her life on Mars, while Trent only sees snippets of his life, or Aiden's life, there."

"When Captain Wood was revived, she mostly remembered her life on Mars, but she knew Taylor, Trent, and Maya," Melissa said. "She didn't recognize Tai Su until just before she died. She seemed to be struggling to keep herself rooted on Mars."

Maya lowered her head when Melissa mentioning Wood's death. Alexa looked at her and said, "Maybe Maya shouldn't be here for this discussion. It could be a little intense for her."

"Maya, are you okay with listening to our discussion?" Trent asked.

"Yes."

"If something bothers you, just tell me, and we'll leave," Trent said.

"It's okay. I've heard people talk about the loss of crews before," Maya said.

"You have?" Trent said.

"It's a fact of life on Mars. There have been several accidents where people have died. My dad and I almost did when the airlock malfunctioned. We were lucky."

"Hank, anything new on the gravity bursts that were detected during the abductions?" Starke asked.

"I have someone at Hanover working on that," Maxwell replied. "That's why I'm hoping Trent will be able to provide some insight when I show him my work."

"Hank, could the white holes that you think the aliens are producing be responsible for the exotic matter burst Maya's told us about?" Sanderson asked.

"Unknown," Maxwell replied.

Maya leaned forward, put her elbows on the table, and said, "I remember my dad talking about white holes."

"What did he tell you?" Maxwell asked.

"I don't remember much. He did say that white holes power the universe. I know it was an important part of his work."

"Trent, is there anything you can add to that?" Maxwell asked.

Trent closed his eyes, then said, "Cascading microbursts of white holes may have been what triggered some of the disasters on Earth, but it could never be proven." He opened his eyes and added, "My visions must be being triggered by this discussion."

Starke stared at Trent, then glanced at Maxwell. "Well, that was different. Hank, could white hole microbursts trigger volcanic eruptions?"

Maxwell rubbed his chin and said, "A strong enough gravitational burst could trigger earthquakes and eruptions and disrupt the atmosphere, possibly even cause a magnetic polar shift, but I'm not sure how it would happen with microbursts."

"Trent?" Starke said.

"Sorry, that's all I got."

Maxwell rocked back in his chair. "General, if Trent, or rather Aiden, was doing theoretical work on white holes, that could be why he was taken. Maya could be here to help him connect with that knowledge. If the aliens are controlling something akin to a white hole, they could warp spacetime within a multiverse continuum. Trent may be the key to helping us unlock that technology."

"How?" Starke asked.

"Creating a time dilation event could theoretically allow the aliens to see what the future holds for humankind," Maxwell said. "Were any of the others that were taken scientists?"

"I haven't gotten the complete bio packets for the abductees from China and Russia," Starke said. "None of the American abductees' professions are of interest." He read all of their names aloud, then added, "There's a stay-at-home mom, a career banker, a realtor, an insurance adjuster, and a pharmaceutical rep."

"What about the one taken from the ship?" Alexa asked.

"Her name is Naira Kavena. I don't have her full bio yet."

"And the others from Canada and England?"

Starke pulled up a file on his tablet. "The English woman is in publishing."

He continued to scroll through the file. When he stopped, his eyes lit up. "The Canadian is a volcanologist. She was stationed in Iceland as part of a scientific team studying Icelandic volcanic activity."

"So we now have two indications that we're dealing with volcanos," Alexa said. "There has to be a connection. Trent, Taylor, did either of you recognize any of the names?"

"I don't know any of them," Trent said.

"Me either," Taylor said.

"Maybe Trent, Taylor, and Maya should look at the photo files," Melissa offered. "They may recognize someone."

The general slid the tablet across the table. It displayed a list of names with corresponding photos. "Well?" Starke asked.

"Nothing," Trent said, after scrolling through the pictures.

"Same for me," Taylor said.

Maya studied the photos. She stopped a few times on different photos, then moved on. When she looked up, she smiled and said, "I know some of these people." She pointed at the first photo on the list and turned the pad around so Melissa and Starke could see it. "This is Dr. Tanisha Jenkins. She's a higher education teacher at Ares Prep at Colony Four. I think she teaches math."

Melissa looked at the photo Maya had identified. "That's Amara Williams from Ft. Myers, Florida. She's a stay-at-home mom. Someone take notes."

"I will," Sanderson said, pulling an old notepad from his pocket.

Maya scrolled down and pointed again. "This is Miku Akiyama. I talk to her when she does the safety inspections around the station. I like saying her name. It's Japanese."

Melissa looked at the photo and said, "That's Chiyo Hayashi, a realtor from Seattle, Washington. Any others, Maya?"

"I think this is Mrs. Camden. I don't know her first name. She's a surface explorer. She has the most beautiful dark skin, and she's really nice."

"That's Gloria Brown, the insurance adjuster from Waco, Texas." Melissa confirmed.

"And this is Chandra," Maya said. "I think her last name is James. She has an English accent. I think she's in atmospheric engineering."

"Deanne Dutta. She's in publishing in London, England."

"Oh, and this is Dr. Brynn Bush. She teaches chemistry and geophysics at Elysium College. She's put on demonstrations at my TEK school. I really like her."

"TEK?" Starke asked.

"I attend Titan Essential Knowledge School."

"Cecilla Tanner," Melissa said. "She's our Canadian volcanologist."

"You're doing great, Maya," Starke said. "Anyone else?"

She reviewed the photos, then said, "No. Those are the only ones I know for sure."

"Five positive IDs," Starke said. "That's impressive."

"I'd say it's imperative that we get Maya fully debriefed," Maxwell said.

"You think?" Starke said sarcastically. "I want to know everything that Maya knows about Mars, the colonies, and Earth's history. I want specifics on everyday life, including operations, housing, staffing, food, power, military, political and educational systems, historical events, plus anything else relevant. I want to know what Maya remembers from her earlier childhood, including classes she's attended. I want her to paint us a picture of her life on Mars. Is that clear?"

"Yes, sir," Melissa replied.

"We need to get started with in-depth interviews," Maxwell said.

"I agree," Melissa said.

Taylor said, "We should limit the time and the number of people asking questions."

"Agreed," Melissa said. "Hank, how do you want to proceed?"

"I'll take the lead. In addition to what General Starke has asked for, we also need to talk about scientific and medical technology advancement."

General Starke leaned forward and said, "Maya, can you provide all of that information to us?"

"Yes."

Alexa said, "General Starke, it will take time for Maya to give us that much information. She can't do a data dump."

"Then you better get started," Starke said. "Maya, I bet you're hungry."

"I am."

"Alright, then let's take a short break and grab a bite. When you're done, I want someone to do a full comparative analysis of the people Maya knows on Mars and the abductees. Look at their family history, including medical. These people are linked somehow, so I want to know everything about them. Hank, you start interviewing Maya."

"You can use my office," Melissa said. "It has a large conference table. I can listen in while I work on the analysis."

"Okay," Maxwell said.

"One more thing," Melissa said. "Why do all of these people on Mars look like they do here?"

"I can think of a number of reasons," Maxwell said. "In a multiverse scenario, they could be living a completely different life. A different reality. They could even be genetically modified versions of their ancestors."

"Why would the aliens do that?" Starke asked.

"So that Maya would recognize them."

"Again, why?"

"To provide additional credibility to Maya's warning."

"I still don't understand why they would want to go to all that trouble," Starke said, shaking his head. "Let's break. I need to check on something before Barrington arrives. Colonel, I'll forward any additional information I receive about the abductees to you."

Brown Level — Melissa's Office — 1335 hours

Maxwell, Maya, Alexa, Taylor, and Trent sat around a large circular table in Melissa's office. Melissa worked at her desk.

"Maya, tell us about where you live," Maxwell said. "Describe it to us."

"Do you want to know about the station or just where we live?"

"Both," Maxwell replied.

"I'll start with our module. It has two bedrooms, a bathroom, a kitchen, and a work area."

"That sounds sizable," Maxwell said. "How many modules like this one are there at Hecates Tholus Station?" Maxwell asked.

Maya scrunched her brow, then replied, "I don't know the exact number. We live on sublevel seven, Aldrin wing, white area. Our station is built into the side of a crater. There are eleven sublevels at the station and two surface levels that are covered by a thick layer of dust and rock to protect us from radiation and micrometeors."

"Does each sublevel have living quarters?" Alexa asked.

Maya giggled. "No. There are only four sublevels with housing modules—five through eight."

"How large are each of the sublevels?" Maxwell asked.

"Um, there are four wings per level. Each wing has four habitats— white, green, red and blue—and each habitat has twenty housing modules. Some modules are bigger than others, depending on the family's needs. We only need two bedrooms, so our module is one of the smaller units."

"The station has to be huge," Alexa said. "That's three hundred and twenty housing units per sublevel. Maya, how many people are assigned to Colony Four?"

"It fluctuates because people are always being reassigned. I think our station is designed for five thousand."

"How many stations are there on Mars?" Maxwell asked.

"Stations or colonies?"

"There's a difference?" Maxwell asked.

"Yes. There are four colonies, each with three permanent research stations like Hecates, and there's two additional colonies under construction."

"Can you give us an idea of what's on each level of your station?" Maxwell asked. "If possible, start at the crater rim."

"That's easy. Above the crater rim there are several surface modules. That's where the command and communications centers, access hangars and explorer vehicle storage, and surface observatories are located. I've only been to an observatory a few times. I'm too young to visit the command and control center or the communications facility. You have to be in ninth grade before you can go there."

"What grade are you in?" Alexa asked.

"Fifth. There's an LLZ three kilometers away from the central access hub."

"What's an LLZ?" Alexa asked.

"It's the Launch and Landing Zone. Someday I hope to go to one of the satellite stations."

Alexa leaned back and shook her head in disbelief. "Let's back up a second. I want to make sure I understand. There are four colonies and a total of twelve stations. Is that everything?"

"No. There's also the exploratory outposts and mining facilities." Maya thought for a moment, then added, "There are three agricultural centers with eight processing plants and four polar magnetosphere outposts. There will be six more permanent stations at the two colonies that are under construction."

Trent asked, "Is your station the largest on the planet?"

"No. We're one of the smaller stations."

Maxwell asked, "Is there anything in orbit around the planet, like satellites?"

"There are twelve orbital spaceflight launch platforms, four observatory stations, a bunch of weather and communications satellites, and two large HABs."

"What's a HAB?" Maxwell asked.

"Habitable satellite stations."

"How many people live there?" Alexa asked.

Maya sat back in her chair. "I'm not sure. I think about twice as many as at our station."

"What do they do there?" Trent asked.

"A lot of things. Some people work in the spacecraft manufacturing, assembly, and repair plants. There are research labs where scientists conduct zero gravity experiments. The spaceflight operations command is also there, and most of the astronauts and support personnel live there."

"You said there are twelve orbital spaceflight launch platforms." Trent said. "Why so many?"

"We have a lot of spacecraft that take food to Earth and bring supplies and equipment back to Mars and the orbital stations. There's a launch and return flight at least twice a week. It takes time to prepare for an Earthbound flight, and to unload the cargo ships when they arrive from Earth. The cargo ships are really big."

"How do you get equipment and supplies to the stations?" Maxwell asked.

"Shuttles ferry them to the different stations."

"Do you know how long the transit time is from Mars to Earth?"

"It varies from five weeks to two months. It depends on the distance between Mars and the Earth."

"That's amazingly fast," Maxwell said. "How is that possible?"

"I don't know."

"Probably an advanced engine to go along with the larger spacecraft," Trent said. "Maybe the aliens provided the technology."

"Is all this information something you were taught in school?" Alexa said.

"Some of it. Some of it you just learn. I learned the history of Mars and the stations' development two grades ago. I know why each station was built and what mission each of them is responsible for achieving. Do you need to know that?"

"Not right now," Maxwell said. "How do you know when space flights are scheduled?"

"The schedule is posted on the information channel. Sometimes we have to ration certain supplies, so it helps to know when the next supply ship is landing at the station."

Maxwell leaned in, then said, "Maya, do you know how many people live on Mars?"

"Hmm." Maya tapped her fingers on her chin. "I think there's about ninety thousand on the surface. Some are Martian-born, like me. Then there's about ten thousand people living on each HAB. There's supposed to be nearly two hundred thousand people on or in orbit around Mars after the two new colonies are completed and another HAB is built."

"That's quite an amazing feat, considering we haven't even been to Mars yet," Taylor said.

"Yes, it is," Maxwell said. "The transit times between Earth and Mars are far less than what the current technology will allow. The frequency of the trips means that food production must be working well."

"It is," Maya said. "My real mom told me that she is developing a system that will increase food production threefold. The oxygen the crops produce will provide us with a self-supporting oxygen system in case of a major disaster, like a meteor strike. She is really excited about getting it up and running."

Taylor said, "I wish I could see what Mars looks like."

Maya said, "Compared to what I saw outside earlier, there's really nothing to see there."

"Anything else you can tell us about life on Mars?" Maxwell asked.

"I didn't tell you about the Triple-A's."

"What are those?" Maxwell asked.

"Autonomous Articulated Androids. They're the latest in artificially intelligent robots. They do most of the work outside of the stations. They're building the new stations almost entirely on their own. The Triple-A's are physically stronger and taller than us. Dad says he thinks they're smarter than us."

"What can you tell us about the spacecraft you use to move supplies?" Maxwell asked.

"I don't know very much about the ships."

"Maya, the information you're providing will assist us in leaping ahead in our preparation for going to Mars," Maxwell said. "Let's get back to the stations and their history."

Maya told them what she could about when the different stations were built and where they were located.

Alexa asked the question that no one had asked yet. "What's Earth like in your time?"

Maya looked at each of them in turn. "From the pictures I've seen, it's not like this anymore."

"What do you mean?" Maxwell asked.

Before Maya could answer, the phone rang, and Melissa answered. "Yes, sir. We'll be right up." There was a short pause. "I understand." After hanging up, Melissa said, "We need to go meet the Secretary of Defense. Maya, you've done an amazing job. We'll have to pick this up later."

TWENTY-ONE

Brown Level — Conference Room — February 6 — 1430 hours

Secretary of Defense Colin Barrington stepped from the cloaked vehicle, which had just parked in the hangar. He'd landed at Mountain Home AFB thirty minutes earlier and had been escorted to the transport.

General Starke and Colonel Endo stood at attention as he walked toward them.

"It's good to see you, General Starke," Barrington said. "I hope you have some answers for me."

General Starke saluted, then shook his hand. "We do. Mr. Secretary, this is Col. Melissa Endo. She's been working to find those answers."

"Pleased to finally meet you in person," Barrington said.

"Sir, it's good to meet you as well," Melissa replied.

"Let's get to it then," Barrington said.

"Yes, sir," Starke said. "Everyone is waiting for us in a conference room in the Nova Annex. If you'll follow me."

"That's some door," Barrington said as he approached the entrance to the Altair Annex. "How did the aliens get through it?"

Melissa knew the secretary had set the tone for the meeting already. "They didn't need a door, Mr. Secretary."

"How'd they get in?" Barrington asked as they walked into the atrium area.

"They used a beam of light that we don't yet understand. Dr. Maxwell has a theory."

"You mean to tell me that they used a transporter like on *Star Trek?*"

"It was nothing like that," Starke said.

"We spent a lot of money on this facility. I don't want to hear that they arrived in a beam of light. I want to know how that light works and if we can stop them."

"We'll explain it in greater detail after we get to the conference room," Starke said. "I'm sure you're going to have more questions, and the people you'll meet will provide some answers. There have been some additional developments in the last hour."

"I don't want *some* answers. I want *all* of the answers, as does the president. I read the reports. They lack the detail we need to make good decisions."

A few minutes later, the three of them entered the conference room. Dr. Maxwell, Dr. Sanderson, and Captain Su stood. The others followed their lead, and introductions were made.

"Sit down, everyone," Barrington said. "I understand that Trent, Taylor, and Captain Su are the abductees and that Maya is our guest from the future. I want to hear your accounts, your ideas on what we're going to do from today on, and I want direct answers."

As the briefing progressed the secretary looked less than satisfied.

"So you're saying that we really don't have anything concrete to tell the president or the other world leaders about how to defend the planet or stop the events that have been foretold by this ten-year-old?"

"Mr. Secretary, we've learned quite a lot over the last few hours," Melissa said. "And Maya has given us some insight into the future that humanity will build on Mars. We need more time to gather additional information."

"Dr. Maxwell, do you really think an alien species would go to the trouble of warning us about a cataclysmic event by having a little girl deliver the message?"

"I can't say with any certainty why they're using Maya, or the other abductees. From what she's told us, combined with what we do know, I'd say we should listen to her."

"Dr. Sanderson, do you concur?"

"I do, sir."

"Colonel, why now?" Barrington asked. "Trent, Taylor, and the others were abducted years ago. Why not have them bring us the message sooner and in a way that would give it merit?"

"Who would have believed them?" Melissa asked. "We only recently developed the medical technology to find the implants. They are invisible to everything we've used in the past, and they dissolve almost instantly when exposed to air."

Barrington pounded the table with his index finger. "These damn aliens could have found a way to tell us sooner, and they could have done it themselves. This catch and release program doesn't make any sense to me."

Melissa's anger surged. "Secretary Barrington, how would you explain to a chimpanzee that it was going to be moved to a new zoo? A chimp may understand what a picture of a zoo is, but not that it's going to be moved to that zoo in the future and how it's life is going to change when it gets there? A chimp can bang away at a keyboard, but it won't understand why pictures on the screen change."

"Don't you dare be condescending to me," Barrington boomed. "Comparing us to monkeys isn't relevant."

Obviously the secretary was under intense pressure, Melissa thought, as were they all. "Mr. Secretary, I wasn't being condescending. We have been given pieces of a puzzle by an advanced species. Like the chimp, we can see the picture, but we have no idea what it means. Maya and the other abductees are being used to provide context for what they're showing us without provoking us. Alexa believes that the aliens understand human nature, so they know that when we are faced with something that threatens us, we usually respond with force first."

Barrington said, "Trent's girlfriend is offering explanations about why the aliens are acting this way. You're taking advice from a civilian that shouldn't even be here to begin with. What do *our* experts think?"

"Mr. Secretary, the aliens are an incredibly advanced species, and I agree with Alexa's assessment," Sanderson said. "We know from Trent and Maya that these creatures can manipulate matter through time. Dr. Maxwell's theoretical research is just beginning to scratch the surface of this capability, while they're using it." He wiped the sweat from his forehead.

"They abducted other people after Captain Wood's death. They made the last group of abductions very overt. I think that was done to make sure we received their message and so we'd start connecting the dots."

"Why would they wait to take more people?" Barrington asked. "Why not snatch them all at once?"

"I believe Captain Wood's death was an unforeseen event which prevented them from sending us the information they want us to have," Sanderson replied. "One thing Captain Wood did before her death was verify Trent's account of the future."

"I concur," Melissa said. "Captain Wood couldn't deliver the message they wanted us to have, so they took the other eleven people. I don't know what role they play, but Maya has identified several of them from her time on Mars. We can say with absolute certainty that Maya is from the future or a different dimension."

"That's a strange way for an advanced species to communicate," Barrington said. He looked at Melissa, then said, "And don't give me another monkey analogy."

"Secretary Barrington, it could be as simple as they don't have a way to communicate with us directly," Maxwell offered. "By using people known on Mars, they can show us the future as it relates to those who are here in the present. I believe what Trent and Maya are telling us is true. A cataclysmic event is on the horizon and Mars is our salvation."

Barrington said, "If that's true, we will need to warn the leaders of the world. We also need to have the means to prevent future alien abductions if we hope to gain there support."

"We can't stop them," Trent said. "I agree with Melissa and Dr. Sanderson. Maya is here to tell us what I can't see in my visions or to put them in context. I only get fragments from the other time, or Aiden Cooper's time, on Mars. Maya has only known Mars. She has no reason to fabricate anything."

"Interesting hypothesis," Barrington said, using a disbelieving tone. "I need to convince the president, and the world, that this isn't a prelude to an invasion. For all I know that implant in your brain has given them all the information they need for the best way to attack us."

Trent said, "Sir, these people are doing the best they can to find the answers you need." Then in a more forceful tone, he said, "This is not a prelude to an alien invasion. We *are* going to experience a catastrophic event that will alter our civilization significantly. Billions of people are going to die. Maya's warning gives us time to prepare and give humanity hope. We can't stop what's going to happen, so you'd better listen to us."

The SecDef clenched his jaw. After a moment, he said to Trent, "I appreciate your candor, but not your tone."

"Mr. Secretary, I really don't care what you think of my tone," Trent said. "Taylor has been studied for two years. It wasn't until Maya and I were brought here that the pieces starting coming together. You wanted answers. Well, you're getting them."

Melissa stifled a smile, then said, "Mr. Secretary, Trent is correct. If the aliens' intention was to invade, they would have done so by now. There is no call for alarm. These abductions have been occurring for at least thirty years. Probably longer."

"Colonel, do you honestly believe that these creatures abducted these people so they could just give us a warning?" Barrington asked, shaking his head as if he was disgusted. "We have a crisis on our hands, and you really want me to tell the president that a ten-year-old has delivered a prophecy of doom and we'd better *listen?*"

"Yes, that's exactly what you need to tell the president," Melissa replied. "There's a catastrophe of biblical proportions looming, and these beings want us to survive."

Barrington huffed. "You want the president to go on television and announce to the world that little green men are real and that we can't stop them from abducting people?" Barrington cried. "Then a few months later, tell them that in seven years that half of the world's population is going to die from a series of cataclysmic events, and again, there's nothing we can do to stop it. Do you have any idea how that will play with the public?"

"Not to be flippant," Trent said, "but the aliens I remember were brown."

Barrington glared at him. "Do you find this funny, Mr. McDougal?"

"Not in the least," Trent replied. "I'm the one with an alien implant in my head and leg. I just thought you might want to have your facts straight when you tell the president and the world what they look like."

Taylor hid a smile.

"Mr. Secretary," Maxwell said, "we have made some inroads into discovering how the aliens are abducting and returning people. We believe they're able to manipulate and control singularities on a quantum level. The technology to manipulate matter this dense requires a technology so far ahead of ours that it staggers the imagination. We've detected gravitational wave bursts each time they've arrived."

"Yes, I know. General Starke briefed me earlier."

"I believe that in time we'll find a way to determine where and when they are here."

"What the hell good will that do?" Barrington asked. "People on the cruise ship saw them coming, and a light pushed them out of the way so they could take an American off the boat." Barrington glanced at each of them. "Dr. Maxwell, when will you be able to tell me how we stop them? At this point, I'd settle for being able to communicate with them directly."

"I can't tell you when we can do that. Secretary Barrington, we may not want to prevent them from taking more people. I think they're trying to warn us the only way they can. Whoever they take may play an important role in how we react or receive information that we will need to survive. What I do know is that we need additional personnel assigned to the project."

"I was certain that funding would become an issue," Barrington said. "How much will it take to expedite your research?"

"Funding would certainly help," Starke said, "but what we really need is more people to address the problem. We can't begin to gather all the information, much less analyze it, with the staff we have at this facility. The information is too sensitive to go global or to use university staff. Dr. Maxwell has sought help as best he could without divulging our existence, but it's slow going."

"Excuse me, General, but we *do* need a global effort," Maxwell said. "Which means declassifying information or granting more clearances to people to work on the project."

"Perhaps," Barrington said.

"With Maya's help we've made significant progress," Starke said. "Although we can't say with a hundred percent certainty that a global event is coming, you should know that I believe Maya. Mr. Secretary, we need to get the American public prepared to handle the fact that aliens exist. Then we need to tell them that they're helping us and that we are going to need to do a lot of prep work to survive as a species."

The secretary leaned back and steepled his fingers in front of his lips. After a few moments, he said, "It won't hurt to make some preparations. They'll need to be covert. Dr. Maxwell, I'll see what I can do about getting you more staff. I want all of you to keep in mind that these creatures may have less than altruistic motives for doing what they're doing."

"I always have that in mind, sir," Starke said.

Barrington looked at Maya. "Young lady, are you sure about your facts? Are there aliens on Mars?"

Maya sat up straighter, then said, "There aren't any aliens on Mars. There are people on Mars. And yes, I'm sure about everything I've said."

"I know you believe that, but sometimes things in life get twisted, and our perspective becomes clouded. Colonel, you're certain that she doesn't have an implant?"

"Very sure," Melissa replied.

"Then how did the aliens know to bring her to this facility?"

"They know where I am," Trent answered, "and they brought Captain Wood here. Bringing Maya here shouldn't be that hard to understand."

Barrington shook his head. "Smoke and mirrors. For now, I'm going to recommend to the president that we tell the world that these abductions are the result of a military experiment with a new defensive weapons system that malfunctioned."

"I knew that I was going to be made the scapegoat," Maxwell said.

"I won't name anyone," Barrington said. "We'll just tell them that it involved a quantum experiment with a consequence that wasn't foreseen."

"I don't believe the public or any other world leader will accept that explanation," Melissa said.

"Probably not long-term," Barrington said, sounding disheartened. "But for now, that's all they're going to get. Like the general said, we need to gradually prepare the leaders of the world. Dr. Maxwell, what other staff do you need?"

"We can use physicists, geologists, volcanologists, botanists, and medical personnel, just to name a few. I will give General Starke a detailed list of everyone and everything we'll need to get started."

"I'll work up a preliminary budget for your approval," Starke added.

"That's a start, at least," Barrington said.

"We also need to accelerate our space program," Melissa added.

"One step at a time," Barrington said. "Pouring more money into that program will only spark more rumors. We need to see what happens over the next few months. I need to get the general his funding and staff. If you people can provide some concrete answers, maybe then we'll take the next step."

"Understood, sir," Starke said.

Barrington sighed, then said, "I must be crazy. You know the president might just fire me on the spot for telling him about Maya's story and your theory. If any of you discover anything else, I want to know about it immediately. Is that understood?"

"Yes, sir," Starke replied.

The secretary stood and looked at Maya. "Maya, I hope you're wrong."

"I'm not," Maya said.

"Then God help us all."

Brown Level — February 7, 0800 hours

General Starke was sitting at his desk when his external phone rang. "Starke," he answered.

"Well, the president didn't fire me, and the Russians and the Chinese want a seat at the table," Barrington said, getting right to the point.

"The president believed us?" Starke asked.

"Yes."

"I thought he was going to keep this quiet and slowly ease the world leaders into what's happening?"

"The president wants to explore all options. The Russians and Chinese want to send their scientists to Sawtooth. They want to see the evidence firsthand and to speak with the abductees and Maya. So do the English, Germans, French, Japanese, and Canadians."

"I gave you a list of the people Dr. Maxwell wants on his team. I'll see if there's anyone from those countries he'd like to have on-board."

"Dr. Maxwell's people will begin arriving at your facility tomorrow afternoon, as will all of the others the president has agreed to sending."

"I'll need additional supplies and security as soon as you can provide them."

"I know," Barrington said. "The president wants you to give the new staffers all the information you have about the aliens and the abductees, including research results. This includes the Chinese and Russian representatives. You're to leave nothing out."

"Sir?" Starke said. "Why would we want to show them everything?"

"Because the president is going on television this evening to tell the world that an alien species is responsible for the abductions."

"He's what?" Starke cried. "That's insane. He'll start a global panic. What happened to telling people that it was an experiment gone wrong?"

"He decided not to lie to the public. He figured that with the videos going viral, the media coverage, and all the speculation about how the aliens are responsible for the abductions, that the truth would leak anyway. He's not going to mention the doomsday event or time travel. He wants the media to focus on the alien contact and what we're doing to get those who were taken returned. That will give us a cover story in case anyone gets wind that we're looking at building underground shelters and stockpiling food, seeds, and everything else we'll need to survive."

"Telling the world that aliens are abducting human beings and that we can't prevent it from happening is wrong. You're going to need to beef up security around Groom Lake because every conspiracy theorist, alien hunter, and crazy in the world is going to descend on that site."

"We're aware of that. To put your mind at ease, no one is going to know where Sawtooth is located. The personnel coming to you are being flown to airbases along the West Coast. They'll be transported by ground at varying times. If anyone gets wind of the scientists headed your way, we'll claim everything is being run out of an underground facility at Mountain Home AFB. The media and whoever else can camp out there as long as they want, and they won't find a thing."

"This is a bad idea. The media will find budget allocations destined for the cataclysm preparation work. Then what's the president going to say?"

"The decision has been made."

"What else is the president going to tell the world?"

"POTUS is going to announce a global cooperative effort to stop any more abductions. He plans to tell the world that we've been aware of an alien presence for years and that we have been trying to make contact. The aliens abducting so many people at once is a sign that we're making progress."

"I thought you said he wasn't going to lie," Starke said.

"It's not really a lie."

"This is going to get ugly," Starke said. "Our cover story would have played better."

"He's concerned that if we discover other evidence of a pending global catastrophe, aside from Maya's tale, that learning about aliens and the event at the same time would be worse. This way we can simply tell people that the aliens made contact to warn us."

"I still don't like it."

"Well, then you definitely won't like what else I'm going to tell you. He's going to tell everyone about Taylor, Trent, and Captain Su and how they were returned unharmed."

"Why would he do that?" Starke exclaimed. He couldn't believe what he was hearing.

"His advisors convinced him that it's best if the public thinks the aliens will eventually return the abductees, alive. He thinks putting Trent, Taylor, and Su on television will reduce panic."

"What about Captain Wood?"

"He's not going to mention her."

"And Maya?" Starke asked. "How do we explain her?"

"We don't. She's not to be mentioned."

"Mr. Secretary, disclosing that Taylor is still alive and has been held in captivity for two years will not sit well with her family or the public. We went to great lengths to confirm her death. And what happens if Trent has another episode during the broadcast and collapses on national television? Moving any of them out of the facility is a bad idea. People will remember seeing them. The lid won't stay on this for very long. I think this facility will be compromised."

"General, you will do the broadcast from the facility," Barrington said firmly. "The president wants Taylor and Trent to tell the world that they were abducted more than once, starting with when they were children, and that they have always been returned unharmed. Trent, Taylor, and Su need to emphasize that there is nothing to fear from these abductions and that the aliens are . . . friendly."

"Mr. Secretary, as I said, Taylor was declared dead. Her family will know that we lied to them to cover up her abduction and return. Most people would consider that a harmful outcome. The media will turn our story into shit in a heartbeat. Can't we just use Trent and Su?"

There was a short pause. "Good point. I'll tell the president that the optics will be bad if we use Taylor."

"I could have Trent and Su say that there are others who have been returned, but out of concern for their privacy and safety, we are withholding their names."

"That's good," Barrington said. "Do you have anything new to report?"

"No, sir. Maxwell has reached out to his contact at LIGO. There's been no new activity. Dr. Sanderson has nothing new to offer, either."

"The aliens will show themselves again?"

"I have no doubt that they will."

"Good luck, general," Barrington said. "I hope you have something new to report soon."

"As do I, sir."

TWENTY-TWO

The Hangar — February 7 — 1230 hours

A blazing white light invaded the sanctity of the hangar, then disappeared a moment later. Alarms blared as red intrusion lights strobed. Marines and technicians scrambled and took up defensive positions to secure the hangar. Two women sat cross-legged in the middle of the floor. Both of them appeared to be dazed. They looked around in apparent confusion. Their movements were slow and unsteady as they tried to stand.

"Stay where you are!" a Marine shouted.

General Starke ran to the elevator, where Melissa met him.

"It appears that our visitors have returned," Starke said. "I was advised that we have two returnees. They've been ordered not to move, and they have complied."

"Good," Melissa said. "A team will meet us at the security door. Have they been identified?"

"Not yet. I think we should have the others join us."

After getting off the elevator, Starke called Trent. "You know what the alarm means, right?' Starke asked.

"Yes, general. How many have been returned?"

"Two. They're in the hangar."

"I'll call Alexa. Do you know who they are?"

"Not yet," Starke replied. "I want all of you, including Maya, to join us to meet them."

Trent and the others descended to Green Level and hurried through the Altair atrium to the hangar security door.

Trent looked at the security monitor. The two women sat on the floor, looking frightened.

Starke asked Maya, "Can you identify either of the women?"

"Haven't you identified them yet?" Trent asked.

"We have, but I'd like confirmation."

"I see Miku," Maya said. "I don't know the other oriental woman."

"Correct," Starke said. "Miku's name here is Chiyo Hayashi. Maya, you're certain you don't recognize the other woman?"

"Yes. I'm sure," Maya replied.

"Trent, maybe one of them will recognize you. When the door opens, step inside and call to Chiyo."

The seal hissed when the door opened. Both women stared at Trent, Taylor, and Maya as they walked into the hangar. A medical team was poised behind them.

"Don't be frightened," Trent said. "Are you Chiyo?"

"How do you know my name?"

"Who's your friend?" Trent asked.

Chiyo looked at the woman next to her and replied, "I don't know."

The other woman looked terrified.

"Try the names Mei Lien Wan or Chyou Hao," Melissa suggested. "Those are our two Chinese abductees."

"Taylor, you and Maya wait here," Trent said. He took a few steps toward the women. "Are you Mei Lien Wan?"

She nodded.

"You're safe," Trent said. He looked back at the door and asked, "Does anyone speak Chinese?"

"We've sent for an interrupter," Starke said.

Trent took a few more cautious steps toward the women, and then he heard the sound of footsteps approaching him quickly.

"Maya, come back here!" Taylor cried.

"It's okay," Trent said. Maya took his hand when she reached his side. *Good idea. People aren't afraid of children,* Trent thought.

"Colonel, I guess biohazard protocols are a thing of the past," Starke said.

"Yes, sir. I see no reason for them at this point."

When Trent and Maya neared the two women, Maya said, "Miku, do you recognize me?"

"My name is Chiyo, and no, I don't recognize you. Where am I?"

"You're safe," Trent said again, then offered his hand to help Chiyo to her feet. "Please, come with us."

Chiyo didn't move. "Tell me where I am."

Trent smiled and said, "Strange as this might sound, you're in Idaho. We'll explain everything later."

Maya approached Mei Lien and extended her hand, then said, "I'm Maya. Do you speak English?"

Mei Lien stood. "Yes. I'm in Idaho? In America?"

"Yes, you are," Trent answered. "General, she speaks English."

Starke joined them, and said, "That'll make things easier. I guess we don't need the interpreter."

Trent asked, "Are either of you injured?"

"I'm not," Chiyo answered, "but I'm confused. How did I get here from Seattle?"

Mei Lien said, "I'm okay. I was in China."

As Melissa and the medical team approached, Trent noticed that Taylor had stayed with Alexa by the door. Taylor looked upset, but he didn't know why. Trent turned back to the two abductees. "Ladies, this is General Starke and Colonel Endo of the United States Space Force."

"Trent, we need to get them medically cleared," Melissa said. "Chiyo, Mei Lien, may I please have a look at your left tibia?"

The women looked puzzled by the question, but complied. They both had a triangular scar on their leg.

Trent smiled and pulled up his pant leg and pointed to his scar. "We have much in common, and we need to talk. You'll be well taken care of here."

"Unbelievable," Starke muttered. "I need to know if Maxwell's team at Hanover registered the return event. Mei Lien, what's the last thing you remember?"

"I don't know how you did this, but my government won't stand for it."

Starke nodded. "Mei Lien, your government knows all about your abduction. We'll explain everything once you're medically cleared, but I'd like an answer to my question."

"My abduction?" Mei Lien said.

"Yes, you were abducted, now answer my question," Starke said more forcefully.

"I was preparing to go to work at my clinic. Then there was a flash of light, and then I'm here."

"I remember a flash of light, too," Chiyo said. "Then I woke up here. What's going on? Was I abducted?"

"Yes," Starke replied. "This may sound strange, but do either of you remember being on Mars?"

"What?" Chiyo said.

"Please answer," Starke said.

"No," Chiyo replied.

"No," Mei Lien answered. "Is this a military exercise?"

"Colonel, I want their medicals expedited," Starke ordered.

"I want some answers," Chiyo insisted.

Maya took Chiyo's hand and said, "You don't know me here, but I know you on Mars. Your name there is Miku Akiyama. You are here because you live on Mars in the future. Mei Lien must be there too, but I don't know her. You are both here in this time because that's where the aliens want you to be."

Trent wasn't surprised by the look of utter disbelief on both of the women's faces. "She's telling you the truth. The scar on your leg is from an alien implant that was put there when you were children. We have to get you to medical right away. Then we can talk at length."

They walked to the first set of elevators in the Altair annex. The women looked around in stunned disbelief. Trent and Maya stood with Alexa and Taylor by the elevator door as Starke and the others boarded.

"We'll catch the next one," Trent said as the elevator doors closed.

"Taylor, are you alright?" Alexa asked.

Taylor shook her head and said, "I'm not sure."

"What's wrong?" Trent asked.

Taylor sighed, then said, "I know the others will be brought here. When they're all back . . . I think the aliens will take me back with them."

"What are you talking about?" Alexa said.

"Maya's given the general the warning, and Trent and Maya will be of value to Maxwell and the others in preparing for the event. I have no role to play."

Alexa shook her head and said, "That's not true. It's very unlikely the aliens will take you away."

Taylor looked at Maya. "You're beautiful, smart, and I adore you. But in this time you're not my Emma. I miss her and my husband deeply. I want to see them again." Taylor's eyes filled with tears.

"That's understandable," Trent said. He put his arm around Taylor's shoulder. "Maybe you should tell Melissa how you're feeling." Trent thought that Taylor was having an emotional meltdown. He'd never seen her like this before.

Taylor pulled away from him. "I want to go home. I want to get off this merry-go-round and go back to a normal life. Trent, you've only been at this for a few days. How would you feel if you'd lost everything you loved and had been held captive for as long as I've been?"

"Taylor, I can't begin to understand the emotional trauma you've experienced," Alexa said. "Understand that we're here for you. We need you. Maya needs you. If you don't want to talk about it with Melissa, then I'll listen. We all will."

Trent looked at Maya. She seemed to be taking this discussion better than he would have expected. As she gazed at Taylor, the look in her eyes was filled with compassion. He figured she was trying to think of a way to make Taylor feel better.

Taylor sighed again. "Maya, I'm sorry. This isn't fair to you. It isn't fair to any of us, and that's my point. I've survived on anger for as long as I can remember. Now all I have is the reality that everyone has served a purpose except for me."

"That's not true," Alexa said.

"If you need someone to be angry with, be angry with me," Maya said. "It was my fault the airlock malfunctioned."

Taylor knelt and took Maya by the shoulders. "You didn't cause the airlock to malfunction. Maya, I could never be mad at you. You should be mad at me for being such a wreck."

"You have every right to be a wreck," Alexa said.

Taylor looked up at her. "Forgive me—all of you. I'm just exhausted, and it all just came burbling out of me. All of these people have a life to return to. Even you and Trent have a future. I can't go home to my family, so the only useful purpose I can serve is to the aliens." Taylor sniffled. "I need some time alone. I'm going back to the apartment. You all go check on the new arrivals."

"Mom, I'll go back to our living quarters with you," Maya said.

Taylor smiled at hearing Maya call her Mom. "You're welcome to join me, but I won't be very good company. I need some time to think. You'll have to find something to do and be quiet. Let's take a walk first."

After Maya and Taylor walked away, Trent and Alexa boarded the elevator. Once the doors closed, Trent asked, "Do you think I should mention Taylor's meltdown to Melissa?"

"I wouldn't," Alexa replied. "Taylor has some issues to sort out. She was just expressing her feelings. That's all."

Altair Annex – Red Level – February 7 – 1325 hours

Melissa had just finished the AMRS scan on Mei Lien. Neither Chiyo nor Mei Lien had any implants other than the ones in their leg. She'd taken a DNA swab, run EEGs, EKGs, and drawn blood from both women.

"I wish the region of China where I work had half the equipment you have here," Mei Lien said. "Very impressive."

"Thank you," Melissa replied. "I was told that you're a physician, but I don't know your specialization."

"General medicine. I'm a family doctor in Dunhuang."

"Where is that exactly?" Melissa asked.

"It's in northwest China, near where the Taklamakan Desert and the Gobi Desert meet. It was once a great trading city and a part of the ancient Silk Road."

"Pretty remote then?"

"Yes. The area is home to only about two hundred thousand people. Visitors come there to see the Mogao Buddhist caves."

"Have you lived there your whole life?"

"It's where I was born, but I left to attend university for my medical training. Then I went back to do what I could to help."

"So you were in Dunhuang when you were abducted during your childhood?"

Mei Lien smiled and said, "I must have been, but I don't remember it or how I got the scar on my leg. Now you tell me that there's an alien implant in my tibia. I'm at a loss to explain any of it. I was in Beijing before I ended up here."

"Why were you in Beijing?"

"I was receiving training in the latest neonatal care. The clinic where I work was to receive our first incubator."

"Really?"

"Yes. Medicine in China is good, but not yet where we want it to be. We have many more people to treat than you do in this country."

"That's true. Your English is excellent."

"Thank you."

"Where did you learn it?"

"In medical school. Many of the older journals are written in English and French. I thought it would be good to know the languages."

"You speak French, too?" Melissa asked.

"Yes."

"I'm impressed. Please get dressed. We need to join Chiyo in the interview room."

Ten minutes later, Melissa and Mei Lien met with Chiyo, Sanderson, and Starke in an interview room. Alexa and Trent watched from the observation room.

"What were your initial findings?" Starke asked Melissa.

"They both have implants in their left tibia, but nothing else. Brain activity and cardio are normal. No sign of any radiological or pathogenic exposure. They're healthy."

Starke nodded, then waved at the mirrored glass to summon Trent and Alexa.

When they entered the room, Chiyo asked, "Where's the little girl?"

"With her mother," Trent said.

"Trent, I'd like you to brief these two women about what's happening," Starke said.

"Alright." For the next hour Trent told them everything he knew, including Maya's being from a future time, when she was living on Mars.

Considering this news, Melissa thought both women had taken it well. She told them that their immediate family would be notified that they were safe, but no contact would be allowed for a few days.

"Does your brain implant cause you any pain?" Mei Lien asked Trent.

"Not at all. I was surprised to hear I had one."

"What do these creatures want with us?" Chiyo asked Starke.

"We don't know. We thought you could have something to do with confirming a global environmental event. I'm not sure where you fit in since neither of you knows Trent or Taylor, and you don't know anything about Mars."

"Trent, you said Maya told you that I'm a safety inspector and computer technician on Mars," Chiyo said.

"Yes. She remembers you because she liked saying your name there—Miku."

"That's a lot different than being a realtor," Chiyo said.

"You haven't told me what I do there," Mei Lien said.

"Maya doesn't know you, so we don't know that," Trent replied. "It's possible you're assigned to a different station. You look familiar."

"Ever been to China?" Mei Lien asked, then smiled.

"No. You must mean something to me on Mars. Wait a minute." Trent closed his eyes. "Now I've got it. We work together. You're Xia Li, an astrophysicist."

"Really?"

"Yes."

"Did you just get a vision?" Starke asked.

"Yes. They're becoming more frequent and are more focused. I think her work is very important to me, but I don't know why."

"How is it possible that you can live in both places at different times?" Chiyo asked.

"That's the question all of our governments are trying to answer," Sanderson said. "Dr. Maxwell said that Hanover LIGO recorded a gravitational wave, followed by an echo wave, when you two were returned."

"And the others that are missing, do you expect them to be brought here?" Mei Lien asked.

"I do," Starke said.

"We're still trying to figure out why the rest of you were taken," Melissa said. "Since neither of you remember being abducted as children, we hope to find a common trait in your DNA that will explain why all of you are connected."

"When are all the DNA results due?" Starke asked.

"Later this afternoon," Melissa replied, canting her head toward Trent and Alexa. "Mei Lien's and Chiyo's will be ready tomorrow morning."

"What happens now?" Chiyo asked.

"We try to make both of you as comfortable as possible," Starke replied. "We'll just have to take this a day at a time. Let's get you to orientation, then settled in your rooms. You'll be staying in the Nova Annex near Trent and the others on Gold Level. Since we're anticipating more abductees and an increase in medical and scientific staff, you'll have to share a two-bedroom apartment. Any problem with that?"

"I think it would be comforting," Chiyo said.

Mei Lien nodded in agreement.

"Good," Starke said. "Alexa, you've been very quiet. Do you have any questions for either of them?"

"No."

Starke said, "Why don't we meet up for dinner at 1800 hours. Colonel, see that they get settled in."

Nova Annex — Brown Level Conference Room — 1630 hours

Melissa still couldn't believe the DNA results. She'd already briefed General Starke about what they'd indicated, and he was watching Maya in his office. Melissa thought that under the circumstances it would be best for Trent and Taylor to tell her about the results.

She'd asked Professor Maxwell and Dr. Sanderson to attend. Taylor, Trent, and Alexa sat together across from Melissa.

"I've asked you all here so that I can share some interesting news."

"It can't be good if Maya isn't here," Taylor said.

"It's not bad, just unexpected. The second sample set of the DNA taken yesterday has been completed." Melissa took a breath. "Maya is definitely Trent's daughter. No doubt about it. The confusing issue arises as to her mother."

"How could that be?" Trent asked.

Melissa turned on the wall-mounted screen across from the table, and a chart displayed. "Maya does have Taylor's mitochondrial genes, but this is where it gets interesting." Melissa highlighted a DNA sequence. "This sequence matches Alexa's."

"What?" Alexa cried. "I don't see how that's possible."

"The results are conclusive. I didn't believe the results the first time. That's why I ran the samples again. There's no question Maya carries both Alexa's and Taylor's DNA."

"How could that have happened?" Taylor asked.

"I don't have the answer to that question. I know there has been some groundbreaking work where artificial chromosomes and stem cells are used to allow same-sex women to produce a child. I have my genetics team working to find out more about the process. I'm thinking that at some point in the future Alexa's ova will be harvested, so to speak."

"But Maya looks like Taylor and Trent," Alexa said. "She has Taylor's hair color and facial features. I don't see any of me in her."

"Based on Trent's visions of the future, I think Taylor's genes were genetically mapped or cloned to create Shona," Melissa said. "In fact, I think that's how all of your counterparts ended up on Mars. That would explain why all of you look the same on Mars but have different names and lives."

"I have to agree with the colonel's conclusions," Sanderson said. "It's very odd, but I'm certain that the aliens took DNA samples during your childhood abductions.

Alexa sat back in her chair, then asked, "That doesn't explain my genetic code being a part of Maya's. I was never abducted."

Melissa said, "True. Not yet anyway."

"That's not funny," Alexa said.

"It wasn't meant to be. Maya's genetic sequence is a certainty, which means at some point in the future they will take your ovum."

"Trent, do I get abducted?" Alexa asked.

"How would I know? None of my memories include you on Mars, or anyone that looks like you."

"I think there's more in play than we can begin to imagine," Melissa said. "Maybe Alexa's alive in the future or on another timeline or in a multiverse, but you're not aware of her being there. It's possible that we're dealing with a medical technology that uses cloned cells. Trent, during your last abduction, perhaps they found Alexa's DNA on something you had with you. But it needed to be a larger sample in order to add Alexa's genetic code to the mix."

"I wish we had a sample of Shona's DNA," Sanderson said. "I wonder if Alexa's DNA was passed down to her. If Alexa is Shona's ancestor—a child she and Trent produced—then that would make sense."

Taylor looked at Alexa and said, "Just when I thought it couldn't get any stranger."

Melissa said, "Here's another interesting tidbit I learned from the DNA study. All of you, including Captain Wood, share a common ancestor. Captain Su does not. I suspect that when Chiyo's and Mei Lien's results are in that we will find that they also share a common ancestor."

Trent said, "How could the three of us share a common ancestor with Mei Lien or Chiyo? They're both of Asian descent."

Melissa chuckled. "Excellent question. Genetically speaking, there was a massive diversification in the species during the last ice age. Light-skinned people sprang up in Europe, Asians in the orient, and darker-skinned people in Africa and the Middle East. Migration of the species isolated many of the early human tribes, while others came across the land bridge that's now the Bearing Sea into the Americas. Evolution and genetic changes were passed down, resulting in the diversity we have today. Look at this." She displayed another picture on the screen. "These five panels of sequencing represent one ancestral line. The three of you and Maya had a common maternal ancestor. My best guess would put her as living around ten to fifteen thousand years ago."

"Colonel, who belongs to the fifth panel," Maxwell asked.

"That panel shows Captain Wood's ancestral line. I'm not usually a gambling person, but in this case I'm willing to bet that the other abductees will all have an implant, and they will all have the same common ancestral link."

Sanderson said, "Perhaps their ancestral mother's genes are significant in the survival of the human race."

"So these creatures would have to have been here for a much longer time," Alexa said.

"Right," Melissa said. "It's possible that they're only abducting people from a particular ancestral line that they know will survive long into the future or who have traits that are necessary for human survival, as Dr. Sanderson said. Perhaps Maya was sent here not only to warn us, but to provide insight into what genetic qualities will be needed in the future."

"You think they've known what's about to happen for that long?" Trent asked.

"It's possible," Melissa said.

"It's also possible that if we dig back far enough, we might find a common thread that'll link all of the tagged abductees to another catastrophic event," Maxwell proffered.

"Interesting thought," Sanderson said. "I'll have a research team review cataloged DNA samples taken from specimens that lived prior to the last ice age and see if we can find a common ancestor."

"I'd have the samples compared to everything on file going all the way back to the earliest ancestor we all share," Maxwell said.

"Why would they pull us together after all of this time?" Taylor asked. "What could we possibly have that would be so important for the genetic line continuing? And what about my daughter, Emma?"

Trent frowned. "Maybe we're all linked along a stream of time that brings us together when humans need us the most?"

Taylor said, "Are you suggesting that we've lived in many different times over tens of thousands of years?"

"I wouldn't rule it out," Trent said.

"The Neanderthal became extinct before the end of the last ice age," Maxwell said, sounding as if he was thinking aloud. "Then the population of the modern human beings began to spread and diversify faster than at any other time in human history. If there is a doomsday scenario lurking in the wings, perhaps all of you are being brought back together to ensure the survival of a specific mitochondrial line that the aliens don't want to lose."

"Interesting," Melissa said, "But why? What would be so important that their mitochondrial line needs to continue more than others? If we go back far enough, we're all linked."

Maxwell opened his laptop and said, "If my memory serves, seventy thousand years ago hominids nearly went extinct. Give me a second." He began typing furiously on the keypad, his excitement evident.

"I didn't know that humans almost became extinct," Alexa said.

A moment later, Maxwell said, "Here it is. Seventy-five thousand years ago, the Toba volcano in Sumatra erupted. It was so large that it created a volcanic winter that lasted a decade, and it cooled the planet for a thousand years. It was one of the largest eruptions on Earth. The human population was reduced to less than thirty thousand, creating a genetic bottleneck which allowed only those that were the fittest to survive."

"Another cataclysmic geological event," Alexa said.

"This seems to be a common theme," Trent said. "Only this time we're adding a magnetic polar shift and a burst of unknown energy to the equation."

"So Maya was more than just a messenger?" Taylor said.

"She may be the key to the survival of the human species, and the aliens need us to connect the dots," Trent said. "Bringing us together will prepare our descendants so they can survive. I believe that with what we know about our genetic similarity and some of our future professions that it's pretty damn conclusive evidence that we are the key to survival."

"But hasn't more than one genetic line survived since the last bottleneck?" Alexa asked. "Why take only those specific genetic traits this time?"

"You're right," Melissa said. "Maya said four billion people survive, so it won't be just the one maternal genetic line that continues. So *why* are they connected?"

"Maybe only one common genetic group ends up on Mars," Sanderson offered.

"We don't know that for sure," Melissa said. "There are still a number of other abductees we haven't tested."

Maxwell said, "We need to ask Maya whether only certain people are allowed to live on Mars."

"That would bring up a new ethical discussion," Sanderson said. "Maya said that the pioneers are trying to create an atmosphere on Mars. Could any specific genetic traits make us more adaptable to environmental change? Perhaps a certain trait can help people survive in a thinner atmosphere in order to expedite colonization of the planet."

"An interesting thought, and something I'd like to explore," Melissa said. "I'll have Mei Lien assist me with that research. Does anyone have anything else?"

No one said anything.

"I'll brief General Starke about our discussion. Trent, you, Taylor, and Alexa need to talk to Maya."

"Yes, we do," Trent said.

"Dr. Sanderson, could you check and see if any of the abductees have their DNA on file in any database?" Melissa asked.

"Certainly."

"Then let's adjourn."

Trent's apartment – 1730 hours

Maya sat at the dining room table with Trent, Taylor, and Alexa.

"We need to tell you something, Maya," Taylor said. "It may not make sense to you, but we'll do our best to explain it and answer any questions that you have."

"Is this going to be like the last time when you told me you weren't my real mom and dad?"

"Not exactly," Trent said. "It seems that you have my genes and Taylor's genes. Do you know what genes are?"

"Yes. So *you* are my mom and dad?" Maya asked.

"No," Taylor replied. "Aiden and Shona are your biological parents, but they're related to us in some way."

"So you'd be my grandparents?"

"We're not sure about that either," Trent said. "All we know is that somehow Aiden and Shona must have our DNA, which was passed on to you. They could have been cloned. Do you know what that is?"

"Yes. Mom does that with plants. Some of the animals we use for food are cloned."

"Interesting I don't think you told us that before."

"Sorry. I can't remember everything."

"There's also another wrinkle," Trent said.

"Okay."

"It seems that you also carry Alexa's DNA."

Maya looked at Alexa and said, "So you're also my mom?"

Alexa replied, "That part is also fuzzy. We don't know how, but Shona passed down my traits to you, too."

"So you could be my mom's relative?"

"We don't have all the answers, but we wanted you to know what the DNA tests showed," Alexa replied. "It may mean something to you in the future."

"Maya, do you have any questions?" Trent asked.

Maya frowned as if in thought, then said, "I don't know what to ask. It all sounds very strange to me."

TWENTY-THREE

A week had passed without any further alien abductions. That was the good news. As expected, the president's announcement about the existence of an alien presence had resulted in a global panic, a financial crisis of unparalleled proportions, and a hoarding of food and weapons, all of which had taken the world to the brink of disaster. People had formed militia groups to protect the hoarded supplies. World governments were trying to put together a coalition to establish a unified front to quell the panic.

Melissa knew it was good that the president had withheld the knowledge of the even greater pending crisis. Trent and Captain Su had made several public service announcements urging calm, with limited success.

There had been a dramatic increase in suicides and a rise in recruitment by several cultlike groups. Churches, mosques, temples, and other religious centers were packed with worshipers praying for a divine intervention. Some religious sects were preaching that the end times were upon us.

Various sources had leaked information about where most of the scientists were last seen, and Mountain Home AFB was besieged by thousands of people and the media. Melissa knew it would only be a matter of time until someone stumbled onto the Sawtooth facility. Then all hell would break loose.

The DNA test results on Chiyo and Mei Lien showed that they possessed what some had started calling the Martian Gene. Melissa had run additional DNA comparative studies using the staff's DNA. No one, including her, matched the Martian genetic markers.

Major Striker had returned to the facility, and General Starke had asked Melissa to keep an eye on him. He'd told her that Striker wasn't himself and that he was making inappropriate comments concerning Trent and Taylor. She'd heard about a division between some staff members concerning the best approach to what many of the military members were calling an alien threat. There were also rumors that the military was going to attack the aliens when they returned. Some members of the scientific team claimed that the aliens were responsible for the coming catastrophe and were adding to the festering animosity toward those with the Martian gene.

Some of the scientists had been confronted by staff and accused of being too soft and naïve about the aliens. This had only further divided those working on the project. Melissa knew that Maxwell was doing his best to squash any real issues.

Melissa caught Starke at the door before he entered the conference room. "General, I just learned that Su and Striker have been spending a great deal of time together and that they seem to be at the center of the spreading discontent."

"I've heard the same thing," Starke said.

"Perhaps you should have Striker and Su speak with a staff psychologist."

"That won't do any good. Striker's a warrior. I'll speak to him before we start the meeting. You can order Su to see one. Have Striker meet me in my office, now."

"Yes, sir."

General Starke's Office — 1000 hours

Striker knocked, then entered Starke's office. "You wanted to see me?"

"Yes," Starke said, standing to greet him. "Close the door. We have some things to discuss."

Striker shut the door, faced Starke, and asked, "What things?"

"It's come to my attention that you disagree with my approach to dealing with the aliens. I've also learned that you and Captain Su have been spending a great deal of time sowing dissent among the staff and undermining me." Raising his voice, Starke said, "I want to know why you've become openly insubordinate and why I shouldn't have you removed from the program."

Striker stiffened. "I admit that I don't agree with your approach to dealing with the aliens. I've had discussions with others who feel that you're opening us up to an attack. General, Trent's a spy. That the thing in his head is transmitting everything that he sees, hears, and does. His presence in this facility weakens our ability to fight. I felt that I should inform the security forces to be prepared to engage when it became necessary—and it will become necessary."

"I see. You think that I'm mishandling the situation?"

"With respect, I do. I know how Trent acts during meetings and that he's receiving messages in real time. They know what we're doing. He's an information pipeline and you're doing nothing to curtail it. You're not taking any precautions to exclude him from sensitive discussions."

"So you've decided that Trent's a serious threat?"

"Yes, sir."

"And what would you suggest we do with him, Major Striker? He's providing us with information that will be helpful in the future."

"Lock him up. Then use him to force the alien's hand. Make them come to us when we want them to, and then capture or kill as many aliens as possible to send a message that we don't take kindly to invaders."

"Invaders? Seriously? You really think that an advanced species needs Trent to open the gates for them?"

"Yes. They want to kill us and blame it on a bullshit cataclysmic event."

"You don't think the dark times prophecy is real? Hell, I didn't believe it at first. I also thought we had defenses in place that would shield the facility, but I was wrong. I even wanted to capture the aliens two weeks ago. But things have changed. I've learned that our best course of action is to make contact and open a dialogue. We need Trent to do that."

"General, I supported you when we were going to take positive action. I believe that talking will get us nowhere with these beings. We must respond with force. Our security forces need to be told what's really happening so they can defend us."

"I don't know what's happened to you, Major. I remember when you'd think things through before jumping to conclusions, and you would never think of undermining me." When Striker opened his mouth to speak, Starke raised his hand. "Don't try my patience any further. We have a briefing to attend, and then we'll talk again. If you're still adamant about an aggressive posture, I'll need to find someone else who'll support me in seeking a peaceful encounter."

Striker clenched his jaw. "Yes, sir."

"Dismissed," Starke said.

Brown Level Conference Room — 1010 hours

Melissa eyed Striker as he entered the conference room. He appeared to be agitated. She wondered what the general had said to him.

General Starke entered the room, looked around, and said, "I see everyone is here. So let's have the latest."

Melissa cleared her throat and said, "We've determined that all of those still missing carry the Martian gene."

"How did we get that?" Starke asked.

"From various sources of sample DNA, mostly from the maternal relatives."

"I really don't like it being called Martian," Taylor said. "I'm not Martian. I'm human. Ever since people got wind of how a few of us carry the trait, people have begun looking at us differently. I'm wondering when you'll isolate us from others or move us someplace away from here."

Striker leaned forward and said with venom in his tone, "That's a good idea."

Starke said, "Major, that's enough!"

"May I speak freely?"

"Yes."

"As you know, Captain Su and I have been doing some research." Su looked stunned by the major's admission. "It stands to reason that when the aliens return they'll either bring back more of those they've abducted or maybe take some of *them* back with them." He gave Trent a hard stare.

"Get to your point," Starke said.

"I believe it's in our best interest to move them out of the facility in order to protect our assets here. If we move them to a different site, the aliens will follow. This will preserve our ability to continue working on our preparations for the supposed coming event. The staff will feel safer knowing the Martian people aren't around."

"Major, that's *enough*! They will remain at the facility. These people are not the enemy."

"I believe they are, especially the little one," Striker said. "She's from their world. We need to defend our country and our planet. These beings need to understand that we won't stand by while they destroy our world and put their puppets in command."

Melissa could hardly believe what she was hearing. How could he even be thinking those thoughts? What had Striker and Starke discussed before the briefing?

"That's enough, Major Striker!" Starke shouted. "If they wanted to destroy us, they would have done that already."

"Not if they need these people for their future world," Striker said.

"Major, you're not making sense," Melissa said with a harsh tone. "Trent and the others need to help us make first contact with the aliens. That's what we're all tasked to do."

Striker said, "Well, then let's get on with it. Trent and Maya are special to these creatures, more so than the others. If we want to guarantee first contact, let's put them under extreme duress. When the aliens come to save them, we hit them with everything we have and put an end to them."

Trent said, "General, I think your adjutant has blown a circuit."

Striker stiffened. Blood vessels bulged on his neck as he ground his teeth.

"We will *not* attack the aliens!" Starke said. "And Trent, I don't care for your snide comment about Major Striker."

Striker said, "You know they want to sucker us in by saying they're only trying to warn us. It's nothing more than a ruse to get us to lower our defenses. I've read the classified USGS summaries. Yellowstone is no closer to erupting than it was fifty years ago. There's been no unusual seismic activity or quasar explosions that would send anything toward Earth. Yes, the magnetic poles could shift, but they've been doing that for eons."

"Major Striker, that doesn't mean anything," Maxwell said. "Many of the historical major volcanic eruptions didn't show any warning signs until just hours before they happened."

"Major, you are done here!" Starke cried. "Wait in my office."

"No, sir," Striker said. "I'm just getting started."

Melissa was certain that Striker had become unhinged, but she couldn't understand what would have pushed him to this point. He'd always been a little intense while doing his duty, but this was way over the top.

"What did you just say?" Starke growled.

Striker pushed his chair back. "You heard me. These creatures want Trent and the others to survive, so that's our bargaining chip. Kill one of them and I'm willing to bet that the aliens will come to save the others."

"Have you lost your mind?" Starke asked.

Striker jumped to his feet with a semiautomatic pistol in his hand. He pointed it at Trent. "Let's see what happens."

Melissa froze. She could only watch as Alexa snatched up a coffee mug with incredible speed and hurled it at Striker, hitting him on the bridge of his nose just as the gun fired.

Trent grunted as he was blown backwards from his chair.

Maya screamed.

Alexa was over the table and on Striker before he could recover. She hit Striker's trachea with a quick jab and knocked the gun from his hand. She pivoted and drove her elbow into his solar plexus, then spun back and hit him with a brachial stun strike to his carotid. The large man collapsed to the floor. Alexa picked up the gun, and pointed it at Captain Su who was about to tackle her.

"I wouldn't if you want to live," Alexa said.

Su stopped in her tracks. Starke rushed around the table to secure Striker while Melissa hurried to Trent. Taylor screamed for help as she pushed Maya into the hallway.

Blood seeped through Trent's fingers as he held his shoulder and writhed in pain. "Let me have a look," Melissa said. She examined Trent's wound and felt grateful that the bullet had only grazed his right shoulder. Not life-threatening. "Trent, you'll be fine. Keep pressure on the wound."

"That son of a bitch shot me!" Trent yelled.

Melissa went to check on Striker. She guessed that he'd had a psychotic break. Perhaps the idea that the world he knew was going to end had pushed him over the edge. Even though he was irritated only minutes before, she never suspected that he would shoot someone.

She knelt beside Striker. She knew immediately that he was in trouble. When she rolled him over, she saw that his trachea had been crushed. There was nothing she could do to save him.

Four Marines burst into the room with weapons at the ready.

"Secure the area," Starke ordered.

By the time a medical team arrived, Striker was dead.

Captain Su threw her head back and cried, "For the trumpet shall sound, and the dead shall be raised imperishable, and we shall be changed."

"You're quoting Corinthians?" Melissa said. "You told me that you were a Buddhist or Taoist."

"The end is coming!" Su wailed. "Ask around. Others believe it to be true, and they will rise up against you."

"Get her out of here," Starke ordered.

"Take Captain Su and Major Striker's body to Red Level," Melissa told the Marines. "I want to examine Captain Su. Restrain her."

Two Marines pulled Captain Su from the room. Melissa heard her ranting as they dragged her down the corridor.

"Colonel, do you think she was infected with something during her abduction?" Starke asked. "Something you didn't find earlier?"

"I'm not sure." She looked at Alexa, who was kneeling next to Trent. "Alexa, Trent will be fine. As they say in the movies, it's just a flesh wound. You saved his life."

Alexa looked up at her, her eyes filled with concern. "What worries me is that if Major Striker could lose it, how many others here will try to take some kind of hostile action. You heard Su's rant."

"I understand your concerns," Melissa said. "That's one of the reasons I want to examine and question Captain Su. Perhaps there are others that share Su's and Striker's opinion. General, we need to investigate."

"No shit," Starke said. He turned to the two Marines standing at the door. "Lock the facility down. All personnel are to return to their rooms."

The Marines didn't move.

"Did you hear me?"

"Yes, sir." One of the Marines radioed the order to Security Control.

"This is what I was worried about," Taylor said, standing in the doorway. "Everyone thinks we're to blame for what's coming, and it's only going to get worse."

"You and Maya okay?" Melissa asked her, using as calming a tone as she could muster.

"Yes," Taylor replied, a bit tersely.

"I can't believe Striker caught me off guard," Alexa said. "I could tell he was very angry, but I didn't expect him to pull a weapon. I should have moved sooner. Out of practice I guess."

Melissa smiled. "Alexa, I've never seen anyone move that fast. You must have been an exceptional agent."

Starke approached Alexa. "I don't know what to say, except thank you. Who knows what he would have done to the rest of us." He looked at Melissa. "Colonel, I'll deal with Captain Su after your exam. Any formal investigation of her actions will have to wait."

"General, if others feel the way Striker and Su do, we need to find out who they are and isolate them. We need to get ahead of this before we have a real problem."

"I agree, but interviewing everyone in this facility will take time. You get Trent fixed up and let me know what Su has to say."

"Yes, sir."

Medical — Orange Level — 1100 hours

Trent's arm throbbed. Maya sat next to him on the bed. She'd been very clingy and quiet since being allowed in to see him. He could tell that Taylor was also very troubled by the incident. Alexa and Melissa discussed something in hushed tones, but he couldn't make out what they were saying.

"Maya, everything is okay," Trent told her.

"Why did that man shoot you?"

"He was sick, Pumpkin."

"I'd say he was sick in the head," Maya declared.

Taylor crossed the room and picked Maya up, then said, "You're too heavy to carry." She put her down. "It's a good thing Alexa reacted the way she did or things may have ended differently."

Trent nodded and said, "Maya, can you go talk with Alexa and Melissa for a few minutes?"

"Okay."

Taylor said, "Trent, I know there's chemistry between us. But now that we know we're together in the next life, I really don't know how to feel anymore. It's no longer a simple issue. We don't even know if it's our future life, or an alternate universe life, or what the hell it is. For all we know our counterparts are clones."

"Where is this going?" Trent asked, fearing he already knew the answer.

"Alexa is good for you. I have a family, another daughter here. I need to find a way to live a life with them again. You need to be with Alexa."

"I don't know if that's going to be left up to us."

"We control what we do today. It's our decision to be together or take separate paths."

Trent thought for a moment. He looked into Taylor's beautiful eyes. "I know that I don't want to lose you. You're a part of my life now. One that I don't understand, but no one else can share what we do. Taylor, somehow the three of us came together to create Maya. Our lives are all intertwined, here and wherever else we might be."

"Are you advocating a polygamist life?" Taylor asked. "Because that's not for me."

"No, nothing like that. I'm certain Alexa wouldn't want that either. Maybe we're overthinking this. We may think that we make our own decisions, but I don't think we have control of our destiny. Maya is proof of that."

"I'm not planning on following a script that an alien species has written for us."

"I understand." It could have been the painkillers starting to cloud his thoughts, but he didn't think so. His vision began to blur. It appeared as if Taylor was slowly vanishing. A moment later, he was on a different world with Taylor. He felt a sense of contentment, but he knew it didn't come from Taylor. "Shona?"

"Yes?" she replied.

Trent looked around. "Where are we?"

"Our quarters. You were blown out of an airlock and saved our daughter. You're my hero."

"I'm back," he muttered.

"What do you mean?"

"I'm on Mars, right?"

"I think I'll get a medical tech. You're not making any sense."

"No. Taylor, I mean Shona, wait."

"Who's Taylor?"

"You are. I was just on Earth with you in a different time." He took a step toward her. "You don't remember me then, do you?"

"I remember the past just fine. You must have suffered a brain injury saving Maya."

Trent looked around and saw everything in much more vivid detail than ever before. "Is Alexa here?"

"Why are you asking about her?"

Trent looked around the living quarters again. He didn't know if he was dreaming or living in the present. "I lived a past life with Alexa. You were there with us at the Sawtooth facility. That's where I was a minute ago."

"Aiden, I'm calling a medical team. You're scaring the shit out of me." She pushed a button on the wall and said, "Medical needed at this location. Expedite." A synthesized voice said that a team had been dispatched.

"You remember Alexa, don't you?"

"Of course I do," Shona replied. "The medical team will be here in a minute. You should sit down."

"Where is she?"

"Aiden, stay focused on me."

"Where's Alexa?" Trent demanded. "I need to tell her something."

"Aiden, Alexa is gone. Don't you remember what happened?"

Trent stumbled back against the wall. A moment later, he was back in medical at Sawtooth, and Melissa was staring at him.

"Welcome back," Melissa said. "You left us for a moment. Where'd you go?"

"To Mars. I was talking to Shona. I asked her about Alexa." He looked at Alexa and said, "Shona knows you. You must have been on Mars, but she said that you were gone. I don't know what she meant by gone."

"She knew me?" Alexa asked.

"She did, and by your name," Trent said. Then a kaleidoscope of images flooded his mind, and he lost consciousness.

Confinement Interview room — Red Level — 1230 hours

General Starke said, "Captain Su, you really expect me to believe that you didn't know Major Striker was going to try to kill Trent or one of the other abductees?"

Captain Su was handcuffed to the table. The handcuffs rattled against the stainless steel surface as she lifted her head. "I already told you—No! We talked about how contact with the aliens should be arranged on our terms."

"That's it? All the times you met and spoke in private and with others, that was all that you discussed?"

"There were other things, but at no time did he ever mention killing Trent. I was just as shocked by his actions as you were."

"Yet you tried to help him. You would have attacked Alexa if she hadn't stuck a gun in your face."

Su nodded. "That's true. I wanted to protect him."

"After he'd already shot Trent? Do you know how that looks?"

"Yes, sir."

Starke spent the next hour going over every detail of Su's and Striker's discussions. He'd wished that Melissa could have sat in, but she had her hands full with Trent. Su maintained throughout the interview that all they wanted to do was protect the planet from an alien invasion. She insisted that they never had any seditionist discussions.

"I almost believe you," Starke said.

"Those things killed my best friend. They deserve to die for what they've done. The major wanted you to take a more aggressive stance. I agreed with him. The major thought that you'd grown . . ."

"Grown what?"

"The major believed you were getting too close to the subjects."

"They're not subjects, Captain Su. They're human beings." Starke leaned back in his chair and closed his eyes for a moment. "Captain, I don't have any more time to waste with you. You will be confined until further notice."

"Yes, sir."

Starke summoned a Marine who was standing by the door. "Lock her up in her quarters," he ordered. "She can't have any visitors or go anywhere without my permission."

The Marine said, "Yes, sir."

Starke left the room and walked to the nearest office with a phone and called Melissa. When she answered, he said, "What's Trent's status?"

"He's still out. Tests indicate his brain is hyperactive."

"So he's back on Mars?"

"General, I won't know until he wakes up and tells us. What's Su's story?"

"She swears she didn't know Striker's intention. I actually believe her. I've confined her to quarters under guard. How's everyone else doing?"

"They're good. Alexa seems to be handling Striker's death without any remorse. Maya won't leave Trent's bedside. There was one bit of news."

"What?"

"Trent woke up for a minute and claimed that Shona knew who Alexa was in their time."

"That's interesting."

"General, do you want me to perform an autopsy on Striker?"

"We can do that later. Stay with Trent. If anything changes, call me."

"Yes, sir."

Medical — Orange Level — 1700 hours

Melissa was checking on Trent when his eyes suddenly popped open and he sat up. "Easy there. You've been out for a while."

Trent looked around the room. His eyes moved slowly, lingering on each face before moving to the next, taking inventory of who was present.

"Taylor, take Maya out of the room," Trent said.

Melissa thought his voice sounded strident, almost artificial.

"Come on, Maya," Taylor said, taking her by the hand.

"But I want to stay," Maya said.

Trent blinked his eyes several times, then said, "Go with her. I need to speak to Alexa and Melissa in private."

Once they'd left the room, Melissa asked, "What do we need to talk about?"

"They're coming. Alexa and I must greet them."

"You mean the aliens are coming here?" Melissa asked. "When?

"Soon. Alexa and I must meet them."

"So you said," Alexa said. "Trent, you don't sound like yourself."

"I'm fine. The pain in my arm is gone. Medication will no longer be required."

"What are you talking about?" Melissa asked.

Trent looked puzzled by the question. "I have no pain."

"I'm not liking where this is going," Melissa said. "Lay down."

Trent closed his eyes. "Alexa and I must be at the lake in two hours."

"That's where the aliens are landing?" Alexa asked.

"Yes."

Melissa felt as though Trent was looking through her rather than at her.

"Melissa, you need to accompany us to the lake. The others will be returning. Some may require your assistance." A pale yellow glow appeared on Trent's forehead, and he fell back onto the pillow.

"What the hell is wrong with him?" Alexa asked. "His voice sounded as if he was reading from a script."

"The aliens are using the implant to send us a message. The implant is also probably blocking the pain sensors and altering his voice. Let me check his arm."

Melissa took Trent's shirt off and removed the blood-soaked bandage. The wound was healed. "What the hell?"

"What is it?"

"His arm is completely healed."

"I don't understand," Alexa said. "How is that possible?"

"The neural implant must have accelerated the healing process. Incredible. Trent has just moved to a new level."

"That's for sure. I wonder why the aliens want me to be with Trent when he meets them."

"I'd say the aliens have something they need from you."

"I'll meet them, but I have no intention of going anywhere with them."

Melissa said, "You may not have a choice. I'm going to take another look at the implant."

Trent opened his eyes. He knew he was in the imaging center.

Taylor said to Alexa, "I can't stop worrying about him."

"I know what you mean," Alexa replied.

"Stop worrying about me, both of you," Trent said. "How long was I out?"

"Which time?" Alexa asked.

"There's been more than one?"

"Twice, actually. You don't remember being awake an hour ago?"

"No," Trent said. "What time is it?"

"Just after six," Taylor replied. "I'll go find Melissa before you have another episode."

Trent sighed. "I have a headache, but my arm feels better."

"It should," Alexa said. "It's completely healed."

"What? How?"

"Melissa thinks it was the implant. Trent, you said that the aliens are coming and that we're supposed to meet them. They'll be landing on the lake in fifty minutes."

"Really? I don't remember saying that."

"Melissa thinks the aliens took control of you to send their message."

Images flooded his mind. Voices he recognized spoke as if they'd been recorded and were now being played back to him. "I'm starting to remember some things."

Maya shot through the door, followed by Taylor and Melissa.

"You're awake!" Maya said.

"So it would seem." He squeezed Maya's hand, then looked at Melissa. "I hear that we have an appointment to keep."

"That's what you told us," Melissa said. "Trent, are you sure you're up for a walk in the woods?"

"I'm good. Stop worrying about me, all of you. My head is clear—well, almost." He got off the bed and stretched. "Everything seems to be working. Is the general ready for our visitors?"

"He is."

"Let me get dressed," Trent said.

"Are we going to see aliens?" Maya asked, sounding excited.

"I believe we will," Trent said. "Melissa, will Dr. Maxwell be joining us?"

"Do you think he would miss this opportunity? I think everyone will be anxious to see our visitors."

Trent closed his eyes, then he said, "All are welcome, but everyone must stay away from the ship."

"Did they just send you a message?" Alexa asked.

Trent opened his eyes and smiled. "I guess they did. May I get dressed now?"

"Yes," Melissa replied.

"Hello," Maya said.

Trent gave her a questioning look.

"I want them to know I'm looking forward to seeing my first alien." She waved at Trent.

"Can they see us?" Taylor asked.

"I have no idea," Trent said. "Why don't we ask them when they get here."

TWENTY-FOUR

The delegation was assembled at the edge of the lake. A small platform had been hurriedly erected for Alexa and Trent to stand on. Cameras and recording equipment were in place around the frozen shoreline, and high-intensity lights illuminated the snow-covered lake.

Marine snipers had been positioned in the woods with a clear line of fire, and supporting troops were in positions for a rapid response, if needed. Starke had made sure that Trent didn't know they were there. He'd also informed Defense Secretary Barrington about the imminent landing and had received specific instructions that he was to capture one of the aliens—alive. Starke wasn't sure how they were going to achieve that objective. If the creatures stayed on the ship, storming it wouldn't be practical. Trent had warned them not to go near the ship. Considering the number of fighter aircraft that were circling nearby, he was concerned that the president would order the alien craft shot down to keep it from leaving. Their engines could be heard rumbling overhead in the distance.

Twilight had fallen across Greylock Mountain; the western sky was painted with shades of pale blues and oranges. A few stars sparkled in the creeping night sky. Surveillance cameras on the peak of the mountain captured a three-hundred-sixty-degree image of the area; their signal was being fed to the security area on Green Level within Sawtooth and to the Pentagon and the White House.

Dr. Maxwell had a direct link to Hanover, so he would know the instant they detected the gravity wave. Not that it would provide any advance warning, but Maxwell planned to have their arrival through the white hole captured to the millisecond.

"I don't know about any of you, but I'm a little anxious," Taylor said as Melissa handed her a pair of large sunglasses to protect her eyes from the bright light they expected.

"Me, too," Melissa said. "Everyone listen up. Put your protective glasses on. Team leaders notify your personnel."

"These look like the glasses that people wore during the test detonations of a nuclear bomb," Taylor said. "Which I guess isn't too far from the power we're about to witness."

Twenty minutes later, Starke asked Trent, "Are you sure about their time of arrival?"

"Yes," Trent replied. "They will arrive in thirty seconds. The military jets should not attempt to engage them. Humanity's fate rests on the successful completion of this mission." Trent's voice sounded as if he was reading from a script again.

Twenty seconds later, the stars were blasted from Trent's view. Even the protective glasses didn't much help against the intensity of the light. Then the light disappeared.

"Shit, I can't see a thing," Starke said. "My night vision is a big blue dot."

"You shouldn't have looked at it," Maxwell said. "The burst was in the upper atmosphere."

Starke said, "Where the hell's the craft?"

"There," Trent said, pointing.

A cigar-shaped craft drifted over the southern peak soundlessly as it slowly descended. It was at least three football fields wide and three times that in length. The metallic silver coating reflected the light that surrounded its hull.

"Shit, that's not what we were expecting," Starke said. His voice echoed across the lake as if he were in an amphitheater.

"That's incredible!" Maxwell said. "Hanover advises that they detected both waves."

As the craft glided into position over the lake, an intense white glow formed beneath the ship. A dark hole appeared on the bottom of the hull, and a blue light shot from the craft to the surface. The light slowly expanded until it was fifty feet in diameter.

A moment later, a ball of blue light carried something down from the opening in the hull. It landed softly on the ice. When the light disappeared, two figures stood there, one tall and one short. Starke said, "Colonel, the aliens have landed."

"They both appear to be bipedal with two arms and two legs," Melissa said.

"That one thing is definitely alien," Starke said.

A short, brown-haired, flat-headed creature stood next to a tall humanoid-looking being. The shorter creature looked like a stocky monkey, with a flat, apelike face.

"Wow! Two aliens," Maya said.

"That is one very ugly alien," Melissa muttered.

Starke removed his protective glasses. "Trent, is that a person standing next to the monkey on the ice?"

Trent stepped forward and said, "No. It looks like an android. The little creature standing next to it is the kind I saw when I was a child. Several of those things carried me out of my bedroom and stayed with me until I was in a ship."

The tall being and the small creature walked slowly toward them. As they approached, neither of them seemed afraid. Starke spoke into his radio, "Gunnery Sergeant Radley, do not engage. I repeat, weapons safe. Inform the others."

"Yes, sir," Radley replied.

The two aliens stopped at the shoreline, twenty feet in front of them. The taller being was about six feet tall with a thin build, and it was covered with a tight, grayish-brown suit. He could pass for a human, except for the red, glowing eyes.

The humanoid creature advanced, leaving the smaller being behind. The humanoid stopped a few feet in front of the platform and said in perfect English, although a bit robotic, "Trent McDougal, it is good to see you again."

Trent replied, "Have we met before?"

"Yes. Several times, but those memories have been suppressed."

The being's eyes glowed brighter, and Trent's forehead glowed in return. Trent stepped off the platform.

Maxwell moved closer to the humanoid alien and asked, "Who are you?"

"Dr. Maxwell, I have no need of a name, but you may call me Alpha."

"You—you know my name?" Maxwell stuttered.

"Of course."

"Are you an android?" Melissa asked.

"I am a hybrid. I was constructed to resemble you so that you would be less afraid of me."

"How do you know Dr. Maxwell?" Starke asked, edging closer.

"I know all of you. We have been monitoring Trent since his last return."

Starke said, "You have been spying on us."

"We have been gathering information to determine the best way to approach you."

Alexa joined Trent.

"Can we get closer?" Maya asked.

"No, we're staying right here," Taylor replied. "Trent, I've seen that thing before. It's what has always examined me."

"I remember seeing it as well now," Trent said softly.

Alpha nodded, and multiple blue streams of light appeared on the ice beneath the ship. A second later, nine people stood on the ice.

"Medical teams, move to the shoreline and stand ready," Melissa ordered.

"It looks like everyone from the abductee list," Starke said.

The abductees walked gingerly across the ice toward the shoreline.

"This reminds me of a scene from an old science fiction movie *Close Encounters*," Maxwell said. He had a big grin on his face.

Trent turned to the others and said, "General Starke, Alexa and I will be leaving."

"We are?" Alexa asked with surprise.

"Yes," Trent said. "We are needed. Maya and Taylor will be joining us. Do not try to interfere."

"The hell you say," Melissa shouted. "General, we can't let them leave."

"Trent!" Starke shouted. "You and the others aren't going anywhere."

"We must," Trent said.

"Why?" Starke asked.

"There are things that must be done so that humanity can survive."

As Maya and Taylor walked up and stood next to Trent and Alexa, Starke said again, "No one is leaving until I know what the hell is going on."

"General, how do we stop them?" Melissa said.

A ball of blue light captured the small alien and it glided toward Alexa and Trent. A second later the light encapsulated Alexa and took her to the ship.

"What the hell!" Starke bellowed.

"It's alright," Trent said. "She was needed."

Alpha said, "General, you may join us aboard our ship. We will not harm you. We know that you have many questions. The answers you seek are there."

Starke was taken aback at the offer. A chance to board an alien spacecraft was not what he'd expected. "What about Dr. Maxwell?" Starke asked. "May he join us?"

"He is welcome, but no others. We must hurry. The window cannot be sustained for very long."

"What window?" Maxwell asked.

"I will explain," Alpha replied. "Follow me."

"Wait," Starke said. "Do we need protective suits?"

"No." Alpha turned and walked toward the ship.

"Colonel, you're in command," Starke said.

"Yes, sir."

The Alien Ship

Alpha stood beneath the ship and told each of them where to stand. Several of the small aliens floated down from the ship in a light, each of them extending a hand.

Starke backed off and said, "That thing isn't going to touch me."

"They will not harm you," Alpha said. "You must join with them in order to gain access to the ship."

"Why?" Starke asked. "The others you took didn't have to."

"Yes, they did. The ship is connected to a quantum field that allows our movement on this world and into the next. You must be anchored to one who is of the light. Please, take a hand."

Taylor glanced at Starke and said, "Alpha is telling you the truth. You need a date to go to the prom."

"It appears so," Starke replied as he took a little alien's hand.

A blue light enveloped the group, and they rose into the belly of the ship. Taylor's escort released her hand as soon as she was aboard. She surveyed the unfamiliar surroundings. The aperture on the floor closed.

"Don't be frightened," Alpha said.

"This is a strange place," Maya said.

"Yes, it is, but we got to meet some aliens," Taylor replied, taking her sweaty hand.

The walls, floor, and ceiling were composed of a dark material that wasn't quite black. Strange looking pieces of equipment ran along the walls. They looked as if they were molded into the fabric of the ship. She hadn't seen this place before.

"Where's Alexa?" Maya asked.

"She's safe," Alpha replied.

"Trent, do you remember this place?" Taylor asked.

"No."

"Me either."

"I can't believe we're inside an alien spacecraft," Maxwell said.

"We need to remember everything we see," Starke advised.

"Please follow your escort," Alpha directed.

They were guided to a large door which suddenly retracted into a wall. The small alien escort stopped at the doorway and motioned for them to enter a lightless chamber.

"I don't think so," Starke said. He stepped in front of the others to block their path into the room.

The android's eyes glowed briefly and the chamber became lit with a soft amber glow. "Is that better?"

Starke scanned the room. "Yes." He entered.

"This is a kinda scary," Maya said.

"A little bit," Taylor replied. "We won't let anything happen to you."

A creature suddenly appeared fifteen feet in front of them. It was seated on what Taylor could only describe as a large, cushioned throne, which was illuminated by an unknown source. The being was immense, with a large girth and chest. Its six-fingered hands rested in its lap, and its body was covered with a fine, golden mesh robe. Its two eyes were large, dark, and slightly offset. The beings grayish-brown face had a wide nose and heavy cheekbones, and its forehead was broad, with a heavy bone structure. Its legs were apelike, and its feet were clad in gold colored boots that matched the robe it wore. Taylor couldn't decide if the being was male or female.

The creature motioned for them to come forward. Taylor's heart pounded. She'd also seen this being before. It was responsible for all of her abductions. She became angry.

Trent stepped forward. "I recognize this being from my childhood."

Taylor grabbed Trent's arm and said, "I think we should all stay right here."

"I'm with her," Starke said. "Everyone stay where you are." He stood straighter and said, "I'm General John Starke, United States Space Force. I'd say welcome to Earth, but I know you've been here before."

The being nodded. It tilted its head slightly, and the throne glided forward silently, as if suspended on air, and stopped a few feet in front of them.

Alpha walked to the being, then faced them and said, "I've been asked to extend our warmest greetings. This is our leader. She wishes you to know that no new specimens will be needed from your world. No others will be taken."

"That's good to hear," Starke said. "You took Alexa. Is she your last?"

"Yes," Alpha said.

"Where is she?" Trent asked.

"She is safe and being prepared."

"For what?" Taylor cried. But she already knew what awaited Alexa.

"She is the last that is needed. I will join her shortly."

Alpha turned to the leader and nodded, then turned back and said, "As you know, Trent, Taylor, and Maya have been with us before. Maya is the first human to make the transition across the dimensional boundary.

A very special feat. Alexa made it so. We suppressed Maya's memory of her journey so she wouldn't be frightened by the experience."

Taylor looked down at Maya. Her eyes were wide with either fear or amazement. She wasn't sure which, but she felt Maya's death grip on her hand.

Taylor asked, "Will you be taking Maya back with you?"

"No. Alexa was needed to complete the cycle. A genetic sample is required from her in order to create Maya. We knew Alexa existed after Trent was last with us, but we were unable to locate her until Trent was returned and she joined him here."

"We already figured that out," Maxwell said.

"You need Alexa's ova," Taylor said, feeling her anger intensifying. "Like you took mine."

"Yes. Maya could not exist in either time or dimension without both your and Alexa's DNA. It is imperative that Maya be born and carry forward the DNA required for future human generations. Maya could not have made the interdimensional time transition without the genetic strand from Alexa, and you would never have been given the warning. Death is coming to this world. There is no stopping the destruction that will occur."

"So it's definitely coming?" Starke said.

"Yes." Alpha gave a curt nod, then said, "I will need to expedite the procedure. Our time is short."

"I want to be with Alexa," Taylor said.

"That is acceptable," Alpha replied.

"Trent, stay with Maya."

"May I join her?" Maxwell asked.

Alpha nodded.

"Excellent," Maxwell said. "I want to understand how you control the power that you use for transit through time. I'm betting you're using a white hole. Why did you choose to come in a ship this time? I . . ."

Alpha said, "Technical knowledge will not be shared."

"But I really want to know how you've mastered generating and controlling the power. You said the answers we sought were here."

"They are here," Alpha said. He turned and hurried into the darkness. Taylor and Maxwell followed.

"Where the hell are they going," Starke asked. "I want some answers."

The leader spoke for the first time in a deep base voice. "We have been here since the beginning." The leader's voice sounded as if air was being forced through vocal chords that had been dormant for millennia. "Be assured that we watch over your kind. In time, you will evolve into an advanced species. General Starke, the others will bring back the answers you seek." The corners of her mouth turned up. "But they will only bring more questions." She bowed her head slightly and looked at Trent, then Maya. "You both will leave the ship and return to the surface with General Starke. We must return to our time, but we will come back soon."

Trent nodded his understanding as Maya squeezed his hand.

"You're leaving?" Starke asked.

"Yes. Your aircraft are approaching."

The small creatures entered the chamber and took their hands. Darkness returned to the chamber as they were led back to where they'd entered the ship. A moment later, they stood beneath the ship, and the small aliens floated back into the ship.

Starke took a moment to regain his bearings, then said, "Let's get back to the shoreline."

As soon as they reached the shoreline, the alien craft disappeared into the night sky. A few seconds later four F-18 fighter jets screamed overhead, but Starke knew that they'd only find empty airspace. He spoke into his radio. "Radley, call off the fighters. They're just chasing ghosts. Have everyone stand down."

"Yes, sir," Radley replied.

"Trent, that creature is their leader," Starke said. "What is it?"

"I don't know, like I said, I have a memory of it from my childhood abduction. That's all I can tell you."

Starke said, "I need to brief Secretary Barrington. Any idea when they'll return?"

Trent smiled and said, "Not a clue, but I know all of them will be safe."

Melissa joined them. "Where are the others?"

"Alexa went with them," Starke said. "She was needed. Taylor and Dr. Maxwell opted to stay with her. They'll be back."

Red Level – 2300 hours

Trent stood in the observation room. He looked through the two-way mirror as the others were brought from the imaging center. Some sounded confused in their responses, while others voiced their anger at the medical staff. When the last of the abductees was led into the orientation area, Melissa said, "You look concerned."

Trent replied, "I don't remember feeling disoriented when I was returned, even as a child. Maya wasn't that way when she arrived. Some of these people appear confused."

"I know, and I can't explain why either. They're all in great shape, physically speaking. No neural implants, although their tibia implants are still in place."

"I wonder if they'll remove my implants when they return."

"I don't think that's going to happen. You're connected to them and to both times. You're the only one who is able to convey their messages. Whatever you relay to us as the environmental disaster approaches will be taken seriously. You will be able to provide us with information on how we can better prepare."

"Maybe they just want to see if we actually survive what's coming." Trent inhaled and sighed. "Let's go see Starke."

"Don't you want to say hello to the returnees?"

"No. Chiyo and Mei Lien can explain what's happened to them. I have an important question for the general."

Aboard the Alien Ship

Alexa was stunned by the stark white room, which extended as far as she could see until it diminished to a pinpoint, then blinked out. She felt as if she'd walked into a future world. An odd smell hung in the air. She couldn't quite identify the odor. It was a musty smell laced with a disinfectant. She'd been brought to this place after passing many closed doors that were outlined by an orange light. There were geometric symbols on every door, and they had no handle or knob. She knew that the ship wasn't large enough to contain the space that she was in. An escort—one of the little brown aliens—waited with her in the room. Alexa had lost track of time. She now knew what Trent and Taylor had experienced when they were abducted.

The door opened, and Alpha appeared. Taylor and Maxwell stood behind Alpha.

"They got you, too," Alexa said.

"No, we volunteered," Maxwell said.

"Alexa, are you alright?" Taylor asked.

"Yes."

"Have they done anything to you?"

"No. Why?"

Taylor walked into the room and took her hand, then said, "I know this place. I've been here before." She faced Alpha. "This is where you killed my unborn child."

Alpha stared at her for a moment, then said, "Taylor, the child you carried was not healthy. It would not have survived more than a few hours after its birth, and you would have been at great risk."

"That should have been my decision."

"We did what was best for you."

Alexa waited for Taylor to say something, but she just stared at Alpha. At last, she said, "Alpha, why am I here?"

"We need to harvest some of your ova."

Direct and to the point, Alexa thought. "That's what I thought. Why didn't you just ask me instead of taking me?"

"You needed time to acclimate and be prepared for the procedure."

"I've been waiting here since I was brought on-board," Alexa said.

"You only think you have." His eyes glowed brighter, and darkness enclosed her.

A moment later, Alexa stood alone with Alpha. She felt pain in her left leg and abdomin. "What the hell?"

"The procedure is complete," Alpha said. "We have what is needed. We placed an implant in your tibia as a precaution, should we need to contact you again."

"You're done already? How? I have questions about what you did to me."

"An explanation is not warranted."

"I want to know how many ova you harvested."

"Eleven," Alpha replied.

"Why eleven?" Alexa asked.

"They correspond to the eleven spacetime dimensions," Alpha replied. "We have enough to see us through until Maya's birth."

"Then tell me why you'd need to contact me again?"

"There are many reasons. You should know that your implant is different from the others. With it you will be able to cross through time as Maya can. Your genetic traits permit transition without harm."

"Maya doesn't have an implant," Alexa said.

"Because she doesn't need one. Maya carries the genetic structure needed to transition through the window of time without coming to any harm. Your DNA provided the final piece of the genetic sequence required for passing the trait to her. She will be taught how to use what is within her. Your presence here anchors Maya to this time. With your implant, you and Maya can physically transition through the multiverse. It will connect you to us, and we will channel the power needed to move you."

"You mean I could go to Mars and see Trent and Taylor there?"

"You will see Shona and Aiden there," Alpha said, correcting her. "But your presence there will not be permanent. You are anchored here. To explain in greater detail requires more time than we have left. Your friends are waiting."

A second later, Alexa was back in the massive room. She glanced at Taylor and Maxwell.

"You okay?" Taylor asked.

Alexa pulled up her left pant leg and exposed the new wound. "I know how you feel. Alpha took what they needed."

"Do you need medical attention?" Maxwell asked.

"No," Alexa replied.

"Alpha, what about Trent's neural implant?" Taylor said. "It killed Captain Wood. It fried her brain. Can that happen to Trent?"

"No. Captain Wood had an undetected genetic cerebral flaw that rejected the tendrils."

"So your actions killed another human being," Taylor said.

"The implant should not have caused her any harm. We wish we could have intervened before she expired. When we realized the implant wasn't linking properly on Earth, we tried to return to save her, but there wasn't a window. All life is sacred to us. Our mission is to protect humanity from extinction. Alexa, you and Maya are important to the survival of humankind. Now we must go." There was urgency in Alpha's voice.

"Alpha, you said that you took eleven ova that corresponded to the eleven spacetime dimensions. What did you mean when you said that you'd have enough ova until Maya's birth?"

Alpha replied, "That is all I can tell you."

"That's not good enough," Alexa said. "Are you planning to use my DNA to create other children before Maya is born?"

Alpha's eyes glowed for a moment, and then he replied, "I cannot say."

"I'm not leaving until I have some answers." When Alexa took a step toward Alpha, an electromagnetic field pushed her back. "What the hell?"

"We must leave," Alpha said. "If necessary, I will push you to the disembarkation point. This topic will no longer be discussed."

"Just when you think you can trust them," Taylor said.

Maxwell said, "Alpha, when you said that eleven ova were needed for the eleven spacetime dimensions, are you referring to M-theory?"

"Yes. One is required for each. We must go."

"You've proven that M-theory is the fundamental key to explaining the universe?"

"Yes."

"What are you talking about?" Alexa asked.

"The theory of everything and the altering of the physical laws as we know them."

"You lost me," Taylor said.

"Simply put, there are four fundamental forces that make up the Standard Model," Maxwell began. "Gravity and electromagnetism are relevant to us on a macro level, while the other two forces interact at the quantum level. Gravity, or, more specifically, gravitons, have always posed a problem in unifying all the forces.

"M-theory states that there are eleven dimensions at work and explains that the five different string theories that are in play are really just variants that exist within M-Theory. The strings are like energy tubes that vibrate in multiple dimensions within the multiverse field. It's the vibration that determines whether it's seen as gravity, light, or matter."

"What does that mean?" Alexa asked.

"It means that I'm beginning to understand where we are now. Parallel universes, or quantum universes, can also create parallel timelines and alternate realities. We're between those fields. They create a miniature white hole to punch through what Alpha calls the window. I'm guessing that the windows must align in order for the aliens to transition. They can materialize in any time, within any of the universes so long as they have a window. Is that right?"

"Yes."

"Alpha, why isn't the field stable?" Maxwell asked.

"I will explain as we walk. The fluctuation of the quantum field makes it difficult to maintain stability within any spacetime for very long. We are presently between two parallel universes."

"Amazing," Maxwell said. "How can you transit between dimensions?"

"We create the energy necessary," Alpha explained. "We slip through the fabric of time within the quantum field. That is where time does not exist. You were also correct when you said that the windows must align. This ship is a large quantum generator. It stores energy with a technology that would take years to explain. We create what you call a white hole. This allows us to take the stored energy the ship acquires, and we can focus the energy needed to transition to the time and place we seek, providing that we have a window."

"How can we be someplace where there's no time?" Taylor asked.

"We create pockets within the quantum field between the universes. There are many factors at play that we do not control. We detect when the field will open and when it will collapse based on interlaced vibration calculations. The window can last for minutes but never longer than a few hours by Earth time. If we don't exit a window to an existing time dimension before the field collapses, we will be crushed or expelled by the gravity force we've created."

"You're balancing the gravitational force that exists between a black hole and a white hole, aren't you?" Maxwell said. "They act as portals to the other universes."

"In basic terms, yes. The power of the black hole pulls us into the gap in time. The white hole pushes us out. We can control the balance of the quantum gravity and energy between opposing masses within the dimensional fields for only a limited time. The gravitational fields are in perpetual flux, pushing and pulling at the fabric of spacetime."

"I see," Maxwell said. "Trent has memories of a future or parallel life. Are those his memories or glimpses into an alternate universe?"

"That is difficult to explain in rudimentary terms. His implant allows him to view what is going to occur when he exists within that reality."

"You mean Taylor, Maya, and Trent are all living in a parallel time?" Maxwell asked.

"The Trent, Taylor, and Maya that you know live in your present. They are also connected to other universes and realities, some concurrent, some in the future."

"How is that possible?" Taylor asked.

Alpha picked up his pace.

"I do not have the time to explain. What I can tell you is that we are locked in a perpetual tug of war between the multiverses. We usually only observe, but because of the environmental catastrophe that awaits your world, we chose to intervene to preserve your species."

"Could you transport people from Earth into a parallel universe?" Alexa asked.

"No. It doesn't work that way. We can take people onto the ship, but we can only return them to their source. Maya was the first to make the transition across spacetime. Her DNA is perfectly matched to the vibrational resonance required to allow her to physically travel between times. Alexa, that is why your DNA was so critical. As I said, you were the key. Maya needed an anchor to this world to complete a quantum pathway. In time, her offspring will evolve and have the ability to exist in parallel universes."

Maxwell said, "What difference does DNA make in the interaction between multiverses at a quantum level, especially as it relates to gravitational fields and time dilation?"

"I cannot explain," Alpha replied. "Understand that what I have told you is accurate. We must hurry."

The pace Alpha had set quickened.

"You're living in an extended present time of your own making," Maxwell stated.

"That is one way to describe it," Alpha replied.

"And you can travel within your extended time between the multiverses?"

"Yes."

"Pacha," Maxwell muttered.

"What?" Alexa said.

"The Inca regarded space and time to be a single thing. They called it Pacha. Einstein and others confirmed it exists, but only where there isn't any time."

"I don't understand," Taylor said. "You're talking in circles."

"I need to think about this for a while," Maxwell said. "I need to rest a moment. Go on. I'll catch up."

Alexa said, "Alpha, why couldn't you have told us about the cataclysmic event without using such a protracted and convoluted process?"

"We did tell people about it. This time we did what was required so that you would believe us. It seems human beings require urgency to act. So we waited."

"Alpha, Dr. Maxwell had to stop."

"I am aware of that. He will catch up to us."

"How did you know that you needed my ova?"

"During Trent's last abduction we discovered that *you* could provide the genetic material required to sustain humanity within the multiverses."

Alexa stopped and shouted, "Where did you find my DNA? How could you tell that my genetic composition was needed for human survival?"

Alpha stopped abruptly. "Several strands of your hair were found in the cabin of Trent's plane. Your mitochondrial DNA revealed the genetic marker needed to create Maya."

"Why didn't you abduct me sooner?"

"We weren't sure where you were. The most efficient means was to return Trent with his new implant and allow him to lead us to you."

"But you've known where Trent was for weeks."

"Yes. We decided to study you."

"Why couldn't Trent have just conveyed the message to us?" Taylor asked.

"No one would believe him without proof."

"Maya's only purpose for being here was to warn us and to act as a lab rat to see if her genetic traits would allow for transition?" Taylor asked. "I think you want her for something besides passing on her inherited genetic traits."

"Yes, she is here to offer proof of what is to come." Alpha's eyes glowed for a moment. "We must hurry. The window is going to close soon, and our leader wishes to speak with you again." He strode away.

"He didn't answer my question," Taylor said to Alexa.

"He can be evasive when he chooses, so I'd say there's more to the story," Alexa said.

Maxwell came puffing to catch up with them. "I'm sorry. I'm a bit out of shape."

"Have you figured it all out yet?" Alexa asked.

"I have a kernel of an idea," Maxwell replied. "I need to slow down."

"Alpha, Maxwell has to slow down," Alexa said.

"Very well," Alpha replied slowing his pace.

"Thank you," Maxwell said. "You see, if you entered a black hole, all of the physical laws we understand won't exist anymore. There's a whole different set of laws governing the space between the multiverses. If gravity compresses matter until it reaches a finite point within the quantum world, time and space in the quantum gravitational field is relative to only those observing it within the field. This only happens where the singularity and divergence occurs. The aliens control movement within the spacetime between the multiverses, but only to a point."

"I understood that from your discussion with Alpha earlier," Alexa said.

"Yes, but in order to continue working within the quantum world, and to be able to transverse across parallel times and multiverses, the aliens can't anchor themselves in one time or universe. I think the aliens want to save our species so that we in turn can find them a home. Or more specifically, for Maya and her descendants to help them. That may be the answer to Taylor's question."

"Why would the aliens need to settle somewhere?"

"I don't know. Maybe they've grown weary of traveling. By studying Maya and you, they could conceivably find a way to alter their DNA so they can anchor in a particular multiverse and time."

"You are partially correct," Alpha said.

"You're anchored somewhere between the multiverses, just as we are anchored to our universe," Maxwell said.

"That is true," Alpha said.

"You can't land?" Alexa asked.

"No. The ship is protected by a quantum energy field that allows us to cross into your time while remaining in ours, which is to say, we are always between times."

"That explains the light around your ship," Maxwell said. "It's an extension of your quantum field. But that also makes it a fluctuating field. So the little creatures were created during our present time and are here to retrieve the people that you need."

"Exactly. They are held in a time stasis until needed to make contact in this world. The ship you see isn't really in your time at all." Alpha stopped and opened a door, then stepped into the chamber where the leader was seated earlier.

"Wait a minute," Alexa said. "When we first met, you were able to stand on the lake. Does that mean you were made in this time?"

"Parts of me were. I cannot remain outside of the field for very long."

"And your leader is locked between universes?"

"Correct. Our leader travels through spacetime across multiverses, and can never go back to the world she left behind. It no longer exists. As I explained, we only travel where there is no time."

Alexa stepped into the chamber. The leader was illuminated. Alexa was surprised to see a different kind of alien. "You must be the leader."

The leader's throne glided forward soundlessly. She said, "You are an inquisitive, unpredictable, and interesting species. Alexa, you have done what was needed to give humanity a new beginning. Taylor, you, Trent, and the others have provided us with all that we need for the future."

Alexa said, "We really didn't have a choice, did we?"

"No. You did not. We will monitor your progress through Trent's implant until it's time for us to return to you. It will cause him no harm. If he chooses, we will remove it when next we visit."

"What about Maya?" Taylor asked. "Is she going back to her universe?"

"She will stay in this world for now so that she will learn what is required of her in the future."

"And what will that be?" Taylor asked.

"We will learn more about her genetic string vibrations and perhaps, as Dr. Maxwell has postulated, we will find a way to escape our perpetual life between universes."

"When will you return to take her back to her time?" Alexa asked.

"That has yet to be determined."

Alpha said, "Humanity will find more roots within this universe. Your bloodlines will create a different future for those that survive the event this world will experience. A new future will be one of peace and exploration. Maya's unique genetic signature will allow your species to evolve to where, one day, humanity in this time will meet other beings from different worlds. Her generation will discover things that have yet to be envisioned."

"Dr. Maxwell, a word of caution about pursuing the technology you seek," the leader said. "Life is precious. Do not sacrifice your humanity for technological advancement. Enjoy the world you have been given. Cherish it. Everything and everyone I once knew is gone. I serve a greater power now, but hope that someday I will stand on a world like yours again." Her throne slid back into the shadows, and an electronic screen materialized, hiding her.

"Wait!" Alexa shouted. "What about Shona and Aiden? Do they know where Maya is?"

"They will know when it is time," the leader said, her voice fading into the distance. "Until then, enjoy Maya's company and educate her well."

Alpha escorted them from the chamber and back to the portal. Alexa looked at him and asked, "How long have you been watching humanity?"

Alpha cocked his head in a most human manner, then said, "There is no absolute simultaneity within our spacetime, so I cannot answer that question. All of spacetime is a collection of past and future events and those that are neither past nor future. Time is only relative to those being observed in the present. You have been given a glimpse into a new reality. Prepare for what cannot be stopped while you can. Goodbye."

Alexa looked at Maxwell and said, "Quantum arrow."

"Exactly."

Escorts arrived and took their hands, and a bubble of light formed around them. When the light subsided, Alexa stood on the snow covered lake. Maxwell and Taylor stood next to her. The alien ship was gone. She looked up at the clear blue sky and smiled.

TWENTY-FIVE

"We're back," Taylor said.

"Yes, we are," Alexa said. "It looks like a beautiful morning."

"And here comes the welcoming party," Maxwell said, gesturing at the Marines running toward them.

"Stay where you are!" a Marine shouted. "Command and medical have been notified."

Alexa waved in acknowledgment of the order, then asked Maxwell, "Well, did you get the answers you wanted?"

"Some of them."

"How do you feel?" Taylor asked Alexa.

"Different. I know that I've served a valuable purpose and that there's hope despite the cataclysm that's coming."

"What do we do now?" Taylor asked.

"We make plans and more plans, bring together all the best scientists and engineers that we can find, build bunkers and stock them, then hunker down," Maxwell said.

Maya and Trent ran to greet them. Starke and Melissa were right behind them.

"You're back!" Maya cried out just before a Marine stopped her at the shoreline.

"We are," Alexa replied. "What day is it?"

"You left last night," Trent said when he joined them.

"We have much to tell you all," Maxwell said.

"I'm sure you do," Starke said. He turned to the Marine. "They're cleared."

Maya ran to Taylor and hugged her, then hugged Alexa.

"I think we need to get you medically screened," Melissa said to Alexa.

"I actually would appreciate that," Alexa said. "You'll find that I have an implant in my leg. I was told the implant is different from the others, so you may have more to learn."

"Do I need to remove it?" Melissa asked.

"No. This one needs to stay. Can we go inside? It's freezing out here."

"Certainly," Starke said.

Medical – Orange Level – 0900 hours

"It's definitely different," Melissa said, after looking at the imaging results of Alexa's implant.

"Different how?" Alexa asked.

"It's larger and more complex than the others," Melissa replied. "It has tendrils similar to the ones in Trent's neural implant, and they're buried deep in your bone marrow. Do you have any pain?"

"No."

"What's it supposed to do again?" she asked.

"It not only tells the aliens where I am, but it's supposed to allow me to transition through a multiverse."

"You can go to Mars?"

"That's what I understand."

Trent said, "You will go to Mars. You will meet Aiden and Shona."

"How do you know that?"

"Because Aiden asked about you, remember? You were with them, and then you were gone."

Brown Level Conference Room – February 16 – 1600 hours

Alexa sat next to Trent at the conference room table. All the abductees were there. Alexa didn't know why Su needed to be there, even if she was handcuffed, but General Starke had wanted everyone involved to be present. SecDef Barrington was due to arrive at any minute. Her stomach growled. She'd grabbed only a few snacks during the hectic day. She took Trent's hand. Trent smiled at her and squeezed her hand.

SecDef Barrington walked into the room and took General Starke's usual seat. Starke and Melissa followed Barrington and sat next to him.

"In light of the events that have unfolded over the last forty-eight hours, I've been directed by the president to meet with you personally, to welcome you all back, and to thank you for your sacrifice," Barrington said. "You have shared something none of us could possibly imagine. Your abductions and interaction with the aliens, along with Maya's warning, have confirmed that there is a disaster of biblical proportions on the horizon. Dr. Maxwell's summary report leaves us hopeful—and scared as hell. Trent, I hope the aliens are listening."

"I'm sure they are," Trent replied.

"We've decided to begin making preparations, as have some other nations. Maya, I've been informed that you're providing valuable information about the colonies and life on Mars. That information will assist us in designing future structures. Thank you."

"You're welcome," Maya replied.

Barrington smiled at her, then said, "Unfortunately, some world leaders remain skeptical. Some of them think this is a sham. They have even accused us of trying to consolidate our power. We've shown them the visual recordings of the alien craft, but some think they are fabricated. I guess some people still believe that we haven't walked on the moon."

A few people chuckled.

"I know that many of you have communicated with your leaders and have explained, in detail, what Maya has told us." He looked at everyone in the room. "We even told them about the Martian gene." He raised his hand at Taylor when she began to protest, then said," I know that's not politically correct, but it simplifies conversations. I'm sorry I offended you."

"So you heard I wasn't crazy about being called a Martian?" Taylor said, then glanced back at Su. "It tends to set us all apart from everyone else."

"I know all about it," Barrington said. "We're all one species, regardless of genetic diversity. I believe that if certain people can adapt to a future world better than others, then we need to leverage that trait to our advantage for the sake of humanity.

"I find it interesting that all of the abductees, regardless of national origin, speak fluent English. I can't help but wonder if the aliens did that deliberately. Maya has told us it's the official language of Mars. All of you, except Captain Su, carry the unique Martian genetic traits." He took a quick look at his notes. "We will need all of you to help us convince the holdouts that this event is going to happen by sharing your experiences."

Maxwell said, "I believe that many in the scientific community will also help with getting the message out."

"Excellent," Barrington said. "Trent, have you had any new visions lately?"

"No, sir."

"Dr. Maxwell, what else have we learned about the mysterious energy burst? None of our astronomers have detected anything that indicates a gamma burst of an extinction magnitude. Certainly nothing that will reach us and cause massive earthquakes and volcanic activity in seven years."

Maxwell said, "We've learned nothing new."

"Not the response I was hoping for," Barrington said. "Did you ask the alien leader about the burst during your visit?"

"No, sir," Maxwell replied.

"Why not?" Barrington asked.

"Because we didn't have enough time before the window closed. We had to leave. I didn't even find out if the aliens have a name for themselves."

"I see," Barrington said.

"Mr. Secretary, it's possible that the energy burst could come from the collapse of a massive star we haven't identified yet. Maya said that no one really knows what it was composed of or where the exotic burst originated. Major gamma bursts only impact Earth once every billion years. But a high-energy burst combined with the polar shift and the other natural disasters would cause a geological tempest."

"Young lady," Barrington said, looking at Maya, "are you sure you can't tell us anything else about the energy burst?"

Maya shook her head and said, "No, that's all I remember. It was only described as an exotic matter energy burst."

Barrington said, "Dr. Maxwell, could an exotic matter burst be different from a gamma burst?"

"I don't know."

Barrington took a deep breath, then said, "The geological tempest will destroy the world's infrastructure. That's why we need to be on the same page as all of the other nations. From what Maya has told us, we will eventually trust each other, and we will survive."

"Hopefully," Maxwell muttered.

"What do you mean?" Barrington asked. "Speak up."

Maxwell said, "Quantum universes can have parallel timelines and alternate realities. The alien leader confirmed that they are, in essence, nomadic spacetime travelers. The aliens exist between the multiverses on a quantum scale. Maya was the first to transition from a future reality. In theory, it's possible that Maya and the others are survivors of a different reality or parallel universe."

"What?" Barrington cried. "That wasn't in your report. You're telling me that our Earth could cease to exist?"

Maxwell replied, "I'm just telling you that it can't be ruled out. The aliens have gone to great lengths to warn us. I'm optimistic this reality, this planet, in this universe, survives."

"Could a parallel Earth in another multiverse be destroyed?" Starke asked.

"It's possible," Maxwell replied.

Alexa glanced around the room at the others. Maya's expression told Alexa that she had something on her mind. "Maya, do you want to say something?"

"Yes. Where I live, we all work together for the betterment of humanity. The sooner you work together, the sooner everyone will understand what it will take to survive."

"Spoken like a true leader," Taylor said. "General, maybe we should put her in charge. I bet Maya could get the world to pull together."

A few people chuckled. Barrington didn't look as if he found any humor in Taylor's statement.

"I'm not old enough to be in command," Maya said.

Everyone in the room laughed.

Barrington's hard façade softened, and he said, "I'm leaving for Washington in a few minutes. I hope all of you will convey the words of this ten-year-old to your respective national leaders. I will relay it to our allies.

"General Starke, I want this facility to be expanded and reinforced. This is the best place we have for weathering the storm. I want all of the abductees to work together, compare experiences, and see if we can obtain any additional intelligence."

"That sounds like a good start," Starke said.

"General, I want all of the abductees protected at all costs."

"I understand, sir," Starke said. "I'll see that they stay safe."

Everyone followed Barrington out of the room.

Trent asked Alexa, "Aren't you coming?"

"I want to sit here for a minute."

"Everything alright?"

"Yes. Go on. I'll catch up with all of you later."

"Okay." Trent left the room.

Alexa pulled up her pant leg and looked at the scar. *What do they really have in store for me?* she wondered. The aliens would come back for Maya, but would they want her to go with them? Regardless, she decided to make the most of their time together.

Sawtooth Lake — March 10, 2030 — 0630 hours

Alexa and Trent stood alone by the lake.

Trent told her that when she went to Mars, she would have an extremely tight window for delivering the message. She would meet Aiden and Shona Cooper just before Maya's accident in the airlock. It was her visit that would put Aiden where he could save Maya.

Suddenly Alexa felt the pull. The light grabbed her. The alien ship did not materialize. A moment later, she was in Aiden's and Shona's apartment.

"Don't be afraid," Alexa said. "You are both safe."

"What the hell?" Shona said. Fear was etched in her face.

Alexa couldn't believe how much Shona looked like Taylor, and Aiden looked like Trent. "Aiden, Shona, my name is Alexa Padgett. I'm from Earth before the dark times."

"Call security!" Shona shouted.

"Please listen. I don't have much time. Maya is going to be transported to Earth later today." Alexa handed Shona a picture of Maya standing in the woods by the lake. Snow covered the ground. "She will be safe and well taken care of."

"Who the hell are you?" Aiden asked. "Our daughter isn't going any-where. How did you get in here?"

"She will be taken shortly. You can't prevent it."

"Aiden, call security," Shona said again.

"I'll be gone before security arrives. There's going to be an accident involving Maya. Aiden, you'll be instrumental in saving Maya when an airlock fails. Keep the picture as proof that she survives and is alive on Earth. Only show the photo to Dr. Stefanie Morgan. She will help you explain Maya's absence."

"Aiden, go get Maya," Shona shouted.

"I'm not leaving her here with you," Aiden said.

"We will see you again," Alexa said.

The light took her and she was back with Trent at the lake. "How long was I gone?" Alexa asked.

"About two minutes. How was it?"

"Quick. You look exactly like you do now. So does Taylor. I hope he saves her."

"He will."

Alexa noticed Trent's understanding look. She felt an overwhelming sense of relief when she saw Maya and Taylor walking toward them.

"Now you know what awaits you," Trent said.

"Yes, I do," Alexa replied. "All is as it should be."

"Time is information we don't have.
Time is our ignorance."

ROVELLI

EPILOGUE

"Are you ready?" Maya asked.

"Yes," Alexa replied. She couldn't believe how Maya had grown. At seventeen, she was Alexa's height, with her athletic build, but with Taylor's thick, auburn hair, which hung past her shoulders. "Are you?"

"Honestly, no, I'm not, but I know what's required of me. I haven't been on Mars since I was ten. I'm excited to see my parents again."

"I'm sure they'll be happy to see you. Trent, you're certain about the time of their arrival?"

"Yes. The message was quite clear. They'll be here in twenty-two minutes. Alpha said that you both need to be at the lake when they arrive."

"Then it's time we leave," Alexa said.

Tears tracked down Taylor's cheeks. "We'll miss you guys."

"We'll be back," Maya said. "I'm just not sure when."

"I know," Taylor said. "Still, this is very hard for me."

Alexa hugged Taylor.

"I wish we could go with you," Trent said. "But we don't have the genes for it."

"No, you don't." Melissa said, walking into the ready room. She'd been promoted and had taken General Starke's job at the Sawtooth facility two years before. "Not to mention the possibility of a quantum time paradox. At least that's what Maxwell claims could occur, although I don't know how."

"Where's Maxwell?" Alexa asked. "We wanted to say goodbye."

"He's buried in the lab. Reports of seismic activity are increasing around Yellowstone, and the magnetic poles are showing imminent signs of reversal. Starke sent his regards from Washington. As Secretary of the Mars Expeditionary Force, he had other pressing matters."

"I imagine everyone is very busy," Alexa said.

"I'll miss both of you," Melissa said. "I wish you safe travels, and I look forward to hearing your stories about your life on Mars. Do you have all of the questions that we need answered?"

"Yes, I know what we need." Alexa replied.

Trent said, "You'll have some serious explaining to do on Mars."

Alexa said, "I believe we're prepared for all inquiries. I only hope the information we've been provided about the events on Mars are accurate enough to convince the others about who we are and where we're from, or else we'll look pretty foolish."

"Maya, I wish I understood more about how your DNA is so perfectly matched to the vibrational resonance of the quantum field," Melissa said.

Alexa said, "Maya is the critical link to this world and theirs, and hopefully she'll find the quantum pathway for the aliens to anchor to."

Trent said, "Maya, we're very proud of you."

"I know that," Maya replied. "Let's not get all emotional. I'll be back."

Taylor wiped the tears from her cheeks again and said, "It's still hard. You know we love you."

"Yes, I know that, and I love both of you."

"It's been a little unsettling that I haven't had any visions or memories of Aiden's life on Mars for so many years," Trent said. "All I get are the messages from Alpha. I still don't know what they call themselves or if their leader has a name."

"You worry too much," Maya said. "I'll tell my other parents all about you and show them your pictures. And besides, you said that the alien ship is going to make an appearance. That'll help cement our story on Mars."

"That could also work against you," Melissa said. "Everyone but Aiden, Shona, and Dr. Morgan think you're dead."

"They'll believe us," Maya said with confidence.

"Alexa, I wish you the best of luck," Melissa said. "We'll want a full debrief when you get back."

"I know you will," Alexa replied.

Alexa and Maya stood together beneath the ship as a small group of well-wishers looked on from the shoreline. Alexa put her arm around Maya's shoulder and said, "So our adventure begins."

Maya looked at her and replied, "Yes, it does."

As they were lifted into the alien ship, Alexa and Maya waved goodbye. The ship rose slowly, then shot into the sky and disappeared.

"Well, my wife, they're gone," Trent said.

"Yup," Taylor said, hugging his waist. "We need to get back inside."

"Let's stay here for a while and smell the fresh air. The time for the geological tempest approaches, and we won't have this opportunity much longer."

"We've prepared the world as best we can," Taylor said. "I know that Emma, Rick and his new wife will be safe in one of the bunkers. I was happy to hear that Starke was going to tell Emma and Rick the truth about me after the dark times begin. I hope to see Emma again."

"I think General Starke will do the right thing."

"All we can do is wait and see what happens. Maya and Alexa are safe."

Trent took one last look at the blue sky, then inhaled a deep breath of the crisp, clean air. "It'll be decades until we see this sky again."

"I know," Taylor said. "Life will go on. We've done our duty, and that's all we can do."

They walked toward the facility.

Greylock Mountain — February 24, 2037

The geological tempest began as predicted. Yellowstone exploded. The advance warning of the disaster had allowed for the evacuation of the predicted blast area. The Sawtooth facility had been hardened and expanded, and it suffered no damage from the eruption. Ash blocked the sun above the facility and rained down, covering the snow.

It was late in the afternoon three days later when the exotic matter blasted through the Earth's atmosphere. Maxwell's team had not detected its coming, and they had no idea what it was, as Maya had predicted. The microburst of energy caused the magnetic poles to reverse, and the tectonic plates shifted hundreds of miles in the span of a few days, triggering massive eruptions, earthquakes, and floods unlike anything Earth had experienced in a billion years.

Sawtooth remained isolated from the rest of the world, suffering minor damage during the worst of the tectonic shifts. The work they were doing would take many people to Mars and save humanity. The first astronauts, or pilgrims, as they were being called, would reach the new world soon.

Trent, Taylor, and the others worked and waited for Alexa and Maya to return, hoping they would bring technological information that would accelerate their reaching Mars. Or maybe destiny would keep Maya and Alexa on the future Mars. They could only wait and see.

ACKNOWLEDGEMENTS

I want to sincerely thank all of the readers who have taken the time to turn the pages or tap the screen as you read *Quantum Arrow*.

For my wife, Terry, thank you for being so supportive.

Thanks and appreciation to my beta readers, Abby High, Darlene and Richard Kingas, and Chris Gurley. I know that this novel was different from the ARKLIGHT series. You all have been extremely generous with your time, faith and trust for this journey.

Thanks to my editor, Paul Thayer, of Thayer Literary Services.

Thanks to Kimberly Martin, Jason Orr, and Stephanie Anderson, of Jera Publishing, for the interior and cover design work.

FROM THE AUTHOR

I hope you enjoyed the novel. If you would be so kind, I'd appreciate it if you'd take a moment to leave a rating or review on Goodreads, Amazon, or your favorite review site to let me know what you thought of the story.

When I started *Quantum Arrow*, I wanted to write a story that didn't fit the traditional mold of alien encounters or invasions. I laced the account with some hard science so that the action and scientific discoveries were believable. Obviously, I took some liberties with M-theory and quantum mechanics so that the characters could travel through time into the multiverse realm.

Extraterrestrial contact of any kind is a fascinating possibility. Unidentified sightings are the most prevalent, while reported alien abductions are rare. Research into the alien abduction phenomenon revealed that there are very few cases that appear to be substantiated. Some abductees have reported having alien implants, which is why I included them in the story.

You can connect with me at my website, www.gbholley.com or on Twitter at GBHolley1. If you're on Facebook, I can be reached at GBHolley or Spirit Owl Books, LLC.

A NOTE ABOUT THE AUTHOR

G. B. Holley is the author of the *ARKLIGHT Ancient Alien Adventure trilogy.* He is a native Floridian and a retired law enforcement commander who spent more than three decades serving with a Florida Sheriff's Office. He's a pilot, a former adjunct instructor at St. Petersburg College and a leadership and law enforcement high liability trainer. He earned his MPA and BA degrees from the University of South Florida, Tampa, Florida. He loves reading science fiction and adventure novels, and enjoys flying when he's not writing.